WHAT
WE
RECKON

WHAT
WE
RECKON

ERYK PRUITT

The following is a work of fiction. Names, characters, places, events and incidents are either the product of the author's imagination or used in an entirely fictitious manner. Any resemblance to actual persons, living or dead, is entirely coincidental.

ISBN 978-1-943818-64-8

ISBN 978-1-943818-82-2

Library of Congress Control Number: 2017946113

First trade paperback edition October 2017
Polis Books, LLC
1201 Hudson Street, #211S
Hoboken, NJ 07030
www.PolisBooks.com

POLIS BOOKS

For Jennifer,
Geraud, and, as always,
Lana

"Watch and pray so that you will not fall into temptation.
The spirit is willing, but the mind is weak."

—Jesus Christ, to his Disciples at Gethsemane

"Find what you love and let it kill you."

—Charles Bukowski

"You know, a long time ago being crazy meant something. Nowadays, everybody's crazy."

—Charles Manson

PART
I

1

IT WILL END MUCH LIKE THIS, thought Grant as the fire flickering up his nostrils gave way to a slow, mellow drip down the back of his throat. No sooner had he chased away the sweats, the whispers, the steady but fevered panic that so often wrapped its fingers tight around his windpipe than did he eyeball the rest of the kilo—still shrink-wrapped with only a jagged hole, hardly big enough—and consider into what further mayhem he might find himself.

It was good coke, sure, but Grant had no reason to think it wouldn't be. Back in South Carolina, Bobby had been his best friend and would hardly look sideways at shit that wasn't of a particular quality. *You want to put bullshit powder into your face,* Bobby used to say, *then go down past Decker Boulevard.* Bobby had a reputation. Folks around town knew he had the good shit. They knew how to get a hold of him night or day. What they didn't know was where he stashed it, but Grant did, so a fool and his narcotics were quickly parted.

The only thing better than good cocaine, he thought as he plucked another pinch from the hole in the package, *is stolen cocaine.*

Any tranquility, perceived or otherwise, came crashing to a halt with a knock at the motel room door. Grant quickly shuffled away the brick of cocaine into a hollowed-out King James Bible, then scooted it beneath the bed. He perked an ear. Listened. Held his breath.

"Hey, Grant," called a voice from outside. "Open up. I ain't standing out here all day."

Craig.

Relief.

Grant reached into a paper bag for a brand new bottle of brown liquor and two plastic cups that came with the room, then set them on the tabletop where once sat the contraband.

Craig did not enter when the door opened, but rather stood at the threshold.

"Thanks for coming," said Grant. "Means a lot."

"You look like shit," said Craig. He nodded his head to Jasmine, sitting on the bed, not looking up from the television set. "Both of you."

"And you've lost more hair since last I seen you," said Grant. "Come in. Have a drink. Been a while."

"Not long enough." Craig took a step into the room. Only one.

"Jasmine, say hey to Craig," called Grant. If she heard him, she didn't let on. "You remember Craig, don't you?" When still she said nothing, Grant narrowed the distance between the two of them and said, "Jazz, you are being rude."

She turned only her head, made perfunctory eye contact, then returned to the television. The sound was off and the picture looked like shit, but still held her full attention.

Before Grant said anything more, Craig waved a hand and called him off. "Don't worry about it," said Craig. "I ain't staying long."

Grant rounded the little table in the corner and sloshed whiskey into the plastic cups. About two fingers' worth. He swallowed one before pouring himself another, then handed one to Craig.

"How you been?" he asked.

"Got divorced," said Craig. "About six months back, I reckon."

"Real sorry to hear that. I thought you two made a good couple."

"You never met her." Craig sipped from his cup. "We married long after you skipped town."

"What I mean is, I seen photographs of you two. One of y'all dancing. I thought she was hot enough, even for you."

"Our wedding," said Craig. He shifted his weight from one foot to the other. "Look, if it's all the same—"

"Why don't you sit down?" Grant kicked out a chair, but Craig only looked at it. "Seriously, take a load off. This here is a fresh bottle and I already tossed out the lid. The least we should do is throw a dent into it. Talk old times."

Craig crinkled his nose like he smelled something funny. "I'd rather not talk old times, to be honest. It took damn near an hour to find this place and I ain't looking forward to the hour back."

"I sure appreciate it." Grant held out his palms. "Really, I do. It means the world that you'd do the work and make the drive. I'd come to you if I could, but it's best if I steer clear from Lake Castor for a spell, if you know what I mean."

Craig nodded. He looked across the room at Jasmine and watched a single tear quiver across her cheek. He watched it a long time, then turned back to Grant.

"This is it, you hear me?" he said. "This is the last time."

"Craig…buddy, I—"

"I'm serious. You ain't an easy person to say no to. So, after this, you'd best forget my phone number. Forget about me and anything I ever done for you."

"That's a tall order," said Grant. "Without you, I'd probably be dead. Dead or in jail, so forgive me if I don't up and forget everyth—"

"I'm not joking around." He wasn't. He'd hardly touched his corn liquor. The cup rattled as he slapped his hand against the table. "This is the last time."

"Okay."

"I need to hear you say it."

Grant licked his lips. "This is the last time."

Craig let the moment linger. Silence hung between them like a sinner. He let it linger a bit more before he reached behind himself and tugged a brown envelope from the waistband of his work khakis. He set it on the table between them, minding the liquor. Grant held his breath a bit before snatching it. He tore it open and dumped the contents onto the table.

Drivers licenses. Two of them.

Social security cards, also two.

A pair of birth certificates.

Two entire lives, scattered across the scuffed tabletop alongside a cheap bottle of liquor.

"Dear Christ," Grant whistled, "this is great work." He picked up one ID, then the other. He held each to the naked bulb hanging between them, then lowered them to the table. He couldn't take his eyes off them. "I mean, this is really good work. Jasmine, come check this out."

She didn't move.

"This time, you outdone yourself," said Grant. "Jack Jordan. My name is now Jack Jordan. Will you get a load of that, Jas—I mean, *Summer*? From now on, I'm Jack Jordan and your name is Summer Ashton."

And so it became thus.

"Who are they?" asked Jack.

"Jack Jordan was just a kid," answered Craig. "Grew up around Amarillo, in West Texas. Ran his car into a tree a few days shy of graduating high school. The girl, she died of leukemia about six months ago. These should pass an ordinary traffic stop or credit check, but if I were you, I'd stay out of the emergency room or anywhere asking after medical records."

Jack pat his old friend on the shoulder. "You are wasting your talents down at that copy shop. I've met some folks who'd pay a pretty penny for a fella like you."

"From what I'm to understand," said Craig, "they'd pay a pretty penny to get hold of you too. Both of you."

Jack let that settle a bit before he up and poured himself another shot. Dropped a jigger's worth into Craig's cup as well.

Said, "If that's the way you want to play it, then fine. I won't call on you no more. After you leave here, you and me is done. But I won't forget you. Not ever." He cocked his head toward the cup. "Now, drink with me and let's get on with our goodbyes."

Craig eyed him over the top of his cup as he slowly sipped. Immediately, he coughed. He choked down what he could, then broke into a clumsy laughter.

"Should've known the stuff you drink would be shit." He took another swallow. "I swear, I don't think you could surprise me anymore."

"I got a kilo of cocaine stashed beneath the bed."

"Goddammit, Keith…" Craig stood, knocking over the chair.

"You want to see it?" asked Jack. "I'd never seen that much blow before. We hollowed out a Bible and jammed it—"

"Hell no, I don't want to see it. I don't even want to be in the same room with it."

Jack tried to block him from leaving. "Craig, wait…"

Craig stopped. Looked his old friend in the eye.

"I need you to help me sell it," said Jack.

"Go to hell, Keith, or whatever your name is. You know, for a short piece of shit, you really—"

"I ain't kidding around, man." Jack put his hand on the knob before Craig could reach for it. "I need to move this shit kind of quick. I could use the cash. Hell, who couldn't? You stand to earn a nice chunk of change for yourself if—"

Craig slapped Jack's hand off the knob, then opened the door. "I'm leaving," he said to the room, "and I don't want you calling me. Not for cocaine kilos, not for fake IDs…not for nothing."

Jack followed him into the parking lot. The night had turned cool, as the promise of autumn set upon them. Craig stopped shy of his pickup truck, then spun on his heels to face his old friend.

"How much longer you going to keep her on?" he asked.

"Jas—I mean, Summer? She can leave anytime she wants."

"You and her fucking yet?"

Jack laughed through his nose. "No, we ain't fucking, and we ain't about to start." He scratched at the asphalt with the toe of his shoe. "That's the last thing I need right now."

"Then maybe you ought to see about cutting her loose," said Craig. "She looks like she could use a little break."

"She's fine," said Jack. "If you remember, she always had a flair for the dramatic."

"It's really none of my business, but I mean it when I say the two of you have seen better days. Y'all been eating?"

"Things got a little messy, leaving the Carolinas." Jack rubbed at the scar alongside his hip, still amazed at the feel of it. "I'm afraid our girl, she didn't—"

"I said I don't want to hear nothing about it," said Craig. "You asked me to get you some Texas IDs, so I imagine that's where you're headed next, if I wanted to imagine anything at all. Which I don't. But if you plan to get lost, then I recommend you stay lost. I don't want to know nothing about where you're coming from, and I damn sure don't want to know nothing about where you're going."

Yonder, a stray tomcat emerged from the brush and crept silent and slinky across the parking lot in search of food. Jack watched it a spell longer than he'd planned and snapped out of it only as Craig opened the driver's door of his pickup. Jack shuffled after him.

"Remember how you and me and Davey used to stay up all night drinking coffee in the truck stop on the far side of town?" asked Jack. "What was it called, The All-Niter? What if I told you I saw a joint just like it about two exits up the highway? We could head up there and fetch us some hash browns and shit coffee and—"

"Man, I've got to go."

"Say, how is Davey? You ever see him anymore? He still around Lake Castor? I ain't—"

"Keith, I've got to go."

Jack's hands dropped to his side. He took two steps back and stared at the truck tires. He shrugged.

Craig climbed behind the wheel, then rolled down the window. He nodded toward the motel door and said, "Look, I don't plan to get in the middle of nothing. But if I were you, I'd clean up your act. That girl in there ain't nothing like the girl I met, what, four, five years ago. You ain't neither, but you've always been a smart fella. Too smart, sometimes."

Jack bit his lower lip.

"What I'm saying," continued Craig, "is maybe you two ought to take some time off. I can't help but think this whole mess you've brought down on the both of you is going to do one or the other of you in. If you care about her as much as you say, maybe you ought to think about that."

"You're right about all of it." Jack touched each of his fingertips with his thumbs, popping several knuckles in the process. "That being said, it'd be a lot easier for you to sell off an ounce, were you just to ask around—"

Craig threw up a hand. "You've got a way of dragging people down with you and, if it's all the same, I want to be left out of it. One day or another, someone's going to get a hold of you. The law or worse, and I can't have it leading back to me." He slipped the truck into gear, then didn't so much as nod as he backed out of the motel lot and, in a spray of gravel and rock, got himself onto the freeway.

Jack stood there a spell. First, he felt awful. Craig's words, like ricochet, pierced him and knocked him senseless. Then, up came the fury. He'd become quite skilled at starting anew and wasn't accustomed to someone popping in from his past to throw fast a finger in judgment. It was all he could do to keep from climbing into the shitty Honda they'd just bought and chase down his old friend to run him off the road, give him the what-for he'd probably had coming since they were little.

Eventually, all of that settled and left him standing alone with only the florescent hum of the street lamps and the faraway din of traffic. It was easy to hate, thought Jack. It was easy to fly off the handle and take your eyes off the prize.

More difficult was to keep focus.

To learn from one's mistakes.

Perhaps Craig had a point. Perhaps things had run somewhat off the rails. Perhaps time for a change beckoned. Perhaps it was time he shed himself of Summer or Jasmine or whatever her name was, lest she drag him down.

But he had many things to do before that day came. For one, he had a stolen kilo of cocaine to unload. For another, he had to carefully map the quickest backwoods route into East Texas. And, more pressing, he had about three-quarters of corn liquor left in that bottle back in the room.

He slapped his palms against his thighs, as if brushing them clean, then headed back inside to see if maybe Summer would snap out of it long enough to help him finish it.

2

The smell of gasoline.

Cicada, whip-poor-will, and the sweet symphony of late August.

Summer came to in the passenger seat of their shitty Honda, on the
far side of a gas station parking lot. Maybe three, four in the morning.
Roadside, but not another soul to be found. No one in the driver's seat.

Alone.

No Jack.

No keys in the ignition. If he'd finally up and abandoned her, he
would have left her the keys. A little bit of money. Perhaps even...

In a bluster, she thrust her hand beneath the passenger's seat. Rifled
through empty go-sacks and plastic soda bottles.

Not there.

Summer dove into the backseat and cast aside one trash bag full of
her clothes, then a knapsack. Kicked errant books and CD jewel cases
to the floorboard.

Still nothing.

In a fit of desperate inspiration, she reached beneath the driver's
seat and didn't realize until finally her fingers found it, that she had

forgotten to breathe.

There it is.

She exhaled.

Jack would never leave without it.

Summer leaned her head against the backseat window glass. There were lights on in the gas station. Streetlights, florescent and throttled with flies and moths and gnats swarming in angry spasms.

She wiped sleep from her eyes.

Summer had been dreaming of farming. Of raising carrots and beets and cabbages and wandering fields of produce. Rows upon rows, sprouting from good, honest dirt collecting between the toes of her bare feet, then sprinkling back to the earth to birth more plants. She had been dreaming of the barn, of the farmhouse, of the chickens and cows and even a rooster, which she named Gordon. In the end, it was Gordon who woke her. Gordon's crowing, telling her and the rest of the world to wake up, lest they sleep through End Times.

Jack...

Maybe he'd gone into the gas station to shake a leak. Maybe he'd gone inside for another bottle of those trucker pills he often thought he could hide from her.

Maybe he'd only be a minute.

Summer housed no doubt that Jack Jordan would one day make a run for it. She also assumed there'd be no ceremony when finally it happened. She could very well find herself ditched roadside far, far from home. Cold, alone, and in some state of disarray. But she also knew he'd come running at the first sign of trouble. He'd fall in with another girl, one who couldn't keep up with his shit—they never could—then realize what he and that girl had wasn't love at all, not anything like what he shared with Summer. He'd get around the corner and finally believe all the hype he'd been spoon-feeding himself didn't mean a hill of beans, because he was nothing without Summer. Nothing at all. Then along he'd come, tail tucked.

Not even Jack Jordan could convince himself he could move a kilo without her.

If she'd done anything, it was prove she could make it on her own. She could live on the street, if push came to shove. One night, a year or so back, she'd taken off for a couple days with some guy and, just to see if they could, they camped beneath a bridge. They'd lit fires and ate hot dogs and stood out on the off-ramps, holding signs and asking for money. They'd spanged eighty-six bucks in three hours. That's $25.50 per hour, and they weren't even trying. On the third night, it got cold, so they went back to his apartment and tried black tar heroin.

Best she knew, Jack had never noticed her gone.

Summer leaned forward, between the driver and passenger seat. She thought more than once about wandering into the gas station to see what he'd gotten himself into, but didn't so much as pop open the door to the backseat. Instead, she sat still, staring at the dashboard and trying like mad not to get lost in her thoughts but losing, losing desperately until she noticed a commotion yonder and found Jack, shuffle-stepping across the parking lot, holding his britches bunched at the front. Behind him, a fat older man chased him to a spot shy of the gas pumps. A man holding a baseball bat.

Jack threw open the driver's door and slammed the key into the ignition, started the car, then got them on the road. He never once looked at her through the rearview, never once asked why she'd climbed into the backseat. He was a mess of sweats and shakes and kept both hands firm on the wheel, lest he vibrate out the door. All that cacophony, yet how still were his eyes. How still and even. Summer watched him a long moment to make sure he was okay, but soon bored of it and returned her dead stare to the dashboard.

"Slow down, Jack," she said. "Speed limit is fifty through here."

He did, a little. Summer couldn't see past the high beams, the twin yellow lights stretching into yonder night.

"Where are we?"

"Texas," said Jack.

She blinked. "How long have we been in Texas?"

"Too long, it feels like."

Summer squeezed into the front seat. Craned her neck until it nearly touched the windshield, then turned her head upward to the heavens. Or what she could see of the them.

"How much further we got to drive, you reckon?"

"Another hour, at most," he said. "We'll get another motel and hole up for the morning. Tomorrow, we'll grab some lunch, then go check out a place I found on the internet."

She sighed. "Another place. You know, I really liked the last place we had. The one in Columbia."

"The duplex?"

"Yeah, that was real nice. Washer, dryer…dishwashing machine. I think of all the places we've stayed, the duplex was the nicest."

"You were hardly there at the end."

She drew a half breath and held it. "That doesn't mean I didn't think it was nice."

The air soured and Summer could tell he was sorry to have brought it up. He knew it'd get her thinking about Scovak. She'd thought plenty on him since leaving South Carolina, and very little on anything else. Mostly, she thought about the last time she saw him, how his eyes narrowed to slits when she told him she was only going to be gone an hour, that she'd be back as soon as she could. How he'd squinted and gently stroked his beard, pointed at the chin, and said nothing as he looked away and returned his attention to his brand new tattoo. The one with her name on it. Like he knew she was lying to him, like he knew she could never lie to him. He allowed it. If for no reason other than he was certain she'd change her mind, he allowed her to leave, and no sooner had she driven over the Savannah river had—

"Hey, you in there?" Jack snapped his fingers, inches from her nose. "Stay with me. It's late and I've been driving, what, nine hours now? I've been going nuts and you've had enough time in that little head of yours. Come on, wake up. Talk to me."

"I miss him," she said.

She could hear his eyes roll in his head. He said, "Summer…
don't—"

"I'm not, Jack." She turned in her seat. Her breath fogged the
passenger window glass. She reached out a finger to mark it, but
stopped short. She had no idea what to write. "All I'm saying is I miss
him."

He sighed. For the first time, he took his eyes off the road, hands
off the wheel. Summer didn't know if his trembling hand reached
to stroke her hair or pat her shoulder or possibly even strangle her
neck, but instead, reached inside the breast pocket of his flannel shirt
and wrestled free a wrinkled pack of smokes. He tapped one out and
offered it to her, but she refused. The driver's side strobed furious
orange as Jack fussed with the lighter, finally sparking it. He drew and
blew deliberately on his cigarette. Drew and blew.

"You know," she said, "I'd prefer not to say his name again either.
In fact, as of this moment right here and now, I will never again utter
his name. You hear me?"

"I'd be more than fine with that, if it were true."

"It's true and you'll see." She sat still, as long as she could. She
watched the road a good while, the names of the towns on signs
popping up alongside the road. Names like San Augustine and Macune.
Chireno and Etoile. Towns that could only be gas stations at highway
intersections, open or closed, but mostly closed, and billboards that
should have long ago been painted over. Pine trees sentinel and
stretching well into the night like crooked fingers, blocking out moons
and stars and letting through no light, nor any out. Summer watched it
all and wished there were more, but there wasn't, so she spoke.

"But one thing the man whose name I won't say used to tell me
was there weren't no use in being sad when there were so many other
things on the planet to be."

"Weren't he just a poet, then."

"It may sound simple to someone like you," she said, "but it's
actually very wise if you break it down."

"I'm sure it is."

"I know you never did like him," she grumped, "but you didn't know him. Not like I did. He said I was the only person he'd ever met who wasn't afraid of him."

"I wasn't afraid of him."

"You can't even say it without cracking your voice."

"I'm telling you, I wasn't scared of him." Outside Jack's window, the world whipped past in a blur of starlight and streetlamps. "Part of my act was pretending he intimidated me."

"You did a mighty fine job." Her voice could have been draped with tinsel. "Especially the parts where he came in the front door and you slipped out the back."

"Half the things they said about him weren't true, I'd bet."

"How much?"

"How much what?"

"How much would you bet?"

Jack licked his lips. "I'd bet that entire kilo under the seat that he never did time for killing nobody. I'd bet that's all something he dreamed up so folks would take him serious. That one tattoo he had above his elbow... You remember it?"

"I remember his every inch."

"He said it was how they mark someone in the Aryan nation after they'd killed somebody for the cause. And by *somebody*, what they mean is—"

"I know what they mean."

"I'll have you know I googled it and that weren't no Aryan tattoo," said Jack. "It's some bullshit he and a couple drunk peckerwoods carved into his arm with a safety pin and some India ink and now he's trying to play it off like he's hard, and all you kids lapped it up. People can be full of shit sometimes."

She crossed her arms. "He didn't let a whole lot of people close, not like he did with me. That's why a lot of people... Hey, Jack, will you please slow down?"

"Will you please not tell me how to drive?"

She said, "There's a kilo of cocaine under your seat and you're going twenty over the speed limit."

Jack did. He pushed his sweat-mottled hair out of his face with a twitchy hand. Summer noticed for the first time he had yet to buckle his belt and zip his fly. She studied him through eyes squinted.

"You were having one of your fits back there, weren't you?" she asked. "Back in that gas station bathroom?"

"Summer, please…"

"You act like it don't affect you none, that I'm the odd one for getting sore about things. That all the sneaking out in the middle of the night and changing names and the lies and looking over our shoulders, all that rolls off you like water off a duck, but these fits you get say something quite different."

"If it's all the same," he said, voice cracking, "I'd rather think about something else. Anything else, to be honest."

Summer nodded. "Fine. Not talking about it don't make it go away, but suit yourself."

"You ain't the only one who lost someone," muttered Jack.

"Oh ho!" It was Summer's turn to roll her eyes. "I bet if you tried, you couldn't remember her name."

"Her name was Michelle and I miss the ever-loving shit out of her. I had something awful special with her and I'm afraid I might have broke her heart. You never know how something like that could affect a person."

"She's young, she'll get over it." Summer twiddled her thumbs. Through the windshield, the sky colored purple and resplendent. Up came the sun. "Besides," she said, "if what you two had was so special, you wouldn't have lit out with her student loan money, would you?"

Jack took the last drag from his smoke and tossed it through the window. He didn't bother to roll it up, instead let the wind roar through the opening.

"Summer," he said, when finally he spoke, "all that mess is in the rearview, and that's where it should stay. We have a unique opportunity lying before us. We each can start anew, a clean slate. How many people get a chance like this? When we cross into Lufkin, I suggest we drop all our troubles and burdens at the border, leave all those hard times behind us. Because from here on out, it's going to be roses and sunshine."

"You think so?" Summer asked with a whisper.

"I know so."

Jack leaned back in his seat and slipped an arm around her shoulders. She tucked herself into him, suddenly warmed. But at the door there beckoned yet a chill. One that nobody, not even Jack Jordan, could ward away. So she sat silent and filled herself with his smells: the cigarette, his sweat, the fresh stench of panic. She matched, best she could, the rhythms of his unsteady breathing. For even if she couldn't say it out loud, even if she wouldn't allow it past her tongue, she'd still say it over and over in her head.

Say it so loud in there that sometimes, she could hear nothing else.

Just his name.

Over and over.

Scovak.

Scovak.

Scovak...

3

SUMMER DIDN'T BELIEVE HIM, but Jack stood convinced there was a science to laying low.

Never contact anyone from the past. Let sleeping dogs lie.

Once you crossed the state line, stay across it.

Don't give anybody reason to question your story. This means keeping wild tales of hoorah to a minimum. Skim the details and leave little worth research.

And pay cash as often as possible.

The current political climate did not fare well for folks caught acting shady with credit cards and identities, so it was best to keep to the back roads. No point filling out an application to some fancy apartment complex in town, then subject oneself to background checks, credit reports, and the scrupulous eye of a moneylender.

No, better to find some hillbilly renting a Light House trailer on Craiglist.

They met at the foot of a dead-end road awash in overgrowth and covered by pines. The woman's name was Debbie Delco, and she loved Jesus. Or so she said. She cast a wary eye over both him and Summer, then pursed her lips like maybe she'd just eaten a lemon. She crinkled her nose, then said to Jack:

"I'll have you know, we don't much care for co-habitation of the sexes. I'm afraid that simply won't do. While folks from Dallas and the rest of the country may have adopted liberal values, I assure that we here in Lufkin still lay our claim to what is good and right and dictated in print among the pages of the King James."

"As do we," said Jack in an even tone. "Presbyterian ourselves. Have been for six generations. This here is my sister, Summer, and Mom reckoned it best for the two of us to share a place so we can save what money we can, as well as keep an eye on each other."

Jack winked, then hitched a thumb over his shoulder at Summer. She hopped up and down and spread her arms, then raced across the switchback like she was in a raisin commercial. She shuffled to the trailer, then fell to her knees at the wooden pallet that had been propped up to make a patio. She hugged the very ground she knelt upon and made happy little noises… *squee… squee… squee.*

Said Jack, "She needs…*special* attention, if you get my meaning."

Summer collapsed at the base of a dandelion. She shaded it with her hands from the afternoon sun.

"Bless her little heart," said Debbie Delco.

"My name is Jack Jordan."

Debbie Delco accepted his hand, then wiped it on the leg of her slacks as she slapped on her best Sunday smile.

"And bless yours as well for taking good care of your family."

"Well…" was all he said. He ducked his head, as if he might be allergic to a kind word. "What do you say we see about that trailer?"

"It's a Light House," she said as she waved her arm across its facade. "My daddy bought it new in fifty-four and kept it up until he died forty-two years later. Since then, my momma and I have rented it out to whomever could pay on time, so long as they aren't Mexican. It ain't moved from that very spot since sometime in the eighties. I have to tell you, because of the location, I've grown accustomed to meeting folks at challenging points in their lives." She leaned in close to whisper, "They usually go one of two ways from this Light House. They either join the church of their choice, or, one day, end up clearing out."

Jack nodded his head. He made to say something, but was drowned out by a passing train, the railroad so close that the windows shook.

"This ain't exactly how it looked on the internet," said Jack.

"Nothing looks like it does on the internet," she replied. "You don't expect me to be the one to make sense of that, do you?"

"I'm just saying," said Jack. If there were more to add to that thought, he kept it to himself.

"I'll want first and last month's rent up front," she said. "And the security deposit. In cash."

"Not a problem," he said. But he said it to the five-foot poke weeds scratching along the back half of the trailer, the half which had rusted to a shit-brown.

"And you will be responsible for the upkeep," she said. "It said so on the advertisement. I'm certain you saw it."

He nodded and swallowed tight. His wheels spinning.

"It's fine," he said, "so long as the AC works."

"It works." She stood still as a statue. "You a handy guy around the house?"

"Not in the slightest."

"In that case, it might not work all the time," she said. "That going to be an issue?"

"It ain't, if you agree to knock a hundred bucks off the place."

"I will do no such thing."

Jack sighed. "Then I reckon it won't be a problem."

"Shall we take a look inside?" she asked, leading the way.

Summer met them at the front door, hopping up and down on the wooden pallet like a little girl in love. When Jack approached her, she clasped his hand to hers and held it to her heart. Debbie scowled, and Jack flinched at the sharp tang in her eyes.

"She's my half-sister," said Jack. "Different daddies. I'm not sure what's legal and ain't out this way, but I know what it says in the Bible and those are the instructions I tend to follow."

Debbie Delco nodded, but that didn't mean a thing. She opened the door and followed them both into the unit.

"This old thing has been furnished with things folks have left behind over the years," she told them. "A carpenter looking for work once left behind yonder love seat. A traveling preacher who tried and failed to start a church for the Pentecost left behind that kitchen table and a handful of silverware that don't match. The downstairs bed was forgotten by a wayward writer. This whole thing is a mosaic of castaways and hand-me-downs."

Jack ran a finger along the top of a rickety metal bookcase, then immediately wiped that finger across the back of a tattered Naugahyde easy chair.

"There's an upstairs and a downstairs," Debbie said, more to the living room than to Jack and Summer, "but mind the ceiling. It's a bit low on the bottom floor."

However, she needn't have said a word. Jack, as short as he was, could stand upright with nary a need to duck as he walked through the cramped living room, the tiny kitchen, and up the stairs to the front bedroom, then the rear. He made it a point to linger at the loose board at the bottom step, to gesture at the mildewed tile in the corner of the bathroom. The rot soaking the linoleum near the tub. He had half a mind to tell the good Ms. Debbie Delco he planned to take his act on into town, but Summer set again upon the walls and floors of the tiny trailer.

"This is where I want to sleep," she said, pointing to the aft bedroom. "And downstairs is where you can sulk in your easy chair while you drink your bourbon liquor and practice your curse words."

Debbie Delco arched an eyebrow and narrowed her eyes. She silently mouthed scripture as Jack whispered something sharp and fricative to Summer. When finished, he turned to Debbie with a grin, which favored shit-eating.

"We love it," he said. "How soon until we can move in?"

☀ ☀ ☀

No sooner had the good Ms. Debbie Delco quit the dirt lot in front of the trailer than did Jack get right to work. He fetched the Bible from beneath the driver's seat and dropped cross-legged with it to the floor of the dusty living room.

He was still staring at it when Summer entered on her third trip to and from the car, carrying clothes, books, and other whatnot bundled into her arms.

"You going to sit there and stare at it like it's something holy or are you going to get after it?"

Jack snapped himself to. With trembling hands, he opened the front cover. He fingered through the flimsy pages, first one by one, then by the dozen, then finally in handfuls, skipping verses, chapters, entire books until near about Judges where suddenly the pages had been cut into, the center of them removed and hollowed out, replaced only with a paper bagged, shrink-wrapped kilo of cocaine.

Jack unwrapped it like it was the last Christmas present he'd ever receive. As if aware the moments before and the moments after would forever be defined in relation to the ones in which he found himself.

Behind him, Summer dropped two trash bags full of clothes to the floor.

"It always looks smaller than I remember it," she said. "A kilo."

She tried the word over and over. Each time, it sounded more alien to her tongue than the last.

"Kilo. Kilo. Kilo."

Jack pulled a pocketknife from his boot and cut away the shrink wrap. He took a short breath, held it, then broke the kilo in half, or as close to *in half* as he could. A mess of it crumbled to the plastic below.

"This stuff is compressed to all hell," said Jack. "I'll need a jackhammer to break this son-bitch."

Summer lay spread eagle on the linoleum in the kitchen, not two feet away. She flapped her arms to the side and out again, making little snow angels in the dust and grime.

"How do you want to play it?" she asked.

Jack was too busy with the mysteries in his hand to hear her, or to answer her if he did. He did math in his head. He bought and sold empires there as well.

"Did you hear me?" asked Summer. "I asked how you wanted to play it."

"What do you mean?"

"You and me." She sat still and counted the ceiling panels. *One… three…seven.* "How are we going to be, you know, in this town?"

"I don't follow." He ran the blade of his pocketknife along the jagged edge of the broken kilo. An errant rock flicked somewhere in the corner, against the step with the loose board. "What do you mean, how are we going to play it?"

"I mean, we've done it all sorts of ways. Brother and sister. We said we met as strangers back in South Carolina. All kinds of ways we could play it, so were you thinking on how we'd play it here in Lufkin?"

"We already told that landlady we was brother and sister."

"Yeah, but I bet we never see that landlady again in our whole lives, so long as we pay on time."

"Do-gooders have a way of showing up unexpected." Jack wiped perspiration from his hands, then went back to breaking up the kilo with his knife. "Don't be fooled by the likes of that old landlady."

Summer laughed through her nose. "Besides, if you look at our IDs, they say we're from different places. Yours says Amarillo and mine says…" she tugged it from the back pocket of her corduroys and looked at it, "… Duncanville, Texas. I don't even know where that is."

"I looked it up in the atlas. It's south of Dallas." He glanced around the room. "Hey, I think I need to be wearing rubber gloves."

Summer belly crawled to her knapsack and rustled around until he found a small shaving kit, which she slid across the floor to Jack. Inside was everything he'd need: Digital scales. Little baggies. Bigger baggies. Rubber gloves. He slapped a pair at his wrists to knock free a cloud of talcum powder.

She sat up and watched him operate a moment before saying, "It's just…I was thinking this time we'd play it a little different. Maybe this time, this one time, we could play it so I was your girlfriend."

"We can't do that, Summer." He didn't so much as look up from the scales.

"Just hear me out, Jack." She rose to her knees, rested her palms atop them. "We've done it all those different ways, all different kinds except that one. We should try it. You know, once."

"That's not a good idea," he said.

"Please…we don't even have to screw. You don't even have to be in love with me. You can fool around behind my back, even. Do you hear that, Jack? I'll even let you cheat on me."

Jack stopped what he was doing. He looked from the bigger baggies to the smaller ones. "You think I can get an ounce into that?"

"Don't cut them into ounces," she said. "Do eight-balls."

"To hell with that talk," said Jack. "I ain't running all over town slinging eight-balls. There's, like, three hundred eight-balls in a kilo. It would take us a year to sell that many eight-balls."

"Two hundred eighty-five," said Summer. "That is, if you don't step on it some. I suggest we step on it some and stretch it to four hundred. I have the B12 in the shampoo bottle."

"We'll never sell four hundred eight-balls, Summer. That's just asking for trouble."

"What's asking for trouble is walking around with ounces in your pocket," said Summer. "Come on, Jack. You know this. We're strangers in this town. We go around asking people if they want to buy an ounce, they'll peg us for troublemakers from the get-go. No, you start small. Grams, eighths… Be patient. Soon enough, I'll have us in a room where someone will say, 'hey, I wish we had an ounce right about now,' or, 'man, I just came across five hundred bucks and I got no earthly idea what to do with it.'"

"I'd like to see what might happen if we approach it a little differently this time," he said. Yet still, he reached for smaller baggies. "Maybe attract a different crowd than we're used to."

"Speaking of different…" She pulled around her legs and sat Indian-style, unconsciously mirroring him. "Maybe we could go about attracting that different crowd if we went at it like boyfriend and girlfriend. Think about it, we could have couples nights and play board games or things like that. It could be nice."

"Forget it, Summer," growled Jack. "We got enough on our minds to have to worry about any kind of romance. It'll only—"

"Not a real romance, Jackie," she said. "A pretend one. Just putting on a front. Like we always do, but this time a little different. Different, because I don't really want to date anybody this time, but you know how it goes. These dirty hippie guys thinking they've got some connection with me because I'm somebody they can hang out with, and I'm such a free spirit, blah, blah, blah, so the logical progression is they've got to stick their smelly pecker in me, then next thing you know they're telling me where I can go and who I can't talk to. No, Jack…I can't do that right now. Not so soon. Not after—"

"I thought you weren't going to say his name."

"But, Jackie, it hurts…" She held herself tight with her own arms.

"It hurts only because you let it." He pointed a finger to her face, like maybe he was her daddy, or better still, her step-daddy. "So don't let it."

Summer's lower lip quivered.

"You just got the blues, that's all," said Jack. "You've got to cheer up. And I know what will cheer you up."

He chipped at the corner of the larger brick with the knife until a tiny mountain piled at the tip of the blade.

"You said this go-round we weren't going to do any more of that," Summer said, straightening her shoulders and tucking her hair behind her ears. "You said this time we were going to keep our heads about us."

"A celebration," he said.

"What are we celebrating?"

Jack held the knife out before him, offered it first to her. Said, "We liked to not got out of South Carolina."

He locked eyes on her until she looked away. Looked down, dammit, like she was a dog caught pissing the carpet or the bed.

Said Jack, "But we did get out, Summer. And we're here now, starting over, and I believe that calls for a little hoopla. Something to cheer you up and get us started on the right foot."

Summer took the cocaine up one nostril, then covered the other and sucked it back through rotten cartilage. Rather than meet eye contact, Jack busied himself chipping away another bit—just a little, bitty bit—with the knife and perhaps he busied himself a bit much with it because Summer swatted his hand away and pulled the kilo closer to her side of the room. Gone was droopy Summer, gone was the sad sack. Summer was all business. Summer had skin in the game. Jack ran his fingers along his gums and watched as Summer, being steadier of hand and quicker to eyeball, scooped detritus from the plastic wrap, from the paper sack, from the floor, and dropped it in clumps to the top of the digi-scales. Three point two grams. Three point four. Bingo. She was good. She'd always been good. He watched as she portioned out two eight-balls. Three eight-balls. Five. Watched as she finished, swept the remainder into a larger bag, one that held the two broken pieces of brick, both whittled smaller but still Everests. Grand Canyons. Great Walls of China. Then she returned it to the hollowed-out Bible into which it had been hidden. She tended to it with such detail, with such precision, that he found himself hating it. *It* being the kilo of cocaine, in all its components, the Bible in a paper sack, then lowered into the loose board at the base of the stairs, the one he'd pulled free, nearly slicing off his damned finger and he realized what a fool he was, what a stupid, stupid fool he was for feeling as such toward something so innocent as a kilo of cocaine, and wished instead he could take a hammer to the back of Summer's skull.

"Be real careful how you dip into that," said Summer. "You know how you get."

Jack cast narrow eyes upon her. "You talk to me like this is the first time we ever sold coke."

"I'm talking to you like it's the first time we sold a *kilo*."

Summer fit the shaving kit and the shampoo bottle of B12 alongside the Bible full of cocaine into the hole at the bottom of the stairwell. She replaced the board just so, then leaned back to admire her handiwork. A moment passed and soon Jack realized she was not laughing, but sobbing.

"Summer, you can't keep this up for much longer," he said. "No one wants to hear a story about a girl crying over a guy she can't have no more."

"I know." She wiped her nose with her bare forearm. "It's just…it's just…I just don't know who I am anymore."

Jack could hear her breathing. A fine whistle in, a rough chafe out. Then, a commotion as he crawled two feet from the stairwell to the tiny kitchen, banging his shoulder into one wall and his knee into the other. Her chin oddly cold as he took it between his thumb and forefinger and turned up her head to face him. Her pale blue eyes saw through him, and out the other side.

"I know who you are, Summer. Don't that matter?"

"Oh, yes, it does, Jack. You have no idea."

"Good." He rose to his feet. Like a lord, he stood over her.

"Jackie?"

"Yes?"

"Can you tell me?"

"Tell you what?"

Summer measured her breaths in tiny pinkie nails.

"Can you tell me…who I am?"

Jack exhaled all the air from his lungs. She sat at his feet like a leper and he bent down to pat her head with one hand, to pluck the twin eight-ball baggies from her palm with the other. He dangled them before her eyes like a pair of Christmas ornaments.

Said Jack, "You're the one who's going to help me sell off this kilo of cocaine to a bunch of college kids."

4

JACK JORDAN SAID THINGS to her like *There's a science to it* one minute, then would say *Come on, Summer, this ain't brain surgery* the next. Before coming to a new town, he'd sit her down and analyze each and every step they'd taken, as if he were the only one taking it. He'd talk about the data he'd collected, or try to draw a correlation between how much money they'd made against how much trouble they'd stirred up. However, truth be told, they both stood in the same rocking boat. They both flew by the seat of their pants.

Summer knew better: there was no goddamn science to it at all.

If anything remotely resembling a formula to success existed in this racket, Summer felt she could chalk it up to *Being a Good Person* or *To Thine Own Self Be True*, but even she saw through that line of bullshit. Wasn't nobody true to nothing, least of all thine own self.

Jack, bless his heart, hadn't the same head for it that she did. Oh, he had a pretty face and was great in a nightclub or a college classroom, or someplace more genteel. He had a head for numbers and the clandestine arts, such as *marketing* or *branding*, but put him in a room with more than two people and a mess of drugs and he'd find himself stranded. Alone. He'd get the sweats, or a bad case of the fidgets. He'd draw into himself and suddenly the sharks would circle. He'd be ripe for the picking.

For this reason, among others, Jack insisted he stay behind at the trailer while Summer set out to ply her trade.

"I don't think your friends care too much for me," he said as he collapsed into the sofa once they returned to the living room. He reached beneath it and produced a small tray scattered with stems, seeds, and maybe a little shake. "If it's all the same, I'll wait here while you run back and sell them those two eight-balls."

"It's only been a week," said Summer. "They hardly know you."

"So they won't miss me if I stay home and get high."

Summer rolled her eyes. "I'm not stupid, Jackie. You have no intention of staying home. I bet I'm not halfway down the road before you're up and dressed and headed to that enchilada joint to talk up that waitress. We've eaten there every night since we came to Lufkin and I know Mexican food don't sit right with you. You came back here so you could see her. Admit it."

"I came back here so they won't know we had the shit on us," said Jack. "Remember, everybody wants to be a coke dealer but don't nobody want to sell coke."

Summer nearly tripped over her own feet at Jack's wisdom.

"Last thing we need," he continued, "is the phone ringing off the hook at all hours of the night because some redneck hadn't the wherewithal to properly plan his evening."

"Unfortunately, that's the nature of the business."

"But it don't have to be our business." Jack packed a bowl and sparked it. "I say every time somebody wants to score, we tell them we have to get it from our guy. We wait an hour, then roll back with the shit."

"I thought you were against doing things the hard way."

"I'm against somebody getting coked up and brave, then deciding to roll over here to try to take it from us." Jack took a hit and passed the pipe. Summer waved it off. "With any luck, we won't be driving across town for eight-balls and grams much longer. Hopefully, we'll be shed of this kilo and settled in with something sustainable."

Summer did what she could to talk him into riding with her, but it was no use. Once his yen for chips and queso took hold of him, there'd be no shaking him loose of it. She knew there'd be trouble the first time that waitress laughed at one of his shitty jokes. How he'd gone clear out of his way to mention he and Summer were family, not the other. How he'd get up to shake a leak and be gone longer than fifteen minutes sometimes, and Summer would have to fetch her own refills.

So be it. She and Jack had different principles, different goals. They were two different animals. If she fancied she were a creature with a natural habitat, that habitat would be living rooms. Apartments, houses, trailer parks…didn't matter, so long as it had a living room, cram-packed with people, thick sheaves of green smoke, and idle chatter. Maybe a mirror or a picture frame laid out on a coffee table or text book, with a skinny finger of white powder carved atop its surface and a rolled-up dollar bill. Not Jack. He had considerable more trouble with environments such as those. The first time they'd met, back in Charlottesville, had been in a living room. In he came, wide-eyed, with pockets full of cash, sent by some other boys from the dorms to score. With a different name back then, but in over his head all the same. The two guys in charge were a couple no-counts, and they'd isolated her in the kitchen. *Keep him stoned*, they told her, *and we'll jack him, then split the money three ways.*

In rooms such as these, Summer could maneuver. Hunt. Thrive.

Getting in was hardly a problem. Earlier that day, she'd thrown on her dirtiest Grateful Dead t-shirt, then marched down to the campus commons area to dance to no music until finally a white boy in the midst of a Rasta phase stopped to compliment her on her hat. She latched onto him, refusing to let go until he and a couple of his pals brought her to an apartment on the edge of town so they could smoke out.

At the door, Summer ran through the same routine as always. A finger parting the shades, then an eyeball.

"You know you have to tell me if you're a cop or not," said the girl who answered the door. Kathy. "It's the law."

That was not true and Summer knew it. "I know," said Summer, "and I'm not a cop. Would a cop have a sack full of this?"

And she was admitted into the apartment. Kathy's boyfriend was a guy named Matt, three sizes scrawnier than she. Scared of his own shadow, poor thing. He took the bowl she'd packed and hit it, perked up his eyes and said, "This is good weed. Where'd you get it?"

"Duncanville, back where I'm from. It's south of Dallas. Hey, you're supposed to pass it to Crunch. Always pass the bowl to the left. Only pass to the right in a time of fight."

"What?" asked Kathy.

"I learned that following Phish," said Summer.

"Whoa," said the boyfriend, Matt. "You followed Phish?"

"For a few years," said Summer. "No big deal. And I'm not talking about that thing running around right now calling themselves Phish, although I love Trey and Jon and Mike very much. I'm talking about the *original* Phish. You know, before all the hipsters starting following them."

Everyone nodded.

"What was it like?" asked Crunch's friend, Lance.

"It was wonderful," said Summer. "Imagine, like, all of the love in the entire world, but humming and vibrating inside one amphitheater. It's like a song heard for the first time, but thirty thousand people know the words to it. It's like a big hug from Jerry. A big, warm, cosmic hug."

"Jerry?"

"Oh dear," murmured Summer, "how old are you kids?"

Kathy butted in. "No, no, no. I mean, why did you call him Crunch? His name is Dario."

Summer looked at Dario/Crunch and shrugged. "When I met this crazy cool cat back on campus, I told him he didn't look like a Dario.

He looked more like a Crunch. So I named him Crunch."

"I like this girl," said Kathy as she took a hit off the pipe. She took another, then passed it. "Let me ask you a question. If you and me were to swap cells one by one, at what point do you suppose I would stop being me and you would stop being you?"

"You just blew my mind!" squealed Summer. She threw her arms around Kathy. "Crunch, you guys told me your friends were cool, but you never told me they were like *Tundra* cool!"

"Crunch…" Kathy turned her head to the side. "I like it. No, I love it."

Queen Bee: neutralized.

For the next order of business, Summer turned her sack upside down and dropped the clumpy green buds to the tray full of stems and refuse. "We can smoke this entire sack," she told the room, "but first we need to make sure I'm able to get more. So who's got the hookup?"

Summer found these rooms easy to command. At that age, most folks' belief in who they were or would become was malleable. Even if they had a firm grasp on their identities, who they were *while high* could still shift like putty in Summer's hands. Take for instance Crunch's friend Lance. That guy had been Mr. Chatterbox while on campus, but once inserted into the smoky living room amongst a few folks he knew, a few folks he didn't, Lance had nothing to say. He took a bit longer to get the joke. He'd stare at things with more intensity than necessary. He'd start sentences, only to abandon them.

Or Dealer, once they'd journeyed to his apartment. Dealer, not because it was a nickname, but rather a surname. Kevin Dealer. He'd said upon meeting her, "If you're looking for a hookup, I'm in the phone book under Dealer." He laughed at it a bit harder than the rest of the folks in his apartment, those who had heard it several times before.

Kevin Dealer was the kind of guy who liked to keep people around him. People like the two guys with multiple piercings through their faces who chattered nonstop in the kitchen. Or the couple townie girls who stared, glassy-eyed, at the other fella who sat alone at the coffee table, meticulously rolling a joint. Summer, Crunch, and her present company increased the population of the tiny apartment by six.

Dealer liked to keep folks entertained. He didn't care who did the entertaining, but he couldn't handle a lull in the conversation. Summer had no problem obliging. She understood there was no such thing as *too high*. If folks weren't high enough to do her bidding or find her interesting, she'd pack another bowl. Roll another joint. Rinse, dry, repeat, until she got her way.

Dealer twitched again at the lull and Summer was eager to keep him happy. Him and everyone else, so she sat them down cross-legged on the carpet and promised to tell them something she'd never told anyone. Each of them leaned forward while Summer told them all about Luther.

"Who's Luther?" asked the brunette townie girl.

"Is that the old dude you meet at that Tex-Mex joint over in Lufkin?" asked Crunch.

"No, that's just Jack. My roommate." She put unnecessary emphasis on that last word. "Luther is my guardian. My protector."

"Like a bodyguard?"

"A bouncer?"

"Similar," Summer smiled, "except that Luther is not from this planet."

Some of the glassy eyes—not all of them, some—got glassier. She hurried along another bowl with the shake scattered across the tray, then passed it. To the left.

"How many of you believe in aliens?" she asked the room. Some put up their hands, some didn't. Dealer did his best to steer the conversation toward an episode of *The X-Files* that he sort of remembered, but Summer refused to give up the reins. "I don't blame you for not believing in them," she said. "I didn't myself, not at first. But I don't have that luxury no more. Not since I woke up that night and there was an alien standing next to my bed, and ever since, I believe in them, let me tell you."

"Whaaaaaaaat?" went half the room.

"I'm not lying," said Summer, picking up steam. "And he didn't look like they do in the movies. You know, with big heads and big eyes. No, Luther looked a lot like us, except he didn't have to talk with his mouth."

"What did he say?" asked the blonde townie girl. "Or *not* say, I mean."

"It wasn't words." The bowl made its way again to Summer. She kissed it, barely dragging a hit, before quickly passing it again. To the left. "But I knew Luther wasn't there to hurt me. In fact, he wanted to protect me. And he does, even still. He's saved my life so many times...I owe everything to him."

No one spoke. Not even the ones who suspected she might be full of it.

"And I've never told anyone that story."

Everything out of her mouth, of course, was a lie. Especially the part about not telling anyone. In fact, she'd recounted her Luther story at every drum circle and jam band concert for the past ten years. At tailgate parties and curtained apartments or mobile homes in cities and towns sprinkled across the South. Give them a little crazy, she always said, and they'll love you forever. They'll make you their mascot. She believed if she offered up her flaws from the get-go, they wouldn't rush headlong in search of others.

However, she also understood the importance of leaving them wanting more.

"What do you say we step into the other room?" she said to Dealer. "Take care of business in private?"

Dealer agreed. Much to the chagrin of her new audience, they stepped into a bedroom down the hallway. Mattress on the floor, much like his clothes. Tattered girly pictures masking-taped to the wall. A trashcan flipped to be used as a tabletop, the contents pushed into a corner. Atop the so-called table, a tray full of stems and seeds, and an ethics textbook sporting a rolled-up dollar bill.

"Your girlfriend doesn't live here, does she?"

"Mandy lives in the dorms," said Dealer, unaware of her point. "You said you're looking for some weed. I can get you a slice anytime you want."

Summer was still eyeballing the rolled-up dollar bill, saw the textbook had been licked clean.

"What is a slice?" she asked.

"Eighths," said Dealer.

Summer crinkled her nose and squinted her eyes. "Why do you call them slices?"

"Because they slice into a quarter."

"Why not just sell a teenth?"

"Because this is Nacogdoches, not SMU. Folks around here don't like paying for teenths. They like paying for slices. But I can get you a quarter sack if you want one."

"I'm looking for a bit more than a quarter sack," Summer said. "As you can tell, I got my habits."

"If you give me enough notice, I can maybe get you an ounce. Let me see what I can do." He commenced texting on his phone.

"I don't want to pay for four quarters to get that ounce, if you catch my drift. Shit, I can remember the days when I thought it was called a quarter sack because it cost twenty-five dollars. Those days are long gone, ain't they now?"

"Sweetheart," said Dealer, "this ain't schwag I'm slinging. This is *Snowcaps.*"

"Snowcaps?" Summer shook her head. "Save that chatter for the freshmen, man. I don't fall for cute little names. Why the hell do you call it Snowcaps?"

"Because when you smoke it," he told her, "you get so high you can see the tops of the mountains."

Summer laughed through her nose. "I don't have time for all that. What I want is some real weight. Because I smoke a bunch, man. I smoke a bunch, and if I want to sell off a little to pay for my habit, then what's the harm? Right?"

"I feel you," said Dealer, "but I ain't the one who sells that kind of weight, bro. I'm in grad school. I ain't Joe Pot Dealer."

"Maybe you can introduce me to the guy." She unrolled the dollar bill on the makeshift table and ran a finger along the inside of it. Tasted chalk. Knew she had the goods on whatever shit they rolled through town. "I can make it worth your while."

"I…I don't know," said Dealer. "These guys are real paranoid."

"Everybody's real paranoid," said Summer. "Now hit that pipe again."

☀ ☀ ☀

An hour later found her in yet another living room in yet another apartment, this one across town. Her group, having grown by four members, like a stoner snowball hurtling down a mountain, then shed, as Dealer warned her not to travel in a crowd. Not to meet these guys.

"But Crunch is harmless," said Summer of the people she'd only just met.

"Yeah, but Gumm and Little Jon aren't." Dealer stood on the landing and waited to ring the doorbell. "Best ditch them here and you and me head out alone. These guys here, they're the sort that can get you anything, anything at all. You know, one time I heard they got a guy a kidney." He lifted her chin with his finger, brought her eyes up to his, then said, "A *kidney.*"

This apartment was a world apart from the others. This one, spic and span, everything in its place. The walls, clean and white, with only a framed picture of a velvet bullfighter on a corner wall and a photograph of Nolan Ryan on the opposite. One couch, two recliners, and a TV with a stereo setup from another planet.

Little Jon was Orca fat, a big guy stuffed into a La-Z-Boy with nary a single intention other than the screen of his video game. Gumm was more go-get-em. He dressed preppy. Penny loafers. Khakis. Socks barely kissing his ankles.

Gumm paced the carpet.

"A new year brings new friends." Gumm's voice dripped molasses. "I'd rather live nowhere else than a college town, truth be told. Can you imagine living amongst the same people, year in and year out, until someone was kind enough to sweetly die? Not I."

Summer's fingers fumbled as she plucked from her sack to pack a bowl, but Gumm motioned her away with his hand. He reached into a crinkled brown paper sack and pulled out what had to be a pound, shrink-wrapped tight except for one end which had been torn open, almost as if chewed. Bricked. He scratched off a good bit, then loaded an oversized glass pipe. He handed her the lighter.

"And there will always be a living to be made in a college town," continued Gumm. "So long as there are waiters and bartenders, bouncers and cab drivers. Or hookers, DJs, college professors trying to recapture elusive youth and free thought. Freshmen, burnouts… Young Republicans and Student Democrats. You know what every one of them has in common? They are all looking for new ways to get shit-faced."

"Damn, this is good shit," she said, holding her breath. "Man…it's really good."

"We get it from this old boy down in Austin," said Gumm.

"What do you call it?"

"I don't name weed," said Gumm. "That's for children. You want some? I can get you a great deal."

Summer blinked twice. She blinked again.

Said Gumm, "Anything you want."

"You guys get Molly?"

Gumm nodded. "We get something way better than Molly. We got ecstasy."

"I thought ecstasy and Molly were the same thing."

"No, ecstasy is the real deal," said Gumm. "Molly is ecstasy cut with bath salts or some other bullshit. The stuff we can get is one hundred percent pure."

"Oh yeah?"

"You've got to meet Matlin." Gumm looked over his shoulder at his roommate, yet to look up from the video game. "L.J., don't you think Summer and Matlin would get along well?"

If Little Jon heard him, he did not let on.

"What about coke?" asked Summer, dipping in her toe. "Y'all get into that at all?"

"Who doesn't like coke?" smiled Gumm. "How much do you want?"

"How much for an eight-ball?"

Gumm sussed numbers in his head. "I can get you one for two bills, no problem."

"No problem for you, maybe," she said. "But it's a problem for me if I don't want to pay two hundred."

"This isn't Austin, baby," said Gumm. "You'll have a rough time finding coke on the cheap out here. Maybe every once in a while some undergrad gets in over his head and has to move a large chunk on the fly, sells it cheap. That stuff goes pretty quick, and it doesn't happen often."

"Funny," she said, "but I met a guy today who said he could get me an eight-ball for one-fifty. Anytime, night or day."

"What's the catch?"

"No catch, so far as I can tell," she said. "He said if someone wanted two of them, it's only two seventy-five."

Gumm whistled low.

"Things break down the higher you go, I reckon," said Summer.

"How much for an ounce?"

"I ain't never asked him for an ounce," she said. "Me? I'm kind of small time."

"You mind asking?"

"I don't mind at all," she said. "But he's going to want to know you ain't goofing around."

Gumm side-eyed her. "How do I know you ain't a cop? New in town and all of a sudden you've got the best hookup?"

Summer shrugged and dropped an eight-ball onto the coffee table. She tapped out a touch of blow, scraped a rail with the edge of her driver's license, then took it up her face. She stood, wiping her nostril, and faced him.

"I ain't no cop."

Gumm looked over his shoulder at Little Jon, who had paused his video game.

"Then I suppose I'm not goofing around."

Aaaand just like that: Kingpin.

So yes, Summer knew her way around rooms such as those. When the joint or bowl or bong was being passed, when things like hygiene and pest control and homework went out the window in favor of a good buzz, when folks got chatty or quiet or weird…Summer knew how to handle herself. She could walk into any of those rooms with nothing and step out with a new lease on life. Someone's life, anyway.

For long ago, in a room such as that, halfway across the country, she had met Jack Jordan. And she had called him outside, pulled him into the hallway of a dingy student apartment in Charlottesville, Virginia and told him the score. Told him he may think he knows everything, but he didn't know shit because he and his money would soon be parted. She watched his face burn and his cheeks flush and listened as he made several promises to the heavens about what he would do and how he would do it, but she put her hand on his arm and told him otherwise.

"If you really want to teach them a lesson," she had told him way back then, "you'll let them cheat you this one time. You'll let them cheat you this time and hell, maybe even the next time, and when we're ready to make our move, they won't see you coming."

Stepping outside the door of Gumm and Little Jon's apartment, she felt much the same way. The same exhilaration. One that never got old. The first of many scores in a small town. How she could walk into any strange town, reach down to pull up her bootstraps, and make something of herself.

She ran home to Jack to tell him the good news.

5

SURE, IT TOOK A while to get him going, but once it did, every night she cranked his gumptions straight into submission. She worked him like a sock puppet. She was a good eight to ten years younger than he and Jack counted himself lucky to start the game, not to mention last through the Seventh Inning Stretch.

Jack would never be confused for Don Juan. First impressions certainly were not his specialty. Most ladies balked at him physically. They found him short. They considered his eyes beady. Often, he'd get a bad case of the shakes or the sweats and they'd be turned off like a faucet. Furthermore, the only way a guy his age could score a girl her age was to either pay for it, or lie to her. A thrifty man of limited resources, he often opted for the obvious. Turned out, he didn't have to worry about sleeping at night. Not with a girl of her predilections.

Oh, his poor, battered pecker. Red as a raspberry and rubbed raw in several places, it was tender to the touch and near impossible to tolerate in blue jeans. Some nights, he found no respite. She was so very young, so willing. So eager to please him, and, so far as he knew, only him. He knew not whilst she knelt before his feet if her devotion was a byproduct of the size of his handle—just north of average—or if, more appropriately, it was due to the avalanche of psychological hoodoo he festooned upon her.

For example, one look at her and Jack knew she'd be a Daddy's Girl. Her blonde head was too well-combed and kept for someone immune to the want of approval. When she did something he liked, Jack was sure to kiss her forehead, or administer a loving pat upon her shoulder. When she did something bad, he was certain to shake his head in disappointment, then retire to another room in silence.

"I'm sure you'll do better next time, pumpkin," he would often say in such situations.

Or that she'd once been a much larger girl. Many nights, while she lay asleep in her bed, he maneuvered about her dorm room in the dark. She talked a lot about herself when given the chance, but Jack learned more by going through her things. He'd peek into the drawers of her bureau, or finger through her purse until he found old high school photographs, Daddy's credit card statements, letters from ex-boyfriends, diet pills…yes, *diet pills* secreted away between tons of body lotions and body oils and body soaps. Jack pocketed a handful, sure, but the real bounty was the information he'd acquired.

As of late, he'd become interested in her textbooks. Particularly, he'd taken to the experiments of Pavlov. When she'd direct her sweet, sweet kisses down south, he would click his tongue four times against the back of his teeth. A tiny, imperceptible sound, but somewhere it registered because he noticed later when he clicked his tongue that her tiny nipples hardened beneath her shirt, or her pupils dilated, and soon they would be at it, casting aside their britches for romance.

To keep her interest, he revealed very little about himself. Girls often responded to that. Freshman girls, more specifically. Girls who only recently had shed their small towns and cliques of friends who'd tell the world if they were sluts or prudes, true or not, so they could use a touch of mystery in their life. And after a lifetime of dumbass high school boys, she'd foist a host of Daddy issues and inhibitions and hang-ups all over the first older guy who came along, and why should some seedy liberal arts professor have all the fun?

All she wanted was to be seen for more than a great pair of legs.

Or tits.

Or blonde hair with big eyes and come-fuck-me lips.

Not that she had any of those, but Jack did not mind. She was pretty *in places.* Places like her wrists, or ankles. Places not yet disturbed by time or age or an improper diet. Or knives, god forbid. He understood that she was young, but hoped one day she might grow into herself. Shy of nineteen, according to her driver's license, and yes, he'd insisted she show her driver's license. Too many times he'd been burned in the past, headed for fields far from fallow, only to discover he'd been hoodwinked, hornswaggled by a girl so thirsty for attention, she'd lie about her age. He was one angry parent away from a long, tortured stint in the pokey and understood the importance of casting a net more selective.

Her name was Lindsay. She took classes at the university during the day and waited tables at a Tex-Mex joint down the road a couple nights a week. Her family lived in Houston, where her daddy sold houses and her mother decorated them. One look around her dorm room, or at her car, and Jack knew she was not accustomed to want. Their family was well-to-do, or well-enough-to-do, and he reckoned that provided all the beauty she'd ever need.

One such night in late September, Jack returned to bed as quiet as he could, careful, so she would not stir. To test his current hypothesis, he reached for one of her danger zones. He could have chosen from many—the flesh beneath her chin, or where her upper thigh had yet to draw taut—but he settled upon the spot just above her hip. The love handle. She flinched, recoiled, then retreated into herself. Before she could scramble too far, Jack again grabbed her, but this time drew her closer into him.

"Do you see that?" he whispered.

She did not struggle. "See what?"

"The way the rain strikes yonder window?"

"Yeah." She wiped sleep from her eyes. "I see it."

"It's beautiful."

"Do you—" She crumpled up the words and sighed.

Jack tightened his grip on her naked hips. "No one else sees that but us," he said.

"I…"

"Only us, and only right now."

Silence.

"I will never again see rain fall against a window at exactly that angle at exactly that pitch as it hits, never again like we do—you and me—right now, and every time after that I see rain bounce along a windowpane, I will think of this moment. Even if this is the last time we have together, which I hope it isn't, forever will I think of you in the rain. The way you smell and the way your neck feels against my lips and…the way you taste…the sound of your breath against my ear…the inside of your thigh…at my fingertips…"

With her engine good and primed, Jack reached a hand down yonder. He had every intention to more than fuck that girl, to give it to her not only *down there*, but *up there* as well. He wanted her to never again know such affection, to never again know such manhandling. He wanted to give her a father, a teacher, a best friend, a poet, and a bad boy, all rolled up into one angry pounding. He'd give her everything a girl like that wanted or thought she wanted, then he'd give her so much more. More than she'd ever had. Or could. Or would again, should he have anything to do with it, because if he couldn't make it so she never, ever experienced joy or sadness or the slightest hint of satisfaction without first drumming his face or smell or touch across sense memory, then hell, he didn't want it.

But it didn't happen quite the way Jack planned. Perhaps he tussled too much with the rubber beforehand, or felt weird about scrapping it to ride bareback, or any number of things, because something had gone awry and tinkered with his machinery.

"What's the matter, sweetie?" she asked him. It dawned on her that she was *in flagrante* and offering an angle perhaps not too congratulatory. She covered herself with her skinny arms and pulled tighter the blanket. "Do I not turn you on?"

Nothing could be further from the truth. He clicked his tongue four times against the roof of his mouth and thanked the gods above for the reprieve as she slowly kissed him from chest to belly button and kept right on going until…

"Are you sure everything's okay?"

"Dammit…"

She rolled off him and onto her back. Together, they stared at the ceiling.

"I'm just a little stressed out, is all," he said. "This never happens."

Actually, it happened nearly every night. Sometimes he could slip his own hand between the sheets and try and get things going. Maybe close his eyes to picture the girl in all sorts of dandy poses, or bawdy outfits, or making sultry promises. He knew, over the years, the drugs would be taking their toll on him. He made pacts with a god he'd long ago abandoned: *If you help me this one time…*

"Is this because of earlier today?" she asked.

"What are you talking about?"

"Because I didn't sign up for all those credit cards in the student union?" Her voice sounded faraway, like a little girl's.

"No," he said. He didn't mean it.

She rolled over so her nose nestled his shoulder. "I know you said we could contest the charges and say my identity was stolen, and that my dad would never have to pay for it, but I don't see the difference between that and stealing."

Said Jack, "It's not stealing when you do it to a big corporation. Think about it, those credit card companies are trying to get college kids to sign up. They know those kids don't know a lick about managing money and are out on their own for the first time. What kind of monsters would prey on those people?"

"You're disappointed in me, aren't you?"

Jack shook his head. "No, pumpkin. You know you could never disappoint me."

This led to silence, then sniffling, followed by a big ol' bout of sobbing, and Jack let her have at it a bit before wrapping his arm around her. She put her head to his chest and let it all out. Tiny, high-pitched whimpers, then warm, salty tears and all the sadness anyone could ever imagine, and goddammit if Jack didn't feel himself twitching down yonder.

"Honey..." He rolled her over and climbed atop her. "Keep crying for daddy, just a minute or two longer, will you?"

And afterward, while they lay broken, side by side, he touched her again at the hip. This time, she did not recoil.

Instead, she lay still and silent, until she could no longer. Sighing several times before unleashing what really she had on her mind.

"That girl..."

"What are you talking about?"

"Your roommate."

Summer.

Jack laid his forearm across his eyes. "She's my sister."

"Y'all don't look nothing alike."

"Step-sister."

"You know, it's not important."

"What's not important?"

She slipped her arm around him. Big spoon, little spoon.

"All I'm saying is, she don't seem to like me."

"Don't be ridiculous. Summer likes everybody. If I'm not careful, she'll bring home every hobo from the street corner. I've seen her do it."

"It's different with me," said Lindsay. "And I think you know why."

He wanted nothing more than to end this conversation. To fuck or fall asleep. His weary pecker begged for the latter.

"I think she's in love with you."

Jack swallowed. He could think of no fresher hell.

"I told you, she's my step-sister."

"It don't matter." Lindsay stroked the hair around his nipple. "Sometimes love knows no bounds. Where are you going?"

"I just remembered some things I have to do."

"Where?"

"Back in Lufkin."

"What kind of things?"

"Things." He shimmied into his clothes. "And they're best done on my own."

He kissed her forehead and jiggled her tricep just enough to put her off breakfast. He raced down the stairs and across the lot to the shitty Honda in what felt like only a handful of footfalls.

The drive to Lufkin was a good half hour, and damned if Jack's mind didn't race the whole way. He had enough to worry about. Summer had brought home a quarter pound of weed. *A quarter pound.* As if the kilo wasn't enough, she had to get her fingers into the marijuana business as well, and Jack wondered would there ever be an end to it.

Or what if Lindsay was right and Summer was falling in love? There could be no worse fate for him, no worse fate at all.

Summer had a mean streak in her, thick as a boulevard. He'd seen some of the things she'd done when she got sore at a fella. This one poor bastard back in New Orleans. All he'd done was run around on her. Hell, that wasn't *all* he did, because Jack had seen him do some pretty shitty things. Only back then, Jack had been named Pete, but he saw old boy one time steal from Summer's purse, then lead the search party to ferret out the missing money. He'd blamed this guy and pointed fingers at that guy, but in the end, they all got wasted and forgot about it. He'd done many shitty things, but Summer refused to see it. Refused, until she found out he'd run around on her. And it wasn't so much that he'd run around on her, but who he'd run around on her with, which was another little girl who wanted to be Queen Mama Stoner. Then Summer had it and went after his car—a burnt orange Chevy Chevelle—with a ball peen hammer. A set of car keys. Her goddamn fingernails. She fucked up his wheels good and proper, then made it so he couldn't score drugs in town. No, he'd blown it. She said anybody caught selling him so much as a nickel bag would meet her full fury and didn't nobody want to do that. People made up a story about him being a narc. Wasn't true, but folks all believed it and, soon enough, the poor guy moved. Left town. Upped his whole life because of Summer's angry fatwa.

But she hadn't been Summer back then. She had been Stormy. Storm.

He'd liked Storm. Storm had been a riot. Storm got them invited to all the coolest parties. Everybody loved Storm. You could hand Storm a coffee can at a party when the keg ran low and she'd have it filled with dollar bills in no time. Enough money to run out for another keg with a little leftover so maybe you could grab a pack of smokes. Nobody had a cross word to say about Storm. Not until she'd raised enough money to score eleven pounds of weed, then never came back. Then they had plenty cross to say about her. Not that Jack would know, because Jack's name was Pete and he'd lit out with ten grand on his own.

But Storm was gone. Autumn was gone. Hell, even Jasmine from South Carolina was gone, and all that was left was Summer. Summer, whining and crying. Summer who pouted, slouching about the house, looking for shoes, looking for the t-shirt with the giant pot leaf, looking for the hairbrush…picking up things and dropping them, then stepping over them as she griped and moaned, and when finally it came time to leave the trailer for the day, she'd stomp her feet clear to their shitty Honda, for she'd rather do anything than let him forget she'd been slighted.

Jack had thought it a million times and he was bound to think it a million times more: it was well past time for he and Summer to go their separate ways. However, he knew she'd just as soon see him dead as see him leave, so it was bound to be tricky. Were he to slip free of the ties that bound them, he'd have to plan ahead. He'd have to watch for any openings. He'd have to keep ajar all doors and windows, and most of all, he'd need a little bit of luck.

He hadn't noticed doing it, but before he knew it, he'd whipped the car around and headed back up Highway 59 and had already cruised through the main drag and parked in the wooded lot behind the dorms. He ducked just below her window and tossed stones until he'd rousted her.

"I thought you were going home," Lindsay said from above.

"There's nothing for me there," he called to her. "I fear my only future may lie with you."

6

JACKIE DOESN'T KNOW WHAT'S BEST FOR HIM.

Jackie likes blondes.

Jackie likes pretty young things.

A little diddy...about Jack and some pretty young things.

Summer didn't like the looks of her. The girl who went from bringing them chips and hot sauce to waking up some nights in their Light House trailer, other nights with Jack at wherever-the-hell. The girl who Jack began to take his dinners with. The girl with a rich Daddy.

For all Summer cared, the girl's Daddy could fetch enough cash to retire them all to a hemp farm in Costa Rica, that still didn't mean she liked the looks of her.

She stood beneath the pines across the switchback and stared hate-fire toward the windows of the Light House trailer. She'd watched them come home, then watched them go upstairs and switch off all the lights. She waited to hear the sounds of them crying out, then decided she could imagine nothing worse, and covered both her ears with her arms.

She swallowed a pill she'd gotten from Gumm, a pink one, which meant it was either a football of Xanax or it could have been one of those Adderall knockoffs, either way. That fear took hold of her. Cold fingers of sweat swiped at her back, her throat, and down her legs, so she popped another one, whatever it was.

This shit has to stop.

Summer had no earthly idea when it started to rain, but the inferno within her burned and mounted, mounted and burned until finally the sky cracked in half, shitting lightning bolts this way and that, and she found herself knee-deep within a deluge.

This shit is going to stop right this very minute.

She shimmied up the slick creek bank, then sloshed through the gravel on the road toward the highway. She could very well have swiped the keys to the shitty Honda—that would be too easy—but instead, muddier than a pair of work boots, she stomped the entire way to a truck stop and pestered each and every trucker until finally one said, yes, I will drop you down the road in Nacogdoches.

Once in town, she found the first pay phone and dialed Ben Matlin's beeper number. He arrived ten minutes later, and his face fell upon seeing her.

"I didn't call you out here to sell me drugs," she told him. "I thought it high time you and me get to know each other."

Matlin appeared despondent. "I really don't think… You don't want to buy *anything?*"

"Let all them students and townies use you for your connects," she said. "You and me are bound to be fast friends." She opened the passenger seat of his car. "Let's grab a bite to eat. It's on me."

"But, Summer, you're filthy."

"Don't be silly," she said. "It's just mud. It will wash right out of your car seat."

She offered Matlin no recourse, so he slipped the car into gear and got them on the road.

She'd met Ben Matlin a week or so earlier at a roller disco thrown by the campus gays. Crunch and Lance and Tyler and that girl who'd been hanging around Tyler and Kendall and Jamie climbed into Kevin's mom's minivan, and when they climbed out, it was within a green cloud of smoke and one of them had the bright idea to all drop acid.

Enter Ben Matlin. Up and down the rattleboned streets of Nacogdoches, Texas, only one man had the wherewithal to sling hallucinogenics like acid or MDMA. Others might pop up here or there, sure, but they'd never last due to inferior product, bad word of mouth, or, god forbid, the police. When the weekend came and folks wanted to dance or groove or simply stare, open-mouthed, at their dorm room walls, there was only one number to dial.

While everyone in town knew Ben Matlin, very few knew anything about him. Summer sought to rectify that. She imagined a man like him, with great foresight and wonderful drug connections, could finally free her from the likes of Jack Jordan, for whom she no longer cared a lick.

Ben suggested a restaurant in town named Los Rancheros. No sooner had they been led to their table than did Summer regret their decision. Like Jack, Ben Matlin was a short fellow. Also like Jack, he was incredibly twitchy, with ferret-like eyes bugging this way and that. And, most regrettably, like Jack, Ben had eyes for the server in a Tex-Mex restaurant, only this server had broad shoulders and a tight backside and lovely blue eyes. He looked eighteen if he were a day and Summer reckoned if she was going to make this happen, she'd face an uphill battle.

"To be honest," she said, "perhaps we should skip this joint and fetch something we can take back to your place."

Summer'd never seen an apartment so tidy as Ben Matlin's. He dressed like a skater in high school, but had a keen eye for Asian decor. He had a stereo system so state of the art, she hadn't the foggiest where to begin. He took the wheel.

"I've got some Madonna, some ABBA, maybe a little house music?"

"I want to know everything about you," she said, perhaps a bit too dreamily. "Play whatever you like."

Ben chose some soft disco. Summer never knew there was such a thing, but tried her best to dance to it alone. When it wasn't working, she joined him on the fancy love seat where he picked pepperoni from his pizza.

"Processed meat is like the new wave of designer drugs right now," said Ben. "Nobody seems to care where it comes from."

"I was just saying that the other day," she said. "Wow. It's like our minds are so…wow."

"These kids around here don't know how good they've got it." He ate his pizza with a fork. "Down in Houston, the stuff they've got is only about forty-three percent, if that. They've whacked it over half to shit and those kids are bouncing off the walls, calling it Molly."

"I thought if it was Molly, that meant it was one hundred percent."

"Once upon a time, maybe," said Ben. "Not anymore. These days, when you hear the word Molly, that means it's been cut with crank or ethylone or hell, sometimes I've heard they use that stuff they sell in gas stations. The stuff labeled as pipe cleaner."

Summer felt a pill burning a hole in her pocket. "All of this is so fascinating. Tell me more."

"Me…I hold out for the good stuff. I get it down in Houston and they keep trying to sell me on cheap shit." He wiped the corners of his mouth with a cloth napkin. "I know I could dose these kids with Drano and they wouldn't know the difference, but this is a small town. Word gets out."

"Can I use your bathroom?"

He showed her the way. No sooner had she closed and locked the door behind her than she fumbled out the pill in her pocket and popped it. A green one.

What's the green one?

She went through his shit. Face creams, hand creams, and lots of lubricants. Scented candles. Fussy hair gels and colognes. A vast array of things that glowed in the dark.

Summer knew she had her work cut out for her. She inspected

herself in the mirror, then dry-wiped away a streak of mud from behind her ear. Ran her fingers through her hair to smooth it out. She saw eyeliner on the far edge of the sink counter, but decided to work what she had.

All you really want to do is crush him and take his drugs.

Summer disagreed. The last thing she wanted was for a single soul in the world to feel such pain as she.

Except Jack. And that little blonde girl.

Except, of course, Jack and that little blonde girl.

She reckoned there no use in wasting another thought on Jack Jordan. In her mind, there was no duller story in all the world than a criminal trying to go straight, so perhaps she'd better focus her attention on fields of greener pasture. Perhaps she should seek goals more attainable.

She rejoined Ben Matlin on the love seat.

"You're not like anyone I've ever met," she said.

"Did you put on my cologne?"

"You're not even your own star. You are your own solar system. You are an entirely different galaxy."

"And you are so comfortable with who you are," said Ben. "You seem so free and happy. So often, I see people trapped within themselves. They would give everything to be a fraction of how comfortable you are with yourself."

Summer put a hand to his face. "Beauty is all around us. Sometimes in the most unexpected of places."

"I wish I saw things the same way."

"Sometimes we think we are one way," she said, "when in reality, we are a completely different way."

"Sometimes I'm afraid people don't know who I am."

"I know who you are," she said. "I know you are the kind of guy who will try anything, to see if it works."

"I don't know about—"

"The kind of man who will follow his heart, no matter where it leads him."

Ben slapped a funny look on his face, then drained the rest of his white wine. He scampered to the bottle on the counter to fuss out some more.

"You know what we should do?" she asked as she joined him at the counter.

"What? Tell me."

"We should get married."

Ben nearly choked on his wine. He swallowed a glassful, then chased it with another.

"Did you hear what I said?"

Ben's voice, three octaves higher: "Oh, I heard. Look, I think you have the wrong idea about me."

"But I don't."

"I fear that you just might."

She put her hand on his. She refused him the right to recoil.

"You don't get it," she said. "I can see inside you. I can see you are a good person. You care about your customers."

"I really don't. Not a single—"

"When I look at you, I don't see a drug connection or a hookup," she said. "I see someone beautiful. I see a wonderful, sweet person."

Ben lowered his head. His hand relaxed in hers. Summer wanted to take him in her arms and never let him go.

"I'm not a good person."

"Yes, Ben. You are."

"I've done things…"

"We've all done things." Summer laughed louder, the more she thought about it. "If I could only tell you. I can't tell you, but whoa boy, if I could."

"I do horrible things every day."

"But that's not who you are." Summer took hold of his other hand. "You do what you have to do to survive. That doesn't make you a bad person."

His hip pocket buzzed. He pulled a pager from his pocket and looked at it. He seemed to lose himself to deep thought a moment before asking, "Hey, you want to go for a ride with me?"

"Sure," said Summer. "I'll go anywhere with you." Then, after a second thought, "Where are we going?"

"To work."

☀ ☀ ☀

Damn near the entire county paged Ben Matlin, on account of Halloween was coming. The Rho Thetas had their annual keg party on the books, so they wanted to stock up on Molly. A couple kids in the dorms bought two ten-strips of some paper called Electric Ladyland. While he was there, he got a page from a young couple at the student union who wanted some E. Then to the sports bar across town for a couple of rednecks looking to trip. Then another call, and another, then yet another.

"You must make a lot of money," whispered Summer after all was said and done. They sat parked in the car outside the dorms while Ben counted his money.

"I tell my mother I have a paper route." Ben held up a Ziploc with three sheets of acid. "Get it? *A paper route.*"

She put her hand on his knee.

"Summer…Summer, I—"

"All you need is love, man."

"I don't think—"

She doe-eyed him. "I'll do anything, Ben. Just ask."

"I'm afraid you may have the wrong idea…"

"Don't be silly," she said. "Your walls are up and man, those things are high. You should allow yourself to take them down. You should let someone in."

Ben's smile crooked ever upward. She didn't like the look of it.

"In my experience," he said, "I've found most folks have ulterior motives when it comes to me. I don't know if it's the drugs or—"

"That must be so awful," she said. "I can assure you, my intentions are pure."

"I've heard that before."

She nuzzled up close to him. "We already determined the people in this town are shady and full of shit."

"You know what I do when I find out people are less than genuine with me?" he asked.

"No. Tell me."

Ben looked at his watch, then he looked at her. "Let's make one more stop," he said.

"Whatever you say, Bennie-boy."

Crazy Carter: Thin as a rail. White. Long, stringy hair down to his shoulders. He wore a vest of what Summer could only guess was alpaca. Eyes glazed like donuts. Hunched over a tray riddled with stems, seeds, two empty packs of rolling papers. A razor blade.

Two other girls in the room. Also skinny, also white. One wore a bikini, for some odd reason. Both were made up for a night at the club, not kicking it at some apartment with a stoner tripping balls.

More than once he showed off his lamp made completely from debris from the space shuttle Columbia. More than once he stopped talking or pacing or petting a copy of the *Physician's Desk Reference* like it was a kitten to throw an arm around Ben Matlin and declare him the greatest man who ever lived.

Maybe it was the line of Molly she did off Ben's dashboard before they came up to the apartment. Maybe it was the three Adderalls and the whatever was that green pill she took earlier. Maybe it was an internal sensor sounding the alarm—one of the last still working—because no sooner had Summer stepped inside the door than she felt something had gone horribly wrong.

"Did I tell you or did I tell you?" Crazy Carter said to the two girls. He said it again, then again. Before long, Summer wondered if he'd ever quit saying it and understood why those girls had such troubled looks upon their faces.

"Carter here is chasing a record," said Ben.

"Oh?"

"That's right," said Carter. He slurred his words, not like a drunk, but rather like a boxer who'd thrown too many rounds. "I'll have the record in fifty-four days."

"What's the record?" asked Summer.

"What's the record?" Carter laughed harder than necessary. "This girl here wants to know what's the record. Like she's never been on Twitter or Google or watched the evening news."

The girls in the corner mouthed something that looked like *help me*. Summer had problems all her own. Her stomach began to churn. Her jaw tightened and vibrated like a guitar string.

"Summer is new in town, so be nice, Carter," said Ben. He turned to Summer. "The record for the most days a person has consecutively taken MDMA—"

"Set in 1998 by Larry Williamson in Mill Valley, California," said Carter. "His long quest actually began in December of 1997, but did not reach its finale until early February 1998. This was actually the second of such tries by Williamson, as he also holds the record for second place as well."

"The record is seventy-three days," said Ben. "Carter is on day eighteen."

"Nineteen," said Carter.

"We agreed that the first day didn't count because you got it from that guy who was busted selling methylone. We have no idea if what you took had MDMA or not."

Carter's shoulders sagged, but not for long.

"I'm liveblogging the entire experience," said Carter. "So far, I've been retweeted in forty-seven different countries."

Summer pretended to give a shit. Quite frankly, she wanted out of the room. She thought if she didn't find fresh air and soon, she would spackle the apartment walls with vomit.

Ben gave the man his medicine.

"What about your friends?" asked Ben, motioning to the two girls.

"Them?" Carter laughed. "They're not my friends. They're only here for the drugs. The second you dose them, they'll be out the door and leave me here all alone." Carter slapped his buddy on the back. "You know what that's like, don't you, buddy-old-pal?"

Ben didn't blink. He plucked two tabs from the baggie in his pocket and bestowed them both upon the two girls. With little to no fanfare, they slipped into their britches and out the front door. Carter's face crumpled and he fell to the floor in a conniption.

"This is going to kill my high," Carter wailed. "This is bringing me way down, man."

"How about another?" Ben offered. He'd already fussed out a tab and set it on the coffee table.

Summer wanted to stop him. She wanted to shout him down and remind him that eighteen or nineteen days of consecutive MDMA use was no good for someone's brain or soul or anything in between. That perhaps enough damage had been done and the last thing he needed at this very moment or any other moment in life was another tab of fucking ecstasy because that shit ate holes in your brain. That shit robbed you of serotonin, and after eighteen or nineteen days, there was nothing left in the tank, man. His brain had to be Swiss cheese and, well, come to think of it, what was Summer doing with that shit in her head and was it too late for her? Was she destined to become something like that shivering, huddled mess on the carpet, and speaking of…

Summer launched for the door. She barely made it out in time before all of her insides wretched up and projectiled over the stairway. She fell to her knees, but lurched forward still, hoping to steer clear of her spray and doing a poor job at it. She made it to the parking lot and held her head a solid inch over the gutter, where Ben found her some time later.

"I told you," he said. "I get the good stuff."

There was a twenty-minute drive from Nacogdoches to Lufkin. Ben did most the talking, as Summer fancied herself in no shape for conversation.

"You wouldn't think it to look at him," said Ben, "but Carter was one of the top neuroscience students in the state. He'd had two articles published. Then…"

Summer could barely hold open her eyeballs. She feared she might have chucked up her soul back yonder.

"He'd never so much as smoked pot before he met me." Ben sounded a touch boastful. "He said it was all an experiment."

Summer wished she had the energy to smoke.

"He said he was experimenting with a lot of things."

Ben's sadness filled the front seat of his car, if indeed it was sadness. He stared forlornly out the windshield as they rolled over the river, through the road carved into the forests, and into the outskirts of town.

"What did he do to you?" asked Summer.

"Why do you think he did anything to me?"

"For you to hate him so much."

Ben tried to square his shoulders, but couldn't keep them upright.

"What makes you think I hate him?"

"Why else would you do that to his…" Her lips were oh so dry. She ran her tongue across them. It did her no favors. "Why else would you keep giving him…"

"I'm in business school," he said, "and I'm a drug dealer. Carter is not only my best customer, but he's the best advertisement money can buy."

It took a while for that to sink in. When it did, Summer asked, "Fine. But what did he *do* to you?"

"What did he do?" Ben wouldn't take his eyes off the road. Summer swore she saw his face change from a man to a monster, then back to a little boy. "He told me a lie."

Summer could speak only in a whisper. "What did he lie about?"

Ben's only answer was to turn and face her full-on. Gone was that little boy. He transformed again into a man.

They spent the rest of the ride in silence. Summer couldn't put her finger on it, but never before had her soul taken such a huge hit. A broadside. Her engines had been crippled and she wanted nothing more than to be free of him.

But those drugs...

He had a hookup, sure. Best she could do in that county was get her own stuff, but it'd never be better than what he was slinging. It would always be inferior, and the way it sounded, competitors didn't last in that market. How come every story she heard about some other guy with stuff ended with that other guy in jail? Ben was smart. He'd dime if it meant squeezing out the competition.

From the looks of Carter, *dime* wasn't the worst Ben would do.

Ben maneuvered the switchback and pulled to a stop outside the Light House trailer. He killed the lights, but not the motor.

"I had a good time tonight," he said.

She could barely breathe. "So did I."

"I don't have any real friends," Ben said. "I hope that you and I could—"

"What are you two doing?"

Jack stood in the darkness just outside her window. He smoked a cigarette and smiled Cheshire.

"Jack?"

"Dear me..." Ben licked his lips.

"Jack, we're just sitting here talking. I'll be in in a minute."

Ben's eyelids went a-flutter. "Summer, who is this?"

"Is this... Are you two..." Jack's smile traveled from Cheshire to shit-eating. "Ha-ha. My name is Jack. I'm her roommate. We're *just* roommates."

"Oh, I see…"

"Jack, would you please give me a minute?"

"Certainly, Summer. Most certainly."

And she thought she couldn't possibly hate him more, but she was wrong—dead wrong—because when she saw that look in Ben Matlin's eye as Jack strutted his way back to the Light House trailer, she hated him *ten times* more. Once again, he had stymied her. Once again, he had gotten the upper hand. Once again, he had ruined her buzz.

"That's your roommate?"

"Yes," she sighed.

Ben put a hand faint to his chest. "Is he…is he…"

"A pain in my ass? Yes."

"No…I mean, is he *gay?*"

Summer never felt so used in all her life. Jack used her for drugs, and now Ben Matlin used her for Jack. She reckoned she could plant herself in the best soil on earth and grow apples out her ass, but still no one would see her as the ends, as opposed to the means.

"From what I'm to understand," she said, "he's the biggest cocksucker in all of Angelina County."

Ben drew his hands to his mouth and shuddered.

"If you want," she said, "maybe I'll introduce you."

"Would you really?"

"Sure," she said, her face turning upside down. "I bet the two of y'all would get along just fine."

7

JACK LIKED TO HAVE blown his top when he put eyes on the Light House trailer the night he'd come home from Lindsay's dorm room. He'd spent half the evening trying to subliminally hint to her and her roommate that a threesome would be a wonderful idea and the other half trying to stop her from crying. He so looked forward to a nice, quiet night at home. Maybe a little time with a book, which he hadn't done in ages.

However, he came home to find a party. Not a chips-and-dip and let's-have-a-few-beers get-together, but a full-on rager complete with a keg and about three dozen co-eds spilling onto the switchback, drinking beers and passing joints.

Inside, the trailer looked like it'd bust at the seams, there were so many people crammed inside. Jack stood at the door and pushed aside first one, then another, then yet another still as he squeezed through the horde until he could make the stairs. All the way upward to his bedroom, the people shouted *hey, watch it* and *what's the big idea?* But finally he got to his room and, after kicking out a couple trying to make time, he closed the door so he could—in private—enjoy a minor conniption.

Once all that was good and settled, he shouldered his way down the stairs, braving a chorus of *hey there, asshole* and *who do you think you are?* before he arrived in the living room. He elbowed his way to the light switch where he flashed the lights on and off, but instead of getting attention, he got applause. Someone cranked louder the dance music and the throng of people partied on.

Able to take no more of it, Jack muscled his way into the kitchen. There, Summer Ashton nursed a beer and chopped way-too-fat rails of cocaine across the kitchen counter.

"What the dog-shitting hell do you think you are doing, Summer?" he wanted to know.

"I'm throwing a party," she said. "What does it look like I'm doing?"

"A party?" Jack seethed in his boots. "In our trailer?"

"I'm always impressed with your intellect." Summer leaned forward to take one of the powdered lines up her face. "And a damn fine party at that, considering the size of this joint."

Jack clenched and unclenched his fists. He gritted his teeth.

"Summer, need I remind you that not only have we got damn near a half kilo of cocaine in this trailer, but—thanks to you—we've also got a quarter-pound of pot and pills of every color. What if the cops come?"

"It ain't a party until the cops show up," she said. "But don't sweat it. All they'd say is how we should turn down the music and send these folks home. Don't act paranoid."

Summer knew a surefire way to cut him at the knees was to call him paranoid. Jack was paranoid, sure, but calling him such could twist him into a reckless frenzy. She took a moment to savor his frothing at the mouth. Jack thought he could stomp a hole in the trailer floor.

"You should have your head examined, throwing a party with all these drugs in the trailer."

"If anybody around here should get examined," she growled, "it's you."

He shook his head like a dog in from the rain. "What are you talking about?"

"We've been in town two months, Jackie. You go off with that little blonde for make out sessions and I'm the only one bringing in business."

"I told you, I'm working on it."

A stoner crawled across their path on all fours. He backed into Jack, who thought very little before casting him aside with his foot. The stoner rolled over on his back and kicked both arms and legs like an upturned cockroach.

"Is that what you'd call it?" Summer crossed her arms and upturned her chin. "Because I'd call it something else. You and me, we're supposed to be working together. Instead, it's me making all the money and connections while you run around to make time with the anorexia poster child. We both are supposed to have dirty faces."

Jack pointed to the counter top. "You do more coke than you sell!"

"You can't make an omelet without first cracking open a couple eggs. You're the one who taught me that."

"Summer…" Jack struggled to keep composed. "You have to get these people out of this trailer."

"I'm not breaking up a party, Jackie."

Jack felt those cold fingers of fear inching their way up his backbone. They took hold of his lungs, his shoulders, all his upper body and squeezed tight until he labored for breath. He rolled his neck from side to side, trying like hell to loosen his tendons.

"Summer…*please*…"

"Nope."

"I can't breathe…" Jack tugged at his collar with a finger. "They'll put us in jail…"

She sucked up the second line off the countertop, then, after much deliberation, took pity on him.

"I will send home all of these people," she said, "so long as you do one little thing for me."

"What?"

She frowned. "It shouldn't matter. You should be happy to do it because it's high time you shouldered some of the load around here."

"Fine. Name it."

Summer's smile could have burnt toast.

※ ※ ※

Jack would never have ridden to Houston had Summer not put the screws to him. *Really* put the screws to him, because not only did he agree to ride shotgun while Ben Matlin re-upped his packages, not only did he agree to try to negotiate the purchase of a couple sheets of acid and perhaps an ounce or two of Molly, but he also agreed that to do it, he would perhaps need to play along with Matlin's affection for men.

"I'm not going to blow him," Jack had told his roommate. "And no way in hell will I let him stick anything up my keester."

"You don't have to be gay," Summer had countered. "All you need to do is make a little mystery of it. The only thing a gay dude loves more than drama is a little mystery."

Jack reckoned he could do as much, so the entire way down Highway 59, he kept the conversation toward such things as fussy restaurants, movie star gossip, and the musical stylings of such luminaries as Madonna and Cher.

Still, Matlin played it safe. He toed the edge of the water. He kept his hands firm on the wheel. A slick sheen of sweat spackled his forehead and his eyes, although twitchy, rarely left the road. Matlin tried his damnedest to keep his cards close to his chest, but instead laid them out across the table, faces-up, to Jack.

"So...Summer is your...what?"

"Beg pardon?"

Matlin swallowed something imaginary. "Is she your...girlfriend?"

"Not hardly," said Jack. "She's not exactly my type, if you know what I'm saying."

Rather than admit he didn't, Matlin let a few miles pass before he mustered the courage to speak again.

"So…what type is that?"

"Is what?"

"Your type."

Jack shrugged. "I've found it more advantageous to keep my options open."

Matlin let his foot off the gas just a moment, and for the first time since they'd left Angelina County, they dipped below eighty miles per hour.

Once he'd collected himself, he stammered, "D-d-do you like breakfast tacos?"

"Who doesn't like breakfast tacos?"

"Carter didn't."

"Who is Carter?"

Matlin quickly shook his head. "Nobody. Just the guy who used to make these runs with me."

"He sounds like an asshole." Jack couldn't for the life of him remember Summer saying anything about anyone named Carter. "Anybody who don't like breakfast tacos sounds to me like an asshole."

"I know the best place in all of Houston for breakfast tacos. It's only open on Saturday and Sunday mornings."

"You'll have to tell me the name of it. Next time I'm down here on a Saturday or Sunday morning, I can fetch me some."

"Because…I was thinking…" Matlin took his sweet time with it. "Maybe we could get a room…you know, so we don't have to worry about the drive back. Maybe drop a little E, party some, then wake up and get some breakfast tacos."

Jack made a brief list of all the people he'd like to strangle. He put Summer at the top of it.

"We don't have to wait until we get into the city before we start the party," Matlin said. Jack turned sideways in his seat to see he'd wiggled free a tiny baggie of purple pills from his pocket. "We can get it started right now. By the time we get to Manson's, you'll be seeing monkeys."

"Who the hell is Manson?"

"It's a nightclub." Matlin thumbed a pill onto his own tongue, then chased it with an energy drink. "It's where we pick up the shit."

"You buy this shit from some asshole in a club?"

"No," Matlin said, "I buy it from the asshole who owns it."

☼ ☼ ☼

No lie. That asshole was named Beef Guidry, and no closet could possibly contain him. When Jack first met him, he'd thought he was a she, as the person to whom he'd been introduced was lit up like a Christmas tree. She wore feather boas and stiletto heels, but not just any stiletto heels would do for Beef Guidry; no, these stiletto heels contained the image of the Statue of Liberty and the torch lit bright orange with each footfall.

She'd worn a long, slender gown and Jack watched her backside like it was a metronome as they were escorted to the office in rear of the club. Once they'd arrived and the door clicked shut, Beef set about making things right by plucking off the wig, the feather boa, the Elton John sunglasses, the long, long eyelashes and, before long, Jack wondered what in good hell he'd been thinking.

Another thing Beef removed was the pencil-thin moustache of white powder, which he cleared with his finger and licked clean with an abnormally long tongue. Jack swore the office had gotten smaller and the walls of liquor boxes and file cabinets grew tighter around the three of them.

Beef wagged his spit-slicked finger at Jack, then wiggled it at the knuckle.

"Benjamin," he said, "who is your little friend here?"

"This is Jack," Matlin said. "He's from Nacogdoches."

"And is his costume supposed to be *ironic*?" Beef wiggled his nose.

Said Jack, "I don't follow."

"Your outfit." When still Jack offered nothing, Beef rolled his eyes and sighed. "Benjamin, you certainly have your peccadilloes."

Beef sauntered around the desk where laid a framed picture of Ava Gardner. He took a seat and lowered his face to the glass and sucked up his nose a line of powder off Ava's long legs. He cleared his nostril with a finger, then leaned back and slithered a smile.

"What happened to Carter?" he asked.

Matlin shook his head.

"That's too bad." Beef crossed one hammy leg over the other. "I liked Carter. How long did he make it? Eight weeks?"

"Ten."

Beef raised his eyebrows, impressed. "Ten weeks? Wow, Benjamin, you must really be turning them out. When I first met that little boy, I thought there'd be no way he'd last ten weeks, but you certainly are full of surprises."

Beef rose from the chair and swept across the floor until he stood alongside Jack. He slipped an arm around his waist and nuzzled his freshly shaved cheek against Jack's.

"What do you say, Jackie-boy?" he whispered. "Don't you think our boy Benjamin is full of surprises?"

Before Jack could speak, he was guided by the waist toward the photo of Ava. Two hefty lines of powder stretched across her lovely face. Beef waved his hands across the glass as if he were a model at a trade show.

"I'd better not," Jack mumbled. "I don't think cocaine will play well with the shit I done already took."

"Oh, this isn't cocaine," Beef tittered, "and it plays well with everyone."

Jack got the funny feeling he shouldn't argue, so he lowered his nose to the glass and sucked up first one line, then the other.

"So happy to have you aboard," said Beef with a zealous squeal. "So tell me, Jack: what's your fancy?"

"My fancy?"

"Your pleasure."

"I'm not sure I follow."

"Do you like boys, or do you like girls?" Beef's smile carved his face in half and froze that way. "Or perhaps you prefer something in between."

"I…I, uh…"

"Oh…" Beef took a step backward. He had a look like he'd been told it was malignant. "Dear me."

Beef turned with a flourish and reached his desk in two grand steps. He swept up a cellphone and tapped the screen a number of times, then returned his piteous stare to Jack.

"And what will you be having to drink?"

Jack wondered what he had done wrong. What he had said or done or—

Beef snapped his fingers. "Honey," he said, "folks are busy."

"Orange juice, I guess," Jack said. "Maybe a touch of vodka."

Matlin's head hung low, fists jammed into his pockets. Jack had no idea if it was the drugs, but he felt the heat off the little man. He didn't care much for the vibe.

Beef tapped further into his phone, then waved him away with the back of his hand.

"Off with you, then," he said. "You run play with the kiddos while Mommy and Daddy handle business."

"Where do I—"

The answer came when the little door to Beef's office swung open and in walked the twins. Twins, as they looked exactly the same. Both burly, hunky dudes wearing nothing above the waist save a bowtie and about two pounds each of hair gel. Both smooth as otters and eyes hungry like jackals.

"These are my beefcakes," said Beef. "I'm sure they will find something appropriate for you to play with."

With that, Jack found himself whisked by the elbow down the

skinny flight of stairs and across the crowded dance floor to the bar, where waited both a cocktail as well as a cocktail waitress.

"My name is Sheila," said the girl as she removed the drink from the tray. "Beef said you and I are destined to become fast friends."

Once Sheila stepped out of her apron, Jack saw she had crippling curves and came with no instruction manual. He hated to dance, but wouldn't dare leave her side on the dance floor. Something took hold of him and he blamed it on the E or whatever he'd taken up his face back in that tiny office upstairs. He could not keep still. He shuffled his weight from one foot to the other, somewhat in time with the music.

To speak, they had to lean into each other and shout over the music.

"This is good shit," he said.

"You keep saying that." Her hips lost no shimmy. She ground against him with her back, her front, and whatever else at her disposal. "Do you want to sit down?"

"I can't dance worth a shit."

"You're holding your own."

"All I'm doing is watching you."

"Like I said…" Her eyes were the color of fox hair. They sparkled like disco balls. "But we should get some air."

He agreed. He floated behind her like a balloon on a string as she led him by the hand out a side door marked NOT AN EXIT. Outside was crisp. Lit yellow by halogen street lamps. Yonder, two hobos bickered over what sounded like five bucks. Jack's hands shook like the Parkinson's as he tugged two cigarettes from a crumpled pack.

"So, are you a farmer or something?" she asked.

"What do you mean?"

Her eyes trickled the length of him, then retraced their steps. She shook her head.

"Never mind."

"You work here?" he asked her.

She answered, "I'm a waitress."

"Part of a waitress' job is to eat Molly and dance with who the boss tells you?"

"It's a pretty easy job." Sheila held her cigarette to a flame and sucked it lit. "You don't like how I do it?"

"Oh, I like it just fine."

She batted her eyelashes. "When you fill out a comment card, tell the boss you think I deserve a raise."

"Are we supposed to…you know…"

"Screw?" Sheila flicked an ash with her forefinger. "Not at this rate, we aren't. What, are you not having a good time?"

"I'm having a great time—"

"Then chill." She resumed dancing in the parking lot, although the music could barely be heard through several layers of concrete. Some peckerwood in a pickup truck hollered catcalls. Nobody minded the rat scurrying from yonder dumpster. "How long have you known Ben?"

"Ben?"

"Matlin." Her hips continued their hypnotic rhythm. "The horse you rode in on."

"Oh…" The drugs rolled his eyes back to their lids. His teeth chattered on a creaky jaw. "I only met him yesterday."

"You guys rode all this way to Houston to score from Beef?"

"For a waitress," he said, "you sure know a lot."

"Maybe I'm looking to be more than a waitress." She nuzzled tight against him. "I've seen Ben come and go with lots of characters. But somehow…somehow you don't seem the sort."

"What do you mean, *the sort?*"

Her entire body laughed, starting with her eyes. "What are you, a parrot?" Her hands grabbed both of his. "We were better off dancing."

Sheila had a point. He'd lost his way with words, but not for standing still while a girl danced against him. She had something going for her. He couldn't quite put a finger on it, but she had it where Lindsay didn't and Summer for damn sure didn't, and maybe not even Melissa back in South Carolina, or the host of girls in New Orleans. Maybe nobody he'd ever met, because as he handled this girl along her waist, her hips, or the small of her back, he found the possibilities infinite, all horizons within reach, and the stars countable. Needing only the tip of his finger, he drew her into him.

"You are a narcotic," he whispered.

She thanked him with a smile. A pair of parted lips. He needed no translator for that.

"Baby, come get your fix."

※　　※　　※

Matlin flew to fury. First he raised a finger to the heavens and declared misdeeds. Jack could see the *et tu* all across his face and how this must be the deepest cut of all. Jack thought nothing of the woman in his arms, who suddenly felt pounds—no, *tons*—heavier, so he released her, then felt like he might melt like tar into the earth.

"I thought you were different," Jack said through clenched teeth. "I thought you were not like the others."

No matter how angry Matlin was, Jack kept his wary eyes upon the twins, grinning like hyenas. Shimmering from the oils applied to their pecs, their abs, those arms…looks on their faces like they'd spent more than a week in the desert and now stood at the front end of the buffet line at Golden Corral. They stared a hole in his stomach, so he promptly crumpled to his knees and vomited pills and jerky into the gutter.

"I expected more from you." Matlin carved half-moons into the pavement around the mess with his tiny, sneakered feet. "You disgust me."

"What did I do?" Jack panted, still on his knees.

"You must think we're idiots." Behind them, sirens sliced the night. "You think I would let you get away with this?"

"Please…I got no idea what you're talking about."

Sheila could not be bothered with any of it. She'd lost the rhythm. She reckoned it was somewhere beneath her fingernails, the way she studied them. The proceedings—Jack on the floor, Matlin losing his shit—held no interest for her whatsoever.

"Boys…" Matlin snapped his fingers. "Let's check him for a wire."

"A *what*?"

Before he could further protest, the twins clutched him at the elbows. They went to work ripping the buttons from his shirt.

"Wait…"

No dice. Soon, his hairy chest was bare and the autumn evening blew chilly kisses along his back, his midsection.

"No wire, Ben," said one of the beefcakes.

"Nothing here," said the other.

"I'm not convinced." Matlin's face crumpled to a frown. "Let's get those pants off him."

All of Jack's world became pectorals and cocoa butter. Hot phlegm wretched from his insides. He scuffled, but he could do no good as he was pinwheeled. Telescoped. Crisped. He could be made of Styrofoam or tissue paper. There would be no one to mourn him. His marker would be a fake ID found in an alleyway. Stain caked on the back wall of a discotheque.

He wondered who would take care of Summer.

The beefcakes manhandled open his britches, then yanked them off his legs.

"All of it," growled Matlin.

One of them held him flat against the cracked concrete while the other wrested free his skivvies. Sheila took a peek at what she might be missing, then returned her attention to her cellphone. A smooth hand grabbed hold of his nethers at the base. Another slipped a sneaky finger between his cheeks and, once finished with him, awaited further instruction.

"He's clean, Ben."

"Nothing so far as I can tell."

That wouldn't cut it for Matlin. He stepped half in shadow and grumbled from somewhere deep.

"Check him again."

This time, the beefcakes were far more thorough. Jack struggled, sure. It would do no good, but he at least wanted to be able to say he struggled.

"Be sure to check everywhere, boys," said Matlin. "This one is very slippery. There may be no depths to which he would not stoop."

Sheila held up her phone and snapped a photo of the tableau. She returned with a smirk to fingering her screen.

"I will make you beg me for mercy," said Matlin. "I will make you crawl on your hands and knees."

"I ain't no cop!" Jack shouted into the abdominals of his attackers. "I may be a lot of things, but I ain't no police!"

"I'd rather not hear another word from this piece of shit," Matlin said as he turned his back. "Perhaps you boys might find something to stick into his mouth."

"Not a problem, Ben."

"We'll take care of him for you."

Jack had never been closer in all his life to another man as he was in that moment.

Yet never in his life had he felt more alone.

☀ ☀ ☀

"Ben, what in great Gloria Gaynor are you doing to that poor man?"

Matlin backed off him from the front. In the other direction, Jack felt air pass between him and the beefcakes for the first time.

"Tell me, please, that things are not how they appear." Beef stood at the side entrance clad complete with wig, evening gown, the whole nine yards. She held a little Derringer pointed toward the air like an afterthought. "Tell me this is all a horrible misunderstanding."

"This guy is lying," Matlin panted. "I'm about to prove it."

"Lying about what, Benjamin?"

Jack did his best to shimmy free from between the beefcakes, but they kept him put.

"I ain't lying Mister…uh, *Miss*…I mean—*Dammit*, I ain't lying." Jack added, "By all things holy, I swear I ain't a cop."

Beef rolled his eyes and slapped Matlin's shoulder. "Bengie, you and I both know good and well this here boy could not be an officer of the law."

"I know no such thing!" Matlin stomped his feet like a petulant child. "I don't know the first thing about this guy except everything he's told me so far has been a lie!"

"He's taken far too much E to be a policeman." Beef took Matlin's cheeks into his cupped palms. "This happens every time, Bengie. You always think these boys are cops and they never, ever are."

"This one was supposed to be different!"

"You are such a sweet, sweet darling."

Matlin sagged, but Beef kept him upright. Behind them, Jack felt the beefcakes lighten their grip. Jack remained where he was, but began the nervous business of collecting his pants.

"You know these boys can be so mean," whispered Beef. "However, that does not make them police."

If Matlin understood, he did not let on.

"And you certainly cannot do those things I saw you doing," Beef said, more stern. "Especially not behind my nightclub."

Said Matlin, "This one was supposed to be different."

Beef answered, "They are all the same." He kissed the little man on the nose. "There's only one person you can trust in this mean old world, Bengie. That's your good aunt Beef."

Beef released Matlin's cheeks. The little man did not sink to the ground, but rather remained before him with his shoulders slumped until finally he straightened them, smoothed the wrinkles from his shirt, then turned to face Jack.

"Business here is done," he said. "If you're not in the car within five minutes, you can walk back to Lufkin for all I care."

The last bit he said over his shoulder. Jack took advantage of what little time he had. He found Sheila leaning against the side of the nightclub. She finished her cigarette and dropped it to the ground where she let it smolder, rather than toe it smushed.

"Listen," Jack said, "I ain't got much time. If you tell me not to get inside that car with him, then I won't. You say the word—that's all you've got to do—and I'll stay with you. I don't have much to my name, but I know how to get what I need and I swear to God on high you will remember this moment for the rest of your life as when you finally began to make better of yourself."

Sheila arched an eyebrow. "You're kidding me, right?"

The air let out of Jack's sails. He considered points on the compass long ignored, or perhaps never considered.

Instead, he and Matlin spent the entire distance from Houston to Lufkin in silence.

8

JACKIE CAME BACK TO the Light House trailer from Houston and said to hell with it—to hell with all of it—he was settling down. No more. Never again. He'd seen the light. He'd stayed too long. He was the old guy at the party.

Summer asked him what was the matter.

"I don't want to talk about it." Jack stopped what he was doing: putting away his wallet, his cigarette lighter, a handful of pocket change. He looked Summer square in the eye, to let her know he meant business. "I don't *ever* want to talk about it."

Summer gave him his space. Jack could get a wee grumpy if she remained in his face after he'd started to sputter. However, she would prefer no chance of miscommunication.

"What do you mean, you're done with *all of it*."

"The whole kit and caboodle." Jack pointed toward the loose board hiding the King James Version at the bottom of the steps. He pointed to the tray on the coffee table which had been reduced to stems and seeds. He pointed at the aspirin bottle filled with Valium. "I'm through with it. I want nothing more to do with it. I've said it before and I'm going to say it again: it is over. I'm going clean. I don't want to so much as touch the shit. No more pot dealers. No more coke dealers. No more trips out of town to buy quantity and shitting my pants the whole way back because what we got in the trunk could make things federal. I'm settling down."

Summer portioned her words piecemeal. "You're settling down how?"

"I'll tell you how." Jack raised a finger to the air, as if teaching a class. "I'm going to ask Lindsay to be my steady lady. I'm going to start a life with her. Not a transient life full of fake identifications and idiot marks, but a *real life*. One where we go to a church we don't believe and make friends with folks we don't like and laugh at jokes that aren't funny. Like normal people do."

"Are you sure you don't want to talk about what happened in Houston?"

Jack cut a glance at her, but said nothing. He crawled into the kitchen and poured himself a glass of water. Summer watched as he drank it to the last drop.

"What about the rest of that kilo?" asked Summer. "What about all the marijuana? We've still got more than a pound."

"It's yours," said Jack. "I hereby renounce any and all claims to the contraband purchased before this moment in time." He checked his watch against the clock on the microwave. "You're selling it all anyway. I want nothing more to do with it."

"I think you need to sit down."

Jack put a finger to his chin. "However, I am a bit low on funds, so if you could front me a hundred bucks until my first paycheck…"

"Paycheck?" Summer dropped her head into her hands and collapsed against the wood-paneled wall. "How the hell are you going to get a paycheck?"

"I'm going to get a job."

Now, she'd heard it all. She looked him over—twitchy, sweaty, beady-eyed, and scared to all Armageddon—and couldn't imagine a single white employer who'd take him. She thought hard about what skills he might possibly have. Sure, he may have thought he hung the moon, but last she checked, that got no man a job.

"I'm going to wait tables," he said. "Or tend bar. I could do that, tend a bar. I'm real good at getting people fucked up so it's high time I try it legal-like. Folks in need of a good time, look no further."

"The decrease in pay will likely leave you rankled."

"That's what you think," said Jack. "Bartenders make good money. And they don't have to worry about going to jail or friends who will stab you in the back or…"

His eyes went somewhere far away.

Summer snapped her fingers until he drew focus on her.

"You should sleep and revisit this subject when you are sober."

"I am sober." His frisbee pupils told another tale. "Last time I snorted any E was hours ago and I took an Adderall to snap me awake."

He'd never make it a week out there.

Summer had to agree. How long would Lindsay stay with him after she saw him fall into one of his fits? He'd go dipping into the cash register behind any bar he worked, so that plan was bound to fail as well. Summer knew he could do anything he set his mind to, but not *anything*.

He wouldn't last a day.

Jack squeezed up the stairs, then back down and took a seat on the blue beanbag. He'd brought with him a picture frame, the one formerly holding the picture of Keith Richards he had cut from a magazine. With shaking hands, he removed the picture and carefully set it aside. He replaced it with a printed screenshot of Lindsay. It was a selfie. He rested his elbows on his knees and his chin within his hands while admiring the hell out of it.

Perhaps it's best if we let him try.

※ ※ ※

Summer wished him well, but on the inside, wished he'd go fuck himself. She dialed Crunch and asked loud enough for Jack to hear if he'd come pick her up. Said she wanted to spend time with her real friends. Said she wanted to go somewhere to feel safe. Said she'd wait for him out front of the trailer, because she could no longer stand the air on the inside.

No sooner had she stepped into the moonlight and the stars and the last of the cicadas than did Lindsay come traipsing up the walk. She carried with her a bottle of wine which she held like a holy relic.

"Jack is making his special chicken," Lindsay said. "I brought a Chardonnay because it goes well, but also because Jack said he likes a good Chardonnay."

"Does he now?" snapped Summer. "Ain't he full of surprises?"

Lindsay smiled, probably thinking she had one over on Summer. Probably thinking she knew Jackie better than anyone else, if for no other reason than because they'd swapped saliva and seminal fluids and god only knew what else. Probably thinking Summer wasn't nothing but unwashed, surly shit.

But Lindsay was an idiot. Summer knew more than what he liked—*swinging out over the creek in a tire, the Carolina chickadee, minor league baseball games, macaroni and cheese from a box, coffee with lots of cream and sugar, old sit-coms from the 1980s, fresh peaches, driving at night, the Pixies, that one time in Mississippi when they ate fried alligator tail and listened to an old-timey blues band and he got drunk and said, "Stormy, this is the best night in the entire world," History Channel, bourbon, air-conditioning, classic rock, smoking from a pipe instead of a joint or a bong, being in control, thumb tacks instead of push pins, mayonnaise instead of mustard, boxer briefs instead of choosing one of the two, quiet in the mornings, shirts with collars…not a one of them being a bottle of bullshit Chardonnay*—she knew his name. Not off the top of her head, but she knew it, and it for damn sure wasn't *Jack Jordan*. Lindsay could stick his every appendage into her grimy little slit and would never know a fraction of what Summer could tell her.

Summer put a hand to Lindsay, at about the love handle. Felt the girl flinch.

"I don't care what he says," said Summer, "you should feel free to eat as much as you want. Don't listen to how the media believes women should look. I bet you're so much happier now—so much freer—since you no longer worry about your body image."

Lindsay recoiled, as if slapped. She covered her midsection with her bony, bulimic arms.

"Us girls got to stick together," Summer told her with a wink. "Don't let the men tell us where to find happiness. Am I right, girl?"

"I…I, uh—"

"But if you ever did want a, you know—" she sniffled her nose two times hard "—then I'll hook you up. Friend prices."

Lindsay opened her mouth. She closed it.

"Enjoy your dinner."

Summer waded down the switchback to wait for Crunch, closer to the highway, rather than do what she wanted, which was stomp out of the shadows and back into the Light House trailer. To throw a finger to his face and accuse him of bullshittery. For him to claim something so clearly devious as an affinity for Chardonnay—*the smell of leather, paperback pulp novels, girls in sweaters, girls in yoga pants, girls with pigtails, driving ten miles over the speed limit, talk radio at night, winter as opposed to summer, rain as opposed to shine, not standing in line, the Rolling Stones, drinks with lots of ice, dirty jokes*—only told her he was taking this to another level. This time, he might actually be serious.

No matter how much dope she and Crunch and Mike D and Crazy Carter smoked, no matter how many YouTube videos they sat around and laughed at, no matter how many times they listened to Summer's extensive collection of bootlegged Grateful Dead cassette tapes…no matter how much coke or pills or booze…she could not shake it from her head.

He's back there right now. He's cooking that goddamn chicken dish, which is the only thing he knows how to cook. The one I taught him to make. The one he only makes for girls and sits about, listlessly bragging his statistics on how many times he's cooked it versus how many times it's gotten him laid. That stupid little girl will put that food in her stupid little mouth, then put her stupid little mouth on my Jackie. And soon they will be rutting away on the couch or, god forbid, the carpet, and next thing you know they will have a stupid little baby and move to a home closer to the school.

"There's still a way to stop this," Summer said aloud, and only one of the boys so much as cocked an eyebrow.

"Stop what?" asked Crunch.

"I need to borrow your car," she told him. He lay supine on the run-ragged carpet of Dealer's apartment and only stared at the popcorn ceiling as Summer rummaged the keys from his pocket. "I'll bring it back torreckly."

It's so easy to forget Jack can't read minds. It's all a parlor trick. He's anticipating basic human emotion and calculating the reactions. But just in case…just in case, think only about something else. Think about anything else… How about that time in New Orleans when we went out for drinks and the band came back to the house and we threw a party so big and they let him sing a song in the microphone and he said over and over it was the best party he'd ever been to and wouldn't you believe, we threw it together? Remember how fun it was to watch him smile. Think about that, instead of the other, because what happens if you're wrong and he really can *read minds?*

Summer found herself not back at the Light House trailer with Jack, but instead at the Circle K, and behind the counter was that old Muslim son of a bitch who never was any fun to run into after a night out. Bastard used his position behind the counter to cast judgment upon folks out for a good time, and some nights she could deal with it.

Not this one.

"Give me three packs of those things back yonder," she said as she pointed a finger behind the counter. "That stuff they call Ivory Wave."

The Muslim frowned. "Do you know what that is?"

"I ain't got time for your bullshit tonight," she snapped. "Shut the hell up and fork it over."

The Muslim furrowed his dark brow and looked her over once or twice. His eyes shone like rubies. He had a snowy beard and he rubbed his palm into it.

"Satan's plan is to excite enmity and hatred within you," he said. "With intoxicants. To hinder you from remembrance of God and prayer." He put both hands on the counter. "Will ye refrain?"

"Just give me the goddamn bath salts," she spat. She turned her back to the counter and watched his reflection in the beer cooler glass down the aisle. She waited until he collected her purchase and rang up her order. She paid and left.

She didn't care how she found them as she kicked open the door of the Light House trailer. Should they be fucking in some corner of a room or cooking their damn meal or canoodling out on the goddamn back stoop…she didn't care in the slightest. She had a mission. She would not be sated.

Summer found them at the dinner table, supping by candlelight.

Bless their fucking hearts.

Jack stood from the table, a paper napkin still tucked into his belt. He raised out both hands like maybe Summer carried a scattergun, instead of two fresh-rolled joints.

"Summer," he said, "please don't start nothing. We're having a nice, quiet dinner, and we—"

"Jackie, how dare you?" Summer smiled best she could, but this settled Lindsay none the better. She gathered what possessions she could and quarried them into her lap. "You always think the worst of me."

"Well…I—"

"I've turned over a whole new leaf, Jackie." She held out the two joints. "I meant to give you these earlier. Just something to help the two of you relax on your wonderful date."

Jack cocked his head to the side. "What are you up to, Summer?"

"You hurt my feelings, Jackie," she said. Through clenched teeth, she added, "Sometimes I think that's all we do: hurt each other. This is where I put my foot down and end the cycle."

She stole a look toward Lindsay, frightened in the corner. Her big eyes threatened to melt even Summer's angry heart. Her grip on the twin joints weakened. She closed her eyes and swallowed at the nothing in her throat, and when she opened them again, she shoved the joints into Jack's outstretched hand.

"And when you smoke them," she said, "I want only that you should think of me."

"Thanks, Summer," said Jack.

Summer said not another word, simply went out the way she'd come. She drove directly to Matt and Kathy's apartment, but did not get out of the car. Instead, she sat in the parking lot and rolled everything over and over in her mind. She could barely sit still, her ass shifting about and covering every inch of the driver's seat. She squeezed her hands around the steering wheel and wished to the devil she could rip it directly from the dash. She thought of every message she'd ever received in life and weighed it against her own actions.

"Luther?"

She said it to an empty car. Her voice sounded alone and quiet, like a whisper in a cavern stretching from the very bowels of the earth to the first kiss of fresh air. It sounded like the last thing man would hear before the world was brushed into the dustpan.

"If you're there, Luther…"

What are you doing?

Summer rubbed her eyes with her fists. She ran her fingers through the tangles in her hair and wished to tug it from her head in tufts. She lowered her face to the steering wheel and thought more than once about driving until she reached the ocean, then driving yet even further.

There is no Luther. That's a story you make up for the tourists. That's something you tell the kids. You don't believe it because it's another of your lies. It's a fun lie, but a lie all the same, and the second you start to believe in it is the second you are no better than…

…Jack.

She felt it deep within her heart. She sat upright. It was like a voice had come from somewhere within the car—not a voice inside herself, mind you—but somewhere like the backseat or the hatchback or perhaps even from the air vents, but it was a voice tried and true and it said the words echoing through her brain like a thoughtless ricochet.

Jack is in trouble.

Summer did not stop to think. She nearly broke the key turning it in the ignition. She released the parking brake with all her might and thrust the car into drive. She aimed to kill any and all bystanders should they stand in her way as she careened down one street and then the other, and in no time whipped the car around the hairpins of the switchback then saw all she needed to see to make herself sick.

The front door of the Light House trailer stood wide open. The front windows were broken and the window shades had been pushed through the shattered glass.

Inside was dark, save for the flickering blue light from an overturned television set. They had been watching a sit-com with a laugh track, though Summer could find nothing funny as she crept on the balls of her feet toward the front door.

"Jack?" she called into the room. The only response was canned laughter from the television.

Summer did not realize until she stepped completely inside the trailer that she had yet to breathe since leaving the car. Glass crunched beneath her feet. The wood-paneled walls of the living room had been marked by hands and fingers with something a dull shade of red. Jack's easy chair had been tossed aside.

"Jack? Dammit, Jack, if you two are funning with me..."

It was blood. The drops on the floor were blood. That which ran led to the kitchen was blood, and from the pale light of the TV, she could see a pool of it. So was that which smeared its way upstairs.

He's up there.

In the kitchen, she heard a drawer slam shut. She heard another ripped from the counter, followed by a shower of forks and spoons and...

You'd better get upstairs.

She bounded up the steps on all fours.

"Jack! Say something if you're okay!"

From Jack's bedroom: "Summer?" He sounded weak. "Summer, please…"

More canned laughter from the television set.

"Jackie, hold on!" She reached the top of the stairs. "I'll save you!"

Summer, behind you…

She spun and nearly fell. There was no use trying to keep air inside her throat. Below her, at the foot of the steps, was Lindsay. Or what Summer reckoned used to be Lindsay. Already a whip of a thing, she looked twenty pounds slighter soaking wet. Soaking wet with what was anyone's guess, but if Summer had to put money on it, she'd suspect it was blood. Whatever it was, there was lots of it. It streaked her hair down the sides of her muck-spattered face. It drenched her shirt straight through to the skin. It dripped and puddled upon their linoleum floor.

Lindsay cast down her head, so that her eyes looked up with hate-fire. She carried something in her hand that caught the light of the TV screen. She showed teeth in her smile and it was with a voice summoned from the nethers that she grumbled:

"I'm a stupid, fat whore."

Summer steadied herself by placing a hand on each wall of the stairwell.

"Come again, honey?"

Said the demon Lindsay, "I'm a fat, fat whore."

"That's no strike against you, girl." Summer gulped. "With proper diet and exercise, you'll clear that right up. You can have any man you want."

Lindsay pointed toward the top of the stairs with that thing she held in her hand.

"What if the man I want," she said, "got himself bled out like a pig?"

Summer bit down hard on her own tongue. The water in her eyes boiled hot.

"He was trying to control me," the girl growled like a dog. "He was fattening me up so I would do what he commands."

Summer swallowed. "That's not true. Jack would never do that."

"*Are you calling me a liar?*"

The mirror cracked on the wall beside Summer. The power flickered, causing the television to strobe. Summer closed tight her eyes and curled into a tiny ball. She remained as such until she heard the demon Lindsay slough away through broken glass and debris.

She's gone.

Summer took no time rushing the length of the tiny hallway and hurtling herself through the particle board door of Jack's bedroom. It was dark, so she had to feel her way through the room, but it wasn't long before she laid a hand upon his boot, then his leg, then for the love of all things holy, upon his sticky, slick midsection from which he bled like the dickens.

"She stabbed me, Summer." He didn't sound well. Jack's voice trembled out his throat. "I don't know what happened."

"Jackie, I need you to hold still." She put two fingers to his throat. His pulse ran races. "I got you."

"I don't know what I said." He began to sob. "She just flipped out."

All around them, the carpet grew sticky. She cradled his head against her chest. She stroked his hair. She hummed the melody to "Brokedown Palace."

Mountains instead of beaches, blues music by black guys instead of white ones, guitar solos instead of drums, cherry-flavored lip balm, cherry-flavored sno-cones, cherry-flavored cough syrup, horror movies, breakfast sausage, driving through Kentucky because everything looks like a postcard, going fast, fast, fast…so fast…

"You have to help me," Jack moaned. "You have to make it all better."

"Summer's got you," she whispered between verses. "And I'm not going to let anything hurt you ever again."

9

Tweekers were all the same.

In every town, Jack Jordan noticed no difference. He believed there only were variations of the same behavior. Whether in Lake Castor, Charlottesville, New Orleans, Columbia…Lufkin… Someone would invariably stand vigil at the window blinds. Would thumb upward a single slat to watch what lie behind the smudged glass. Dear god, someone would forever pace. There'd be a guy who couldn't shut his mouth, would just jabber, well into the morning sun. Something—an earlobe, a nipple—inevitably would get pierced. A tweeker's apartment remained clean.

And without fail, there was a guy holding out. Looking to the future. Thinking of words like *coming down* or the cries well beyond the dawn of why didn't they get more, oh, where could they score some more?

More often than not, Jack was that guy. He had a slippery side to him. All across the South, he'd sneak a little out of each rail, whittling them thinner throughout the night. He told himself they would thank him later. When he stood proud before them as day threatened to break and held high the remnants of his embezzlement, they would cheer his foresight.

But things were rarely thus. As day turned to night and night again to day, someone eventually would offer him a slight. Someone, particularly in a room full of hopped up boys or men, would call someone else a pussy or insult their mother and Jack would find it ample grounds to excuse him from his pillaged booty. And then another would barrage his taste in music or film, and they too would be excised. Before the last whip-poor-will, Jack would stand alone in his victory and carry it to the bathroom, lock the door, then quiet as a mouse, suck it into his face.

Much the same was JoJo's tiny apartment in Nacogdoches. Jack hadn't moved much from the futon in the corner while he waited with the others for JoJo to return with more shit. All night he'd been up to his old tricks—cutting open a straw to scrape clean the residue; cleaning the mirror with his driver's license, then cleaning the license with a razor—and amassed a solid quarter gram for the long day that lay ahead. JoJo's girl constantly clacked her tongue ring against her teeth and offered a couple times to show Jack the other places she'd been pierced.

Their friend Gabe: "...why I'm voting for the Third Amendment. Listen. To. Me. They can't take away our guns, bro. They can't. You ever listened to the Constitution? It's in there. I've seen it. Scroll down under Amendments. The Third One. Thou shalt not impede the right to bear arms. But the president doesn't care about the Constitution. He cares more for preserving a bipartisan system of government that spends more time coming up with new ways to stop good, law-abiding citizens like myself from protecting themselves. Like my man Jack here. My man Jack gets attacked in his home by a bunch of Mexicans and can't nobody do nothing about it."

JoJo's girl put a hand to Jack's arm. In the corner, the dude named Sam turned dark in the face. A hate had taken hold of him and wouldn't let go. He was a man who needed something small to beat on or else things might get broken.

"That was bullshit what happened to you," he said.

Jack nodded. Not his favorite topic of conversation. None of it, of course, was true. However, he did not feel like the good people of East Texas needed the truth when it came to what happened in the Light House trailer that night Lindsay had gone ape shit. Had he told them it had been a ninety-nine-pound coed who had thrown their sofa through the window, they never would have returned to work the next day. Forever they'd try, same as him, to make heads or tails of it, when there was no heads or tails to be made. So instead, he told them all a bunch of Mexicans had broken in as he slept, tore the place asunder in search of contraband, then stabbed him in the gut with a dinner knife.

In fact, Jack did quite a job of convincing himself Mexicans had done the deed that perhaps the only person who knew any semblance of truth was Summer. Summer, who'd cradled him like the Virgin and poured her special jar of clear liquor—she called it her Jerry Water because she swore someone or another in the Grateful Dead had drank from it—onto his wound until she insisted it was clean.

"I need to go to the hospital," he'd told her over and over. "I'm going to fucking die."

"You're not going to die," Summer had told him throughout the night. "You always think you're going to die and what do I always tell you? Huh? Every time you get like this, don't I tell you that you're being ridiculous?"

"I think this time is different."

"It's no different. We only have two rules, you and me. That's why life is so simple. Two rules. Do you remember what they are?"

"Yes."

"Tell me. What's Rule Number One?"

Jack had licked his lips and looked her in the eye. "Cops are the bad guys."

"That's right. Cops are the bad guys and we never tell them shit." Summer wiped most of the blood clear from his face with the tatters of his shirt. "And what is Rule Number Two?"

"No hospitals."

"That's right."

"But, Summer—"

"To go to the emergency room is to go to jail." Summer applied a touch of pressure to his gut and pain had shot through him like a bolt. "Under no circumstances are we to ever take the other to the hospital."

Jack could feel infection settling into the jagged hole in his belly.

"Not even if I'm dying," Summer had said in a more than firm tone. "We never take each other to the emergency room."

So instead, Jack treated his injuries with her Mason jar of Jerry Water. He changed his bandages often as he could. When he felt the fidgets threaten to deliver him to his knees in an itching fit of panic, he fought it off and said to himself that pain was only his body healing itself. It would all pass in time. Soon, he would again be whole.

In the apartment, Gabe showed no sign of letting up: "I personally come from a time and place where if you don't care for someone's conduct—specifically how it pertains to you—then you may invite said person to step into the street. But we live amongst those who would *freak out* at such noble behavior, and that, my friend, explains more than half the messes we as a people find ourselves in."

It had been Summer, of all people, who'd suggested he take up methamphetamine. Again.

"If any one human being on this planet can keep his shit together while tooting ice," she'd told him, "it would be my Jackie boy."

"I don't know, Summer," Jack had countered. "You know how things get when I'm on that shit."

"It's a multi-billion-dollar industry…"

Summer had let her voice trail. She didn't need to finish the sentence. Anything else that needed to be said was between the pages of the hollowed-out King James beneath the steps. What had once been a mighty kilo of cocaine had been whittled down to baggies. Quantities of marijuana had come and gone, but the profit margins were shit, mostly because everybody and their dog had an out-of-state medical hookup that was supposed to be *the bomb*. All that remained of the sheet of blotter acid was a couple ten-strips, and Jack had no plans of crossing paths with Ben Matlin ever again.

"Meth is the rage these days," Summer had said. "Haven't you seen *Breaking Bad?*"

Which dropped him flat into the lair of JoJo Randall. A good time for the past two or three days, whichever, but as of late suffered from a sort of comeuppance, as they found themselves with only mirrors licked clean and tiny baggies turned inside out. A feral energy had taken hold of the room. The circles under the bug-eyes had grown darker. Their fangs, longer. JoJo stepped out to talk to his guy about getting more.

"He's been gone three hours," said Sam. "Where the hell is he?"

He'd been gone not fifteen minutes, but Jack didn't bother to correct him. Jack hit some of the refuse in his pocket, planned to hit it again in a couple minutes. He could keep the panic at bay at least until JoJo returned, then he could start the process all over again. This stuff kept him on his toes. Why did he ever quit doing it to begin with? Maybe he'd gotten in a little over his head in New Orleans with it, but he had three years' experience since those days. He was a completely new person with a different outlook on life. Those days only made him stronger. Smarter. He looked around the room and couldn't find a single equivalent, not a peer among them, and his pride soon gave way to resentment.

Yes, resentment. For two, three days—whichever—he sat and watched them do stupid things, things like finish a sack before they had another in hand or starve themselves or maybe pick for hours at a scab they shouldn't be picking at. And he took comfort in saying he was smarter than all of them because he fancied himself the smartest guy in the room. Any room, for that matter. Even a room full of Harvard graduates because fuck them, they were a type. They were types and they didn't know it. Sure, they were East Coast, pseudo-feminist uber-liberal pain-in-the-ass hypocrite types, but they were types all the same. Stock characters. Caricatures. And what got Jack the most was that the Harvard grads didn't know it, but he did, which made him smarter than the Harvard types and therefore he was the smartest guy in the room.

But JoJo's apartment didn't have any Harvard types, so it was only JoJo's friends, and Jack needed feel no intellectual heat. Especially from Gabe, who, while pacing a hole in the floor, decided to open the front door when he heard a knocking, and not the door in the back which led to the parking lot and which everyone who was anyone used, but rather the door to the front, where only came cops and pizza delivery guys and hey, didn't nobody order a pizza, but before Jack could say a word, the population increased by five and one giant German shepherd.

"Everybody stay right where you are and things won't get silly," said the first cop. They each wore black windbreakers over Kevlar with the words EAST TEXAS TASK FORCE in yellow across the back. "But if you'd prefer things get silly, then keep acting like assholes."

Asked the second, "Where's Joseph Randall?"

Most nobody in the room knew JoJo's real name, so it took them a minute to get their acts together and their stories straight. Jack did what he could to hide the mirror, the rolled-up dollar bills, the scales… but no going. Cops Three, Four, and Five swept the room carrying assault rifles and soon sequestered them all from the paraphernalia.

"We ain't got nothing on us," Gabe challenged from the corner. He'd been positioned to his knees with his hands above his head. "We're clean, man."

Jack could speak on no such authority, especially after the German shepherd next to him began to bark.

The police decided it was best to speak with them one at a time. They chose first to speak with Jack.

✺　✺　✺

"You're a dumb motherfucker, you know that?"

They had him in the bedroom JoJo shared with Lorie. Actually,

Lorie's room since her name was on the lease and JoJo didn't really live anywhere. They sat him on the unmade bed while they took turns sitting on an upturned guitar amp.

"We're not here for you," said the second cop. "You are the least of our concerns."

That cop was "the nice one." The other cop put the shit they'd found, plus some other shit, in a giant Ziploc with the words JACK JORDAN written in Sharpie and waggled it in Jack's face. While he ranted and raved about how Jack would be locked up with Big Black Bubba for twelve to fifteen years because of this statute or the other, the nice one spoke in calm, even tones.

"We're here for JoJo," he said.

"I don't know where he is," said Jack.

"Maybe we can work something out."

"Something like what?"

The nice one winked at the other one, then gave him his seat on the guitar amp.

Said the mean one, "You strike me as the kind of guy who knows how to get things."

Jack's stomach turned. This could go only one direction.

"You strike me as the kind of guy we can send into one of these parties, accompanied by an undercover officer, and point out exactly who it is we ought to get to know."

Fuck...

"I really don't know all that many people," said Jack.

"That's too bad," said Good Cop. "Because I really don't what to see you get into any trouble. You seem like a nice enough guy."

"I bet if we run him," growled Bad Cop, "we'll come up with some wants or warrants. You want me to run him?"

"I don't think we have to do that right now." Good Cop arched an eyebrow to the heavens. "Mister Jordan here is being a real good kid. I think, the rate he's going, his record stays clean a long, long time. What do you think?"

"I think he ain't so clean at all," said Bad Cop. "I think a guy like this has something we can find if we look hard enough."

Fuck, fuck, fuck, FUCK

The shakes settled into Jack's hands. "I don't know nobody," he said. He said it again. In fact, he said it so many times, he started to believe it. "This is all so new to me. I never tried this shit before. This is for real my first time to do drugs and I promise you, officer, I ain't never going to try it again."

"*Officer?*" Bad Cop stood from the amplifier. Good Cop rushed alongside and held him back with a meaty forearm. "I'm a *detective,* motherfucker, and you want to know what I'm starting to detect? I'm starting to detect a piece of shit lowlife who needs his face punched into the carpet. I'm starting to detect a guy who must like getting gang-raped by Big Black Bubba and his friends, every night, for eight to ten years—"

Good Cop ordered his partner to stand down. He had him pressed against the wall until finally Bad Cop's breathing regulated. Before they could get back to business, in came a third cop. Third Cop gave Good Cop a slip of paper and suddenly they were all smiles. After a bit of backslapping and fist-bumping, Third Cop was on his way and there stood Good and Bad Cop, happy as devils.

"We've been talking to your friends in the other room," he said.

"Yeah?" Jack's mind raced. "So? What did they say?"

"What do you think they said?" asked Bad Cop.

"They don't know nothing about me," said Jack. "I only just met them."

"That's not what they say."

"Then they're fucking lying. I only just met them." He licked his lips, which made them worse.

Bad Cop whispered in Good Cop's ear.

"I don't know what's the deal," said Jack. "You walked in that door looking for JoJo. You wouldn't be here if it weren't for JoJo. So why you busting my nuts? Why not go fetch JoJo?"

"Are you telling us Joseph Randall is your connection?" asked Good Cop.

"I ain't telling you shit," said Jack. "The only thing I'm telling you is you came looking for JoJo, and I ain't JoJo."

"That's right." Bad Cop poked his finger at the slip of paper, still in his partner's hands. "Your name is Jack Jordan."

"That's what he tells us."

Jack didn't like the way they said it. Said it like it was the punchline for a joke he'd taken all day to set up. Didn't like those looks on their faces either. They smiled like a kid with a whoopee cushion.

Jack did the math. Could they have gotten news over the radio that he was not who he claimed to be? There'd be so many channels to go through before his subterfuge had cracked. Unless, of course—and he wondered why he'd never thought of it—the real Jack Jordan's father worked as a cop somewhere. Maybe someone had gotten hold of him or dispatch knew a guy who knew a guy and now they stalled for time so Mr. Jordan could arrive at JoJo's apartment to deliver an unholy what-for to the impostor who'd stolen the name of his dead son.

All he needed to do was get out of that apartment and he'd be in the wind, man. He'd be gone. Nacogdoches and Lufkin and all of Texas would be in the rearview.

"If I were you, boy," said Bad Cop, "I'd give us a name."

"A name?"

"Tell us who's got the shit."

Again, Jack shrugged. "I don't know nobody."

"Then we take you downtown with this big baggie." Bad Cop held up the giant Ziploc with his name on it. "It don't matter if all of this belonged to you or none of it, you're getting pinned to it."

"Unless, of course," said Good Cop, "you give us a name."

Jack counted maybe four steps to the door out of the bedroom. On the other side, there'd be another twelve down the hallway, then six more would get him to the back door and out onto Pearl Street and he swore he'd run the entire way back to Lufkin. Sweat all that shit out of him and never touch it again. Never touch any of it. Just run and run and run and no sooner would he come upon that Light House trailer than he'd be packed and into the shitty Honda and on the road to some place far, far away where he could never be found.

All he had to do was get out of that room.

"You're saying all I got to do is give you a name?"

Bad Cop's showed teeth. "It can't be any name. We're looking for a name that can open doors."

"I talk to you and I'm dead in this town."

"You don't talk to us and you're dead," said Good Cop. "You used to be in the drug business. You ain't no more."

Said Bad Cop, "Now you're in the business of getting fucked by me. If you don't sing me a song that gets me dancing quick, then I swear to god the second you get out of jail, I will be at your house every day. I might not get something on the first day, maybe not even the first month, but I'm coming up with something that will put you inside for so long you'll be begging for sunshine."

"Do you want to go to jail?"

"Do you want to spend eight years with Big Black Bubba?"

Jack thought he might cry. "No," he said. "I don't."

"Then give us a name."

"Ben Matlin."

"Who?"

Jack couldn't fetch it back to his mouth, even if he wanted to. It was out there. It hung in the air like fresh cigarette smoke.

"Ben Matlin," he said. "You nab Ben Matlin and you've shut off the spigot."

10

THE LEONIDS.

Summer and Crunch snuck onto the intramurals to lie on the grass and stare into the heavens. One of them brought a joint they passed back and forth until it was little more than a stubby roach, then quickly discarded into the freshly mowed grass. Most the time, what they saw was not a meteor at all, but an airplane, or a satellite.

"All that world up yonder," said Summer aloud.

She let him cop a feel. She bandied about the possibilities before throwing on the brakes and telling him whoa. He pouted a bit, but overall acted like a gentleman, which rarely anybody did with her, so she placed his hand back upon her tit and reckoned what the hell. After a good bit of making out, she stopped him before he could oust her shirt.

"It don't feel right," she said. "Not out under all these stars."

"Feels pretty right to me," said Crunch. "We don't have to tell nobody."

"I don't care about that." Summer shrugged and scooched an inch or so apart from him. "It's just that I don't think he would like it none if you and me hooked up. Not even once."

"Jack?" Crunch rose to one elbow and leaned into her. "I thought you said you two wasn't fucking. That y'all were all friends and no benefits."

"We are. And I ain't talking about Jack."

"Then who are you talking about?"

Summer pointed a finger to the sky.

"Jesus Christ?" Crunch put out his hand.

Summer swatted it away. "No, silly. Not Jesus."

"Then who?"

"Luther," she whispered.

"Who the hell is Luther?"

"I told you about Luther," said Summer. "The one up there."

Crunch rolled into the grass on his back. He laid his arm across his eyes. "Oh yeah," he said. "The alien. I forgot."

"He's not just an alien," said Summer. "He's like a guardian angel."

"Yeah, you told me already. I remember."

"He never meant to hurt me," Summer explained. "That's what he wants me to tell everyone. They never mean to hurt us."

"Sure seems like you tell a lot of folks." Crunch scoured the blades of grass with his fingers for that roach they'd discarded. No dice.

"That's why he chose me."

Crunch seemed to weigh things a bit in his head before he hefted himself first to his knees, then to his feet and, dusting off the seat of his britches, said, "Maybe we ought to get you back home. I don't think we're going to see any meteors tonight."

"I think you're right about that," said Summer as she accepted the ride back to the Light House trailer, where she found neither hide nor hair of Jack Jordan.

"Jack?"

Summer stepped easy into the living room, then the kitchen. Nothing had been cooked, nothing had stirred.

"It's been a weird one," she called to the empty trailer. She crawled to the stairs. The loose board had not been moved, so she could tell. Inside, she found the hollowed-out King James and what was left of the goods. "Crunch tried to make out with me."

His bedroom empty. Hers as well.

This isn't good.

"Not that I don't think Crunch is a good guy. I mean, let's be honest, Crunch is a pretty man. Too pretty, if you get my meaning. There's just something not there with him. Like a screw came loose upstairs. Like maybe somebody should have told him a long time ago to stop taking acid. His soul is beautiful, but I think if I had to spend a considerable amount of time next to something that beautiful, well, I think I'd crumple up and die, if we were being honest with one another. Jack, where are you?"

She slept fitfully through the night. She'd wake to find herself on the floor and in a fit of sweats. When the horizon purpled, she swallowed two Xanax and wondered why she'd waited so long to do it.

The next night, she went to the protests on campus with Chase, Tony, and Dealer's girlfriend. They carried Day-Glo waterguns under their jackets, just in case. That was the first time she'd heard of what happened.

"What do you mean the cops got hold of Jack?"

Chase knew more than the rest. "I heard he was up at JoJo's girl's place and the cops busted in with a dog. Sam Tuley put up a fight, of course, and things got a little nasty. I heard they took Jack into a bedroom and nobody ever saw him come out."

Summer's knees nearly gave beneath her. "Are they saying he's dead? Jesus, please don't tell me—"

"They ain't saying nothing except they never seen him again."

If he was alive, he would have taken the cocaine. There isn't much left, but he would never leave it behind.

While at the kegger in a trailer park east of town, Dirty Bill posed an alternative scenario.

"He could have ratted, for all we know."

"That's impossible," said Summer. "I've known Jack for a million gazillion years and he would never talk to the cops. He hates cops more than anybody. You know, this one time, before we moved here, Jackie got pulled over for a busted license plate light. He's got three pounds of really sweet weed in the car, but, you know…a busted license plate light. I'm sweating bullets, but this guy…this guy—"

Dirty Bill's brother scratched his head. "Say, where did you and this fella meet, anyway?"

"Jackie?" She nearly choked on her keg beer. "Hell, I've known that crazy cool cat for maybe…gosh, I guess it's been three years now. If he was a cop, I'm pretty sure I would have figured it out, don't you think? I mean, who in their right mind would go undercover for three years just to catch little old me? Right? Like I'm the hippie Pablo Escobar or some shit. Man, that's, like, a really paranoid thing to say, don't you think?"

Dirty Bill had just finished a joint, so that gave him plenty to consider. Before he could duck his head out of that wormhole, Summer launched into a story about this one time in New Orleans when she and Jack—

The last thing you should be talking about is New Orleans. Where is your head right now?

Later still, when she crossed town and finished the last of an eight ball with two guys she met at the grocery store, other options were proffered.

"He's always had a bad way with meth," she told them. "He thinks he can handle it but he gets in there and before you know it, three days have passed and he ain't slept or fed. I used to could bring him down by forcing tomato soup down his throat and dosing him with a Xannie. But for a couple days still, he'd act a fright."

Neither boy paid much attention to what she said, so she didn't mind saying it. Instead, they both pawed at her tits while she spoke, then later her belt and zipper.

"More than likely," she said, "he just up and went. Maybe he figured what happened with that little blonde girl was a sign. Maybe he was telling the truth all these years and finally did what he's been saying he was going to do and left me high and dry. Maybe he finally cracked up."

One of the guys was rough, but the other took it easy on her. She found it hard to remember a gentler hand and wondered if he could find the value in someone like her. How she might try harder to act normal, if he would only give her a chance.

No such luck. The next morning, they rushed her from the back door of their A frame and, rather than risk being seen on the streets in such disrepair, she took to the woods.

When she came to, she had no idea how long she'd been out. What day had she gone down?

Friday? Saturday?

It took twenty minutes for her phone to charge enough to check the calendar, which was how she discovered sometime in the night she had made four phone calls to South Carolina.

All the blood in her body stood still.

South Carolina.

Who the hell would you be calling in South Carolina?

Summer needed to sit. She limped to the couch, collapsed, then searched like mad between the cushions for a cellophane full of Valium that she was certain to have hidden. Then checked the medicine cabinet. Then each room of the house until finally she found an Adderall tucked between the pages of *Still Life with Woodpecker*. She ate it and immediately began to feel better.

You're avoiding the subject.

Summer remembered the time in Charlottesville. The first time. Jack had packed all his things and would have been a shadow, had she not come to the door. All day, she'd thought over and over how tonight would be the night. He liked bourbon, so she'd brought a bottle and hadn't so much as touched the stopper before knocking at the door of his dorm room. She found him hardly in the mood, as he'd nearly finished packing all of his things into three flimsy duffel bags.

Mostly she remembered how she would have said or done anything to keep him from tucking tail and running, so she asked him more than once what he wanted. Out of the whole wide world, she asked him, what could she give him to settle his nerves.

"A brand new start," he'd told her. He'd said it through a mess of tears and coughing, but she'd heard him loud and clear. "I just want to do it all over again, and this time, I wouldn't let no woman make an ass of me and I wouldn't let no fella think he could cheat me. I'd start over and make them all sorry they didn't kiss my ass when they had the chance."

Summer never thought she'd care more for another human being. That night, same as many others, she'd held him in her arms and promised him the world. She knew then and there he'd stick himself in and out of many, many women, but never would he find another half as good as she.

"If it's a brand new start you want, Keith," she'd told him, "then a brand new start is what you'll get."

You knew it was going to happen. This was a long time coming.

Summer crawled to his bedroom and threw herself across his mattress. Although he passed out most nights downstairs on the couch, she could still smell him on the blanket. She closed her eyes tight and nuzzled the pillow.

You were the one who taught him to do it.

Summer couldn't stand the quiet. She hopped out of bed and tore apart the trailer until she found Jackie's iPod and scrolled to the Grateful Dead she'd uploaded over the years. She played it as loud as it would go then ran upstairs to rip the bedsheets from his bed. She carried them in her arms as if they were a baby. She danced with them and sang "Sugar Magnolia" at the top of her lungs.

You are the one who made him this way.

"Shut up!"

She restarted the song, then fell to the floor in a heap beneath Jack's bedsheets. Twelve or so hours passed before she moved from that spot, and only then it was because she'd heard someone stirring in the trailer. She sat up, slowly at first, and wondered would her day be turning to shit.

"Summer, what the hell are you doing?"

Jack?

She ripped the bedsheets off her and found her old friend, much worse for wear, crouching in the doorway of the kitchen. He had a look on his face like he'd watched her give birth to a litter of kittens right there on the living room floor. She fought the urge to squeeze the life from him.

"I thought you were gone for good."

"I thought about it," said he.

"Why'd you come back?"

"I couldn't leave you behind."

Summer could no longer look at him. "That's a good one, Jack. Maybe if you put that to music, I could dance to it."

"It's not a lie." He shuffled into the living room and knelt down to eye level. "There's no way on this earth I could do that."

Summer knew somewhere was another shoe. She held her breath and waited for him to drop it.

"I knew," he said, "that I was powerless without you."

She reckoned it no better than this, then set about scavenging enough money for them both to fetch a bottle so they could talk.

"I'm halfway to Kansas," he told her, "when a funny thought struck me. We always say the worst thing in the world we can do is talk to the cops, but we have to ask ourselves, is it really?"

This one was a no-brainer. "Yes," she said. "It is."

"Sure…if the person we were talking about is each other, there's no way I would say jack shit to the police. You can count on that. Look me in the eye and tell me you believe me."

She did.

"What I'm saying is, what if I got myself into a situation, and the only way out of it was to give them a name?"

"Then you go down," Summer said in a low voice.

"I go down for some other guy? Some piece of shit I hardly know?"

She crossed her arms. "You go down because it was you who was stupid enough to get pinched. The other guy, he might live the rest of his life without a run-in and it's no fair he pays for your mistakes."

"What if I told you there was plenty opportunity for a man who got a little loose with his lips?"

"Then I'd tell you he was a piece of shit and I didn't have no quarter for him."

Jack fell back on his haunches and leaned against the wall. His skin had set deep against his cheeks, his jawline. She often thought he looked his best after he'd been run ragged.

You have your own bad news to deliver. When do you count on discussing that with him?

"Summer, there's one man in all of East Texas with the great Molly hookup. The holidays are coming. Spring Break is coming. It will be like hitting the lottery, if all of a sudden that man ain't around anymore to collect the check."

"Ben Matlin?" Summer scrunched her nose. "What do you mean if he ain't around anymore? You aren't talking about…"

"Stay with me," he said. "I'm talking about if somebody put the screws to me and said I got to give a name, and then I gave up a name…"

She thought she might be sick. She had a bad feeling she knew where this was going.

"So I drop a dime on this guy who, believe me, we don't owe no favors, and now he's gone and there ain't nobody left to sell drugs to all these college kids. We created a vacuum, and now, if only we knew a guy who knew Matlin's connection and could handle business after he'd gone. Hmm, who do we know around here who's met Matlin's guy? Can you think of anyone?"

You have to admit…

"I did this for us, Summer." Not a shred of him came off

disingenuous. She reckoned he'd practiced sincerity in the rearview mirror. "I thought it over and over and there ain't a thing in Kansas City or St. Louis or Lincoln, Nebraska, better than what I got with you right here. I figured we pull this off and we can be kings. We can control things, you and me. Remember how long we've been talking about that? All the things you said you could do if only you ran the drugs in a town this size? Now we can finally have it."

You've got to tell him.

Summer's hand crept across the carpet, precariously close to his. At the last minute, he jerked it away to push back the hair from his forehead.

"And once those cops do what they've got to do, I'm in the clear. They get their guy and won't have any more use for me. We can do as we please."

Summer balled the bedsheets in her fists. She put her head between her legs.

Tell him what you've done.

"What's the matter?" he asked. "You don't seem very excited. You're not acting like I just told you that all the dreams we've had for the past, what, five years, hasn't paid off."

"Jackie…"

"What is it?"

"I may have done something…"

Jack shrugged. He would have arched his shoulders and strutted like a peacock throughout the trailer were his insides not likely to burst from the poor stitch work.

"We've all done something," he said. "Trust me, ain't nothing been done by you or me that can cause the other to throw a finger blame's way. Both you and me have dirty faces, which I suspect is why we get along so well. I tell you, Summer, we got—"

"I think I may have got a little friendly on the phone last night."

Jack didn't follow, or, at least, his face didn't follow, because he had that question mark splashed across it for a good ten minutes after

Summer told him what she thought had happened. He stood there a bit, soaked it all in, then screamed bloody murder to the ceiling panels.

"*My empire is crumbling!*"

She saw first the blood darkening his shirt alongside his torso, then watched him double over in pain. He held himself as if his insides might spill onto the floor.

"Jackie, let me get the Jerry water—"

"To hell with your Jerry water," he spat. "I'm stepping out for a goddamn drink."

He did, and Summer thought to follow after him. She would have, but for the ringing of her cellphone. She didn't need to look at it to know who would be on the other end.

South Carolina.

It rang again. Her hands shook so hard she nearly dropped it.

On the fifth ring, she clicked *answer*. No one said a word on the other line, as was his custom.

"It's me," she said into the receiver. "It appears I talked to you the other night."

Breathing: the only sound from the other end for a few moments before finally he said, "You were pretty messed up when you called."

"Are you still mad at me?"

"I could never stay mad at you," he whispered. "You're my special Jasmine flower."

"My name's not Jasmine anymore."

"Oh?"

"No. It's Summer. After my favorite season."

"You told me your favorite season was autumn," he said. "I thought of you when the leaves began to change."

The tremor melted from her voice. "Oh…"

"Summer." He tried it a few more times, tossing it across his tongue like pasta sauce. "I like that."

"So you're not mad at me?"

"No." Silence a moment. "But I'm still coming to see you. The other night, you said you were all alone. You said you needed me by your side."

She closed her eyes and tenderly touched the receiver with her fingertips.

"It's true, Scovak," she said. "I'm afraid I don't have nobody else."

Summer collapsed onto her phone as if it were the one thing promising her so much as a hint of the very salvation she'd spent the better part of her life trying to find.

11

THE NIGHT THE COPS came for Matlin was supposed to be a celebratory one. For the students, it was the last day of classes before Thanksgiving break. For the local dealers, it was the second busiest weekend of the fall semester, second only to Halloween.

Jack spent the pre-gaming portion of the evening in the back of a white van with the windows blacked out. They'd parked down the street from a house party. Detective Rapino sat in the back, twisting the knobs and levels, and playing with his headset. Detective Keisling affixed tape to a small microphone, then the microphone to Jack's pasty chest. Jack did not enjoy the close proximity to cops—he never had—but passed the time by thinking of what he would do with his newfound riches.

"If my nipples fail to harden, detective," he said with a smile, "please do not take offense. I've yet to cotton to fellas and I reckon to stay that way."

Neither cop laughed. They gave no sign they'd even heard.

"I only got one chest hair, so be careful not to pull it off with that tape."

"If you find the adhesive to be uncomfortable," said Keisling, "then be sure to file your complaint either through the department website, or with the duty sergeant down at the sheriff station."

"I'm just messing around," said Jack. "Just being funny."

From the backseat, Rapino said, "Could you say that one more time?"

"Beg pardon?"

Rapino tapped one ear of his headset, then motioned for Jack to repeat himself. Jack nodded, then lowered his lips closer to the microphone taped above his left nipple.

"I said I was only jerking around."

Keisling and Rapino were good old boys, born and raised beneath the Piney Woods of East Texas. Keisling from some place called Huntington and Rapino from further out. Both wore plaid shirts tucked into their dress slacks. They kept their badges on their hips and cowboy boots on their feet. Felt hats, except when indoors. To everyone else, they said "sir," "ma'am," and "thank you."

They did not say it to Jack.

To Jack, their every word was punctuated with a tone that said they couldn't give a shit if Jack liked what was going on, that he was going to do it. They could back it up with billy clubs, service weapons, or even their bare hands if need be. This was not the first rodeo for either of them.

"Our objective for this operation is to net one Benjamin Garrett Matlin," said Keisling. "This operation does not end until we have a transaction totaling more than three hundred dollars. Is that clear?"

"Loud and." Jack sat up straighter. "Yes, sir."

"If the transaction does not equal three hundred dollars," continued Keisling, "then the operation will be aborted and your participation, although noted, will not have concluded in our investigation."

"Trust me," said Jack. "I'll get you plenty more than three hundred bucks."

Said Rapino from the back as he again tapped his headset, "Could you say that one more time, please?"

Jack had plenty reason to believe they'd conduct more than a couple hundred bucks of business that evening. While he had no intention of cozying up to Matlin again, to get in a room with him and a large quantity of product would be next to impossible. However, he had an ace up his sleeve.

Summer.

It took Summer all of thirty minutes to set up the deal. How she'd put it into her friend's head, he'd no idea. Hell, for all he knew, part of that money was hers. All that mattered to her was getting done what Jack said needed getting done.

She'd said, "You can always count on me, Jackie-O."

If the cops had set it up, it'd be entrapment and the whole case would be kaput. But the cops hadn't set it up, that had been Jack and Summer. Both of them counted the imaginary piles of money they'd accumulate once Ben Matlin was out of the picture and, for the next two days, talked nearly of nothing else.

However, time passed on tiptoes throughout the week until finally the day of the party came and all the light quit Summer's eyes. No longer was there a spring in her step. No longer had she the urgency of those earlier times. Jack imagined it to be hard on her.

"They assure me no one will ever know it was me who wore the wire," he'd told her over and over.

"You and me will know you wore it," she said in a low voice. She swallowed one of a row of pills she had lined up along the overturned cardboard coffee table. "I guess that's all that matters."

"Hardly," said Jack. "You and me can forget all about it after a couple weekends of partying hard. I plan to forget about it after we buy a new place. Somewhere a little closer into town. What do you think about that? Finally getting out of this here Light House trailer?"

"Huh? Yeah, sure."

"Buck up, Summer," Jack had told her. "Things are about to change for you and me."

For the rest of the day, she acted like she had something more to tell him, but Jack paid it no never mind. Instead, he put on his game face. He popped an Adderall, then decided that would never do, so he snorted a wee bit of yay. Still, unconvinced, he dipped into the leftover crank he'd ferreted between the pages of his copy of Timmy Leary's *Book of the Dead.* He mellowed all that out with a joint the size of a breakfast sausage before stepping out to meet the cops.

☼ ☼ ☼

All mic'd up and raring to go, Jack stepped inside the party. It was a good one. A proper mix of girls to boys, enough sampling of classic rock by the DJ to keep it steady, and free flowing beer from two kegs in the backyard.

Jack said his perfunctory hellos, but he was there for business and not pleasure. It wasn't long before he'd gotten hold of Dealer and Dealer's friend, and then was soon joined by Ben Matlin. Jack had not seen Matlin since their jaunt to Houston and found himself more than uncomfortable at the sight of him.

Matlin could have been juggling cats for all Jack knew; he wouldn't look up from the carpet.

"We ready to do this?" asked Dealer.

"Let's go," said Jack.

Not so fast. Matlin snatched him at the elbow and motioned him into the hallway shadows. Jack struggled and brought up a knee, but Matlin had him pinned to the wall.

"I ain't going to hurt you," said Matlin. "I just want to talk."

"We got nothing to talk about," Jack whispered. "If it's all the same, I'd rather the money do the talking."

"I want to talk to you about..." Matlin cocked his head to the south, "...you know..."

Jack damned the microphone beneath his shirt. "I don't think that would be appropriate conversation right now."

"It's something I feel should be addressed." Matlin looked up one side of the hallway, then the other. They were alone. "I was out of line."

"Look, we can forget about it."

"No, I can't forget about it. I—"

"Well, we don't have to talk about it." Jack's voice leveled-up. "Not right now. This is not a good time to discuss this. I don't want it discussed."

"I'd like to get it off my chest."

Matlin waited for a drunk girl to slip past them on her way to the restroom. He said, "I haven't had the best luck with interpersonal relationships."

Jack blinked once. He blinked again.

"It's no secret that I like to party," said Matlin. "I can skip all the coke and booze, but I can't say no to a good tab of E. I eat it, snort it... my biggest fear is one day I'll finally break down, cook it, rig it, then shoot it straight into the veins beneath my nutsack."

Matlin's hot breath smelled of corn chips and energy drinks.

"You know how people get off on that shit?" he asked Jack. "Biochemically, I mean. It eats holes into your brain. MDMA does its job by eating tiny holes through your dura matter. I think about that every morning when I wake up and I think about it every night when I go to bed and I'd be lying if I told you I wasn't afraid it affected my decision making."

"I don't know what to say..."

"You don't have to say anything. I just want you to understand I know what I did in Houston wasn't right. People shouldn't do things like that to each other."

"Nothing happened, man." Jack fussed with his shirt, about where the microphone sat. "There's nothing to talk about."

"What kind of person does that to another man?"

"Nothing was done, Matlin. Technically, nothing was done, so can we please drop it?"

Matlin drew even closer and his whisper steamed Jack's eardrums.

"But I swear to God, Jack," he said. "If you give me a second chance…if you let me take that back, I'll make it up to you ten times over. I'll make you the happiest man in all of Lufkin. I'll make you rich…"

Jack opened his mouth.

"Just give me one more chance, okay?"

Jack closed it.

Said Matlin, "How about we talk about it later? Over a taco? For now, let's sell some fucking drugs."

Matlin slapped Jack hard at the shoulder and nearly knocked loose the transmitter at his belt. He left Jack leaning against the wall, rubbing the wound in his side, which lately had begun to itch. He watched Matlin disappear into the bedroom, where waited Dealer and his buddy.

On instinct, Jack looked at the front door. He could still make a run for it. He could rip free the wire and be halfway to Louisiana before the cops knew he'd gone rabbit. But he'd decided before turning his head back the direction Matlin had gone that he would go through with it. He had to, if for no other reason than—

Jack looked again to the front door. He rubbed his eyes with his fists.

It can't be.

It was.

It's impossible.

It wasn't.

Having entered the front door, he stood out among the throng of college-aged party-goers. Alan Scovak stood six feet four inches and his gingerbread hair hung past the middle of his rail-thin back. He was bearded, tattooed, and sported a thousand-yard stare. Scovak saw Jack long before Jack saw Scovak, and already he'd cut the distance between them in half.

"No, no, no…" Jack could barely contain his panic. "Not today."

"Hey there, buddy-ro," said Scovak. "Long time, no see."

"What the hell are you doing here?"

"I heard there was a party," he answered. "I like to party."

"You know what I mean. What the hell are you doing here? In Lufkin?"

"She called me."

"The hell she did."

"You really believe that?" Scovak pulled the pack of smokes out of Jack's shirt pocket. He lit one, then crumpled the rest and dropped them to the floor. "I'm real sorry about that."

"It's okay," said Jack. "Those things will kill you."

"Not if something else don't kill you first."

Nobody knew if half the shit Scovak told them was true. Rumor had it he'd been to prison in Florida. Or Georgia. For murdering a man, or two men, or maybe for simple possession. It could very well all be an act, but one that could win an Oscar, so Jack cut him a wide berth.

"How's Toby doing?" Jack asked.

"You know, Toby and I weren't on the best of terms after the two of you hightailed it out of Carolina. Let's just say that was the beginning of the end of my business with him."

"I'm sorry to hear that."

"Are you?" Scovak smiled sideways. Jack's stomach flipped. "In the end, Toby and I had a difference of opinion that couldn't be reconciled."

"On what?"

"On the value of my work."

"So what did you do?" Jack didn't want to know.

"I decided to test the market."

"To what result?"

"Fuck the market." Scovak held up a tiny plastic keg cup full of piss-yellow beer in mock toast. He drank it dry, then tossed the cup aside. "I swore up and down a million things I'd do if I ever laid eyes on you again. I lost a lot of sleep thinking about it."

Jack's ear twitched. His side hurt. The microphone up his shirt felt heavy enough to bow him over.

"Why don't you keep that to yourself for now?" asked Jack. "In the meantime, if you need directions to the quickest route out of town…"

"I'm not going anywhere, Grant," said Scovak. "Me and Jazz got a fire to rekindle. And she's told me what all you got fixed around here and I'd say, the very least, you owe me one."

"How much did she tell you?"

Scovak's smile slithered ever upward. "She loves me. She told me that much."

"If that were true," said Jack, "you'd shut the fuck up and be on your merry way."

Scovak's ice-blue eyes went to Jack's midsection, his chest, then his throat. Behind him, Matlin popped his head out the bedroom door.

"Jack…"

Said Scovak, "We ain't done by a longshot, you hear?"

"I don't imagine we are."

"I'll see you later tonight." Then, the kick in the gut. "When you get home."

☀ ☀ ☀

How it went down depended on who you asked.

There were maybe eight, nine people in that back bedroom, counting Dealer's buddy, Matlin, and Jack. Mostly stoners from around town, nearly all of them with skin in the game.

No sooner had money and drugs been transacted than did the population increase by six more, these men all with badges.

Dealer's buddy had eyes in the back of his head. He was one of the more paranoid people in a sea of paranoid people.

"I had a bad feeling about the dude," he said, long after. "He was nervous and skittery. His eyes bugged and he was sweating a mess. Johnny tells me that's because of all the Molly the guy took, but I bet it was something else."

If Dealer's buddy thought Matlin was in on the sting, he kept it to himself. No one would dare make such a claim after what happened that night.

"Next thing you know, in come the cops. All of them screaming get down, get your ass on the floor…don't make me shoot you. You know, cop stuff."

Another guy who had been in the room was Lance, who was with his girlfriend, Sheila. They'd already dropped a couple tabs of Molly and were looking to score some more.

"I thought they came in a bit extreme," Lance later said. "You have to ask yourself why cops think they need riot gear in a college town."

"Especially the size of Nacogodoches," said his lady.

"I'm no lawyer or nothing," he said, "but I've been out drinking with a couple of law students and they all agree with me: civil rights were violated."

No one denied the cops were ready when they came through the door that night. Rarely had they an occasion for their Kevlar vests and riot shields. So often had they lasciviously eyed the boxes upon boxes of zip-ties, the canisters of tear gas, the batons and billy clubs. How hard they'd charged into the black part of town, begging for someone to get antsy, but that end of Nacogdoches was too sleepy for anyone to get antsy.

Ben Matlin, it turned out, was their dream come true.

Crunch had not been in the room. Hell, Crunch had not even been at the party, on account of he had left town to see his grandma, but he rarely let that fact get in the way of his telling of the events.

"Matlin prepared his entire life for that very moment," he'd often say. "It's anybody's guess how many times he'd lived it in his head. Couldn't nobody ever open a door too fast in a room where he transacted business, on account of you might send him scurrying for a back door somewhere. That squirrelly bastard mapped the ingress and egress of every room since he'd sold his first ten-strip, I'll bet you."

Perhaps. The only other entrance or exit in that bedroom were the windows against yonder wall, and Matlin had made for them.

Said Dealer's buddy, "That little guy ran so hard against those windows, you'd have thought they would have broke. They didn't. He bounced off them and landed on the floor. It was like a cartoon, man."

"Of all people," Lance would often say, "you'd think a gay fella would take less issue with a long stretch in prison. Me? My number one fear is getting locked up with a horde of slavering buggers who'd barter me like cigarettes."

"That wasn't the case for old Ben Matlin."

The folks on the local news had questions. So did the upper echelons of command within the police and sheriff's departments The committee that oversaw the joint task force held several reviews. The official version came from the point man on the operation, Detective Keisling.

"The suspect was ordered to remain on the floor. He did not. He made a second attempt to evacuate through the far window, and again was unsuccessful."

"At this point, how was the suspect's behavior?"

"He had become agitated. He then began a confrontation with another of the occupants of the room."

"This occupant was your confidential informant, is that correct?"

"Yes, sir."

"And what was the nature of this confrontation?"

That was the one of the points most often contested. No one denied that Matlin made for Jack's throat, but the cause for such an attack was left to mere speculation. Dealer's buddy said Matlin had gone plain rabid. That his fear of incarceration outweighed his use for reason. Jeni, a raver chick who had been in the room, said Jack was only trying to calm his friend, to prevent further harm from coming to him.

"Regardless of why he did it," Lance would later say, "all we know for sure is what he did. That little dude jumped on Jack Jordan and put both hands around his neck and started bashing his head into the floor. Over and over, screaming something like, 'What did you do? What did you do?'"

Most everybody agreed those were the words said as Matlin commenced a melee upon their counterpart.

Said the cop, "That's when he went for his pocket."

"All of a sudden," said Sheila, "the cops were shouting for him to keep his hands in the air, don't move, don't move…"

Looking back, there should have been no question that Matlin was going for his phone. After the cops lit him up, they'd had to pry it from his fingers, he gripped it so tight. But hindsight was twenty-twenty, and no sooner had Matlin pulled his hand from the pocket of his blue jeans than the entire room was filled with gunfire.

"The suspect was hyper-aggressive in that moment. We saw no other option."

"It was a volley of gunfire, man. They took him out high."

"They killed him in cold blood, right in front of our eyes."

Asked the investigative committee, "Was it a justified shoot, detective?"

Keisling's reply: "The officers and myself felt that in order to sidestep any further injury or bloodshed, deadly force was necessary."

One question on everyone's lips was why Matlin elected to go for his phone in the middle of a bust. Some speculated he was calling for a lawyer. Others thought perhaps his intention was to tip off his suppliers of a potential raid. No one had any concrete evidence one way or another.

But the biggest sticking point came with what happened next. The version given by the cops never mentioned it, but they weren't the only ones in the room that night. At every keg party, campfire, or living room where passed a joint from one stoner to another, there existed a different ending.

"They've got us all on the ground," Lance would often say. "They've got our arms behind us and they're zip-tying us at the wrists. Checking our pockets. All the while, Ben Matlin bleeds out on the floor."

"They're dragging Jack out of the room," said Dealer's buddy. "His face is busted up, one eye swole shut."

"Jack's screaming, 'Let me see him, I want to see him.' He's screaming it at the top of his lungs. He's bucking and grunting, fighting off the cops until finally they heft him closer to where Matlin is dying."

"We're pretty sure he's still alive at this point. He's almost to the door, but not quite. You can see loogies of blood coughing out of the holes in his chest."

"It was nasty."

When asked what happened when Jack was delivered to the side of his fallen friend, everyone agreed that he stood over him. That the two men locked eyes. That, as Matlin left this earthly plane, the bloodied and beaten Jack Jordan shouted angrily into his face until finally all of the little man's lights had gone out.

What he screamed to the dying man depended on who told the story.

"He kept screaming *you fucking killed him*, over and over," said Lance's girl, Sheila.

Lance argued, "No, he said something like how he now knows what it is like to lose someone."

"Whatever it was he said," Dealer's buddy would tell folks, "he said it over and over until they carted him out of the room."

Unbeknown to everyone involved, Jack still repeated it, days and weeks later. Most often, he did so as he stood before his bathroom mirror, or the rearview in his shitty Honda, or any reflective surface he came across. He said it in his mind and he said it with his mouth. Anytime his eyes caught the reflection of his own eyes.

"Now it's your turn to get fucked."

12

WHEN THE DAY CAME for Jack to make his first solo trip to Houston, he hopped to it. He packed a couple changes of clothes and lit out the front door and would have gotten halfway to Livingston had Summer not stopped him shy of the car door. He'd grown twitchier than usual. He regarded even the wind with suspicion.

"When will you be back?" she asked him.

"After I score the drugs, I reckon."

"How long will that take?"

Jack shrugged. "Beats me. The only time I went down there was with Ben Matlin. With him gone, it may take some doing to convince them to open trade with a new partner."

"So, what? Be back tomorrow morning?"

"I could be back tonight. Maybe it will be later. I reckon if three days pass and you ain't heard from me, then I'm not coming back and, well, I guess there's your answer."

"Are you sure this is…" She swallowed thickly. "Jack, what if these guys are dangerous?"

"Trust me: they're dangerous."

"But what if—"

"Summer, don't chicken out on me now." He opened the hatch of the shitty Honda and threw in his duffel bag. "We've got one play and we worked real hard to get it. The only other choice I got is tossing nickels and dimes and waiting for that hard rain to fall, and I ain't doing it with Alan Scovak breathing over my shoulder."

"You're not happy he's here?"

Jack cut her a look that told her a thousand different things, chief among them that no, he was not happy to see Alan Scovak.

Before he could hit the road, she pulled him to her and held him tighter than she ever had. Were her tear ducts not good and used up, she'd have sobbed like a silly schoolgirl, but instead said over and over for him not to do anything stupid. For him to keep his eyes open for any trouble.

"Make sure you come back for me."

Jack nodded, said *yeah, yeah, yeah,* and left her in a cloud of dust as the shitty Honda rattled down the switchback.

At first, Summer didn't miss him. In fact, she thought it heaven to be out from under his oppressive keep. His judgmental stares. Those heavy sighs and teeth ground to nubs every time Summer played her Phish bootlegs, or talked to no end about her good buddy Luther, or organic coffee beans or the connections between each human being and the universe, or how much exactly did the soul weigh. No longer would she worry about ending her damn good time for fear of finding him shaking his head and clicking tsk, tsk, tsk.

That lasted all of a couple hours, for suddenly she missed him so after Scovak asked where the best place might be for him to find a gun. Preferably without serial numbers.

"I mean, if it's the You and Me Show from here on out," Scovak told her, "then it's best if we hit the ground running."

Where to get a gun? Funny, she'd never once thought about it. She fancied herself hooked into the East Texas underworld, but had not the first idea how to procure firearms. At that moment, she cursed her peace-loving, hippie ways. She hated herself for claiming Democrat. She wished she could make but one phone call to Crunch or Mike D or Downtown Tony and produce for her steadfast lover a Tommy gun or the like.

Instead, she drove him down past Butt Street. She drove him in and out of the Lufkin trailer parks. She took him out to the woods where JoJo was last known to be hiding. Finally, she stumbled upon Noah and Gabe, walking out of the forest, stoop-shouldered and hangdog.

Turned out, with JoJo in the wind, didn't nobody respect his outfit any longer. No more could the underweight or lower-classed present themselves with dignity in the crack houses and alleyways of Nacogdoches, not without the protection of JoJo's name.

"We got jacked," Noah explained.

"What happened?" asked Scovak.

"We tried to score off a couple black dudes," said Gabe. "What do you think happened?"

Scovak lowered his head and shook it. The longer he kept his eyes pointed toward the fiery depths of hell, the more his body vibrated. He stomped his left foot against the red dirt road and rocked back and forth. When finally he looked back up at the three of them, his eyes had run red.

"We got to send these boys a message," he said. "We need to show them there's a new sheriff in town."

Scovak drove them back to JoJo's girl's apartment so they could load guns with bullets and powder rifles. Summer bit each of her fingernails until finally she worked up the courage to confront her man.

"Alan, baby, don't you think maybe this—"

"Don't you worry about a thing, buddy-ro," he said. "Why don't you hang out and do one of those drum circle things with the girls yonder? Let me show the children how it's done."

She did as she was told and took her seat on the futon with two other women.

"That's my boyfriend," she said to either or both of them.

"He's fucking scary," said the prettier of the two.

And later, when they returned with tales regaling Scovak's bravado as he put the gun in the tweaker's face and demanded retribution, she sat in what she reckoned was pride and wondered what, if anything, Jack would do if he were there. Most likely, he would suggest they get some pills instead, or move to another town.

No, she thought, Scovak was finally there and the days of running were long behind them. Perhaps she should think of finding a house and building a life in Nacogdoches.

First thing she did when she got back to the Light House trailer was turn up some Jerry on the stereo and put on a pot to boil. She danced by herself as she pulled out not one but two boxes of macaroni and cheese, then danced even harder after she'd dropped the noodles into bubbling water. There were no neighbors along the switchback to complain about the noise, but so what if there were? Scovak would handle it.

Scovak would handle everything from here on out!

However, when he stepped into the trailer and first thing he did was turn down the music, her first instinct was to protest.

"Hey, what are you doing?"

"I can't handle all that noodle guitar shit, toots," he said. "You know that."

Instead, he ejected the cassette and slipped one of his own discs into the stereo. He replaced all the good vibes with the angry pulse of speed metal guitars. Summer stirred the pot with a plastic spatula. As the bubbles riled again, so did she, and before she knew it, she was up and in his face. She threw a finger at him. She talked out the working side of her mouth.

"You listen here," she said, "I won't have you treating me like you did in South Carolina. I should have set some boundaries back then and I didn't do it. That's on me, but this time, things are going to be different."

Scovak looked like he might kill her. First, he closed his eyes.

Mouthed *one, two, three*, then slowly nodded his head. He slipped a finger into the secret pocket of his jeans and scooped out cigarette cellophane. From it, he dropped into his cupped palm two gigantic orange pills.

"Look what Daddy got for you."

She eyed them like a fat girl over donuts. "Where did you get those?"

"Membership has its privileges."

They weren't all the way down her throat before she said, "Jackie will freak if he finds out I'm taking these again."

"Jackie don't need to worry about shit anymore," said Scovak. "You're my problem now."

Summer threw herself at him. She hugged him tight as a boa constrictor and kissed at his chest like a woodpecker. She danced herself back to the macaroni noodles which had long gone soggy and tossed them into the sink. No colander. She doubled over in laughter at her mistake and set about pecking out the good pieces.

"Dinner's going to be a little crunchy, baby," she called from the kitchen.

Scovak chewed on the side of his tongue, then put his foot down. "You know what? Let's not eat in tonight. My baby's not going to be doing all the cooking around here. Let's you and me go out to eat. How does that sound, buddy-ro?"

"Are you serious?" She nearly swooned. "I never get to go out to eat."

"New management." Scovak slipped into the Army jacket they'd stolen from the surplus store the day previous. "Only I ain't got a lot of scratch to speak of right now, so be sure to fill up on bread sticks instead of ordering an appetizer."

"We can always dine and dash!"

Scovak pinched her chin. "Our time will come."

He had more to that thought, but he'd already stepped out the door. Summer thought more than once about grabbing a jacket for herself, but didn't want to fall too far behind. She scurried along after him, nearly forgetting to lock up.

That night, she danced until she plum wore out. The next morning, on the other hand, her spirits were far shittier. She sat atop the sofa and stared at a blank television set for better than an hour before Scovak woke, came into the room, and offered her another pill.

"Take half now and half later," he said.

And just like that, she hated his guts. She took the goddamn pill and within a half hour she thought it the best idea in the world to clean house, top to bottom. And play some Phish on the stereo while doing it. Loud. Scovak stepped out of the bedroom, dressed and ready to go.

"Where are you going?" she shouted over the drum solo.

"I got shit to do," he said. "Don't forget to do the bathroom, but give it a minute or two to air out. I got no idea how you and Jack live in such squalor."

He was gone five minutes before Summer got to moving again. She dropped the broom where she stood and stomped over to where she kept her cellphone. She didn't know if Scovak had taken it or if she'd done something stupid with it the night before. Instead, she threw on her britches and marched barefoot down to the corner gas station and chucked quarters into the payphone.

"Crunch," she said into the receiver, "come pick me up. My spirits are getting low and I need you and me to party."

"Nuh-uh, Summer," said Crunch. "That boyfriend of yours scares the shit out of me. I ain't getting in the middle of none of that."

"None of what? He's not the boss of me."

"Look," said Crunch, "he gave us all a warning. He said sometimes people get high together and then end up getting ideas in their head about doing things they shouldn't. Then he said sometimes people get found in cotton fields or weighted-down at the bottom of a creek. If it's all the same, I'm kind of busy today."

Summer held the receiver at her side long after the line disconnected. She couldn't decide to be thrilled or angry. She didn't know a damn thing, she reckoned, and probably wouldn't until she'd come off the half-pill she'd taken. She rushed home quick as she could so as to be there when Scovak returned to give her the other half.

That night, she danced like her pants were on fire. The next morning, however, the only thing she felt even close to joy was when Jack walked in the front door.

"He's trying to kill me," Summer said, grabbing at his boots. "You have to help me."

Jack cast a wary eye upon her. There would be no fooling him. He rolled his eyes and pushed her away.

"Jackie, I'm serious," she said. She followed him through the living room and into his own bedroom. "I wish I never called him. I wish I never asked him back."

"What are you on, Summer?"

"Nothing."

He stopped and gave her that look.

"I only dropped half a football yesterday," she said.

Still, that look.

"And then the other half last night."

He turned and opened the second drawer of his bureau. He looked under his dark socks. Relieved, he closed the drawer.

"You two can live however you want," said Jack. "You two can eat all the pills from here to the Gulf of Mexico, for all I care."

Jack took the backpack off his shoulder. He set it gently on the rumpled bed, then took out a pleather shaving kit. Summer tried to think when she'd ever known him to own a shaving kit, then put two and two together.

"Is that what I think it is?"

"Depends on what you think it is." He cocked his head at her. "Summer, I got to ask you a question. And I need a serious answer. And most of all, I need it now."

"Sure, Jackie. Anything. Ask me anything."

Jack opened his mouth, but the only sound was Scovak behind

them.

"Glad you got back okay, Jackie-boy."

Jack and Summer turned to see him standing behind them in the doorway. Shirtless. His chest and stomach a litany of his love for skulls and all things Caucasian.

"I guess this means things went well down in Houston," Scovak said. "Seeing as how you came home in one piece."

"Well enough, I reckon."

Jack scooted the shaving kit behind his knapsack, but not slick enough. Scovak's eyes pointed that direction.

"How much they give you?"

"Look," said Jack, "this ain't got nothing to do with you. I figure you and Summer are set up pretty nice to go fuck yourselves up and down North Street. This thing here is what I got going on and maybe it's best if I handle it alone."

"I don't know if you got the news," said Scovak, "but it's a team sport now. Render unto Caesar."

Jack put his hand on the shaving kit, but didn't move it an inch.

Said Scovak, "Render, or I'll put new holes in your head."

Summer's heart broke at the sight of the wind leaving Jack's sails. And it left them, taking with it all the vim and vigor and even Jack's posture to boot because he wilted like a flower and stared forlorn at the shaving kit as he passed it over the bed to Scovak.

Her Scovak.

Scovak unzipped the shaving kit and took a peek inside. His beady eyes brightened. He tucked a lock of hair behind his ear and lowered his head to the abyss for a better look.

"I've never seen so many tabs in my life," he said.

"Next week is finals," said Jack. "Make hay while there's sunshine."

"Last time I seen this much sunshine, I got burnt." Scovak slipped the kit full of tabs under his arm. "If you don't mind, I'll hang on to these."

13

BEEF GUIDRY SKIPPED THE French vanilla creamer in his coffee that morning. Ever since Ben Matlin went down, he'd felt he deserved no luxuries. He could afford no pleasure. He took that coffee extra bitter and *sans accoutrement.* He took it straight to the face. He had it coming.

However, he had a sinking feeling he should share the blame, and that was what he explained to Jack Jordan, standing before him, sandwiched between the file cabinets and boxes of liquor in Manson's back office.

"I have no problem taking up business with you," Beef explained. He wore a see-through, sequined evening gown that showed off everything except Upper Mongolia. "I told you from the moment we met that I liked you."

They were far from alone. Cramped into the office with them were the beefcakes, slick and aromatic. They crossed their meaty arms over barrel chests and grinned like gargoyles.

"Thank you, Mr. Guidry."

"Please, honey," he said. "I've told you to call me Beef."

"Beef, sir."

Pleasantries exchanged, Beef handed him the pleather shaving kit. Jack opened it and peered inside. It was not the reaction Beef expected.

"Usually, Matlin said he would bring back three times this much."

Beef tittered and sipped his martini through a blinky straw. He winked at both beefcakes. He smiled wide enough to reflect every neon light in the room.

"Matlin? That name, it sounds so familiar…" Beef danced his finger through the air. "Oh, that's right. He's the little fella who left for Nacogdoches with a bag full of my shit and never returned. He's the one who was nearly arrested by the police."

Jack's Adam's apple jiggled in his throat.

"Don't you worry about me," said Beef. "I, for one, am not a girl who believes she should dance all night with the beau who brought her. There are many hours to a successful evening, and if we're lucky…" he dismissed Jack with a flick of the wrist, "…many beaus."

"I assure you," Jack said, "we're far from sunup. There's a good thing going on down there in Nacogdoches and I assure you, I'll have what's in this here bag sold out before the weekend. And it's going to be a big weekend."

"Then come back before the weekend," said Beef. "A fool and his trip are not soon parted. I already lost enough money off the last package I sent north on Highway 59. I'm not ready for my heart to get broken again."

"Thank you very much, Mr. Beef," he said. "Go ahead and have that re-up ready for me. I'll be back here come Friday with your money and more. You'll see."

"I'm sure you will. You know why?"

Jack shook his head. Beef leaned over and cupped Jack's cheeks with his soft, clammy palms.

"Because you're a good boy, that's why."

Jack thanked him. He wondered how he would react, should Beef put lips to his. Could he manage himself from the room through yonder beefcakes, or would he take the easy way out?

Lucky for him, Beef decided against further tomfoolery and instead let loose his hold on Jack's face.

"What's so special about this weekend?" he asked after he'd resumed sipping his shiny martini.

Jack sighed a thousand sighs.

"It's finals," he answered. "All those college kids party after finals."

Same as he said it to Summer and Scovak hours later when he returned to the Light House trailer. Cramped inside his bedroom, neither of them able to function because of the dollar signs in their eyes.

"Finals week?" asked Summer. "Nobody's going to want to party during finals. They're going to want speed so they can study."

"Speed's my area of expertise," said Scovak. "Keep your hands off my shit."

"I'm not talking about while they are taking the tests," explained Jack. "I'm talking about after. I'm talking about long after. Most these kids are going home for Christmas vacation. I don't want them to spend their daddy's money in Dallas or Houston, I want them to spend it with me."

"You're a genius." Summer snapped her fingers. "All we got to do is convince them we have the best shit around and they won't be able to find it nowhere else. They're going to want to snatch it up before they go home to party."

"Not to mention the ones who are going to want to blow it out for end of the semester parties," said Jack.

"No one but me sells speed," declared Scovak.

Summer ignored him. "We're going to need a lot more than what's in that sack."

"Tell me about it," said Jack. "But this is all I could get him to front me. If we sell out by Friday, I can go back for a bigger package. Then maybe a bigger one still after that."

"We're going into the ecstasy business?" asked Summer with a smile blooming. "How *ex*-citing!"

"I see what you're doing here," said Scovak. "I see what's going on."

"We've got to create a social media campaign," said Jack.

"This is the same fucking thing you did in South Carolina," said Scovak. "Except that time, I was the connection who got screwed."

"We've got to give it a good name," said Summer. "Something catchy."

"You know how everybody always talks about how the E back in the day was so much better, nobody trips like they used to?"

Summer tossed ideas into the pot. "Back in the Day? Retro? Vintage…" She scratched her head, then her eyes lit up. "Old-School!"

"Old-School Ex!" Jack smelled what she was cooking.

"That's it!" Summer high-fived him. "We'll call it Old-School Ex!"

"We can hashtag it up! Think about the possibilities!"

"Start a conversation about things we remember fondly on the internet, then use it to promote our brand!"

"Hashtag OldSchoolEx!"

"Oh my God!"

"I'll handle the chat rooms," said Jack. "You know I'm good at that."

"I'll handle word of mouth."

"I'll create a couple Facebook pages, a couple accounts. Get folks talking about it."

All of this drove Scovak up a wall. He harrupmhed and pouted about the Light House trailer as the two of them plotted away. Occasionally, he blasted the stereo speakers with his shitty glam rock, but neither Summer nor Jack could be deterred. Unsatisfied with the state of things, he stepped out to hurt someone. By the time he came back with his shirt bloody and torn, they'd found a way to get him involved.

"Right now, the kids are digging on those hydroponic mushrooms coming out of Tyler," Summer told him. "We can't let everybody spend their money on mushrooms. We've got to shut them down."

"Want me to head over there with a baseball bat and tell them to quit selling?"

"Jesus, no," said Jack. "What's wrong with you?"

"Aw, Jackie..." Summer shook her head. "He wants to help. We need to let him."

"I was thinking more along the lines of a smear campaign," said Jack.

"Smear them into the road with my baseball bat?"

"I couldn't do that to Downtown Tony," said Summer. "He's been so good to me."

"We don't smear Downtown Tony," said Jack. "We smear *hydroponic mushrooms*."

"You're crazy."

"We manufacture outrage. Make a big stink about how the mushrooms have been loaded with strychnine. That they're not organic."

"MDMA ain't organic," said Scovak.

"Whose side are you on?" asked Jack. "All we got to do is make a bunch of bogus accounts across the internet chat rooms. Talk a little shit at parties and coffee shops. Put down mushrooms and praise Old-School Ex. Hashtag it up. We'll move this stuff in two days."

"And we sell out, then get more?" asked Scovak.

"That's the plan."

"And when that happens," said Scovak, "this time I will be riding out with you."

Jack clenched his teeth.

"Like I said, buddy-ro: this is a team sport." Scovak stood nose to nose with Jack. "The next time you point your car toward Houston, you'll have me riding shotgun."

Jack said nothing. He lowered his eyes and gave in, like he always used to do when Scovak started pushing him around.

However, this time, it was an act. One well designed and rehearsed over the long drive up from Houston. Jack, for once in his life, had Scovak right where he wanted him.

"Baby steps. I'll take you with me, but only after this next trip," he said. "And only if Summer says it's okay."

That Friday, he got to Manson's early, just after sunrise. He carried with him a shaving kit full of money and a bottle of champagne he'd bought from a gas station. His plan was to celebrate a new union between successful businessmen, but Beef immediately let him know he had other ideas.

When finally he arrived—thirty minutes late—to let Jack into the club, he'd brought with him the beefcakes. This time, they wore twin jogging suits. Beef, himself, was dressed in bright purple sweats. They all appeared to have either arrived from a strenuous workout, or were preparing for one.

Jack tried to ignore his own shaking hands as he let go his hold of the pleather shaving kit, dropping all that money to the floor.

"I'm so proud of you," said Beef. "You sold all those pills in so little time. Just like you said you would do."

"Yes, sir, Mr. Beef."

"You strike me as the kind of guy who will stop at nothing to get done what he says he will."

"Thank you, Mr. Beef."

"So I'm going to give you a little something to do," Beef said. He traipsed behind the bar to help himself to a shot of something green. He sipped at a second one. "Next time you come here, you are going to bring me the man who delivered Bengie Matlin to the police."

"I got no idea who—"

The beefcakes were at his side. They didn't touch him. They didn't have to.

"Maybe you do, maybe you don't," said Beef. "But you strike me as the ambitious type."

"Put your mind to it," said the beefcake to his left.

"Visualize it happening," said the one on the right, "then make it happen."

"Let's say I bust my ass and find out who done it," said Jack. "How do you expect me to get them all the way out here to Houston?"

"I really don't care," he answered. "And neither should you. All you need to worry about is bringing that person to me. We'll take care of the rest."

It took all he had, but Jack finally managed a weak "Thank you, Mr. Beef."

Beef received the pleather shaving kit from him and replaced it with another that a beefcake kept in the pocket of his jogging suit. Jack didn't bother to open it, and Beef didn't bother to count.

"If you don't bring this man to me in three days," said Beef, "I'm going to assume the worst."

"What's the worst?" asked Jack, over the lump in his throat.

Beef stepped up, nice and tight, into Jack's face. He didn't say a word. Just eyeballed him from top to bottom. When finished, he smiled at the corner of his lips, then disappeared into the back shadows of the nightclub.

"See you in three days," said one beefcake.

"Have a great weekend," said the other.

※ ※ ※

Jack had a wonderful weekend. Of all the scores in all the towns in all the world, Jack never saw so much money in one place at one time. The first Monday after the madness, he counted it not once, not twice, but three times, each time slipping another twenty from the stack into his pocket because didn't Summer nor Scovak deserve an extra lick.

He'd been counting it a fourth time when Summer wandered into the kitchen near about one in the afternoon. Her hair was askew and her face looked as if she'd been through the wringer. She staggered across the carpet and into the kitchen where she stared at the coffeemaker far too long before screaming at the top of her lungs.

"What the hell is your problem?" Jack demanded.

"Why is there never any fucking coffee when I wake up?"

"Because these days you don't wake up until after one in the afternoon," said Jack. He was dressed and had already been in and out several times. Summer collapsed into a dining table chair and hated his guts. "Seriously, how do you propose to sell shit full time if all you do is sleep?"

"Scovak does all the selling," she said. "That's our part of the bargain."

"I thought that was your favorite part," he said. "Mixing with the people, making friends. And what do you do instead these days?"

"I do plenty, thank you very much." But neither of them bought it. She festered a bit before puffing up her chest. "I'll have you know that Scovie has been very good for me."

"Is that a fact?"

"It is." She gathered steam, but did not rise from the table. "I have been incredibly focused and…I've taken a lot of time, you see. A lot of time for myself and it's helped me get my shit together."

"And is it together?"

"I reckon it is." Across the kitchen, a tiny cockroach made a run for it. She watched it until it disappeared behind the microwave. "Used to, I'd run like a wing nut from party to party. I'd talk all kinds of trash, and who needs that, Jackie? How does anybody get to know anyone when they're running their mouths, doing all kinds of drugs, and getting drunk all the time? Now that I've taken some time for myself, it allows me to focus. To get to know who I really am."

"And it's Scovak that helps you with that?"

Summer nodded. She thought it over. She nodded again, but harder.

"Then congratulations," he said. He excused himself, then crawled up the steps to his bedroom. Once inside, he fished again the wad of paper bills from his jeans and began to count again. He wasn't halfway through the stack when Summer entered the room.

"Jackie?" she said from the doorway.

"Yes, Summer?"

"You remember when you came home from Houston?" She fingered a trail in the wood of the doorframe. From about her head down to her waist.

"A couple of nights ago? I sure do."

She crinkled her face, then straightened it again. "You said you had something to ask me."

"Did I?"

"You did," she said. "But you didn't never ask it."

Jack shrugged. He took a seat at his desk and started counting the money back at the beginning. "Then I guess it was probably nothing."

Summer stepped slowly into the room, eyeballing everything like she'd never seen it before. Jack never looked up. He continued counting the cash. He'd nearly finished when finally she said, "I'm just saying…if you were to ask something important and you got interrupted, I wish you'd go ahead and ask it."

Frustrated, Jack set the money back to his bed. He half turned to her. "If I remembered, Summer, I'd be sure to ask you. Now do you mind letting me count this money? I got a long drive tomorrow."

"You know, I get interrupted all the time," she said. "I don't think Alan's let me finish a sentence since he moved in."

"You're the one who summoned him."

"Yeah." She pulled her pipe from her pajamas pocket and loaded it with some shake from the bottom of a sack. "You're right about that one, Jackie. It's all my fault."

Jack started counting again.

"I don't feel like I have any friends no more," she said.

Jack nodded, kept counting.

"I never go out anymore." Her bottom lip stuck out an inch beyond the rest of her. "I never do anything."

"Seven fifty…eight hundred…eight fifty…nine fifty…"

"You know what," she said, her voice dragging behind her, "I ain't even heard once from Luther since a couple days after Scovak got here."

"Summer, do you mind?"

She never so much as looked up. "I think you're the only person who listens to me."

Jack set the money on the bed. He spun around on the blanket and faced Summer. "If that's the case, I need you to hear what I've got to say," he said. She didn't act fast enough, so he took her chin and lifted her eyes to his. He saw all he needed. Her eyes were the Great Lakes.

He sighed.

"Those guys want somebody to answer for what happened to Ben Matlin."

Summer's pupils jiggled.

"You understand what I'm saying?"

She pulled her tattered shirt sleeves down over her hands.

"Summer, you should let me take Scovak to Houston with me."

She nodded, her head going all the way back and all the way down.

"I think you should," she said.

"You know what that means, don't you?"

Her voice was a whisper. "I do, Jackie."

"Do we need to talk any more about this?"

"No, we don't." She shook her head wide from side to side. "Never again, as far as I'm concerned."

"Now, will you please let me count this here money?" She agreed and Jack hadn't got a quarter way through the bills before she spoke yet again.

"Jackie?"

"What?"

"You always do the best thing for us."

Jack didn't dare pick up the money again until he heard her stumble out of the room. Still, he waited another minute, for fear she'd pop her head back to declare some new truth or great discovery, or worse, to change her mind. However, she did not. The next sound he heard was her pill bottle rattling from the back bathroom, then the closing of a drawer. The running of the sink. The setting down of a glass.

The soft sounds of the Grateful Dead from the tinny stereo speakers in her room.

14

SUMMER COULD NOT IMAGINE a better day. Who cared if it was dead of winter? Who cared that it couldn't get above forty degrees and hadn't since the beginning of December? The sun shone. The air smelled crisp and full of pine. The afternoons crackled from fireplaces.

She enjoyed the outdoors like no other day previous as she made her way from Lufkin to Nacogdoches in a series of hitched rides, crossed creeks, and worn-out soles of her shoes. Her plan was to visit each and every townie who'd remained behind for the Christmas holidays. She was bound and determined to smoke out the entire world in contrition for infecting her friends with her crazy behavior of late.

First, she stopped to visit Matt and Kathy, who opened the door rather reluctantly. Katie peeked through the inch allowed between door and frame, eyes just below the chain, still in place.

"Are you alone?" she asked.

Summer nodded.

"Scovak isn't with you?" called Matt from behind a part in the blinds.

Summer shook her head. Kathy carefully unlatched the chain and opened the door a touch wider. Summer threw a tight embrace around her, then Matt, after which she proudly unfolded a thick bag of dank bud.

"Let's hit this shit," she said. She packed a bowl and passed it to the right. She couldn't help but reckon, sure, they were smiling, but those smiles were skin deep. They had ulterior motives—an agenda—but she couldn't concentrate on that. She needed to relax. She reached for a second Xanax from the pocket of her favorite corduroys.

"I drove him to the bus stop," she told them. "I bought him a ticket. Honestly, I didn't care where that bus went, so long as it was away from here. He fell to his knees and said he was sorry and would I please, please take him back. I've done some pretty hard shit in my time, let me tell you—you don't crisscross the country three times following one of the greatest bands on the planet Earth and not find yourself in a sticky situation or two—but this was the hardest thing I ever done in my life, man."

"It had to be done," said Matt.

"He wasn't right for you," said Kathy.

Summer smiled and slipped into Kathy's arms. After a moment, Matt joined them and she felt all the warmth in the world. Love. She felt the waters recede and the universe kneel. Maybe that last pill would do the trick. Maybe she wouldn't need another for the rest of the day. She could do without. All she had to do was not think about…

Before Jack took him to Houston, a strut had settled into Scovak's step. He walked through the trailer like a jailhouse rooster. He'd gotten his way. He was going to meet the big dogs. Once again, Jack had cowered to him.

She'd avoided him all that day. Scovak could read minds. Like that time he asked if she was hungry and she said no, but he knew she was so he bought three extra tacos and said if she didn't eat them, then he'd feed them to the fox who came around out back. He'd known she was lying then and he'd know if he looked in her eyes, so she steered clear.

Except when it was finally time for them to leave and she ran to him, collapsed at his knees, and held onto his ankles for dear life.

"Stay with me," she pleaded. "Don't go to Houston."

"Summer…" Jack stomped his feet at the door.

"I don't feel so good, Scovie," she said in her saddest voice. "Why don't you let Jack go all by himself?"

"I told you, Jazz," said Scovak, "this is our big chance. This is our shot at the big time. We don't want to fuck it up, so you need me in there."

"But—"

Scovak pulled a bagful of blues and yellows and pinks from the pocket of his jeans. He held it shy of her nose.

"I thought you said you didn't have no—"

"What if I left these with you?" he asked her. "You can hold on to them while me and buddy-ro ride down to Houston. I'll be back before you know it."

She'd surprised herself with how fast her hands grabbed that bag. The shame was immediate, but soon deferred. When she returned from fetching a glass of water, both men were gone. No kiss goodbye, no see you later, nothing.

That was the last time she'd seen him.

Summer couldn't handle thinking about that day or anything else for that matter, so she popped another pill from her pocket. She told again the story of the bus stop and this time, added a little more melodrama. She told it again down at Banita Creek with Mike D and Phillip as they skipped rocks across the glass-topped, chilly waters.

"And he looked me in the eye and told me he loved me and wanted one more chance to make it all better. Said he'd be different and I was the best thing that ever happened to him. You know what I said to him?"

"What did you say?" asked Mike D, passing the joint back to her.

"I told him, '*See ya never*.'" She laughed to herself and waved off the weed. "He thought I was joking at first, but he still had that look on his face when the bus left town. I saw him through the window and you could tell that he got the picture."

"That's cold," said Phillip.

"See ya never," she repeated, but this time more reverent.

"You could get that put on a t-shirt."

"He was holding me back," she said. The boys looked nonplussed, so she added, "I never ever told anybody this in the whole world, so you have to keep it to yourself. You promise?"

Phillip nodded. Mike D shrugged.

"No, you have to promise," said Summer. She held out her hand, little finger crooked. "Pinkie swear." They did, so Summer said, "He used to hit me. Call me a whore and stuff like that."

"Dirty mother—" Mike D's face contorted as if he'd just smelled something rotten.

"I'd like to get my hands on him," said Phillip.

"Well, he's gone now."

And he was. She had never said such a thing to him. *See ya never.* Instead, she'd said it to the closed door, long after he'd gone. She said it to the empty bed. She said it to his clothes, which she promptly carried to the woods and burned. She said it to the black onyx pipe he'd stolen from an old friend he'd had. To his cigarette lighter. To all the outdoors, by which she stood at the end of the switchback and screamed it to high heaven.

See ya never.

And if Scovak had any moments of realization, he had them in front of somebody else.

It bothered her, not knowing how it went down. Over and over she told Jack she didn't want to know, but it was a lie. She wanted to know every detail, every word he'd said, but more than that, she wanted Jack to think her noble and stoic, and didn't care to appear bloodthirsty or morbid.

But still, she wanted to know.

When first Jack returned, she kept waiting for Scovak to appear in the doorway behind him. To come loping in with tales of insane action and extreme machismo. But all that followed Jack into the Light House trailer was empty space and lots of it. Jack said nothing, instead squeezing into his back bedroom with his damned backpack. He left open the door behind him, as if he wanted her to follow.

"Do I need to say anything?" he had asked her when she entered the room. His back was to her and he wouldn't turn to face her. "Is there anything you need to hear?"

She thought a long moment. She licked her lips. She tried to sound tough and collected and with it.

"Was it quick?" she asked.

"It didn't happen while I was there." Still, Jack did not turn around. "They took him somewhere else. They told him there was something they wanted to discuss privately. You should have seen his eyes light up. The look he cut me... At least they let him go out thinking he was on top."

"Who was *they?*"

"You don't want to know," said Jack.

She took his word for it. Jack was the smartest person she knew.

See ya never.

She could shake him from her head. She'd shaken Jasmine Atterbury and Stormy Allen and New Orleans and Christy Halifax and Charlottesville and Autumn Sanford. She'd shaken *lifetimes.* Hell, it wasn't the first time she'd shaken Scovak and probably wouldn't be her last.

She took another pill.

And another when she went to see Sammy. She told him all about *See ya never* and the bus stop and how she couldn't believe it was finally over.

And when Sammy said maybe she'd been a little rough on Alan Scovak, she thought she might topple over from laughter.

"If you think Scovie didn't have it coming," she said, "then you haven't heard me tell of that one time he raped me."

"What?"

"I never told you about that?"

"No, man."

"Yeah. I mean, I been raped so many times that I guess it started to make sense. Lucky thing: mostly I haven't been awake for it. I just wake up and realize my britches are nowhere to be found. You'd think at least they'd put them back on, in case it got cold overnight."

"Summer…"

"So when Scovak did it, I actually thought it was kind of sweet. He'd gotten real mad, you know. I don't remember what did it, or if it was even something I did. He could get real heated. Anyway, he comes into the trailer and for all I know, he's going to burn it down. He grabs me by the arm and drags me into the kitchen. He bent me over the dinner table and I swear it was like he grew another three hands, or he had help. Next thing I know he's going at it and I'd taken a couple pills and the room had already gone spinny, so I got sick. I got sick all over the table and this made him angrier so he went harder and I couldn't tell him to stop or else I'd choke on my own vomit. Isn't that the saddest thing you ever heard?"

She couldn't remember what Sammy had to say about that, but it couldn't have been near as sympathetic as Ellie and her brother and the two boys they'd gone to meet who deep cleaned the dorm rooms during holiday break. They'd smoked some sweet bud, but that wasn't doing the trick. Summer reached into the pocket of her dirty corduroys, only to find it empty. She turned it out and looked some more. She fell to her knees.

"We're going to need some more drugs," she said aloud.

"I know a guy who has a lot of that Old-School Ex," said Carlos.

"I think we're plenty fucked up," said Crunch.

"Where did he come from?"

"I don't think you understand," she told him. "I've had a really bad weekend. Hell, I've had a really bad month."

"It's all about to get better," said Crunch.

She cupped his face with her hand. "When you say it, I believe it.

You know why? Because you're real. You're a real person."

Crunch laughed nervously. "You know, I think we'd better call Jack."

"No," she said. Her eyes grew big as dinner plates and her face went just as white. "Please don't call him. Jack will have you killed."

"Shut up."

"No, I'm serious. You don't know Jack. Sometimes, I don't even know Jack."

"Summer, what are you talking about?"

And they were at Denny's. There was more than a handful of them, all crammed into the booth in the back, and a too-skinny waitress stood over them. She had blonde hair, like Lindsay, and maybe it was Lindsay, but there was just no way. No way at all, especially since she said in a louder-than-necessary voice that she was calling the police. That this behavior was unacceptable. Summer thought to remind her that she'd seen Lindsay behave in ways that were completely unacceptable and the last person she should call is the police, but she couldn't say a word because she was laughing too hard.

The bartender at the club refused to serve them, so Summer climbed on top of the bar and kicked over his stack of bar napkins. She upturned his tip jar and shouted, "Make it rain! Make it rain!" until she found herself in the backseat of a car.

"Where are we going?"

"I know where we can get a drink," said Sammy.

"I loved him," said Summer, from the floorboard. "I loved the shit out of him. Did I tell you what the last thing I ever said to him was?"

Outside, there was a fire. About eight or nine people sat around it, some staring into the flames, but most staring at Summer. She danced in a circle. She would never tire. She would never give out. She would have danced all night had she not stopped for a split second to look at the fire. She looked at it for over an hour.

When suddenly the flames parted and out walked Jack, unscathed. Choirs of angels. He put a hand to her forehead and all her blood drained to her feet.

"She's been like this for a while," said Crunch. "She's been talking some pretty crazy shit."

"What did she take?" asked Jack.

"I don't know." Crunch looked anywhere but at her. "She said she got a hold of some acid, but that ain't no acid I've ever seen."

"Thank you," said Jack. He dismissed Crunch with the wave of his hand, then suddenly they were alone. Jack, in all his majesty, bent down low to her and lay both hands on her shoulders. "Summer? Are you okay?"

"I've never been better," she said. "I mean, it was a lance that needed to be boiled. You and me both know it."

"What do you say we head for home?"

"I don't want to go there tonight," she said. She crossed her arms. "I don't ever want to go there again."

"Where do you want to go?"

"You said we could go north," she said. "Somewhere like Wyoming or Montana."

"Not now," said Jack. "You know that thing we've worked for? We're finally there. Maybe you just need to take a little break. You've earned it."

"A break?"

"Give your brain time to catch up with the rest of you."

All around them, the others shuffled like zombies. The fire flickered and popped. She wanted so badly to wash her hands.

"I think I'm going to be sick," she said.

"You need to sleep, Summer," said Jack. "You'll feel better in the morning. You always do. Come on, let's go."

She leaned over and chucked up her insides. She stood. She doubled over and chucked some more. She saw stars. When her vision cleared, they were in the woods beside the house. Jack held aside her hair while she sicked up what remained.

"You've been so good to me," she panted. "You always have."

"Crunch is bringing some water."

"It's been you and me," she said. "You always make the tough decisions. I'm glad you are able to do it, because I would never have the stomach for it."

She laughed as if she'd heard an incredibly funny joke.

"Do you think you can make it to the car?" Jack asked.

"I've made some tough decisions too," she said. "But I can't handle it as smoothly as you can."

"This is hardly the—"

She said, "I know you liked Lindsay, but do you think any of this would have happened if I had let you two stay together?"

"I don't want to talk about her," he said. He gripped his side and winced. "Besides, you didn't do nothing. She went crazy. They always go crazy."

"I mean it, Jack," she said. "After I done it, I felt like shit. I felt like shit for a long, long time. I couldn't look at you for days. All laid up and bandaged… If it hadn't been for Luther, I don't—"

"Did what, Summer?"

"I want you to know, I felt horrible. It was stupid, but there was—"

"Summer, what did you do?"

Summer looked at him like he was something curious on sale in an antique store.

"I put bath salts in your weed," she said. "I dosed the both of you with PCP or whatever the hell those people put in those things, I don't know." She swallowed and steadied herself with a hand to the ground. "Jack, I don't feel so good."

He said nothing she could hear.

"But it's you and me, which is the way it's supposed to be," she said. "Not Scovak. Not Lindsay. Not that redhead back in New Orleans. Remember her? Definitely not her."

Jack stood. He took her by the arm and yanked her to her feet.

"Hey! Be careful."

Along came Crunch, holding a keg cup. "Did you still want the water?"

"Fuck off," growled Jack. He dragged Summer around the side of the house and through the front yard where his car was parked on the street. "Get in."

She climbed into the seat and when next she opened her eyes, she thought she might be in the Walmart parking lot, then the next time, she found Jack had stuck her with a syringe.

"Jack, wait... What's that? Wait..."

The world blurred past the windshield, the side window, the back window, the entire car. Everything raced by so fast and they sat on the other end of town, just past Butt Street. She'd been there before. It wasn't a good part of town, so they should be on the lookout for trouble, but Jack had her, and Jack would protect her, but in the meantime, Jack rolled down the window and tossed out the needle and rolled it back up, which was a good thing because it was cold as a motherfucker out there—real cold—and all the Christmas lights up on the houses, on the streets and all the Santas and reindeer hung from the streetlights downtown. When did they suddenly get downtown? It was getting brighter and even brighter still.

"Where are we going?"

"Shhh," said Jack.

"Jack..."

"We're going to ride a roller coaster. You like roller coasters, don't you?"

She did like roller coasters. She didn't know if she said it out loud, but suddenly things were white. Bright white. Troublesome bright and white. All around her, white, and she fell into sobs. She held tight to the passenger door handle.

"Jack, where are we?"

"Come, Summer."

It was so bright. Jack could read her mind, so she didn't bother to speak aloud. Jack could do anything. One day, back in New Orleans, she saw him fly. He flew and flew and after she told him what she had seen, he denied it up and down. Every once in a while, she would remind him. She would look at him and say, "I saw it. You can deny it all you want but I saw it," and he would shake his head and say she was crazy. All the time, she was crazy. But she saw him do it, and when he said he didn't, he got that look like when he's pulling someone's leg. That smile on his face, and she knew that he knew that she knew that...

"Where are we, Jackie?"

"Do you know what she took?"

"I have no idea." Jack shook his head. "This is how I found her."

"Ma'am? Can you tell us what you've taken? What are you on?"

Summer smiled. "I'm on everything. Everything in the whole world."

Bright light. Dark. Bright light. Dark.

"I'm going to handcuff her to the wheelchair."

"Is that necessary?"

"I'm afraid so."

"Sir, what is your name?"

Jack wiped his brow with the sleeve of his jacket.

"Sir, we're going to need you to fill out some paperwork."

"Jack? Is this a hospital?"

"I don't know who she is talking to," said Jack. "I've never seen her before in my life."

"Wheel her in here. We'll get the doctor to administer some—"

"Jack? Did you take me to a fucking hospital?"

"Ma'am, we're going to need you to calm down."

"Jack? Jack, is this a fucking hospital? What are you doing to me? Why are you doing this?"

"Sir, we're going to need you to step away. Please go to the front desk and fill out the paperwork with the duty nurse."

"Jack! Don't you dare—"

"Ma'am, I'm not going to ask you again."

"Roll up her sleeve."

Cold hands. Warm hands. Hands burning hell-fire hot.

"My god, she's filthy."

"Jack! Jack, you can't do this to me. I'm sorry, Jack. Jack, I'm so—"

"Summer?"

"She's having a reaction."

"Hold her down."

Hands. Arms. Bright lights. Dark.

"Call Dr. Feltner. Stat."

"Summer. Look at me."

"She's going into cardiac arrest."

"Bring the crash cart. Goddamn junkie."

"Jack! Jack!"

The lights got bright and wide. They got brighter. Wider.

"Summer. I want you to look at me."

"Open her shirt. Do it now."

"Summer. Take a deep breath and look at me."

"Who are you?"

"You don't recognize me?"

"I don't. I don't think I've ever seen you before. But you are beautiful."

"So are you."

Both Summer's hands went to her own face. To her cheeks.

"I want you to come with me, Summer."

"But I don't know you."

Yes you do.

"She's crashing. Everyone clear!"

"What is your name?" she asked.

You know what my name is.

"Clear!"

"Luther?"

He smiled. "Take my hand, Summer."

"Luther, I've missed you."

"Come."

And he took her by the hand and led her into the light which blinded them both.

15

THEIR SCREAMS INTERMINGLED ACROSS the night.

The one on top of him—the brunette—had no clue of his distress and, bless her heart, she kept at him, oblivious that rather than pump and grind, he had begun to buck and kick. The blonde beneath him had a front row seat and suffered no such illusions. She scurried out from under him and took cover behind the bedside table which they had already knocked onto its side.

"What the hell is your problem, man?" she wanted to know.

"I can't feel my heart," Jack shouted. He'd let go of the brunette's sweat-slicked hips to grab hold of his own chest, which he kneaded like balls of dough. "This is not like last time. This time, I'm afraid it is for real."

Finally, the brunette ceased with her fucking. She remained astride him, her head cocked to the side.

"Are you playing with us?"

"I assure you," Jack panted, "this is far from funny. Don't worry… this happens all the time. But never like this." He kept one hand fast at his heart, while the other pounded against the mattress. "I can't feel my legs. Jesus Christ, I can't feel my legs."

The brunette looked to the blonde, but the blonde had been thrown for as much a loss. Neither moved from their vantage.

"Am I too much for you, baby?" asked the brunette. She spoke in much the same pitch as when they met: her, slinging dollar bourbons at the sports bar on the far side of town, and Jack with a pocketful of blow. She lowered her lips to an inch from his. "Do you need me to take it a bit slower?"

"This happens all the time," he said. His throat shriveled to jerky. His right hand shook like palsy. "You have to believe me, I'm going to be fine."

He said it as much to them as to himself, yet he convinced no one in the room. His mind raced. Was it the little blue pill he'd swallowed? He'd only taken it because all the liquor and the little bit of coke might have... He'd insisted upon guarantees. To get both those women had been no easy feat, and he'd hate to have wasted the opportunity. It could have been a combination of the three, combined with the rigorous athleticism of the two women who were either younger than he, or even older. He had no earthly idea.

He took comfort that his left arm did not ache. For the left arm to ache meant he could be menaced by a heart attack. But this was not a heart attack, this was *that thing*...this was another of his fits. This was all in his head.

The brunette dismounted, then quickly quit the bed. She braced herself against the wall, as if she might be all that kept it from crumbling to the ground. She bit her lower lip and looked frantically from left to right.

"Should we call 9-1-1?" she asked the cowering blonde. "Should we call an ambulance?"

"I...I don't know..."

"No doctors," Jack squealed. "This...it happens all the time. We just have to let it pass..."

But Jack wondered if that were true. Certainly, it happened all the time, but how had he gotten better in the past? Why, Summer had been there for him. That time in New Orleans, when things had gotten out of control with the crank and Summer held him down and poured flat champagne through a funnel down his throat until finally he quit writhing. Or back in the early days, when she'd insisted he snort Tylenol PMs up his nose before he'd become unhinged. Or the time in Columbia when she played Jerry over and over and ran her fingers over his sweaty head until finally he'd settled.

"I just need…" He could hardly manage the words. "If you wouldn't mind rubbing my temples for me. I think that would do the trick."

Neither girl would go for it. The blonde tiptoed around the overturned bedside table to fetch her shirt, then her britches, and finally her jacket. She held them across her chest, as if to preserve any dignity which may remain.

"Please don't leave," Jack gasped. "Please, please…please do not go…"

The brunette began collecting her things. She kept her wide eyes on Jack, still convulsing on the bed, should he sprout wings and spit fire.

"Are we just going to leave him here?" she asked the blonde.

"I'm not sticking around," came the answer. "This ain't the first time some old guy's had a heart attack while we was…you know. Last time, the cops had me jammed up pretty good over it and it took all I had to keep my name out of the papers. No way, man. If my parents found out—"

"I can't feel my legs," Jack moaned. "I need someone to call my mother. I need to tell her I'm sorry. I'm sorry for everything…"

Said the brunette, "I left my car at the bar…"

"I'll drive you." The blonde had already dressed. She jangled her keys and was halfway to the door. "Let's get out of here before this guy dies on us."

"Please stay." Jack's right hand flopped like a fish at his side. "You can have more cocaine. I've got plenty. If you stay with me…Jesus—"

An eruption again at his chest, at or around his heart. *His heart.* He should have gone easier on it, he reckoned. With no Summer to peer over his shoulder, maybe he'd tinkered a bit much with the blow lately. What he wouldn't give to go back in time and hold off a little, maybe pass on the last couple lines. Maybe snorting the boner pill had been a bad idea. Perhaps, if he just took a minute to breathe…

The two women swapped glances with each other then, as if they had both thought of it at the same time, and set upon his discarded blue jeans. The blonde rifled through the pockets and the brunette searched the floor. When they found no contraband, they set upon his chest of drawers, then the flat surfaces upon his desk. They found it tucked inside one of his cowboy boots.

"Have as much as you like," Jack said. "Just please come lay at my side and sing into my ear. Do you know 'Ripple,' or 'Sugar Magnolia'? Even 'Box of Rain' will do in a fix. You don't understand, it's all in my head…"

Neither woman gave the slightest shit about Jack or his maladies. With the sack of blow firmly in their hands, they gathered the rest of their clothes and made fast for the front door. Jack lay in the bed long after they'd left. He stared at the ceiling until finally his breathing returned to normal.

"See?" he said to the empty room. "I knew there was nothing wrong with me."

☀ ☀ ☀

The dude who opened the door owned the house. His name was Rawlin and he played in a shit band somewhere in town. This meant there'd be plenty of girls around, and where there was girls, someone would want to party.

"Come in, come in," said Rawlin. He had a young Vincent Price quality to him that Jack admired. In the living room, a small semi-circle of co-eds had spilled off the couch and onto the carpet. He said to the girl who'd come in with Jack, "I don't believe we've met."

"Her name is Carmen," said Jack. "She's with me."

"Is she…" Rawlin looked her up and down.

"Cool? Hell yeah, she's cool. You don't have to worry about anything. She doesn't know a lick of English."

"Really?"

"She's Mexican," said Jack. "Can you believe when I found her she was cleaning motel rooms on the edge of town?"

"At the StarLite?"

Jack put his arm around Carmen, who didn't understand a thing they said. He nestled his nose deep into her hair.

"She's the best thing to ever happen to me."

That much was true. He'd freaked out one night and gotten a room outside of town because he was certain the trailer was no longer safe. He'd gotten complacent. He'd grown lazy. They were watching the trailer and he packed everything, then checked into the StarLite. The next morning, he heard the manager shouting outside his door, so he'd lit out the bathroom window, only to find out the old man had been yelling at housekeeping because they couldn't get nothing right. He shouted up and down how it was no fair, he'd given them fake social security numbers and fake papers and the least they could do was mind him when he needed minding.

There had been no question for Jack. He'd never been more in love. He marched up the steps to the second floor and took the little Mexican girl by the hand and never looked back. He'd pointed his finger into that manager's fleshy chest and said she wouldn't be coming back. He could take that job and shove it.

But neither Rawlin nor anybody else in that house cared about Jack or Jack and Carmen or none of that, what they cared about was the shit. Jack's shit. He pulled out an electric blue box of mints.

"Is this that stuff we heard about on the news?" asked Rawlin. "That shit is serious, man. I heard two kids in Arkansas killed themselves taking this shit."

"They always make stuff sound worse on the news."

"I read on the internet that a guy tried to bite off another guy's face after he took one of these."

"Again: you can't believe everything on the internet."

"I know," said Rawlin. "I can't wait to try some."

Jack had stepped on it to hell and back. The kids coming up those days didn't know real MDMA from dog shit. He cut it with some shit speed from Sam Tuley's boys. Sometimes, he cut it with shit he bought in gas stations. If folks spun out too often, he'd relax the cut. Let folks go bonkers. Let them talk it up. Soon enough, he'd whack it again.

"They're calling it Apocolypto," Jack told the underclassmen in the room.

"Why's that?"

"Because it's the end-all, be-all." Jack thumbed open the tin of mints to reveal a pile of capsules filled with sky blue powder. He laid them end to end across the coffee table. He dropped out four more pills than Rawlin had said he wanted, so he fingered them aside. "Oh wait," he said. "You guys only wanted eight."

Before he could slip those four back into the mint tin, Rawlin stopped him.

"I'll buy those four from you too," he said.

"I don't know," Jack said. "The frat boys down the road said they wanted them for the weekend."

"Fuck the frat boys," said Rawlin. "I'll pay more."

Jack loved the sparkle in Carmen's eyes when money came this way and pills went that. She'd abandoned poverty and shit weather and a poor end of the stick to cross deserts and swim rivers and now she'd fallen in with a man of Jack's caliber. He imagined, to her, it must be like winning the lottery.

Overcome with emotion, he took her by the hand.

"If you'll excuse us…"

He barely got her to the passenger door of the shitty Honda before his hands and lips were upon her in a flurry. He could not get enough of her. His thirst would not be slaked. Finally, in a fit, he told her they should be married. He told her he wanted her to father his many children.

"Jack?"

Behind them stood a hippie dude wearing white boy dreadlocks. He hadn't slept well in a good, long while from the looks of him. He had a sadness for the ages in his deep green eyes.

"Can I help you?"

"My name is Dario…"

Like that was supposed to mean something. Jack shook his head.

"You probably know me as Crunch."

"Ah! Crunch. Good to see you, old pal. How have things been?"

"Uh…I don't know, man."

"Don't worry about her," said Jack, nodding his head to Carmen. "She can't speak a word of English."

Crunch kicked rocks. "Have you heard from Summer?" he asked.

Jack could lose his shit. The nerve of this guy asking after a girl while Jack had another on his arm. He always thought there something about Crunch that begged for a jab to the face. However, the current political climate in East Texas said there could be a good chance Crunch had a gun, or worse, a cellphone camera. So Jack took a deep breath and counted *one, two, three.*

"Not a word," said Jack. "But she's got a nasty history of taking off for long periods of time without any notice. It's not outside of her character."

Crunch nodded. "You know, the past couple of months, she used to say things. She'd get really high and talk shit."

"Like what kind of shit?" Jack's fingers tightened around Carmen's waist.

"Mostly stuff about you. She talked a lot about her Jackie. About what we should do if she were to suddenly disappear one day."

"Is that a fact?"

Crunch nodded again. "She was real worried about you. She made us all promise that if anything ever happened to her, we should take care of you."

"Take care of me?" Jack swallowed coke draining down the back of his throat.

"Yeah," said Crunch. "She really loved you and said we'd need to look after you. Said we were to help you with anything you might need." Crunch's eyes flickered to Carmen, then back to Jack. "She'd be so happy to see you're doing just fine on your own."

They nodded goodbyes, then Crunch stepped back up the walk toward the house. Jack watched after him maybe a moment longer than necessary when Carmen put her head on his shoulder.

"*Cansado*," she said.

"Me too." He led her toward the car. "I feel like I could eat a horse."

PART
II

16

THEY CAME UP FROM the highway which led from Rankin and brought with them a mess of East Texas dirt. There were three of them: two girls in faded overalls—young things, really—and the fella behind the wheel of the rusty old pickup truck, himself not a lick older than twenty. When they shuddered to a stop in the Shell station lot just off the main road, they waited a bit for all the dust to settle before clambering out the doors.

The kid's name was Donnie Williams and he'd come through a bit over the past couple months, each time with a different combination of girls. All of them dressed in a pair of overalls and a powder blue shirt. Each time, they'd stick their noses into the wicker bin of handmade burlap dolls near the cash register, then furrow their brows.

The only thing different about that afternoon was the weather, which had turned unreasonably cold.

"It appears you've sold one," Donnie called to the fat man behind the register. He pointed into the basket. "This is great news."

The fat man said, "Actually, I used one to clean a spill after a drunkard made a mess from yonder beer cooler."

Donnie's face fell. "You can't be serious. After three weeks, all we have to show for our hard work is a measly ten dollars?"

"Five, actually." The fat man spit into a Styrofoam cup he'd lined with a paper towel. "I used my vendor discount, as agreed upon, and signed on the line which was dotted."

Donnie could not be consoled. His face wore the weight of a man who'd put all his eggs into one basket. He looked at anything and everything in the store, so long as it wasn't the two girls standing before him with arms outstretched.

"Perhaps you should slash the price," said the fat man. "A dollar or two might make all the difference in the world."

Donnie's shoulders slumped too low to shrug. He peeled two dollar bills from a skinny wad he kept in the back pocket of his dress slacks. He gave one each to the two young girls, who scampered toward the soda cooler. "The Miracle Dolls will take off like a rocket any day now. They're a ship bound to come in. Mark my word, the day will come when you won't be able to keep them in stock."

Said the fat man, "I've sat at this register going on fourteen years and still it boggles my mind what folks will buy and what they're willing to pay for it."

"All we need is a lucky break."

The fat man bothered no more with it once the girls returned to the counter. One had with her a carton of chocolate milk, and the other, a cherry soda. As he took their money and scooped out their change, they swapped glances with each other. They fell into a fit of the giggles.

"I do something funny?" asked the fat man.

Neither answered. They struggled to maintain composure.

"I asked you what's so dern funny?"

When still neither would explain what delivered them to laughter, the man's face turned red as a Coke can and he rapped his stubby knuckles to the counter.

"Listen now, I won't stand for no such—"

Donnie stepped between them.

"Rylah, Marva…" He pointed to the door. "The two of you are to wait for me in the truck, you hear?"

The two girls covered their mouths with their free hands and scurried for the door. No sooner had it closed then their girlish titters again erupted, which could be heard long after they'd climbed into the front seat of the pickup.

"Listen here," said the fat man, "I don't give a rat's ass what y'all are doing up at the old Lucas place. Some folks don't want to deal none with you because they were friends with the old man before he passed on. Me, I know his boy's an idiot and he lost the land to the bank fair and square. Some folks say y'all is swingers, or maybe a cult, or—even worse—a bunch of feminists. I don't care about none of that. All I care about is flipping that sign from the word *open* to the word *closed* at the end of the day. But one thing I won't tolerate is a lack of manners. You might want to straighten out your women, or rethink dragging them into town with you while transacting business."

"We're not a bunch of feminists," Donnie said, his voice rising an octave. "I've told both you and your brother, time and again, that Miracle Ranch is dedicated to delivering young women from the clutches of drug and alcohol abuse, and committed to the restoration of self-esteem—"

"Yeah, yeah, yeah. A sober camp." The fat man plucked a smoldering cigar from an ashtray behind the Lotto tickets and gummed his lips a bit at the soggy end. "I appreciate you. My sister, she had her a little girl, years back. Pretty thing, but she took up with the Oxy. Could neither stay in school, nor keep a job. She washed up one morning on the shores of Lake Bardwell, naked as a jay. She'd been missing a shade over a week."

"I'm sorry to hear that," said Donnie. "That's horrible."

"That's the only reason I let you peddle those things in my store." The fat man pointed his cigar hand toward the bin marked *Miracle Dolls*. "I reckon my niece could have used a sober camp, even if it meant turning her into a feminist."

Rather than further dicker details, Donnie quit the filling station. He pulled hard on the driver's side door handle, only to find it locked. Inside the cab, Marva and Rylah fell into hysterics.

"Girls, I'm not in the mood," he called to them.

"Girls, I'm not in the mood," they called back.

The sound of their laughter drowned out any further protest.

❄ ❄ ❄

Drive south into Rankin and take the last left before town and soon the pavement gives way to gravel. The dusty roads bisect fields of cotton, alfalfa, maybe a little soy. All the roads are named Lucas, after a man who'd once farmed there. Lucas #2, Lucas #3, and so on. Cross two rickety bridges over skinny creeks of mud and soon enough the fields turn fallow, then hang a left before the dogleg curve. There, at the end of a crooked road, sits a farm.

Not a farm, *per se,* but the remnants of one. Pasture land, as far as the eye could imagine, on both sides of a white-rocked road. Not more than three years had passed since Old Man Lucas's son had lost the property to the bank, but time had taken its toll. The barn was falling apart. A work shed had seen better days. Paint peeled and wood rotted on a single, grand, ramshackle farmhouse. The lot between all such buildings was strewn with rusty junk—tractors, plows, an old trailer with hitch—as well as a handful of busted old RVs and campers.

Beneath the shade of a crooked willow tree, Rylah and Marva joined another pair of young women, also dressed in dirty overalls and a tattered blue shirt. Cassie and Suzie quit their singing long enough to receive whispers from their friends, then the lot of them fell into girlish hysterics, their breaths turning to mist before their faces. They continued as such until Donnie approached, whence they suppressed themselves to silence.

"Isn't this your work hour?" Donnie asked of the four girls. When none of them answered, he said, "Aren't you all supposed to be stitching the Miracle Dolls?"

"What's the use?" cracked Rylah Kincaid. "Nobody ever buys them."

"Yeah," wised Suzie Grauwyler, "every time you drive into town you come back with more dolls than you left with."

Said Marva Bottoms, "Barney says it's better to work with our spirit than it is to work with our hands."

"I think you misinterpret a number of Barney's teachings," said Donnie. His intentions were to carry on further with dressing them down for laziness, procrastination, or any number of trespasses they most likely committed, but for his eye catching a flash of flesh from young Rylah. Donnie considered himself principled for a man of his tender, young age, but found every one of those principles tested in the presence of girls as playful and fetching as Rylah Kincaid and her fellow Miracles. He closed tight his eyes and did his level best to think of anything besides the freckles on Cassie's arm or how plush Marva's lips were or what kinds of sins he might explore inside a girl as lissom as Cassie Proffitt. He forced instead images of tractors or contrails or anything, anything at all, save the electricity which hummed inside him like yellow jackets.

Donnie held tight as he could to his resolve, but held onto it by his fingernails. In a fit of wanted distraction, he searched high and low, near and far, until finally he found what he needed. As if summoned from heaven above or hell below, on distant horizon he caught sight of an approaching cloud of chalky dust and the Cadillac it followed. So excited was he, he'd forgotten the degree by which his pants had tightened.

"Where is the old man?" he asked the girls.

They tee-heed a bit more before finally Marva asked, "Beg pardon?"

"Barney Malone." Donnie did not pull his eyes from the approaching vehicle. "Where is he?"

"He's in a Spirit Study with Beth Ann," said Cassie. "He's asked not to be disturbed."

Donnie barely heard the girl. From a great distance, he could still make out the white-walled tires. The fresh wash job and the dealer plates. A scent cast upon the crisp, winter air and that scent was money. Donnie smelled it like carrion.

"I don't care what he said," grumbled Donnie. "Run fetch him."

"Run fetch him yourself," Rylah snapped. "Barney said you're not to push us around like slaves."

"I don't—" Donnie caught himself. He'd no time to fuss with little girls, not when something so fortuitous as the Cadillac drew near. Donnie reckoned he could hoot and holler at those girls until the day drew long, and still move them not an inch, so he hopped to it on his own, same as he always had.

They did not wait until he was out of earshot before they commenced again with their tittered whisperings. It bothered Donnie not in the slightest. He had plenty cause to know what all those girls said amongst each other.

"You ought to see the way he looks at me...I think it's creepy."

"I got no idea why Barney Malone lets him on, do you?"

"I hear it's because he's good with numbers."

"He actually believes those stupid dolls are going to sell."

"Did you hear he wants us to farm crops this spring?"

"It's like all he wants to be is Barney's mini-me."

He reckoned it best not to let it get to his head. Over and over he told himself he had a higher calling, and the murmurs of teenaged girls ought not distract him. Girls of that age thought they knew everything under the sun, and nothing chaffed them more than to be told differently. So be it; Donnie would chaff them.

They didn't know shit.

※ ※ ※

Donnie at first tapped lightly at the Big House door, then beat soundly at it with the meat of his fist until finally it opened and standing before him was young Beth Ann Henderson. Of all the Miracle girls at the Ranch, no one could draw Donnie's breath tighter than Beth Ann. Once slinky and slight, she'd filled her overalls since kicking a meth habit, but filled them out the right way. Her skin showed signs of past transgressions, while her smile offered a hint of those still to come. If she couldn't stop traffic, she'd certainly bring it to a crawl.

Donnie swallowed something which may or may not have been stuck in his throat. He toed the door jamb before him with his boot.

"I need to talk to Barney," he stammered. "It's urgent."

"We're doing a Spirit Study," said Beth Ann. "It's not polite to interrupt a Spirit Study."

"I know…I know…" Donnie wondered if he'd ever find a moment without his motives questioned by a teenager. "Like I said, this is very important. I would never—"

Beth Ann held the door wider and stepped aside. He cursed the look in her eye and, were matters not so pressing, he reckoned he'd have a word with her about it. However, time was of the essence, so he bustled through the tiny kitchen, the cramped hallway, and made his way into the living room where he found at least a dozen candles burning and Barney Malone throwing another log into the fireplace.

The two men could not have been more different from each other. Where Donnie kept his hair trimmed high and tight, Barney kept his tied back in a ponytail. Barney had knuckles cracked and worn, while Donnie's were smooth. Donnie dressed himself in khakis to set himself apart from everyone, to which his denim-clad elder often remarked how much he looked like a bookkeeper. And where the younger man spoke with a breathless urgency, his counterpart spoke in calm, soothing cadences.

"Donnie, my boy," said the old man, "what have I said time and again about disturbing a Spirit Study? I'm trying to break through generations of inherited psychological trauma and it requires intense concentration. We can't afford to have the process—"

"I wouldn't have interrupted if it weren't important." Donnie felt Beth Ann's breath at his neck and took another step and a half into the room. "Can I talk to you alone?"

Barney sighed. He looked to Beth Ann, then to Donnie, then back to the girl. "My child," he said to her in a tone ten times softer, "I beg your forgiveness."

"You are forgiven," Beth Ann said with a toothy smile. That smile fell as she turned to face Donnie, then spirited away in a snit from the Big House. No sooner had she let the screen door swing shut behind her than Barney huffed about the room, making a big deal to blow out each candle.

"It's taken me weeks to crack that one," Barney grumbled. "I don't quite understand the root of her fear, but I'm sure it stems from a chronic lack of self-worth and low self-esteem, something we certainly aren't attending to by constantly interrupting time set aside for spiritual exploration."

"I'm sorry. Really, but I—"

"Sometimes I wonder if it will ever sink in with you."

Donnie felt the air quit his lungs. "I would never have come if it weren't—"

"I made a promise that no one will ever slip through the cracks here at Miracle Ranch." Barney stepped to within an inch of Donnie. He placed both hands on the boy's shoulders. "I wonder sometimes if I'm going to be able to keep that promise."

Donnie nearly doubled over, were it not for the old man holding him erect.

"It's not your fault," Barney said in a low voice. "I blame your mother."

Suddenly, Donnie's knees didn't work so well. He teetered, dizzy, until he backed himself to the sofa at the wall behind him. He collapsed into the cushions and practiced his breathing.

"You got a lot more of her in you than you have me, boy." Barney shook his head as he snuffed the last of the candles. "I saw it the first time you turned up at my door, back in Dallas, and I see it in you now. She was an angry woman, never quick to let anything go. I think I've told you, when first you kept hanging around, I thought maybe she'd sent you to kill me. Twenty years is a long time to hold a grudge, but if anybody could do it, it'd be your mother. Believe me."

Donnie never liked it when Barney spoke of his mother. The old man hadn't been there the day Donnie was born, nor had he been at her side on the night she died. He reckoned it both unfit and unfair for the man to present himself as some sort of expert on the inner machinations of a woman he'd had so little to do with, save for a couple months an entire lifetime ago. Still, Donnie kept his hands in his lap and his mouth shut, for if she taught him anything in life, it was to respect his elders.

Even if the elder was his two-timing, no-account, piece-of-shit, deadbeat dad.

Barney continued. "You do a lot around here, son. You work hard and you've got plenty of great ideas. There are plenty of stinkers, sure, but for every two or three bad ideas there's usually a good one. Those dolls keep the girls busy, but let's face it…" If Barney had more to that thought, he kept it to himself. Instead, he shrugged his shoulders. "The focus at Miracle Ranch is not simply to get these girls off drugs. The goal is to fix what got them started on them in the first place. That's not going to happen with constant interruptions when I'm—"

Behind him came Rylah Kincaid, lithesome and limber. She leaned against the doorway and tapped her fingertips against the wood.

"Somebody just pulled into the lot out front." She said it like it happened every day, which it didn't. "They're driving a pretty nice car."

"Oh?"

"A Cadillac, it appears."

Barney looked to Donnie, still breathless on the couch.

"That's what I came to tell you," said Donnie.

☼ ☼ ☼

Their name was Halifax, and Donnie made them coffee on the stove while they descended to bickering before Barney.

Said the mother, "She's always been a follower. Perhaps she's fallen in with the wrong sort."

"That daughter of yours is no follower, Diane. She's always been a handful. If there's a band of no-counts headed straight for hell, she'd be found at the front of them."

"She's *our* daughter, Larry. When you married me, she became your daughter too."

"If she was my daughter, she'd have a different outlook on life."

"We've sent her to the best boarding schools and we were lucky to see her graduate."

"Lucky nothing." Mr. Halifax showed his teeth. "I paid good money for that diploma."

Mrs. Halifax blew her nose into a silk hanky proffered by her husband.

"For her to have felt unloved would have been an unfair accusation. We've given her everything."

"Not that she appreciates it." To Barney, Mr. Halifax said, "We'd be fools to think she can change. To be honest, I think perhaps it's time to discuss an institution."

"She'd never survive an institution," whispered his wife. "You heard what that nurse said. Our sweet Christy nearly died."

Donnie entered and delivered them each a steaming cup of coffee. Mr. Halifax drained his in nearly one gulp. His wife used her cup to warm her hands.

"She needs something unorthodox," she said. "She needs to be somewhere she can fit in. Somewhere she can belong."

"She could belong just fine to any one of the colleges we sent her to." Mr. Halifax struggled to keep his volume even. "You've no idea what it took for me to keep our name out of the papers after what she pulled in Atlanta. Or what about when we sent her to Europe? You thought a couple weeks away from her friends is what it would take to get her back on track, but how did she thank us? She nearly caused an international incident, is what she did. After that, you'd think there'd be an end to her little stunts, but I see no end in sight."

Mrs. Halifax grabbed hold of Barney's wrist and looked him in the eye. "This is why we need your help," she said. "We've tried nearly everything."

"I don't know what you think I can do for you and your daughter," Barney said.

"The ad in the paper said you could free our daughter from drugs," said the woman. "It said you could bring my little girl back to me."

"The ad in the paper?" Barney jerked his hand from her as if it were hot as coals. "What do you mean? We don't have—"

Mrs. Halifax pulled a wrinkled piece of newsprint from her fancy leather handbag. Sure enough, it featured an advertisement for Miracle Ranch, which promised in bold, eighteen-point type to GET YOUR CHILD OFF DRUGS. Barney blinked no fewer than a dozen times while reading it.

Donnie, on the other hand, didn't need to see it to know what it said. For not only had he already read the ad, but he'd also designed it, and hand delivered it to the newspaper in Ennis for weekend distribution. The mystery was not how the Halifax family received the news, but rather why it took them so long and where were the rest of the families?

Rather than bother himself with the metrics of his marketing, he worried his father would tip their hand by pleading ignorance of the ad. To further prevent this, he snatched away the newsprint from the woman and held it behind his back.

"How you got here is not important," Donnie said, quick as spit. "What matters is what happens next. Especially since your daughter's life hangs in the balance."

However, Donnie knew he'd tipped his hand with his father. The old man's eyes creased at the corners as he stared into the boy and did the math. The look on his face said this would not be forgotten, but first they had to deal with the Halifaxes.

"I'm very sorry for the inconvenience," Barney said to them both, "but there's been some kind of mistake. Miracle Ranch is not open to the public. We're very focused and—"

"We'll pay," said Mr. Halifax. "If money is the issue, then I assure you we'll—"

"I'm afraid this has nothing to do with money." Barney side-eyed his son. "Despite what some people believe."

"Okay, I'll bite." Mr. Halifax whipped out his checkbook. "What's your fee? We'll double it."

"Mr. Halifax, I'm afraid—"

"We'll pay you anything," Mrs. Halifax sobbed. "Just...just..."

Again, Donnie stepped between them. He led Barney away from the couple and said in as low a whisper as he could, "You said the universe has a way of providing, correct?"

"I did," Barney whispered back. "Which is why we don't have to take orders from guys with big checkbooks. I told you Miracle Ranch will not become some counselor-for-hire program run by interests beyond those which are pure. We will sustain ourselves. The universe will provide."

Donnie nodded his head toward the old man's checkbook.

"Looks to me like the universe has provided something pretty substantial," he said.

If Barney had a comeback, he kept it to himself.

"Think of how long that money will stretch us," Donnie said. "Think of all the good we could do with that check. All we've got to do is save one extra child from her own demons."

Barney's neck muscles slackened some. "What we're doing here is important work," he said beneath his breath. "I won't jeopardize it for capitalist gains. I won't be corrupted by a system which created so much hate and distrust in the world, nor will I let it infect my little Miracles."

"Just this one," said Donnie.

"And no more advertisements?"

Donnie held up his hand, as if swearing an oath. "Cross my heart," he said.

Far from convinced, the old man returned to the Halifaxes with his trademark grin. Barney Malone could tame a tornado with his smile. He placed one hand on the wife, and the other on the step-father. He drew them both close, like family at Thanksgiving.

"First things first," he said, "I'll have to have a chat with your daughter. We're extremely selective. The only girls I can help are those who want to be helped. Do you understand?"

"Of course," said them both.

"One thing I can't tolerate," said the mother, "is the spark gone from her eye. I can't stand it one bit."

Said Mr. Halifax, "Personally, I give it a week before we're back on a plane to come fetch her, but I wish you all the best."

Barney shook his head. Again he shot the dirtiest of looks toward his son, then asked of the parents, "What does she liked to be called?"

"Beg pardon?"

"Your daughter." Barney removed the hair from his ponytail and smoothed it with his fingers. As he re-tied it, he said, "Earlier, you called her Christy. Is that what she likes to be called, or does she prefer Christine? Chris?"

"When she was younger," answered Mrs. Halifax, "we would call her Chrissy. She grew out of that in a hurry. When she started making friends in high school, she insisted we call her Tina. All of her new friends did."

"Tina."

"But she doesn't go by that anymore."

Barney arched his eyebrows. "Oh?"

"No. The doctors and nurses from the hospital where she'd been treated for..." Mrs. Halifax could not say the word, so she skipped it. "They all said she'd given them a different name. A nickname, it turns out."

"It's the only name she'll answer to," said Mr. Halifax.

"What is it?" asked Barney.

"She likes to be called Summer," said her mother. "After her favorite of all the seasons."

17

NOT A DAMN THING meant a hill of beans to Summer Ashton. Or was it Tina Halifax? Chrissy?

Whatever.

She didn't fight it those first couple times she'd come to and found her stomach being pumped, or her body fallen to convulsions. When she'd opened her eyes and found the doctor with his knee at her midsection, beating hard on her chest and shouting for her to wake up, please wake the fuck up.

She didn't bat an eye that morning she'd found her mother and Larry standing over her hospital bed. The old lady couldn't keep her hands off Summer's face. Couldn't stop hacking at her hair with a brush she hadn't seen since she was a child.

And she certainly couldn't be bothered with the handsome older fella across the table from her in the little room of that farm house, the one who had been talking for God knew how long before finally she slowed her brain enough to understand a single word coming from his mouth. All she could think about was how the first thing he did when he sat down was take his hair out of its ponytail and shake it loose, so it hung down to his shoulders. How the whole world changed when he did that. It brought out his eyes. Don't get her started on his eyes. His eyes, and how green they were, like twin bottles of Tanqueray, and how they say gin makes you crazy. All the juniper, they say, and maybe—looking back—she could have given up the gin, given her predilection for so many other culprits which daily assaulted her sanity. For want of a glass of gin… Actually, given the chance, she'd forsake the booze for a pill. Two pills. Three pills, which she would grind into a fine meal and snort, for more immediate access to the brain, then quickly followed with another down the gullet. God, what she wouldn't give for a pill. The man before her—droning on and on—looked like a doctor or a shrink or at least someone who could prescribe a pill, so she'd better pay attention to what the hell he was saying, so at the very least she could reckon how best to sweet talk him.

"Could you repeat that last part again?"

"I said you are nothing short of a miracle." Those minty eyes sparkled in the light from the nearby lamp. "To have survived what you did. There are dead rock stars who couldn't hang with half of what you'd taken. Sister, I've got to say, you can sure handle your drugs."

Summer sat straighter in her chair. She thought it best not to look into those eyes any longer.

"I bet there were some weekends you wish Guinness World Records would have been on hand because you might have broken one or two of them. What do you think?"

Summer's lip quivered to an almost-smile. She had to hand it to him.

"I mean, when I was coming up, they had a word for it when you took acid and ecstasy in the same night. It was called candy-flipping. Lord knows what they call it now."

"It's still candy-flipping."

The fella smiled sideways. "Wow. That takes me back." He returned to business. "But they ain't got a word for when you take speed and Xannies and LSD and…what is this other shit they found in your system? Did I see…what is this?"

Summer shrugged.

What's this guy playing? What's his angle?

"Don't they give that shit to hospice patients dying of cancer?"

"It walks them to the door with quite the smile."

The man nodded. "That's a new one on me. What's the high? Is it a body blow, or does it take you out at the head? It says it's opiate-based, so maybe it's like that ecstasy going around back in the day…"

"What do you know about it?"

"What do I know about it?" Barney could not contain himself. "Girl, I know plenty."

He's too pretty to have gone at it as hard as you have. He wouldn't last a weekend.

Summer had to agree. His skin hadn't taken to rot like it would with speed. He was too lucid for Oxy. Not lucid enough for heroin. He maintained a mean front—the ponytail, the beatific grin—like one of those old-timers, always talking about how great the seventies or eighties were, or, in some cases, even the nineties. She tried to picture him in drum circles or political protests or chaining himself to a tree, but she just couldn't, because she couldn't be bothered with it.

"I don't need a rehab," she said. "I ain't addicted to nothing."

Barney nodded.

"I'm sure you get lots of folks in here to tell you the same thing." She leaned back in her chair and kept focused on his eyes and how fine the crinkles around them were. "Isn't that the definition of an addict: someone who says they ain't got a problem? Fine, but that's not me. I'll tell you straight up I got lots of problems, but the drugs ain't one of them. That's something I can kick plenty easy."

Barney said nothing.

"I know this makes me sound like a wing nut, but I didn't take half of what they said was in me. Someone stuck me with something. I was partying, just like any normal, healthy college kid would be doing on a Saturday night, and some asshole came along and stuck me with a hypo full of gunk. Why? Probably trying to get fancy with me while I lay unconscious, if you want my honest opinion. That's between him and me, when I find him. And if you want to know something about me, I'm going to find him. Trust you me, that weaselly bastard won't be able to hide…"

She needed to regulate her breathing. The edges had begun to whiten. Bright whiten. Summer stopped talking and put both hands on her thighs and rubbed them warm. She waited for Barney to say something, but he wouldn't budge. She imagined he could go on like this for days.

So can you.

No, she couldn't. "I reckon you've heard this from here and back, folks saying they don't have a problem. Denial ain't just a river in South America, and all that. And that everything I'm telling ain't nothing more than a junkie's rationalizations, but I'm telling you the truth. I ain't supposed to be here."

When finally Barney spoke, he said, "Summer, you strike me as a pretty smart girl."

"When I need to be."

"I bet you're used to being the smartest person in the room." His hand fidgeted with a leather ball strung by a strap around his neck. "Am I right?"

"So far, I ain't been disappointed."

"How about this room?"

She shrugged. "It ain't that big a room."

"Maybe you think you're in the wrong chair."

"I know what I'd do if I was in the other one."

"And what's that?"

Said Summer, "Prescribe myself a bottle of Valium."

That got the fella laughing and soon she was laughing along with him. They carried on as such for a good while until he came along and ruined it.

"How much longer you think you can go on like this?"

"My back hurts," she said. "It's hard for me to think when my muscles spasm like this. They were giving me something for it at the hospital, but I haven't had it in a couple days."

"You'll find no chemicals here on the ranch." His smile ate the entire bottom half of his face. "We grow our own produce. When we eat meat, it is purchased from a farm up the road. We don't even allow caffeine or nicotine on the premises."

"I'm sure you could get your hands on methadone for the, you know…" She tapped the inside of her arm with two fingers.

"That's not our way."

"You get people off drugs, but you don't use methadone? What do you use?"

"We're straight-edge, man." He smiled like a gargoyle. He twirled that necklace of his round and round his finger. "We are slaves to nothing."

"What, you mean *get high on life*?"

"Now you're talking."

Suddenly, Summer's backbone didn't work so well. Life had dealt her many blows, but finally she had been delivered a knockout. She collapsed from her chair to the floor, where she'd never felt so cold.

"This is cruel and unusual," she howled. "This is the behavior of a sadist. I demand to see your licensure! Terms in the Geneva Convention dictate you must not deny medicine to the sick, and, brother, I am infirmed. What you are doing is a war crime! It is sorcery!"

Barney's arms loosed at the sockets and stretched like tentacles beneath the table until he took hold of her shoulders with both hands and returned her to his chair. After he'd reassumed human form, he maintained his smile, as if what he had done was no great feat.

"Dear God," whispered Summer. "I know what you are."

Barney twirled that necklace, round and round.

"You think I can't see, but I can see."

Barney bit his lower lip and squinched his eyes.

Said Summer in a low voice, "You are an alien."

When Summer got something stuck in her craw, she was like a dog with a bone. She crawled atop the table on her hands and knees until she was nose to nose with Barney.

"Tell the truth," she said. "Are you an alien?"

Barney appeared not able to respond. She had him dead to rights. He'd played one hell of a game of Three Card Monti to get her there, but until now had never faced the likes of her. His mouth hung on a hinge and she pulled him closer by both cheeks.

"Luther," she said to the room, "what do you think? Is he one of you?"

Stand down, Summer.

"Of course, he is," she said. "How else could he know so much?"

Summer, you are beginning to act like—

"I know he's lying about something." She pressed their foreheads together. "Don't you know you can tell me the truth? Don't you know you don't have to lie to me? Tell him, Luther. Tell him we can talk to each other. We don't have to hide, we don't have to play bullshit mind games. If you feel sad, then say you are sad. If you want to laugh, then all you have to do is laugh."

To prove this, Summer detonated a fit of laughter. She went at it so hard, she fell over top of the table and landed flat on her backside. She folded and unfolded herself a dozen times until plum tuckered out.

"See?" She lay her back flat on the floor and stared at the ceiling. "That was pretty funny, but you didn't laugh. Not even once. This is how I know you are lying."

She added through a stream of tears, "Maybe you aren't alien after all."

"One thing I will assure you," said Barney, "is that I am not like everybody else."

"Prove it."

Barney motioned with his head for her to return to the chair. She resisted with every ounce of energy in her body, but could not hold out for longer than a half minute before she found herself seated.

"I'm going to ask you something," he said. "It's something I'll bet no one has ever asked you."

Summer didn't blink.

"If I'm wrong, and someone, anyone in your whole life out there on the streets, getting high, has asked you this one question, then you can leave the ranch."

"Leave?"

"Yep. You can get up from that chair and take off to do whatever you like with what's left of your life. I imagine it to be a short life, but you won't spend another minute of it listening to my blather."

"You will let me bail?"

"I'll hold open the door for you."

Summer liked the sound of that. She nodded her head.

"But if I'm right," he said, "and nobody has ever asked you this question, then you've got to hear me out. You've got to give me a chance to save your life, man."

"A chance? What kind of chance?"

"Thirty days."

"Thirty days for what?"

He had a smile like Jesus. "Thirty days to show you a new way of life. Because the girl I see in the chair across from me is beautiful. She's a fighter. She's always been a fighter. If she wasn't, she wouldn't be here. Am I right?"

Her cheeks burned red. Her eyes stung. She damned this man to high heaven.

"And no fair lying to me," he said. "You talk high and mighty about honesty, so you have to hold your end of the bargain. You might pull one over on me, but you can't pull one over on yourself. No, you will forever know if you have been disingenuous with me here on this day."

Don't take the deal, Summer.

"I can be more honest than you, or anyone else on this planet," she said.

It's a trap. Don't fall for it.

"Then all you've got to do is answer my question."

"Maybe you ought to cut the prologue and ask it."

Summer...

"Are you happy?"

Summer's first instinct was to laugh. She stopped shy of opening her mouth. She covered it with both hands.

Her next instinct was to fight. Those hands turned to fists. She sat on them before they could inflict further damage.

"Think about it," he said, with no idea how close to danger he'd come. "I want you to think long and hard about it. Are you happy?"

Teardrops stung at her eyeballs. A lump the size of Oklahoma took root in her throat.

"I'm not talking about the way you feel after you take a drink," said Barney, "or swallow a pill. I'm talking about how you feel before you do those things. I'm talking about the overall scheme."

Her hands shook beneath her.

"I want you to stop bullshitting me and stop bullshitting everyone else, but most of all, I want you to stop bullshitting yourself. I want you to embrace the next five minutes with absolute clarity and ask yourself if you are happy."

Was she happy? She hadn't time to think about it. Her mind seized upon a million other ideas. Not so much a million others, more like the same one, but a million times. Mostly how the dude was right and hadn't nobody ever asked if she was happy. How well a card he had played and how could he guarantee the outcome? Was there something written across her forehead? Something that said her parents never cared and Jack or Craig or Grant never cared? What about Scovak? Sure, she'd had him killed, but that didn't change the fact that he never once asked if she was happy. This man before her was a charlatan, a false prophet, but he had asked if she was happy, and she was, if nothing else, a woman of her word.

Still, she kept zipped her lip.

"I'll ask you one more time," he said. "Are you happy?"

Her intention was to say it loud and clear. To shout it, perhaps. To leap again atop the table and beat her chest and say of course she was not happy, you idiot. She flat-lined in the emergency room. She saw the bright light at the end of the tunnel. She saw the darkness. She felt the presence of something warm. But she did none of this because she couldn't remember if it was only something she had told the nurses and the doctors and her mother, who wouldn't listen, or if it was something that had actually happened. All she needed was a little time to think about it, to discern what was true or untrue. All she wanted was to put both hands over her ears until she could hear nothing else but her own voice screaming, shouting, hollering to high heaven that no, she was not happy. And from the looks of things, she was bound never to be happy, so she must hope now that, with it in the open, maybe somebody would finally set about fetching her a goddamned pill.

Instead, she crumpled to sobs.

Amidst her hullabaloo, Barney's hand found a way to her head. He stroked her hair and tucked it behind her ears. He gave her time to get it out, there, there, get it all out, before whispering into her ear:

"You deserve to be happy, Summer."

"No, I don't," she choked. "I don't deserve it at all."

"Of course you do. We all do."

"You don't know," she said. In the event he really could read minds, she thought of other things. "You can't possibly know what I've done."

"I know…"

"But you don't. You really don't."

"What you've done is survive," he whispered. "Whatever you did, you did it to survive, because if God did not want you right here, right now, he would never have put you here. Do you believe that?"

"I…I, uh…"

"I'm sure you've been thrown a lot of obstacles, but you overcame them. This is because he was watching out for you. He sent someone to protect you. You know what I'm talking about, don't you?"

She felt all the blood in her body leave out the back door. She stared at him through wide eyes, as if he had ten heads.

"You've been screwed over so many times," he said. "You've been given this raw deal so often that anytime someone has arrived to offer a helping hand, you've got this little voice inside your head telling you it's too good to be true. It *has* to be a trap."

Oh shit.

He put both hands on her shoulders and squared her to him.

"Those voices in your head, where have they gotten you?" he asked her. "They got you here. You don't need them anymore."

Damn.

"You've been in the getting high racket for a long, long while, and look where it got you." He pinched her chin, then turned her eyes to his. "Why don't you let me show you the other half of the racket?"

She could hold no air in her lungs.

"Would you do anything to be happy?" he asked.

Unable to speak, she nodded.

"Anything at all?"

"Yes," she whispered.

"Take my hand," he said.

She didn't.

"In thirty days," he told her, "I'm going to ask you again if you are happy. I guarantee you will say yes. If you don't, I will give you one hundred dollars and send you on your way with the phone numbers of a couple guys in town who will find whatever you want. But you won't take that number because I will show you happiness you have never before felt. I will show you fulfillment and perfection. I will show you the beautiful girl I see before me and soon you will show the entire world because isn't it about time the world got to know Summer for who she really is?"

He held out his hand.

"I just want the pain to go away," she said.

"It will."

"I want it to go away right now."

The light shining off him was so bright, she covered her eyes with her forearm.

"Take my hand," he said, "and all the pain will go away."

Summer waited. She listened for anyone to say something to stop her. When nothing happened, her stomach lurched because she no longer wished to be stopped. Maybe, just maybe, she could never act fast enough.

She snatched up his hand.

18

ONCE UPON A TIME, Donnie Williams knew nothing of his daddy. He'd lived his entire life under the impression his father died before Donnie had been born and that the only worthwhile thing the man had ever done with his time on earth was spill seed into Donnie's mother. He'd carried that lie with him, happy as could be, until the night his momma called out from her bed, where she lay sick with the cancer.

"Donald? Donald, are you there?"

Things got rather rough at the end. Drugs numbed the parts of her brain the cancer had yet to eat, and she could do little more than mumble incoherencies. However, that night, she sat upright in bed and reached her trembling hands deep into the darkness.

"Donald?"

"Yes, Mom. I'm right here."

"I can't see you."

Donnie switched on the lamp. Her face was the color of a cinderblock and her left eye wandered. Her hair only grew in patches. Donnie wondered if, after she passed, he'd remember her any other way.

"Do you need your pills, Mom?"

"I need you to make me a promise."

Donnie nodded his head. "Anything, Mom."

"I want you to find your father."

Donnie reached for her bony wrist. She recoiled from the touch.

"Mom, I—"

"I'm serious, Donald."

Donnie had no doubt. At full strength, his mother had been a fiery type. She'd raised him alone and worked two jobs to do it. She'd sat by the window every night with a bottle of brown whiskey and muttered angry thoughts into the moonlight, for all the things she could have done with her life, but didn't. While the rest of her sapped from sickness, that hatred still burned bright and he watched with detached fascination how it smoldered behind her eyes.

"Mom…Dad's dead. He died before I was born. You said he—"

"I said a lot of things," she grumbled. "Not all of them were true."

"The pills, Mom…the pills, they—"

"Shut up, boy." Her words sounded as if they'd been dragged over gravel. "I need to tell you something and I need you to hear it."

Donnie did as he was told.

"Your father did not die. I told you that so you wouldn't go looking for him. He was a son of a bitch, but that don't excuse me for not telling you about him."

Donnie held his breath and waited for her to continue.

"It wasn't fair what I did, but I…I didn't want you to know…"

"Know what, Mom?"

"That your father was a criminal."

Donnie realized for the first time how wide his mouth could open. He wondered how much a human soul could endure before finally it surrendered.

"His name is Barney Malone. Way back when, me and him were hot as a firecracker. One time, we weren't careful, and next thing you know, I'm flunking pregnancy tests. The night I told him about it, he up and grabbed his jacket. Before he got to the door, I asked where he was going. He said we'd need money for the abortion. That was the last time I ever saw him."

She licked her lips and let her breath catch up with the rest of her. Then she said, "Your daddy was an idiot, despite his notions to the contrary. He took up with two boys from school and they had the bright idea to knock over a liquor store. Like I said, he wasn't too swift."

With no words springing to mind, Donnie kept silent as his mother gathered what strength she had left to finish her tale.

"He didn't do much time, on account of the gun wasn't loaded and he weren't the one handling it." She licked her lips with a grey tongue. "The other two were black boys, so the law went easy on him. All the same, what little time he done for it was spent finding Jesus—or something he reckoned close enough to Jesus—and when he got out, he had no time for a bastard born far from wedlock, nor the whore who birthed him. Which is all well and good because the last thing I needed was some convict showing up and—"

His mother fell into another fit of coughing and hacking. She racked her body sideways trying to sick up the rot inside of her, but there was too much of it. Cradling her bald head with the palm of his hand, Donnie lowered her to the pillow.

When settled, she managed, "I want you to find him."

"Yes, Mother."

"I mean it."

"I will."

She clutched his hand with a skeletal claw. "Promise me," she whispered.

"I promise."

"Thank you." She closed her eyes and opened her mouth so she could better receive air into it. "I can't bear the thought of you living your life like I did…"

"How's that, Mom?"

Donnie's mother barely choked out the word—

"Alone."

—before all the breath left her lungs and she passed into the night.

"You were never alone, Mom," said Donnie. "I was with you the entire time."

But he said it to an empty room.

Thirty days came and went and, just as Barney Malone had promised, Summer did not come crying for that one hundred dollars. However, her first days were far from a cakewalk. She'd often fall sullen upon some stray word spoken in meetings or a Spirit Study. Something would trigger a thought that led to another, which led to yet another, and soon her features would flatten and her eyes would glaze. Her jaw would dangle at the hinge and, soon as anyone noticed, the other girls would set upon her. Hands through her hair, at her back, down her arms. Cheeks pressed against her face, foreheads flat against each other. Whispers fast to her ear—

"You are a Miracle."

"You are perfect."

"You are loved."

—and suddenly she would return to herself, jabbering wildly at another parable of following Phish or Widespread or Dave Matthews on tours across the nation. Or canticles of misbehavior involving vials of liquid LSD poured along the length of her spine or dropped into eyelids or junk shot into the veins behind her ear. Men she'd loved, but mostly left. Places she'd awoken naked, and the lengths to which she'd gone to make her way home.

The girls took to her like a pox. During group, when it was Summer's turn to share, all the nervous energy left the room. Summer told tales of woe more tragic than the others, her heartbreaks more devastating. Her soul had been plunged to depths more dark, her tears cut deeper canyons. As time passed, her turn to share moved closer and closer to the end of the session, as if somehow everyone knew it was an act not to be followed, the grand finale, the moment they'd all been waiting for.

Yes, Summer. Summer who spoke above them all, laughed more robust. She who took to the songs as if she'd known the words all along. Sometimes picking up halfway through a verse with the other girls, and by the end, singing most resonant. She could plant seed faster than anyone, and stitch Miracle Dolls with greater speed. And when her mood was right, could recite Barney Malone's Twelve Principles by heart, learning them quicker than any other girl in the history of Miracle Ranch.

Donnie had no idea how his father did it. The two men spoke different languages. Where Barney weaved wide tapestries with the inner demons of young minds, Donnie had little patience for such frivolities. Instead, he had a head for numbers. He preferred to focus on things which might add up, such as taxes, expenses, and the finite costs of living. Barney cared about no such earthbound matters. Instead, he looked to the heavens.

"Our Higher Power will provide," he often said. "He will put nothing before us that we can't overcome."

An attitude which left Donnie Williams alone to scratch his head and make sense of how best to keep the lights on at Miracle Ranch. Not that they used any lights, as Barney preferred kerosene lamps and candles to electricity, and the hearth at his fireplace or an open window to central heat and air. Nor did he favor running water, choosing instead to fetch it from the well in pails.

"All of modern society has been designed to bring us further from our true spirit," Barney declared when given the chance. "First and foremost, we must shed corporeal desires to discover our true selves."

Something Barney repeated to his son as they stood in a field of fallow corn one brisk February morning. They continued an argument they'd had since the day Donnie showed up on Barney's doorstep nearly a year earlier.

"Dad, I understand what you are saying, but the tax man won't stay a repossession just because you argue that *God will provide.*"

Barney shook his head and waved him off. "I don't say *God.* When will you listen? To say *God* confuses everyone, as our God is an individual understanding with a power greater than ourselves. Instead, we say *Higher Power.*"

"Yes, sorry…"

"Our Higher Power will provide." Barney's smile received the warming rays of morning sun as he turned his head to face it. "Look around you, Donnie. All you need do is look around you as far as your eye can see to realize how much He has provided."

In Donnie's mind, the Higher Power had provided nothing, since it was the money from Donnie's mother's modest life insurance policy which had afforded them the land. Barney would only counter that the universe had delivered Donnie to him, so he saw no point in pressing the issue for the moment. Instead, he waved his hand across the horizon.

"If we sowed seed, we could become sustainable. We could sell cotton and corn in town, and keep Miracle Ranch running for years. Decades, even."

"We only grow what we need to eat," Barney said. "The gardens provide all we need. Besides, I'm fundamentally opposed to making money from what's granted to us by the earth. We only take what we need."

"Think of how many lives we could save with the money."

If Barney's patience flagged, he showed no sign. He put a hand to his bastard's shoulder.

"You need farm equipment to handle that type of production. How would you afford tractors and plows?"

"We have five energetic young women," said Donnie. "With all the unspent sexual energy in these girls, we could have these fields worked in no time."

Barney shook his head. "What you are proposing is slavery. Do you see what the tentacles of capitalism have introduced into your mind?"

Donnie nearly choked trying to backtrack. Barney put his other hand to Donnie's cheek and massaged it with his thumb.

"The further distance we put between ourselves and the world out there," he said, "the better chance we have of restoring ourselves to sanity. Those girls are broken and need to be healed. That won't happen with the interference of a damaged society."

Donnie wished he could break from his father, throw arms to the heavens, and demand the old man take a look at the checkbooks, the bank balances, the cold, hard realities, but his father's touch had warmed him, and the last thing he wanted on earth was to stand again in the cold. Instead, he teetered there with his arms hanging useless at his sides.

"We need to interact with people in order to do business," Donnie mumbled. "We need to show our faces time and again, or else folks will think we're kooks."

"I'm not concerned with the opinions of people in town," said Barney. "I bother only with the safety of my Miracles. I was never excited about you selling those dolls in town, but I allowed it because I believed it helped you gain self-worth, and kept the girls from idle hands. However, I feel I should draw the line with you taking the girls with you to town from now on. They are led too close to temptation. From now on, if you insist on going, I insist you go alone."

Donnie shuddered. He hated no word in the English language more than *alone*. Still, he shook it off and did his best to maintain resolve.

"You know that folks in town use words like *Waco* and *Scientology* when they talk about us," he said. "They snap pictures of us like we're Amish. You'd think we'd want to head that off at the pass before the whispers got out of hand."

"With that in mind," Barney said, removing his hands from Donnie, "I repeat my wishes to remain off anyone's radar."

As if the matter were closed, Barney excused himself and headed back in the direction of the Big House. Before he reached the chalk-topped road leading to the yard, Donnie bounded up alongside him like a puppy at the heels of his master.

"Dad…Dad…if you'll take a look at the big picture—"

Barney turned to face him and, for the first time, his restraint appeared tested. The kind creases at his eyes tightened and wrinkles bunched in his forehead.

"And another thing," said the man, "let's dispense with this *Dad* business. Even in private."

"I didn't mean—"

"It's unprofessional." Barney couldn't look the boy in the eye. "No single individual at Miracle Ranch can be prized above another. That's the First Principle. It's the foundation of our work here. Do you understand?"

"Yes. Of course, but—"

"Which brings me to my next concern." They reached the porch of the Big House. Barney stopped at the front step and blocked his son from it, as if to dissuade him from following him to the door. "I want to talk about Summer Halifax."

"Summer? She's doing great, isn't she? I told you she—"

"I don't think she understands all the Principles."

"What are you talking about?" Donnie shook at his hands and feet. "She can recite all the Principles forwards and backwards. If anyone's made great improvement—"

"She can recite them, but she hardly *lives* them." Barney crossed his arms. "I don't know what it is, but something is horribly wrong with that one."

Donnie blanched. He'd only known his father a short time, but had never heard anything which sounded remotely close to defeat from him. Yet he'd noticed his father as he watched Summer, or how his shoulders tensed when he heard the girl speak. He'd detected flashes of impatience when the two interacted. At times, Donnie reveled in the momentary lapses in patience from a man normally so unfettered, but mostly he feared for the future of the ranch. Donnie tried to stay the panic settling into his stomach by jamming both hands into his pockets, but could do nothing about the tremor in his voice.

"You insist that your God—er, *Higher Power* will provide," he said, "and I'd argue that if he provided any damned thing, it would be Summer Halifax. If the dolls won't sell and you won't plant corn to take to town…if you won't allow us to place advertisements for our treatment program in newspapers and internet ads, then I'm afraid once my mother's money runs out, all we'll have is what the Halifaxes send us. If you have a problem with Summer, you have to get over it, or else Miracle Ranch will have no future."

Barney turned to the boy. He said no words, but none were necessary. All the anger and hate and rage from the man's younger days flared in those mint green eyes of his and any semblance of composure cracked at the seams of his face. Never before had Donnie seen his shoulders so broad, nor the muscles in his jaw so tight. Donnie shielded his face with his hands and bent his back at the waist. He knelt before his father and begged forgiveness.

When finally the air between them settled, Barney let escape a long, sour exhalation from his lungs, then reached down to straighten the boy. Donnie flinched as Barney slipped both hands beneath his armpits and lifted him to face him eye-to-eye.

"I don't believe in letting anyone slip through the cracks," Barney said in a calm but strained voice. "But I won't allow weakness to infect the work we are doing here. If there is a cancer upon this ranch," he said, "it must be cured or cut out."

Were it not for the man holding him upright, Donnie would have doubled over and died. He opened his mouth to protest, but could only manage a weak whisper.

"*Cancer…*"

His father continued. "Some people can't be reached. If any one person on this ranch threatens the greater good, then I must act. If I can't save them, I will hate it more than any organism on this planet, but I will ask them to leave. Do you understand me?"

Donnie could do nothing but nod his head.

"I will do everything in my power to prevent it," said Barney, "but I beg daily for my Higher Power to grant me the serenity to accept the things I cannot change. Negative energy brings about illness, and I won't risk illness."

Donnie's hands shook.

"All illness is mental," said Barney. "All of them."

"I understand," said Donnie with a stammer. "I can help with Summer. I can bring her around."

Said Barney Malone, looking him dead in the eye, "I'm not talking about Summer, son."

Then he stepped into the Big House and closed the door behind him.

Overhead, the skies clouded and cast the earth in a steady shade of grey. The air turned colder around him and not a sound could be heard, save for the snapping of a dry branch lying near where the east wall of the house met the north. Donnie rose his tear-streaked cheeks toward the direction of the racket and found Summer standing before him, twirling the tattered sleeves of her powder blue shirt.

"I feel sorry for you," she said. "Mostly because you have to worry about all that work stuff when all I got to do is watch this here butterfly float past."

She pointed to it. A shiny insect of yellow and blue with grand, gentle wings fluttered upon whispers of updraft and Donnie wondered why he, himself, had yet to notice. He kept his eyes fast upon it, rather than face the girl.

"Did you hear all that?" he asked.

"Yes."

"Can you keep a secret?"

Summer's face was a pylon. "Brother, you've got no idea."

"You are literally the only thing keeping this place afloat right now," he said.

"What can I do?"

Donnie thought about it long and hard. He thought about all the things he could do with his life, out there in the world, without a father or a mother, or anyone else for that matter. He thought about himself, five, ten…thirty years from now, lying on a bed with patches of hair, ashen and grey, and no one by his side to whom he may share his hatred. He thought of all the rancor and regret which might fill that room, and would it be more or less than what crawled and gurgled from his mother's mouth on the night that she died. He thought maybe, just maybe, if he had a little more time, he might keep that from happening. but time ticked and tocked and never stopped, so he feared he must act when given the chance, and if now was the time the Higher Power chose to provide, then now was the time he must act.

"I need you to pay off," he told her. "I need you to pay off big time."

19

BEFORE SHE REACHED THE banks of the skinny creek that ran behind the corn field gone fallow, Summer Halifax received no less than four bona fide messages from God. The first was a black crow which flailed in a pile of golden straw as if in the final throes of death. Once settled, Summer thought no more of it, until she saw it hop to its two feet, then fly away on a late winter breeze. At the time, she had no idea what she had just seen, but it would not be long for her to add two and two.

Next, when a swarm of Texas hornets settled over Summer and the other girls, yet none of them were stung. Then, a three-minute period in which Rylah's shadow did not move. How Summer watched Cassie launch stones into waters which did not ripple. The temperature of the air dropped a good forty degrees.

Summer collapsed upon the muddy banks. Soon, she was awash with broken sobs.

"God is all around us," she cried. "He is everywhere."

The other girls fell upon her and Summer again became warm. She lay there, spackled in mud, and covered by the fingertips and breathless whispers of the other girls and said it over and over:

"God is everywhere."

"God is everywhere."

"God is everywhere."

Until all the girls repeated the words in unison, themselves thrashing about the muck until it oozed beneath every fingernail, smashed into their every crevice. They became one with the mud, and by extension, the earth. They melted into one another. They became part of the universe and its whole at the same time. There was nothing but them.

When finished, they did not linger long before slipping into the cool waters to cleanse themselves. They removed their soggy overalls and soaked-through powder blue shirts and lay them in the sun to dry. They scrubbed each other's backs with the fine silt of East Texas sand. They massaged away any unwelcome stress that might further infect their afternoon.

Then they got right to work.

Each of the girls brought with them a sewing kit and a small sack of rags and burlap. From them, they would stitch Donnie's Miracle Dolls, to be sold in town. Each doll was handmade and different from any other, just like the Miracles at the Ranch. Just like all of God's creatures.

"We shouldn't call him God anymore, you know," Summer suggested to the others as they stitched.

"What do you mean?" asked Rylah.

Summer shrugged. "I mean, in Spirit Study yesterday, Barney went out of his way to preach that it isn't God from the Bible that we worship. Not the Christian or Muslim or Jewish God, or none of the other gods who start wars all over this beautiful planet. He said it's our own relationship with a Higher Power that we should worship and protect."

"It's the Fourth Principle," said Suzie. Then, added with aplomb, "I'm on Principle Eight."

"The point I'm making is," Summer said, "we should change the name of our Higher Power in order to keep us from confusing him with the God of our parents and politicians."

The other girls exchanged glances. Beth Ann shrugged.

"What do you propose we name him?" she asked.

"I'm open for suggestions."

They spoke among themselves in whispers at first, but grew more and more excited with each passing proposal.

"What about Zeus?"

"What about Apollo?"

"Should it be a woman's name? Since we're women?"

"Like Athena?"

"Ooh, I like Athena!"

"What about Venus? Since she's beautiful and we are all beautiful!"

"We are all Miracles!"

"We are all Perfect!"

"We are all Loved!"

"How do we decide?"

"Should we put it to a vote?"

Summer kept her eyes closed, as if in deep thought. Then her eyeballs began to roll wildly behind the lids. Suddenly, she threw her arms into the air, tossing her half-stitched Miracle Doll into the tall grass. She fell onto her back.

"Summer, are you okay?"

"Is she having another vision?"

"Are you talking to...*Him*?"

Summer's breathing took a spell to regulate, but when finally it did, she opened her eyes and stared into the delirious ball of sun.

"Luther," she said.

None of the other girls had the slightest idea how to respond. They opened their mouths, then shut them. They blinked.

"We should name our Higher Power...*Luther*."

Rylah looked to Cassie. Suzie looked to Marva. Beth Ann turned her head to the sky.

The smile spread wide across Summer's face and the second time she said it, she exalted it for all the countryside.

"Luther is our Higher Power. He has been all along!"

The other girls, not knowing what to make of it, nor having any worthwhile substitute, fell to their backs as well. They also threw their arms to the clouds and exalted just as loud:

"Our Higher Power is Luther!"

"Praise Luther!"

"Luther is the name of our God!"

And Summer didn't need to close her eyes tight to see stars. She didn't need to hold her breath until her vision narrowed to pins. She no longer had to pop enough pills to sick up her stomach lining or drink to the bottom of a bevy of bottles.

She could see Luther, plain as day, standing before her.

He smiled and stretched out his hands.

The first few times they did it, Summer suggested it was to test themselves. They'd leave a tractor on the far side of the corn field, then drive it to the filling station off the highway. From there, they'd have no problem finding a ride into town.

"We have to prove to ourselves that we're strong enough to resist temptation," Summer would tell them. "Where else will we learn to defeat a lion, but for the lion's den?"

"But Barney said to place ourselves on the periphery of sin is just as dangerous as sin itself…"

"He also told us that strength comes from within us." Summer was not known to take no for an answer. "That which does not kill us only serves to make us stronger."

Rylah was on board from the get-go. "We hold the keys to the kingdom in our own pockets. No man is ever going to give them to us."

The attentions they received from the men at these bars came as no surprise. The older fellas would shake their heads and return craggy faces to beer bottles. The younger ones didn't need much spurring. One thing Summer learned long ago was that any woman—even ones in dusty overalls and old shirts—could be a goddess this close to last call.

They would tease them and they would flirt, but never would they go home with them. Even Beth Ann, an unusually spriteful type, kept her end of the bargain that was struck: no kissing, no sucking, no fucking. It's perfectly okay to whip these boys to a frenzy, but to give in would break the Principles.

Same with drink, or the offer of a toke off a marijuana joint. They would wave them away with a giggle. The same giggle they shared the entire tractor ride home, where they'd stealthily slip back into their trailers or RVs before Barney or Donnie could wake.

Lately, however, their trips to town had been for reasons altogether different.

"The Twelfth Principle states that it is our duty to share our spiritual awakening with those around us," Summer told the new girl, Brenna Caughey. Brenna was a girl who liked to cut herself, and had been sent to Miracle Ranch to cure her of it. It was her first night to join the girls on their midnight excursions.

"I know you're only on your Second Principle," Cassie told her, "but it don't hurt none to see the road that lies ahead of you."

"If you do not share the love with others," said Marva, "then you are self-centered, and self-centered behavior is what brought us down to begin with."

"Only by giving love can we truly receive it," said Beth Ann.

"How do we share it?" asked the new girl.

Said Summer, "These boys will listen to anything we tell them. It's time for us to spread Luther's Word beyond the confines of Miracle Ranch."

This did not go as they planned. Only after they stepped into the cinder block building off Highway 55, simply marked BILLIARDS, did Summer realize how far and wide her ministry had expanded. Two of the farm boys from Blooming Grove took a shine to Rylah the week previous, and had come to listen to her speak again about God or whatnot. This did not sit well with Rex Larson, who'd driven clear up from Corsicana to have the girl lift his spirit.

Or the fellas from the grocery store in Bardwell, or the ones who'd given them a lift last week, and so on and so forth…

"We've talked about your jealousy issues," Rylah told Rex Larson. "It's selfish behavior, which only leads you further down a wicked path. Who knows where that path may take you?"

"But I've been thinking about you all week," Rex moaned. "I've never been the jealous type with a woman…"

"Envious," said Rylah.

"Beg pardon?"

Rylah smiled on one side of her mouth, something she'd practiced her entire life. "*Jealousy* is when you have something and are afraid of losing it. *Envious* is when you want something you don't have. You're not jealous…you're envious."

Rex had served in two wars, but had never been so broken until he fell under Rylah's spell. The other girls fared no better. Some of the boys with worthwhile math skills put their efforts into the newer girl, suspecting a likelihood of flagging her resolve. It was all Marva and Cassie could do to keep the shots of tequila from flying down her gullet. Beth Ann, who had a hard time turning down a good, hard roll in the hay, had taken to the sweats by all the energy in the room, and Summer prayed for Luther to give her the strength necessary to fight her demons. However, soon they all found themselves swarmed by factions of men who'd taken to them this week or last or the one before that. The heat cranked high and the noise nearly rattled the walls to the ground, but for the crusty old barman stomping around the bar to fire three shots from a snub-nosed into the air.

"I won't have no more of this bullshit tonight," he shouted to the room, newly silent. "You girls ain't been nothing but trouble since you started coming around. You get these boys worked up and tell them alcohol ain't no good for them. We end up with a bunch of pussy-whipped fellas swearing off booze. Now, I'm all for folks following whatever religion they like, but you girls are cutting into my bottom line. I have to ask you to leave."

Gun or no gun, Summer had half a mind to tell off the old barman, but it was not what Luther would have wanted. Here, standing before these poor, lost men, she needed to set an example. What else did she see behind their eyes but hurt little boys who had fallen prey to the anger and insecurity of their parents? Perhaps their daddies had been a bit too severe with the belt, or their mommas had been less than liberal with their love. It was not their fault. Just as it had not been Summer's fault—all those terrible, terrible things she'd done—these men sought salvation, whether they knew it or not. Summer could not lash out. She'd graduated beyond such behavior.

"We respect your boundaries," Summer told the barman. "Although tonight we leave, mark my words: we shall return. Perhaps you men have had your hearts tossed aside and forgotten before, but we won't let that happen. All of you hold value for us, and we shall not cheapen that value with tawdry parking lot affairs."

"You are Perfect," said the girls in unison.

"You are Loved."

"You are Miracles."

The barman cocked the hammer of his firearm and held it further aloft, pointed shaky at the ceiling.

"I'm not going to tell you weirdos again…"

The girls fetched a ride from a farmer headed home and, once delivered back to their tractor, released the ecstatic frenzy they'd hardly managed to contain.

"I never knew I could feel so good!"

"This is the happiest I've ever been."

"This is far better than the best sex."

Summer agreed with them all. She took the lot of them into her arms. They cackled with wicked glee beneath the moonlight as they climbed aboard the tractor. Marva cranked it to life and they were off. They rambled across the rock-strewn paths until they came upon the tree line bordering the alfalfa lot. They hung off the machine and let the midnight breeze blow through their hair.

"Is it always like this?" asked the new girl.

"For so long as you wish it to be so," Summer cried into the night. "There is no such thing as fate or destiny. Only you control that which is before you."

The girl turned her head to the passing ground. "I've had it worse than anyone else."

"No, you haven't," Summer assured her. "We've all been in bad places. But the Twelve Principles show us the light. If you follow them—"

"But aren't we lying by sneaking out of the ranch under the cover of darkness?"

Summer scratched fast at her ear. "Pain is the cornerstone of spiritual growth."

"But, if God...er, I mean...*Luther* really wants us to share his message—"

"Our *awakening* through his message," said Marva. "It's different."

"—and if Barney is the one who receives his message—"

"Barney speaks directly to Luther," Beth Ann offered.

"—then why are we keeping it secret from him that we are going to town to share it?"

The old Summer would have kicked the feet from under the girl, then let her fall below the rumbling tractor tire. The old Summer would have wandered to yonder cow pasture to pick mushrooms from the dung and drop them into the new girl's afternoon tea, then accused her to Barney of a relapse. The old Summer would have done a number of things to Brenna Caughey, but that Summer died on an emergency room crash cart. *This* Summer put a hand to the child's shoulder and spoke in a calm, even voice.

"You're only on Principle Two, so it might be difficult for you to understand everything. By the time you get where I am—which is the Eighth Principle—then you will get it. Until then, I suggest you trust and have faith that Luther won't put anything in front of you that you can't handle."

"I will," said the girl. "I promise."

"Good." Summer took her hand and squeezed it. "Let go and Let Luther."

"Let go and Let Luther."

"Like Luther says: we share the experiences of our newfound awakening—"

"Wait a second…" Marva's face contorted to a tiny ball. "Luther didn't say that. That's from Barney's teachings. It's his Eleventh Principle."

"I'll have you know," said Summer, "Barney isn't the only one who talks to Luther."

None of the other girls could speak. The only sound in all the night was the steady rumble of the tractor engine.

"It's a fact. I used to talk to him all the time."

"Shut up…"

"A few times, I've even seen him."

Summer thought maybe she could let go of the side of the tractor and float high, high above the alfalfa, the creek bed, the whole of Navarro County.

"I'll go one further," she said. "I'd say the only thing that makes Barney so special is he's the one who received the secrets of the universe from Luther, then bothered to write them down. Man, if I'd have thought to do that, then I wo—"

She'd have finished the thought, were it not for a great calamity. Marva, driving the tractor, had long taken her eyes off the landscape before her. She, like the other girls, could not believe what they were hearing from their fellow Miracle, and ran the machine plum off the road and into the darkened creek bed. They caught air as the tires left the ground, then crashed all twenty feet into the ravine.

Summer found herself cast aside into a thorny briar, one of which sliced open her left cheek and nearly missed her eyeball. She lay there only until she could catch her breath, then scrambled further down the cliff to where the tractor lay smoking and upturned.

"Is everyone okay?" she called into the night. She could hear coughing, whimpering, and sobs. "Rylah? Beth Ann?"

The girls had been scattered across the creek bed on all sides of the busted tractor. One by one, they called out to Summer and the others.

"I'm fine."

"Everything is okay."

"That was intense!"

"Thank Luther, we're all alive!"

But not everyone responded. Summer did the quick math and discovered they had yet to hear from Marva. Immediately, they flew to a frenzy.

"Marva!"

"Where are you, girl?"

"I can't see…it's too dark!"

Summer dropped to her hands and knees and scraped her palms against the slick mud. She grabbed hold of roots, rocks, anything, looking for some sign of her fellow Miracle. All the while, her mind racing. What had they done? Could they get out of this? Would she have to run? Saying to herself, all the while, it would be okay, everything was going to be fine, it would all turn out okay.

"I found her!"

"She's over here!"

"Marva? She's not answering me! Marva?"

Summer rushed toward the direction of the voices.

"She's not moving!"

"Marva…wake up!"

Summer's eyes had trouble adjusting. The moon slapped the creek water, which rippled silvery light in a million directions. She still wobbled from the fall. Her cheek burned from the briars. She could make out shapes, could smell the smoke from the tractor. She fell twice making her way to where the other girls stood.

"This can't be happening."

They stood in a circle and Summer shouldered them each aside to better position herself. At their feet was Marva, lying on her back near a swampy puddle of creek water. Even in the moonlight, Summer could see the girl's face had gone blue.

"Get her out of that water!" Summer barked. "Have you no sense?"

"We need help!" said Beth Ann.

"We can't let her die!" cried Suzie.

Summer pulled Marva onto her lap and turned her head skyward. She could not for the life of her remember how CPR was done, but clamped her mouth to Marva's and blew into it.

Rylah scurried up the other side of the creek bed and dashed into the darkness.

"Where is she going?" shouted Summer.

"She's going for help!" Cassie answered. "The ranch is just over the cornfield."

"She'll never make it in time!" Summer could barely catch her own breath. "Everything will be fine. We'll make all this better."

"What do we do?"

"Why is this happening?"

Summer could smash in her own head with her fists. It all moved too fast. What had she done? For the first time in her entire life, she'd found the happiness that had so often eluded her. Now she watched as it slipped through her fingers.

"Marva…" Summer choked on her own sobs. "Please…*please*…"

She could run. She could either head toward the ranch and catch up with Rylah before she woke the others, or head the other way and hope to be long gone before the sun came up and the police were called. She could hitch into Waxahachie and be halfway to Austin before she knew it. She could find a crew of Rainbow People and lay low until the heat died down. She's always wanted to see the desert…

"Luther…"

It came first from the lips of Brenna. Summer might not have heard her, were it not for Brenna's lips being but a whisper from her ear.

"Luther, if you are listening…"

Soon, the other girls as well. Cassie, Beth Ann…Suzie…all of them gathered at Summer's back and pressed themselves tight. Soon one voice became two, and then became them all as they closed tight their eyes, turned their heads to the stars, and said over and over and over:

"Luther, please, please save us."

20

DONNIE SHOT FROM THE bed in a bolt. He slapped both hands to the windowsill where an urgent wind kicked tattered curtains on both sides of him. Upon that wind, he could still hear the cries.

"Help us! Somebody, please...help us!"

Off in yonder distance, he could see a blurry, orange glow. Closer yet, he could make the spindly frame of Rylah in silhouette, rushing wild, flailing twiggy arms above her head.

"Barney! Donnie! Somebody, help!"

Donnie bothered not with the door, and instead leapt from the window. He crashed to the flowerbed below, then took for the cornfield, in the directions of Rylah's cries.

His father, Barney, had already cut the distance between them. He got to the girl first. He took her rawboned shoulders with both hands and pulled her to him.

"What is the matter, child?"

She collapsed her head to Barney's chest. She spoke in staccato gasps. "It's Marva," she said. "She's not moving. She's...she's not *breathing.*"

"Marva?" Barney sputtered. "But…I don't—"

"Where is she?" asked Donnie.

Rylah pointed over her shoulder, toward the flickering firelight. Above them, thunder grumbled in billowing storm clouds.

"You have to help her!"

Still, Barney did not move. "What are you girls doing up at this hour? Why do I smell cigarette smoke in your overalls?"

"We…we were—"

"There isn't time for that," Donnie said. "Rylah, take me to her."

Thunder slapped like a whipcrack and she was off. Donnie kept pace with her and somewhere behind them lagged his father. The sky above them opened and down came a chilly rain, one that would fill the gully in a matter of minutes.

"We have to hurry!" Donnie shouted over his shoulder. Again, he cursed his father for not allowing telephones or internet on the grounds. Without them, they'd find no way to get help without driving into town, and he couldn't remember which was closer: the hospital in Ennis or the one in Corsicana.

He hoped to high hell there'd still be need for a hospital.

"It was an accident," Rylah panted. "I swear to Luther, we didn't mean—"

Donnie had plenty enough on his mind, like how deep his bare feet sunk into the new muck made by rains or how strong was the deluge, to ask who the hell Luther was. When finally he came to the rise of the ravine, he found a small fire roasting the tractor carcass, its flames dancing in the rain. He found a quickly developing stream. He found the remaining Miracle girls, stroking and caressing the body of Marva.

"What the…?"

They laid her in the mud upon her back, and drew her hands to her chest, as if preparing her for the casket. They brushed her long hair with their fingertips. They dried her cheeks from the rain.

"Luther, take Marva into your arms and keep her warm."

"Take her into your arms and keep her safe."

"She is perfect."

"She is loved."

"She is a Miracle."

Donnie barreled down the face of the ravine. Reaching bottom, he slipped across the banks of the rising waters until he came to the girls, who he shouldered aside. He gently lifted Marva into his arms, cradling her head with the back of her hand.

She was gone, sure. Her limbs hung slack and her backbone offered no give. Her mouth gaped and he could see no one had bothered to clear it of water.

From atop the ravine, Barney hollered down, "Don't touch her! She shouldn't be moved!"

"To hell with that," Donnie said. He lowered Marva to the slippery creek bed and tilted up her chin. He put both hands to the center of her breastbone and—*one, two*—pushed inward. He pinched shut her nose. He put his mouth to hers and—*one, two*—blew quick breaths. He repeated the process and repeated it until his father finally reached the bottom of the ravine.

"My poor Miracle," he moaned. "My girls, please…" He scooped them each into his arms where he tried to shelter them from the storm. "You poor children."

"We tried to save her," Beth Ann cried. "We did everything we could."

Between breaths, Donnie called, "Did none of you try CPR?"

"We prayed and we prayed," said Suzie.

"That's all you can do," Barney assured them.

"It literally isn't," said Donnie, gasping for air. "Give me room so I can—"

"God has a plan for us all," Barney said. "Marva is part of that plan. Right now, we all need to—"

Donnie let the girl slip from his hands. He rose to his feet. He split the distance between he and the old man. The rain fell harder, but within the boy raged one fire that would not be doused.

"You think your Higher Power is going to save you from everything," he growled. "I got news for you: he's not. He's not going to save you from the tax man. He's not going to save that girl. And he's certainly not going to save you from her parents' lawyers."

Barney waved his hand as if shooing a fly. "All the world is made of energy, son. The same amount of atoms is in the universe now as there was in the beginning. All that's happened is the shifting of that matter. The same stuff inside of you is the same stuff inside of me, Marva, and all of my Miracles, as well as the air which separates us."

"What does that have to do with—"

"I need you to focus your energy." Barney moved to receive Donnie to his arms. "Only positive thoughts can be allowed here. Marva's soul will redistribute to the universe as only it can see fit, and forever when we look upon this creek, it must be with joy, rather than sadness."

"All the positive energy in the world isn't going to bring her back," Donnie screamed into the night. "Nothing will."

"Our minds are much stronger than we give credit," said Barney. "Our poor, sweet Marva has begun her journey back into the light. Her soul will be recycled and, thanks to the great love she was shown here on earth…*at Miracle Ranch*…some of her karmic duties were fulfilled. With all of our energy and focus, I ask you to—"

"You gave up on her!"

"I fight harder for her soul than I have fought for anything in my entire life," Barney said.

Donnie slapped the water from his eyeballs. "You let her die alone."

"Marva is not alone." Barney waved to the Miracles behind him, all writhing in the mud, mixing moans among the thunderclaps. "She will never again be alone."

"I'm not talking about *Marva*," Donnie hissed. "I'm talking about my mother."

Barney Malone opened his mouth. He closed it.

"I'm talking about how you left her to raise me on her own," Donnie said, "and when it came time for her to die, you were still nowhere to be found. You couldn't be bothered with the thought of her, not even after her son came sniffing around with her insurance check."

"Donnie..." Barney blinked away rivers of rain. "Donnie, I..."

"You talk a mean game about love and understanding and positive energy, but where were you? Where were your rationalizations and justifications then?"

Lightning spider-webbed the horizon with a brilliant orange. Barney waited for the following thunderclap to speak.

"Donnie, you can't let that sickness into your heart," the old man said. "Not right now. As Marva's spirit leaves her body, she needs us to be at her side."

Behind them, Summer dropped to her knees. The rain sluiced sideways, splashing her with wet which she did not bother to wipe away. She spoke in a low monotone which gained momentum like a dynamo.:

"Luther, take Marva into your arms and keep her warm."

"Luther, take Marva into your arms and keep her safe."

Alongside her, Suzie knelt to the mud, which spattered up the front of her overalls. Next, Beth Ann. Then, Rylah. Brenna.

"Luther, take Marva into your arms and keep her warm."

"Luther, take Marva into your arms and keep her safe."

Donnie stepped close enough to his father for their noses to touch. He threw a finger to the man's face.

"So if you're going to keep on with this talk of a positive spirit that can save lives," he said, "then you must admit that you let my mother die."

Barney could not look his boy in the eye, nor could he look to the Miracles, chanting in the tempest.

"Luther, take Marva into your arms and keep her warm."

"Luther, take Marva into your arms and keep her safe."

"So say it," said Donnie.

Barney nodded.

"Say it out loud."

Barney asked, "Say what?"

"You let my mother die."

Barney would do no such thing. Instead, he lowered himself to his knees, much like the girls behind him, and turned his head to the stormy night sky.

Donnie could take no more of it. He returned to Marva's side and cupped her head, much as he'd done with his mother all those lonely months ago. He fingered open her mouth and lowered his lips to hers.

"Son, what are you doing?"

Said Donnie, "Something your Higher Power hasn't the decency to take care of."

Again, he blew—*one, two*—into the girl, then gave another push into her chest. The girls kept vigil—

"Luther, take Marva into your arms and keep her warm."

"Luther take Marva into your arms and keep her safe."

—until, as if on cue, the dead girl coughed water from her lungs and gasped thirstily for the air. Donnie held her until she wriggled like a slippery eel in his arms. Quick as they started, the rains stopped and the thunder shushed to a distant rumble to the east. The only sound was the drippings off yonder pecan tree, and the steady trickle of the stream.

The girls rushed to her and yanked her to their arms. They brushed away soaked strands of hair and smothered her with kisses.

Summer did not join them. Rather, she stood at Barney's shoulder, the old man yet to rise from his knees. She swayed in the memory of the breeze long gone.

"You have healed her," she murmured. "Luther now works through you."

Donnie's eyes blinked faster than he thought possible.

"Who the hell is Luther?" he asked.

Standing in the moonlight, she winked at him and smiled. "Praise Luther," she said.

Said the girls, "Praise Luther."

21

BARNEY HAD NO IDEA what he was doing. The man was lost, floundering in a sea of his own sin and iniquity. His resentments and insecurities had gotten the better of him. What may have been a beautiful man and instrument of Luther, had been crumpled up and discarded. The negativity took root inside of him and festered and spread like a cancer throughout his bones until the good in him floated away on a breeze like the seeds of a dandelion.

What remained was the frightened husk of a man who had taken to the sweats. He now walked with a hunch. His voice pitched at wild octaves and all the swagger had quit his step.

As evidenced when he addressed the girls in Spirit Study.

"We're not going to do this again, ladies."

He'd long stood in the center of the barn with his hands in his pockets, keeping shut his trap while the other girls stared at their palms, kept steadfast in their laps. They looked to each other. They looked to the ground. They looked anywhere but at their leader. His plan must have been to wait out their silence, but his plan fell to the wayside. He didn't last ten minutes before he leapt in front of them in a tizzy.

"This makes four Spirit Studies in a row that you have all refused to share. Do any of you care to tell me what is going on?"

None of the girls spoke. Their resolve could have bent steel.

"Rylah, have you nothing to share?"

She did not.

"Cassie?" His voice remained even, but Summer wasn't fooled. "How about you, Brenna?"

Even the new girl could not be swayed.

"Listen up. You have behaved very strange of late. I've let it slide because of what happened to Marva. Trust me, I understand how traumatic that can be to a person's spirit. After all I've seen in my days… you don't see the inside of a jailhouse and keep high spirits. There were challenges that I faced every day, but—"

Great. Here we go again.

Summer nearly split a gut laughing. She collected herself, quick as she could, then covered her mouth with her hand.

"Something funny, Summer?"

She kept herself still.

"By keeping secrets, you are damaging your own souls." Barney paced the dry dirt in front of them. Outside the barn, the sky was pitch blue with white, fluffy clouds. Somewhere far off, machines tore into the earth. "Secrets get you high. One leads to two, and two leads to three. It's a slippery slope. A downward spiral. You're only as sick as your secrets, and, sisters, I need you to want to get well."

Attitude of Gratitude. Shit or Get Off the Pot. If You're Standing Still, Stand Aside, Because Others May Be Going Somewhere.

Sigh.

Again, Summer stifled a giggle.

"I'm tempted to bump you each down a couple Principles."

Suzie nearly bucked. She was oh-so proud of reaching the Eleventh Principle, quick as she did. She gripped both her knees with white-knuckled fists and bit hard into her lower lip. Summer thought maybe she'd burst, and moved to stick up for her, but a warm hand held her at the wrist.

Suzie is a strong woman. She can resist him.

Summer stayed. She waited. She watched the blood in Suzie's face redistribute throughout her body. For her breathing to return to normal.

See?

"You're always right, Luther," said Summer. "Every time."

Barney cocked his head. "What did you say?"

Summer clamped close her mouth. She returned both hands to her lap.

"This brings up an excellent point," Barney said. "I want you all to stop referring to the Higher Power as *Luther.*"

All the girls drew quick a breath. Rylah looked to Cassie and Beth Ann turned to Brenna. Summer nearly ground her teeth to nubs.

He's bluffing. He wouldn't dare.

"Our relationship with our Higher Power is an individual one," Barney continued. "I'm afraid that by you sharing a common name, you're experiencing an unhealthy—"

Cassie's hand shot up. "But you always say that we all share the same Higher Power, which is why our instinct is to still call it God."

"What I meant was—"

Rylah piled on. "You said that the battle for our sobriety will be uphill, but it won't be alone. We've found our Higher Power and we did it together."

"You're misinterpreting my—"

"He no longer speaks to Luther," Summer said. She stood and puffed out her chest. There was not so much of a whisper of the rage that used to consume her. She'd found peace, but understood the need to defend it. "In fact, I'd challenge that he's not spoken to Luther in quite some time."

Summer, sit down...

"I'll do no such thing," she said. She faced the other girls, turning her back to Barney. A smile took to her lips. "If you really speak to

Luther, then tell me what he is saying right this very minute."

"Summer," said Barney, "sit down."

Summer drew a quick breath and held it. Her eyes darted like fish below the ice. Her arms trembled from the shoulders down to her wrists.

In a weak voice, she whispered, "Tell me what he's saying *now*."

"There is no Luther, dammit!"

This did not sit well with the other girls. Brenna rose, as if to counter, but collapsed immediately to the ground. She flopped about in the straw like a catfish on a riverbank. She frothed at the mouth. She garbled words that were not of this earth.

"What the…?"

None of the girls moved. They kept where they stood and stared hate-fire into Barney.

"You can't keep doing this," Barney said. He put both hands on his hips. "Are none of you going to help your fellow Miracle?"

Cassie fell as well. Like Brenna, she convulsed and twitched in the dirt. Her screams chased bats from the rafters. Spiders from their webs. Sin from the wood bones of the barn and from the still air within it.

Rylah. Suzie. All of them, upon the floor and frothing until there stood only Barney and Summer. They faced each other, as if in a gun duel. They locked eyes until he scanned each and every one of the fevered children, then resumed their staredown.

Said Barney, "I'm beginning to think you are going to have a very bad effect on my Miracles."

"I bet you do," said Summer. "You ain't his instrument no longer. Naw, if it was up to you, Marva would have died there in that creek bed. But Donnie healed her with his touch. If Luther speaks through any of you, I reckon it's your boy."

"Summer…" He couldn't make the words happen. "Summer…I don't think… I hate to say it, but…" He took a deep breath. He collected himself. "I promised myself long, long ago that I would never allow someone to slip through the cracks, but—"

Summer raised high both her arms. At once, all the girls ceased to writhe. They comported themselves, rose to their feet, and stood alongside Summer. Barney looked like he'd gotten hold of something turned. He opened his mouth a couple times, but never managed anything worthwhile. Instead, he clapped his hands against the thighs of his jeans, then stalked out of the barn, toward the Big House.

You stood your ground. You are getting stronger.

The girls watched him until he'd disappeared inside, slamming the door behind him.

"What do you think he'll do?" Rylah asked.

"He'll run straight to Donnie," Cassie said. "He'll order his boy to call Summer's parents and have them fetch her."

"We should stop him," said Beth Ann.

"There's no need for that." Summer took Rylah with her left hand, then Suzie with her right. "Donnie won't follow his father's orders."

"How can you be so sure?" asked Brenna.

Donnie understands how much money you are worth to Miracle Ranch. He hates his father. Donnie will use his newfound power to sate his need for revenge. Donnie will seize opportunity where it presents itself, because he is not a fool. He is smart, like you.

And if all else fails, we'll make him see the light.

"I know," said Summer to the others, "because Luther told me so."

22

Barney burst through the front door of the Big House, already a-frenzy. He yanked his hair loose from its ponytail and shook it so it hung at his shoulders. He paced the floor a bit before finally stalking the room to stand over Donnie, working hard at his desk on bills and whatnot.

"My spirit now is in great peril. I teeter before the precipice of temptation and I've no one to blame but you."

Donnie dropped his pencil onto the ledger over which he'd huddled in the lamplight.

"Me?" he said. "How the hell you figure now to blame me for your predicament?"

"I had a clear path." Barney turned and again paced the floors. "I deviated from it only once and that was to accept the money you offered. You dangled that check before me and I didn't refuse it. Sin laid a trap and, sure as day, I sprung it."

Donnie massaged his temples with his thumbs. "Without that check, you'd still be hollering on street corners and protesting methadone clinics. You'd probably have been carted back to jail by now, for all anyone knows."

"I swear...money corrupts. It serves no other purpose but to lead man into temptation."

"And to pay bills."

"I want not to participate!" Barney punched the air in front of him. His hair stuck out from both sides of his head as his exasperation mounted to a fever pitch. "I want none of it! Those stupid dolls, the fields. We should sell the lot of it and be done."

"Where would you go?"

"We'd take to the forests." Barney pointed wild out the window. "We'd scavenge dumpsters. We'd strip ourselves of any earthly binds that sick, disgusting society tried to slip us into. Civilization is a noose. It strangles our spirit until we're surrounded by pop-up ads and cell phone apps. Billboards and TV commercials. Consumerism! Capitalism!"

"You've got no choice," said Donnie. "That's the way of things, Barney. They've got a word for folks who go that far off the grid and it's not a word you want to be associated with. Not in Texas, you don't. Not in this day and age."

Barney smoothed his hair with his hands, then tied it back with a small strand of hemp rope. He let his breathing regulate. He watched his son grow bored with the performance, as he picked up the pencil to resume his numbers. Donnie let the old man study him a spell until he could no longer stand it. Again, he put down the pencil and sighed.

"What now, Barney?"

Said the old man, "You are no different from your mother."

"Wha—"

"Not a bit." Barney took a seat on the sofa across from Donnie, then crossed his legs. "You've got her eyes. I saw it the first time you came around. You also got her smile."

"Don't talk about my mother."

"Sometimes, in the right light, you're the spitting image of her. Her hair was longer, of course, and a lighter shade of blonde..."

Donnie found himself gripping the pencil so hard, it nearly broke. He'd no idea how long his leg had shaken, but it nearly rattled the kerosene lamp off the desktop. He put a hand to his knee to steady it.

"You know what else you got?" When Donnie didn't answer, Barney continued. "You got her mean streak."

Donnie could not manage an exhale. All that wind sucked up tight in him and had nowhere to go.

"And who do you think gave her that mean streak?" he managed to ask through clenched teeth.

"That woman was an angry person long before she met me," Barney said. "You don't develop a hatred that deep overnight. No, that was something she inherited through generations of broken and damaged DNA. If you don't do something—and something fast—it will continue to spread. Is that what you want?"

Donnie stared at the book in front of him so hard, it liked to have set on fire. He swore to himself that if Barney said another word about his mother, he'd leap over that desk and grab him with both hands and pummel his face with them until the old man stopped moving.

Barney was smart enough to let the air settle in the room. With the powers and energies properly redistributed, he watched his boy wither before him.

"We have to rid ourselves of the Halifax girl," he said.

"Her parents send us another check in three days," Donnie said. "And another one every two Wednesdays after that. So long as we keep her here—"

"I don't like the effect she's having on the other girls," said Barney. "I don't like the effect she's having on me."

"We need to keep her. She's a windfall."

"Windfall…" Barney shook his head and kept his voice level with his breathing. "That's where your trouble begins. You refer to these girls with words like *windfall* and *profit margin*, but they are human beings. That talk may get you far on Wall Street, but not down here at Miracle Ranch." Barney pointed out the open window. "There is something sick about that girl."

"You said we would never turn our back on anyone."

"I said that before I knew what a person could be capable of."
Barney closed his eyes. "I've never before faced something like…"

"Something like what?"

Barney pursed his lips. He swallowed. "Do you believe there is
such a thing as true evil?"

"No." Donnie picked up the pencil again, but could not bring
himself to put it to the paper. "And neither do you. If there's one thing
you've stressed in these meetings, it's that every person on earth is a
Miracle and they—"

"I know what I said." Barney's voice cracked. "But maybe…"

"What?"

Barney turned his face to the wall. "Maybe I was wrong."

Donnie erased numbers. He scribbled new ones. When next he
looked up, the man looked older than Donnie remembered him. He
looked smaller, and beaten more by time and elements. His eyes—
forever green—looked grey in the lamplight and Donnie felt twinges
of remorse mingling with the mirth. He leaned back in his chair and
further inspected his father.

"I think," said Donnie, "maybe you should take a couple days off.
Maybe you should drive into Dallas. Hit you one of those AA meetings,
recharge your batteries…you know, get away for a bit. Nothing is
guaranteed to drive a man batshit faster than a bunch of young girls,
and Lord knows you've spent plenty time around them. How about
you take the truck and air yourself out a little bit?"

If Barney considered it, he didn't do so for long. He shook his head.
"This is no time to retreat. My work is assailed on all sides. I have you
on one side harping about money and Summer on the other. If I left
now, what would I return to?"

Donnie shook his head and turned back to his work.

"What I need to do is pray," said Barney.

"Fine. Then pray."

Barney paced the floor. He appeared lost in thought.

"I thought you were going to pray."

Said Barney, "This was all so much better before you came along."

"Excuse me?"

"You brought pestilence with you, much like the Horseman. You brought disease." Barney pointed a finger to the ceiling. "Sin turned inward, that is disease. Dis *ease*. It's something that can only be cured on the inside, not from outside."

"Except for my mother." Donnie felt his own patience sapping from him. In its place burned something hot. "Say it right now, god damn you. *Except for my mother.*"

"Especially your mother," Barney snapped. "She was a spiteful woman. She was dishonest to the core. She was quick to lie, and quicker to find fault in—"

"Shut up."

Barney showed no sign of stopping. "It's true," he said. "Perhaps a more remarkable person could have healed themselves, but your mother was far from remarkable. She carried with her no insight she didn't pilfer from a schoolbook, nor could she acquaint herself with reason. She was petty, and that pettiness manifested within her a cancer."

"I swear..." Donnie's shoulders squared, heaving. "You'd better shut your mouth this instant."

"In fact, your mother wouldn't have been a blip on my radar, if not for you. Neither before, nor after." Something foreign had taken hold of Barney's voice, his cadence. It was as if the man had been replaced with someone more sinister. He sounded nothing of his former self, especially when he uttered the words, "She was poison then, and she remains to be poison long after her death."

Donnie was over the desk before he could stop himself. He held at his side the pencil by which he daily scratched his numbers and drove its sharp point into his father's throat. This caught them both by surprise, but none more than Barney Malone, who's eyes bugged wide as he drew up both hands to staunch the steady flow of blood.

"Dear God!" barked Donnie. "What have I…?"

Barney kicked the boy off him and jerked from the couch as if yanked by a string. He collapsed, bloodied, into one wall, then raced the length of the living room to throw himself into another. He dropped to the floor, where he struggled and spasmed, working to free the pencil from deep within his throat.

"Don't move!" Donnie shouted. "Hold still and I'll get it."

But Donnie spoke to no avail. Barney wrestled with the confines of the room, as if breaking free might save him from what now appeared certain. He grasped at the air before him with one hand, and threw wild punches with the other. He kicked his feet in the direction of Donnie, as if to keep him at bay. As if to keep him from stabbing him again with more instruments.

Donnie could not be stayed. He dodged one blow, then charged into the melee of Barney's feet until he'd climbed atop the old man and pinned his shoulders with his knees. As his father bucked and hollered below him, Donnie spoke in as calm a voice as he could muster.

"Dad," he said, "you have to trust me."

Barney's eyes bulged white. He sucked air like a catfish on a riverbank.

"Hold still," said his boy.

Barney, seeing little choice in the matter, did as he was told. His face lost color. His left leg twitched slower and slower.

Donnie wrapped both fists around the pencil and closed his fingers.

"This is going to hurt," he said.

Barney opened his mouth in mad protest, but it was too late. Donnie slipped the pencil from the old man's throat, and soon the room was awash in spray. He'd nicked an artery good, and what was inside Barney soon found its way outside of him. The old man clasped both hands to his throat and held on tight. He whispered words that never found their way to anyone.

"No, no, no, no, no, no…"

Donnie ripped his own shirt from his body and held it to his father's neck to stop the life from leaving him. Soon, the shirt purpled and turned heavy, so he tossed it aside and grabbed the pages of his precious ledger, the sofa's pillow, pulled up pieces of carpet, anything to save his father, but all to no use.

Barney Malone could no longer be saved.

23

SUMMER CROSSED THE BACK lot of the ranch with shoulders more slumped than they'd ever been. She carried with her only an apple, rather than the fruits from all her planning, hard labor, and good intentions. She shuffled across the dirt until she reached the far end and sat below what used to be a telephone booth.

Don't sit so close to the tall grass. There might be snakes.

"I pity the snake that sinks its teeth into me," Summer said. "The blood it'd draw would be cursed."

Don't say that.

"It's true." She polished the apple with the front of her overalls. "I'm a black stain. I'm no good to anyone and it's high time I made peace with that."

She bit into the apple. She watched buzzards soar overhead. One bird, then two, all steady on the updrafts.

"Luther?" She swallowed her bite. "Luther?"

I'm here.

"You got quiet, is all." She studied a bruise in her apple. "You know I couldn't handle it if you stopped talking to me."

I just won't play that game. That's all.

"I ain't playing no game."

The pity parties. The self-loathing. I told you, I won't have it. If you're going to talk like that, you might as well talk to someone else. I won't be your audience for it.

Summer sighed. Luther had a point. She'd worked so hard on her self-esteem since coming to the ranch. She'd come so far. She had fifty-eight days sober. She cut through the Principles like they were victims at a massacre.

She was perfect.

She was loved.

"You're right," she said. "You don't understand how hard it is to keep from repeated learned behaviors."

I understand completely.

"Of course you do. You understand everything."

She scanned the horizon. She watched an armadillo hustle from one hole and into another. She took another bite from her apple.

"You're the only one who understands me."

That's not true.

"Oh yeah? Who, then?"

Do I really have to spell it out for you?

Summer opened wide her mouth. She slapped at the air in front of her.

"Stop teasing and tell me."

Think about it.

"Donnie?"

He's cute.

"He's a little straight and narrow for my tastes, don't you think?"

You'd be surprised what kind of darkness he has inside of him.

"I'm tired of the darkness." Rather than finish the rest of her apple, she tossed it into the weeds. "If it's all the same, I'd like to spend a bit more time here in the light."

Summer rose and walked further into the pasture. She ducked

between strands of barbed wire, then kept going. Stepping over petrified patties of cow shit and around prickly mesquite shrubs, she came upon an old bass tank. The waters quivered and quaked as turtles, frogs, and whatnot scattered at the sight of her. A crane took flight. She looked out, over the hilly horizon. The sun was setting. The landscape burned brilliant, a color she'd never before seen.

"You're doing a good job with this one, Luther."

Thank you.

"No…thank *you.*" When everything returned still, she said, "Do you really think he understands me?"

The two of you are cut from the same cloth. Where you are weak, he is strong. And vice versa. You are the perfect complements of each other.

"You've said the same thing before." Summer crossed her arms. "And look where that got me."

Exactly. Where it got you. If it weren't for everything that's ever happened, do you think you still would have ended up right here, right now?

Summer nodded her head. "That's a good point, Luther."

He is a firm, guiding hand. He'll be good to have around in a week or two, because based on my calculations that's around the time you will be—

"Speaking of calculations," said Summer, "he's got a great head for numbers. Let's face it, math is not my strong suit."

Right.

"He's got a good head on his shoulders." Summer's cheeks flushed. "He sure does. You know, I've heard him talk about the plans he has for the ranch. How he says if we planted corn and cotton in yonder fallow fields, we could gin it in town and make enough money to sustain ourselves for years."

If not for his father…

"And how any day, those Miracle Dolls will take off and become collector's items. Any day…I can just feel it."

If only Barney allowed him to market them on the internet. Can you imagine what you could do for the Ranch, if Barney allowed an internet connection?

"I could turn this ranch into something big, you know. They've got no idea what I'm capable of."

When they find out…

"I could bring them into social media. I'd get them on all the latest platforms." It grew dark. She squinted at a fresh star winking overhead. "Maybe fetch us a celebrity to clean up, so we could get on the cover of *People* or *Parade* magazines."

Barney would never go for it.

"That man is a fool," she said. "He's got no clue how to run a sober camp."

He's served his purpose.

"Sure, he did." Summer leaned back in the craggy grass. She stared up to the crescent moon. "Maybe it's high time we move him along."

Focus on a goal with every ounce of love you can muster. Concentrate. Make it so.

Summer closed tight her eyes. She balled her fists. She squeezed the whole of her body so tight, her teeth nearly popped out. When she could tense her muscles no further, she relaxed them with a heavy sigh. Her ears rang long after, and her lungs could not receive enough air.

"I did it." She lay still in the craggy grass. "I focused like a motherfucker."

Good for you. Now you must go to him, because he needs you.

"Who? Donnie?" Summer smiled sideways. "I'm just a washed-up old junkie. What could he possibly need with a wing nut like me?"

Far off, a hoot owl gave plenty warning. A coyote's song filled the arroyo.

"Luther?"

There was no reply.

"Luther?" Summer sat up. Her hands scrabbled at the dry dirt alongside her. "Luther, I was only kidding. I was just funning you. I know I'm more than a wing nut. I'm a Miracle. I'm loved. I'm—"

Summer, I'm serious.

"So am I. I didn't—"

Summer...he needs you.

Summer didn't like the tone in his voice. She cocked her head sideways, like a dog at a whistle. Any hint of a smile quit her face.

"What do you mean? You mean...he's in trouble?"

Summer, now! He needs your help!

Summer needed no further encouragement. She made tracks across the pasture, leapt the barbed wire in a single bound, and headed straight for the Big House.

☀ ☀ ☀

Summer knocked once, but didn't bother to wait as she punched open the back door of the Big House. She stumbled through the kitchen, the hallway, all the way to the living room before she stopped at the threshold, then used it to keep herself upright.

"Oh, dear Luther..." She did her level best to keep it together. "What have we done?"

Donnie Williams stood in the center of the room. His shoulders and chest heaved like that of a wounded animal. The room stunk of fear and something metal, like copper, and the walls had been splattered with blood.

"Oh my—" Summer slipped a hand to her mouth. "I willed this to happen."

Donnie stood over the corpse of his father. The both of them were soaked straight through with enough ink-black blood that Summer could not tell if it came from one or the both of them. Donnie's hands shook so hard she thought his arms might vibrate straight from their sockets. He held a bloodied pencil in one of them, and a gaping mouth on his face.

"I asked him to stop talking about my mother." He could speak only in mumbles. "I begged him."

Bubbles formed and popped at a jagged hole in Barney's neck. It was the only movement from the old man.

"He said she gave herself the cancer," whispered Donnie. "That she'd brought it on herself. He said she deserved to die. He said…" Donnie dropped his head into his hands. "Oh, what have I done?"

"You didn't do anything," she stammered. "It was me. I did this. I swear to Luther, I was just out in the pasture and I made this happen."

"You have no idea what you are talking about."

"I do." Summer hopped up and down, splashing in the gore as if it were rain puddles. "Luther was right. All you have to do is focus your energies and great things will happen."

"I killed my father." Donnie rocked back and forth, as if he'd gone simple. "I stabbed him in the throat with a pencil. That's what happened. He was right: I'm just like my mother."

"I will not attend your pity party." Summer waded into the blood and stepped around one side of the dead man, then the other. She made mental measurements. "If Luther did not want this to happen, then it would not have happened. This is but a single step in a very long journey for you and me."

"There is no journey." Donnie collapsed to his knees, sending a salvo of the old man into both their faces. "I'll spend the rest of my life in a jail."

"I won't let you go to prison."

"When the police hear what happened—"

Summer lowered herself to his level. She cupped his cheeks with both of her hands.

"They're not going to hear what happened."

Donnie stopped his simpering. His eyes quivered, but he kept her gaze.

"No one's going to hear a thing."

"Why do you say that?" he asked.

"Because no one's going to find his body."

Donnie sniffled. He looked her up and down.

"How so?"

"We're going to hide it."

"What do you know about hiding a body?"

Summer shook her head. "Me? I don't know the first thing about it." Behind her, Luther paced the floor. "No, I don't think I've got the wherewithal. But I know someone who does."

Summer...

"Hush, Luther. I got this."

Donnie cocked his head. "Who?"

"Somebody I can't wait to see how happy I am," she said. "Someone who needs to see I could make it on my own after all."

24

IT WAS AN OLD quarry, where they brought Barney. Years back, machines had been used to build highways from rocks they'd yanked from the ground. Since then, it'd filled up with water and local kids used it for a summer swimming hole.

Donnie didn't know much about it, except for what he'd been told, that it was a good sixty, seventy feet deep and the last ten or so was nothing but fine silt and muck. Anything dropped into the bottom of that quarry would never again see sunlight. Not in this lifetime, nor in the next.

"Where is he?" Donnie asked into the darkness. "Where is your friend?"

"He'll be here."

Summer offered him another cigarette. He'd never fancied himself a smoker, especially after his mother had taken ill. However, since loading Barney into the bed of the pickup truck, he'd killed nearly a half pack. They both stood in the gravel lot, precariously close to the tailgate, but neither of them reached to open it.

"What will become of me?" Donnie asked. "Where will I go?"

"You ain't going nowhere," said Summer. "Everything's going to be just fine. In fact, things will be better than they were before."

"I'm afraid that's impossible." Again, Donnie felt himself losing a battle to the coming wash of tears and sobs. He gripped his sides with both hands and grit his teeth. "There's no coming back from this."

Summer took a step from the side of the truck and mumbled something into the night.

"What did you say?"

Answered Summer, "I wasn't talking to you." She pointed to the horizon. "Someone approaches."

She spoke the truth. From a great distance, Donnie could make out headlights. At first, they floated like fireflies on a gentle wind, but they grew, grew into giant suns which the driver did not bother to extinguish, not even after he parked with the bumper inches from Donnie and Summer.

"I'm so nervous," she whispered. She blocked the light from the headlamps with her arm. "This could go so many different ways."

Donnie squinted into the light. "I thought you said you was friends with this fella."

"Best of friends," Summer said. "But we left things a little murky. I'm most curious to see how he's processed them."

The driver killed the engine, but left on the headlights. The car door opened. Summer grabbed Donnie's hand with both hers, then nearly snapped it off at the wrist. Out came one boot, then the whole of the man. Man? Older than a boy, certainly, although he stood nearly as short. His face was youthful, but not for much longer. He'd thickened at the jowls, most likely due to drink and plenty of worry. He dressed casual, but head-to-toe in black. He kept his hair high and greased thick with pomade. He wore sideburns thick as pork chops.

"Jack?" Summer called from Donnie's side. "Is that you?"

"You expecting somebody else?"

She dropped Donnie's hand and ran like a delirious child toward the newcomer. She threw herself into him, catching him off guard, then tumbling them both into the side of the car, like dice. She cackled like a sick hyena. She wailed like a tortured banshee.

"You've come back to me! You've returned!"

They rolled about the gravel for a bit until finally Jack tired of it. He sat up, dusted off his shirt, then accepted her hand when she offered to help him up. He looked her up and down.

"Look at you." He laughed. "These overalls are a bit outside your usual style, but whatever."

"I'm a whole different person now."

"I'll just bet you are." Jack stepped closer to Donnie. Even in the darkness, Donnie could feel he was being sized up. "Step into the moonlight, mister. Let me take a look at who Summer's shacking up with these days."

"Oh, no," said Donnie. "She and I…we aren't—"

"Of course not." Jack smiled. "All the same…"

"He's telling the truth, Jack." Summer leveled her tone. "This one and me, we're just friends."

Jack's eyebrow hitched higher. "What kind of angle are y'all working? Credit cards? Drugs?"

"I've been sober fifty-eight days," said Summer. "Actually, fifty-nine, since it's after midnight. I ain't taken nothing since that last night with you. I mean, they gave me plenty of stuff in the hospital, but I don't really count it, on account of I never asked for it. Okay, I mean I *asked* for it plenty of times, but it was already due to me, with me having withdrawals and all."

"How was it for you," asked Jack, "in the hospital?"

"It got pretty bad." She sounded sad, forlorn. "I died, you know. It's true, whether you want to believe me or not. And I really don't care if you think I'm lying. You can think whatever you want, but I really died and Luther was there and then I was awake. They said I'd been dead for four minutes. *Four minutes.* But ever since, I've learned to move things with my mind."

"Is that right?"

"It's easier than you think," she said. "I can show you how."

Jack said nothing in reply. Instead, he looked Donnie up and down. "And then you took up with this fella?"

"He's an administrator," she said. "He runs the sober camp."

"Sober camp?"

"Miracle Ranch." Donnie reached out his hand. Jack did not take it. "We get young women off drugs, among other things."

The smile stretched ever-wide across Jack's face. "Young women?"

"Typically in their later teenaged years," Donnie said. "Early twenties, maybe."

Donnie did not care for the sound coming from Jack's throat. At first, he thought the man choked on something, but reckoned later perhaps it was laughter.

"And for some reason," Jack said, "you folks at the sober camp need help disposing of a dead body?"

"It's a long story," Summer said. "But you're in luck, because it's a bit of a hike from here to the quarry, so we've plenty of time to fill you in."

Said Jack, "I can't wait.

☀ ☀ ☀

Donnie carried his father at the shoulders, while Jack took him by the feet. As they lugged the old man up the forest trail, Summer filled in her friend. She yapped away about the Principles. She told him all about Spirit Study. She gave him the skinny on each and every one of the girls at Miracle Ranch. Jack never said a word; he carried Barney in silence.

Donnie drifted in and out of the discussion, preferring instead to contemplate how damned was his soul. For even were he to skirt free from this mess...even should he manage to one day not look over his shoulder, he feared forever the last time he saw his mother would be the last time he saw her, as he was certain to burn in the fiery depths

of hell. He needed neither a guru nor a Good Book to tell him he'd
banished himself to an eternity of fire and brim—

"...and Donnie here has tons of ideas, don't you, Donnie?" Summer
had rattled on until she'd become Muzak, but Donnie snapped to at the
sound of his name.

"Beg pardon?"

"Tell him about the Miracle Dolls." She pointed to Jack. "Tell him
about the pastures of crops you want to harvest. Tell him about the
books and lecture tours and TV talk shows you want to host."

Donnie nearly dropped his daddy. "The... Uh, Summer...I don't
think—"

"But *tell* him. Tell him all the dreams you have for Miracle Ranch.
Tell him about the dolls."

"We stitch dolls at the Ranch. We sell them in town." Donnie
suddenly felt short of breath. "Or, at least we try to sell them in town. So
far...Summer, the dolls are the last thing on my mind at the moment. I
don't think you see the big picture here."

"No, hold on a moment." Jack stopped in his tracks. Donnie nearly
lost his balance, but kept upright. Jack dropped the dead man's feet to
the ground. He crossed his arms and refused to budge. "Don't you talk
to her like that. Summer's only trying to help."

"I apologize, Summer. I didn't mean to raise my voice." Donnie
waited for the smile to return to the girl's face. When next he spoke, it
was in a soft but tense tone. "I don't think you understand, Summer.
Without my father, there are no self-help books, because there is no
author. There's no message. Without Barney Malone, there's no Miracle
Ranch."

Summer stared into his eyes a bit longer than necessary. She
seemed to read something no one else could read. Then, as if someone
had whispered a revelation into her ear, she smiled sideways and
nodded her head.

"That sounds about right," she said to no one in particular. Then
she did a cartwheel. She laughed with such wicked glee that Donnie

thought more than once about joining his father down to the bottom of the quarry. When finished with her revelry, Summer rejoined the rest of them and crossed her arms. She spoke with authority, or her best incarnation of authority, and did so at volumes which varied more than the stars overhead.

"I think you are selling yourself short, Donnie Williams. I think you don't see the trees inside the forest. I think that, for a man as smart as you, you sure act awful dumb."

"I don't—"

"I know you don't, but I'm here to break it down for you." She stepped over Barney's dead body and grabbed Donnie by the cheeks. She wrapped both legs around his waist and touched her nose to his. "It's up to you to finish your father's work."

Donnie could not wrest loose from her. "I… It won't… There's no way I could—"

"There's no way you could do anything but," Summer told him. "You're the heir apparent. The same blood which coursed through him, courses now through you. I saw what you done with Marva down by the creek side. Even though you don't hear the words spoken by Luther, he still works through you. He uses you as an instrument. We can get a lot of things done, you and me."

Behind them, Jack scuffed his boots against a rock. He sparked alive another cigarette.

"All those things you want to do with Miracle Ranch," said Summer. "You can do them now. There's no one to tell you it can't be done, except the seeds of self-doubt you sow on your own."

"You don't get it," Donnie said. "I can't do it without him."

"Sure you can," Summer said. "Luther said he was done with Barney anyway."

"Luther? For Christ's sake, Summer—"

He'd have finished that thought, except for Jack had struck him with a mighty right hook. Donnie tumbled into a dead tree trunk which crumbled upon impact. He fell into the leaves and shielded his head with this hands, should any further blows come to follow.

"I told you to watch how you talk to her," Jack snarled. "Don't make me tell you again."

"Aw, Jackie…" Summer swished into the leaves after Donnie. "He don't mean anything by it. Donnie's real good to me. Besides, he just lost his daddy."

She helped Donnie to his feet and brushed off the leaves. Jack stepped over, but offered no hand. "I get a touch sensitive when it comes to her," he said. "She and I have been through a lot together."

"I understand," Donnie said, however far from the truth. "It's okay."

"That's so sweet, Jackie," said Summer. "I knew you loved me."

"Like nobody else in this world," Jack said. "Now let's get this old man up the hill so we can get out of here. I have a hard time with snakes and I'm starting to get nervous."

🌼 🌼 🌼

They reached the quarry after about an hour. Donnie and Jack set Barney's corpse onto a rock overlooking the waters. Below, the moon quivered upon the ripples, and the skyline silhouetted with towering pines and poplar. Around them, the night's cacophony protested the peaceful arrival of the morning sun, as if to say *let it arrive to violence.*

Careful not to turn his back to Jack Jordan, Donnie peeked over the rock. He closed his eyes and lost his every thought to sobs. Summer stepped behind him and ran her fingers through his hair.

"When bad things happen," said Summer, "you just have to block them out. Trust me. I do it all the time. It goes away quicker than you think."

"This will never go away," said Donnie.

"It's going to be just fine," she said. "I know what I'm doing. And we're not alone."

Donnie glanced over his shoulder at Jack, who checked his watch three times in less than a minute.

"That doesn't make me feel any better."

"Not him," whispered Summer. "We have someone much more powerful than Jack on our side."

Donnie felt a chill within him that could preserve a mammoth. He realized that previous to this moment, he'd only thought he understood fear.

"This quarry..." Donnie said. "It's a horrible place. We can't put him in there."

"They'll never find him," said Summer.

"It's not right. I have a better idea. We could—"

Donnie's thought was finished by a loud rustle as Jack sloughed the body of Barney Malone off the side of the rock. All that followed was a hollow splash that could have happened ten miles away, for all anyone knew. It's echo lasted centuries. Millennia.

"You son of a bitch!" Donnie howled. He scrambled to his feet and bum-rushed Jack to the ground. They grappled. "How dare you, you foul son of a bitch!"

Donnie was no match for Jack. While he outweighed him a good bit and had considerable longer reach, he hadn't the back-alley instincts or lack of God which Jack so readily employed as he brought up a knee to Donnie's groin, and a thumb to the socket of his right eye.

"You want extra holes in you?" Jack asked in a rumble. "I can rid you of all but one of your senses, and still sleep this night like a baby. You want that?"

Donnie agreed that he did not. He said so behind a creak in his throat. Jack loosed his hold on the boy's skull.

"Let's you and me stop settling things like this," Jack said. "It won't always end well."

After they'd resumed standing, Donnie asked, "Why did you do that? Why did you dump my father into the quarry?"

"It's what we came to do," said Jack. "Sounded to me like you were starting to waffle. I wasn't carrying that man back through those woods. He was going into that hole one way or another. All I did was speed things up."

"Isn't he the best?" asked Summer. "He looks out for me."

Donnie wished he could vomit. He longed to scream. He wanted to fall to his knees and punch the goddamned earth until his fists pulped to bloody stumps. Instead, he stood in the middle of the trail with his mouth open wide enough to catch one of the fruit bats flipping about over their heads.

Jack no longer considered him. Instead, he turned to Summer. He said, "Hey, girl...you know I've missed you."

"You probably haven't thought once about me this whole time."

"That's a bald-faced lie and you know it." From somewhere on the waters, called a loon. "All I did for the past couple months was check hospitals across East Texas. I listened to police scanners and searched hashtags and whatnot, all trying like mad to track you down."

Summer kicked rocks. "I wish that was true, Jackie. Really, I do."

"It is."

Summer had nothing to add.

"What I was thinking," Jack said, "is that right now, I'm in a transition period. Things got a little hairy with me and the connection down in Houston. It's not a good time for me to stick around Nacogdoches, so..." He let his words hang in the air like laundry. He waited for Summer to pick up the ball and run with it. When she didn't, he added, "I was thinking maybe I come hang with you folks a while. Lay low. You know, get my head together again."

"Jack..."

"I've always said if I could kick for a little bit, things would go back to normal." Jack wiped his nose with the back of his hand. "Maybe a sober camp is exactly what I need."

Summer parsed her words with caution. "I really don't think that's a good idea, Jack."

"Why not?"

"I'm happy now," she said. "For the first time in my whole, entire life, I'm happy. I don't want anything to change."

"You're in a cult," Jack said.

Summer turned her head so her ear touched her shoulder. "Does it matter if I'm in a cult," she asked, "so long as I'm happy?"

"It's not fair," he muttered.

"What's not?"

"You and me went through all that shit together, and you end up in a cult of young, broken girls with no cult leader, and all you want me for is to dispose of the body."

Summer squinted. She crinkled her nose. After a minute, she swept her pointer finger across the air in front of her as if to shush someone speaking. She gathered herself, best she could, but still could manage no words.

Said Donnie, "There's only girls allowed at the ranch. We couldn't possibly—"

"Just girls?" Jack shook his head. "Girls who ain't had the company of a man, except you and your dead daddy?"

"I haven't been in their company…I—"

"What you're telling me is you've got a cult full of girls, but no cult leader?"

"Stop saying that," snapped Donnie. "It's not a cult."

"Maybe it ain't now," said Jack, "but with a little elbow grease…" He dropped to his knees before Summer. He interlaced his fingers and brought them to his chin. "What if I promise to behave? What if I swear to give you anything you want?"

"Jack…" She bit her lip. "We can't—"

"It will be like the old days," said Jack. "Before Nacogdoches. Before New Orleans…"

"It would never work out," said Donnie. "After we announce to the girls that Barney is no longer with us, we'll have to contact their families and—"

"What if we didn't contact them?" Summer thought aloud. "What if we never told them Barney was gone?"

"Wha—?"

Jack shushed Donnie with a single finger. "Don't interrupt her when she's thinking. You'll miss all the good stuff."

"Maybe if we kept Jack around just a little longer..."

Donnie lowered his head to his hands. "Summer, no—"

Again, the little man dropped Donnie with a solid shot to the jaw. Donnie'd hardly time to register the blow before Jack was over him, this time offering to help him upright. Once composed, Jack slapped Donnie hard on the back.

He said, "Don't worry, Donnie my boy. I've done this before. I know how it works."

Rather than speak, Donnie reached into his pocket for the crumpled pack of cigarettes. He tugged a crooked one from the pack and lighted it. Jack pointed to it. "Let me borrow one of those."

"Borrow?" Donnie asked. "Like you're going to pay it back?"

Jack crinkled his nose like maybe he smelled something foul. "Maybe," he said. "We get to know each other well enough and I just might."

"Anybody ever say no to you?"

"Sure," Jack said. "But they're all assholes. You aren't an asshole, are you?"

Donnie handed him a cigarette.

"I didn't think so," said Jack. "Now let's get a move-on."

25

THEY THOUGHT IT BEST to keep Jack Jordan out of sight for the time being, but Summer had no doubt in her mind that would be easier said than done. They secreted him away to the Big House where he found himself most unimpressed with the amenities.

"Is there no electricity?" he asked.

"No," Donnie told him. "Barney didn't care for it. He said it diverted us further from our spiritual center to—"

"That's the first of many things I plan to change," said Jack. "I'm not living anywhere I can't get an internet connection."

"Life has actually been a lot better since leaving the grid," Summer said. "I'm not half as crazy as I used to be."

She must have gotten through to him, because he dropped it, then found something else to keep him preoccupied.

"First things last," he said, "we got to see about that bloodstain."

Donnie turned his back to it, as if he couldn't bear to look at it. "I…I can't…"

"You will," Jack said. "You do the crime, you've got to do the time. First thing you need to do is bring me one of those chickens out in the yard."

"Which one?" Summer asked. "I call the rooster Spatchy and the red one Kendall and I've named the big one—"

"Any one of them will do, I reckon."

Summer did as she was told, stepping into the early morning light to the chicken coop. Inside, the birds still roosted and it took no doing to cradle up the plump yellow one she'd named Luna. She whispered sweetly into the side of its head the entire way back to the Big House. Once indoors, she handed it to Jack.

"Jack, meet Luna. Luna…Jack."

Jack snapped the chicken's neck. It hung limp at its side. Summer screamed like the dickens.

"Jesus, Summer," Jack hissed. "Get a hold of yourself. It's only a chicken.

"She was more than a chicken!" Summer howled. "Why would you kill her?"

"We got to stick her and pour all her blood over this mess made by Donnie's daddy."

Asked Donnie, "Why on earth would you do that?"

"Everybody knows it takes blood to clean a bloodstain," Jack replied. "Plus, if the cops come sniffing around, the DNA will be contaminated with chicken blood. The evidence would be inadmissible."

Summer had to hand it to him: Jack was the smartest man on the whole planet. She'd forgotten how he could free them from nearly every fix, and cure their every ill. Now that she'd rid the poisons from her system, she could think more clearly. Now that she'd turned a new leaf, finally she could see the light.

"What will we tell the girls?" Donnie asked.

"We don't tell them anything." Jack stepped into the kitchen and rummaged a bit until he found a pail. He returned to the living room and dropped the chicken into it. His other hand carried a butcher knife.

Summer couldn't bear to watch. She shielded her hands over her eyes and turned her head to a corner.

"They'll want to know what happened to Barney," Donnie said. "They'll wonder where he's gone."

"Let me handle the girls," said Summer. She peeked from behind her fingers in time to see Jack cut the bird from stem to stern. Its insides splattered to the floor and spackled the walls. It kicked and bucked, much as it would if still alive.

Summer could handle no more of it. She covered both her ears with her hands and squeezed shut her eyes. She stomped her feet against the hardwood floor. She sang "Sugaree" at the top of her lungs, then decided it was time for a long, long walk.

She crossed the cornfields. She traversed the cotton. She wandered flat stretches of pasture. She walked and walked and walked some more, until finally she reached a bridge which stretched far above a skinny creek. She stood beneath a spreading pecan tree and gazed deep into the arroyo.

"Luther," she called into the still air. "How can I tell if I'm doing the right thing?"

At her feet, a bluebonnet sprouted from the dry, hard earth. Another followed beside it, and soon she found herself swimming in a sea of them. She spread both arms even from her waist and soared like a bird above them. She floated a good four inches from the ground. She flitted from flower to flower, much like a honeybee.

"Thank you," she called to the sky. To the ground below. To the horizon, so far, far away. "With all of my heart, I thank you!"

Until one by one, the flowers retreated to the earth from whence they'd come. The ground at her feet again dried to packed dirt and the grass took on a shade of pale. Overhead, storm clouds turned the sky to night.

At her back came the voice of Jack Jordan.

"I was worried about you," he said. "You took off without a word. It's been nearly two days."

Summer collapsed to sobs. "I'm so tired, Jack."

"I know."

"I don't want to think anymore. I'm no good at it."

"You don't have to." Jack took her into his arms. "I've got you."

"Do you?"

He nodded. "Don't I always?"

Summer held her head firm against his chest. She'd never heard his heartbeat so slow. Never heard his breathing so calm. Never felt his grip so steady.

"We have to use this cult to do good things, Jack. Do you understand me? If you're going to use it to do bad things, I won't stand for it."

"I want the same thing you do," he whispered to her ear. "Even if you don't yet know it's what you want."

She yanked herself from his grasp. She stood a good foot away from him and looked him dead in the eye.

"Jack, I'm serious. I'm a good person now. I do good things. I ain't going back."

"We'll both change, Summer." He didn't blink. "You'll see."

Summer stepped backward until she found the bridge. "If you've got designs otherwise, I'll jump off this bridge here and now."

The bridge had no railings. Little more than thick, splintered planks kept her from plunging twenty feet to the dry creek below. She stepped closer to the edge. The wind kissed her cheeks and tousled her hair. It tried to hoist her from beneath her shoulders.

"Summer," Jack said from the road, "step back."

She stayed put. She closed her eyes and turned up her face to better accept the warmth of the sun.

"Summer, step away from the edge. If you're not careful…"

If she put her mind to it, she could do anything. Hadn't she proven that many times before? If she wanted a sack of weed, one would magically appear. She willed Jack back into her life, just as she'd done Scovak or Jackson or any number of folks in her rearview. Should she wish for a million dollars, she damn well might get it, so she asked herself to no satisfaction why the hell couldn't she fly?

"Summer," Jack said in a low voice, "Luther is telling you to step away from the bridge."

The air left her lungs. The blood in her body stopped its circulation. "What...did...huh?"

"It's true. He's screaming at you. Right now. You really can't hear him?"

Summer cocked her head to one side, then the other. A steady wind clapped at her ears.

Said Jack, "He's saying, *Summer, it's not safe over there. You might fall.*"

Summer's feet turned to concrete. "He's not...he... You can't—"

"He's telling me you can't fly," Jack said. "No one can."

Summer focused her mind until it was a dark pin. She kept her eyes on it. She looked at nothing else, and thought of nothing else. She listened hard as she could, but still heard no sound. Nothing. Nothing at all. Not the birds overhead, nor the earthworms digging through the dirt. Not the earth and its rotation upon its axis and, most important, not the voice of Luther. He'd gone silent.

A single tear trickled down her cheek.

She stepped away from the edge of the bridge.

"What else is he saying?" she asked Jack.

"All kinds of things. Come over here so I can tell you."

She did so slowly.

"Why doesn't he tell me himself?" she asked.

"He says you don't hear him right anymore." When she'd gotten close enough, he put an arm around her and drew her closer. "He's saying you're out of gas. You need to let somebody else take the wheel a spell."

"And that somebody is supposed to be you?"

"That's what he says."

She laughed through her nose. "You're lying. He's never cared much for you."

"He sees what I can be. What *we* can be. You and me. We don't have to worry about missing the bus no more because this right here is the bus and—guess what?—we're driving it. That thing we've been looking for this whole time…it's right here. It was never the drugs, or the women, or the money. It's this. Saving people's lives. We can do it. We can be good at it. We can get so many people sober, so they don't end up like us. I've seen the happiness in your face and, if you can do it after all you've been through, then anybody can, Summer. It's up to us to show them how."

"Oh, Jackie…"

"I couldn't do this with anybody else, Summer."

She whispered in reply, "Me either."

Jack looked over his shoulder, toward the direction of the ranch.

"What should we do about him?" he asked.

"Donnie?" Fresh green leaves fluttered about her feet as if a Texas wind carried with it a broom. "He'll be fine. Don't worry about— wWhat does Luther think we should do?"

Jack cocked his head. He squinted both eyes, as if stuck on a puzzle.

He said, "Luther said to leave Donnie to me."

"Don't hurt him," she said. "Promise me."

"I wouldn't dream of it," Jack told her. "Besides, we need him."

Summer peered into his face as if to decipher what might or might not be a lie. She made neither heads nor tails of it. She banged her shoulder and hip against his as she passed him to take a seat at the trunk of the old pecan. Jack took his sweet time joining her. When he did, she leaned her head against his shoulder.

"I don't want to think no more about it," she sighed. "I don't want to think no more about anything."

"You don't have to," Jack whispered. "I'll do the thinking for both of us."

"Just tell me what to do and I'll do it." She thought she could fall asleep and stay there for twenty years. "Just say what you need done, and I'll see to getting it done."

She rested her eyes until her breathing fell into step with his.

※ ※ ※

The filling station off the interstate was the big prize and it didn't come easy. One hundred and some-odd cars rolled through every hour, and if ever there was a spot for Miracle Dolls to boon, it was that truck stop. Summer visited them about three in the afternoon, when business was sure to slack.

With her, she brought Rylah, Marva, and Cassie. Inside, they found a woman behind the counter who kept her lips pursed and her eyes narrowed. She didn't like the looks of them as they entered, nor did she care much for their smell.

"Y'all best not be smoking marijuana cigarettes out behind my place," she barked at them. "I'll have the law up on you so fast, you'll spin like a ten-penny nail."

"We ain't smoking weed," Summer said. "We're sober. We come from Miracle Ranch, out in Rankin. We're here to pitch you on these here Miracle Dolls to sell in your store."

Rylah tugged a rag doll from a burlap sack and set it on the counter between them. The woman looked at it like it might give her rickets. She turned up her nose at it.

"This is hardly an appropriate location for that kind of mess," she said.

Summer looked over her shoulder at a Plexiglass display case stuffed with knickknacks, shot glasses, souvenirs…a replica samurai sword with a mint green scabbard. A desert landscape molded from plastic made in China. She clicked her tongue against the back of her teeth.

"I bet if you took all that junk out of yonder case and replaced it with our Miracle Dolls, they'd sell pretty darn well."

The lady shook her head. "We're not clearing out that—"

"Furthermore," Summer said, "if you trained all your employees to point them out every time they rang a purchase, I bet they'd fare even better."

The lady chortled through her nose.

"Perhaps if they relayed the story to their every charge. Tell them about how these dolls are hand-stitched from local youth who work hard to rid themselves of drugs. That their purchase goes toward helping sustain folks serving the will of Luth—um, I mean...*God*... then I bet these things sell like hot cakes in no time. I'm told they'd make a *perfect* collector's item."

The lady licked the tips of her fingers and traced the perimeter of her mouth.

"We're not selling toys made by some hippie cult," she said. "Now, if you don't mind, I've a—"

Summer's face darkened. Behind her, Rylah, Marva, and Cassie took their positions. All four of them faced the counter with their heads lowered. They said in a low, monotone chant:

"We are perfect."

"We are loved."

"We are Miracles."

They did so a handful of times until the woman genuinely felt a bit touched. She used trembling hands to balance herself against the counter.

"Now, y'all stop that," she said to the girls. "We won't have that kind of talk here in the Grab and Go."

But the girls did not listen. Slowly, they raised their heads, in turn, raising the frequency. The pitch.

"I'm going to call the sheriff..."

Summer stopped, her head fully upright and facing the woman. She shook her head slowly from side to side.

"I wouldn't do that if I were you."

Behind her, Luther knocked items from the candy shelves. He tossed asunder chocolate bars, breath mints, gummi things. He rampaged through t-shirts, kicking over the displays. He ripped newspapers in two, then threw them to the ground.

That's not me, Summer...

The blood ran out of the woman's face. She aged thirty years in a matter of thirty seconds. She lowered herself slowly to the floor.

"We're coming back in a week," Summer said. "When we do, I expect these dolls to be sold. Do you hear me?"

The woman weakly nodded.

"I want to hear you say it," said Summer.

"We'll sell through all your dolls," she said.

"And I don't care how much you charge, but I'll fetch ten apiece for them. You hear?"

The woman nodded quickly.

Summer smiled. "Pleasure doing business with you."

With that, the girls quit the store. On their way across the lot toward their truck, they passed a young boy. Maybe sixteen, seventeen years old, but Summer could tell he'd been around the block. The insides of his arms betrayed him as a user, though still far from becoming a junkie. Summer thought him to have only recently graduated from pills to the hard stuff.

"Can I ask you something?" she called to the boy. When he looked up, but didn't answer, she said, "Are you happy?"

The boy looked from Summer to Rylah, then to Marva. Marva smiled, like a good girl, and Rylah smiled like one who'd gone bad. The boy didn't stand a chance.

"Why don't you climb into the truck with us?" Summer called to him. "You're a Miracle and you belong with other Miracles."

It didn't take much doing. The boy rose to rickety knees and hopped into the bed of the pickup truck.

"Do you know where there's a library around these parts?" Summer asked him. "We need to get an internet connection so we can get the word out."

26

IT STARTED AS A trickle, but soon they arrived in droves. First, it was a runaway someone knew molested by his foster father. Then the girls came back from town with a football player hiding a sensitive side. Hitch-hikers off the highway. Kids bored with the status quo. Summer devised a social media campaign and, after a couple swings, hit a home run. Well-meaning moms and dads turned up at all hours to the door of the Big House thanks to #SaveMyChildFromDrugs.

Soon, nearly fifty Miracles worked the fields or painted the barns or mended the fences across the ranch. The Spirit Studies in the pasture swelled with them, and the night filled with their songs. The Miracle Dolls witnessed a sudden spike in sales, as did internet copies of a pamphlet they published titled *The Miracle of You*. Donnie Williams reckoned they could finally ride Miracle Ranch to prosperity, should they continue along their current path.

Jack Jordan, on the other hand, had other plans.

"The next phase of Miracle Ranch," he told them, "lies within the pages of this book right here."

They stood with Summer in the cramped kitchen of the Big House.

He held before him a ratty, leather-bound copy of the King James Bible. Donnie blinked at it more than once, then scratched his head.

"You want to turn this into a Christian retreat?"

Jack chortled through his nose. "Yeah, right." He opened the cover of the book with his thumb and forefinger, then riffled the pages until he reached the center. Inside, the Bible had been hollowed out to conceal large baggies of pills and powders.

"Is that…" Donnie rubbed his eyes. "That's not…"

"This is our future," said Jack. He slapped shut the book and set it on the counter. He hopped himself onto it, so that his short legs dangled a few feet above the linoleum.

"But we're sober now, Jack," Summer whined. "Remember? We said we weren't going to let the same stuff happen again. You said it wasn't going to be like South Carolina or New Orleans or Lufkin or—"

"And I meant it," said Jack. "These drugs are not for us."

"But I thought…I thought…"

"You said you didn't want to think," said Jack. "So don't."

Summer opened her mouth to speak, but must have thought better of it. She nodded her head, slumped her shoulders, then set about making the three of them a pot of tea.

"If not for us," Donnie asked, "then who?"

Jack watched Summer fiddle with the tea kettle, then allowed a smile to creep the length of his face.

"First," he said, "we wait for the next newcomer to arrive. Next kid trucks through here, we'll dose them on the sly with enough MDMA to make a horse like house music."

"Dose an unsuspecting newcomer?" Donnie couldn't believe his ears. "No. There's a line, and I'm afraid that's crossing it."

"It's part of my master plan."

"I won't be party to it," Donnie insisted.

Jack arched an eyebrow.

"I won't." Donnie crossed his arms. "Nothing you possibly could say will—"

"What do you suppose your daddy would do in this very situation?" asked Summer from behind him. "Oh, wait…he wouldn't have nothing to say because he's dead and you killed him."

Donnie spun to face her. He opened his mouth to let fly a fury, but upon the sight of her, could manage no words.

Said Summer, "If there's one thing I learned, it's that you can't do a darn bit of good in this world without doing a little of the bad. Jackie helps me a lot with the hard part. What do you say you and me do a little good?"

She took hold of his hand.

"Who among us can stand to be alone right now?" she asked him.

Neither Summer nor Jack needed to say another word on the matter, although they did. They plotted and planned and schemed throughout the night, and should Donnie show signs of wear by nodding off to sleep, they would rouse him awake and repeat to him the entire ordeal.

By the next morning, Donnie found himself in quite the state. He had very little fight left in him and could hardly stand on his own two feet. Jack handed him a pair of pills from his sweaty palm and urged him to swallow them.

"What are they?"

"A little pick-me-up," said Jack. "Just to get you through the client pick-me-up."

"We don't do drugs here," Donnie said. "It's a sober camp."

"These aren't drugs," he replied. "You buy them over the counter at a gas station. Truckers use them to stay awake. They don't count because they're not illegal."

Donnie chased them both down his gullet with a glass of warm tap water, then settled in to greet the newcomer family: the Swansons. A nice suburban couple who bustled to and fro with great urgency, fussing over their poor, wretched daughter Lindsay.

Lindsay was a slight girl, given to pitch black circles rounding the hollows of her eyes. She readily licked her lips, as if slavering for the whole of civilization to be brought to her upon a plate. She eyed the slightest movements as would a cat, forever prepared for play or prey.

"They found her wandering the woods alongside the Angelina River," moaned her mother. "They found her in blood and speaking a foreign tongue."

"We've done everything we can," Mr. Swanson insisted. "We've taken her to therapists, we've run tests…"

"We've taken her to a priest…"

Donnie nodded his head. So rarely did the script change anymore. Child after child, parent after parent. *We've done all we could. None of this is our fault. What could we have done? If only…if only…blah, blah, blah.*

"She was always such a good girl," Mrs. Swanson said. "Straight As every year. Student council, National Honors—"

"I blame that school," said the father. "The whole of East Texas is but a black mark on this great state. I wish it would cede to Louisiana. Nothing good ever happens there. I've visited and all I found is darkness. I should never have subjected our little girl—"

Mrs. Swanson placed her hand upon her husband's wrist. He lowered his head and wept heavy sobs which fell onto his necktie. Donnie wiped sweat that sheened his brow and wondered when it got so hot in the room.

All the while, Lindsay said not a word. Her eyes tracked up and down the walls, then back and forth across the hardwood floor. She studied the rugs, the bookshelves. The candleholders and the fireplace.

"We read the pamphlet online," Mrs. Swanson said. "*The Miracle of You.* It's everywhere on social media right now. We believe if anyone could help our daughter…well, it would be Miracle Ranch."

"Who is in charge of things here?" asked the father. "Would that be you?"

Donnie nodded his head, then shook it. Soon, he found himself shrugging, with his neck rolling in circular motions so tight, they could be seen as tics. Spasms. Inner convulsions which might shake him straight to the fetal position were he not solely focused on the task which lay before him.

He said, "Would you mind if I spoke alone a moment with Lindsay?"

Donnie waited to be sure they were gone before smiled softly at Lindsay and spoke to her for the first time.

"Sweetheart," he said to her from a shaky throat, "how would you feel about a cup of tea?"

Herself on the verge, Lindsay slowly nodded her head.

Donnie excused himself to the kitchen. There, he found the cup of tainted tea waiting for him, just as planned. With trembling hands, he carried it to the living room where he set it on the table between him and the girl.

"Drink this and tell me what happened."

She looked into the cup for a long, long time before asking, "What do you mean?"

"In Lufkin," Donnie said. "You can tell me."

She shrugged. She came no closer to picking up the cup than before.

Donnie cleared his throat. Behind her was the spot where he had watched his father bleed out. Across these walls had once been pints of blood caked so thick, they had to be chiseled off with a putty knife. The very room in which they sat had once looked like a Manson family crime scene, and Donnie did what he could to try to force the images from his mind.

"You know," he said, "there's literally nothing you can tell me that I would find too horrible for salvation."

Lindsay was tentative. "Who do you think you are?"

"Just someone who wants to help. Seriously, you can tell me anything, so long as it's honest."

Lindsay breathed in. She breathed out.

"Can I ask you a question?" Donnie said. When Lindsay nodded, he asked, "Are you happy?"

Of course Lindsay wasn't happy, and she demonstrated as such by lowering her head to the table and covering it with her arms, then letting fly a horrible howl which lasted nearly ten minutes. When finished, Donnie handed her a tissue, then pushed the cup closer to her.

"Tell me what you remember."

"I still don't know what happened in Lufkin." She spoke in hushed tones. "I remember some things, but not others. I remember sitting with my boyfriend, then eating with my boyfriend. Not really *eating,* but as close to eating as I allowed myself on a weeknight. Know what I mean? He'd cooked chicken and been oh, so proud of it. So I smiled and stabbed the fork into my mouth—little bites—then surreptitiously spat those morsels into my napkin. I moved the macaroni around my plate until it looked half eaten. I'd gone to great measures to preserve his joy, but why did I have to continue this charade? Why did I have to hide? Why, oh why, should I be the one to cower in the shadows, to secret myself to the bathroom to purge? Why is that men allow their vices and idiosyncrasies to parade the dirty streets of East Texas, but I must seek cover?"

She'd grown rather loud, but didn't realize it until the end. She quantified her surroundings, then took a minute or so to compose herself. She straightened the hem of her skirt across her pretty knees, took a deep breath, then continued.

"I remember all of that—and more—running through my head, then next I remember waking up in the woods, dripping with blood. Some of it was mine, sure; it looked like I'd gone at myself with a shard of broken glass sometime in the night. However, a good bit of the blood could not be accounted for…"

In a quiet, broken whisper, she added, "I think I killed him…"

Donnie realized for the first time he'd forgotten to breathe.

"K-k-killed who?"

"It's *whom,* actually," Lindsay said. "My boyfriend, is who. *Fiancé,* really. We were going to be married. Maybe we already were married. How am I supposed to know anymore? For all I know, he's not even real because they never found a body. They never found anyone with his name…" She turned her head to the ceiling, but closed her eyes. "It's like I made the whole thing up in my head. One minute, I'm having the best night of my entire life and the next…well, the next it's like a nightmare wrapped in a horror show, then dropped into hell. I still don't know what's real. I still don't know what's not. For all I know, you're a figment of my imagination. I could be talking to myself on some farm in the middle of nowhere, or a room at Rusk State Hospital. That's how bad it is right now."

She could no longer stem the tide. She let the tears overtake her.

"You have no idea how the mind slips…"

Donnie let her get it out of his system. When finally she settled, he took both her hands into his and waited for her to again make eye contact.

"I need you to do something for me," he said.

She wiped her nose with her hand. "I'll do anything, just make it stop."

"I'm serious," he said. "I need you to do something and I need you to do it now."

"What?"

"Run."

Lindsay blinked once. She blinked again.

"What did you say?"

Donnie spoke in a firmer voice. "You need to run," he said. "Run as far as you can from this place."

"But…but…" Lindsay broke eye contact. Her sight settled upon the cup of hot tea and she reached for it. Donnie quickly swatted it from her hands. It fell to the floor in a puddle and a billion pieces.

"Hey…!"

He rose from the table. He slapped it with his palms. "You must listen to me. It's not safe for you here. There are agents who conspire to—"

His words were lost to a hustle and a bustle from the kitchen behind him, and with great fanfare, Summer Halifax emerged through the swinging door, carrying a fresh cup of tea upon a saucer.

"How clumsy are you today, Donnie?" she asked the room. "Not to worry, child. I brought you a fresh cup. Why, not too long ago I found myself in that very chair and I had the fidgets something awful. What I would have given for a piping hot cup of—"

Lindsay opened her mouth wide with terror. Her eyes even wider. She pointed to Summer, could make nothing close to words.

"Drink up, girl," said Summer with a wink. "Everything you need to get better is right there in that cup."

"Summer…" Tears stung at Donnie's eyes. "I don't think—"

"Now, now." Summer put the cup in Lindsay's hands. "No need to get so excited."

Lindsay wouldn't settle.

"It's…it's *you*…" she said.

Summer put a hand to her own chest. "Me? No, child. I am merely an instrument. I follow the will of another."

Lindsay rubbed both her eyes with fists. She yanked the ribbon from her pretty blonde hair and wrapped her pointer finger with it so tight, the tip turned purple.

"I think it's happening again…"

Said Summer to her ear, "You are perfect. You are loved. *You are a Miracle.*"

With that, she quit the room with as much cacophony as she had entered. A vacuum of silence settled between Donnie and the new girl until finally Lindsay took the cup with both hands and emptied it down her throat.

Once drained, she wiped her chin and stared in the direction in which Summer had disappeared.

"That girl…" she said. "She means us all harm."

Said Donnie, "You have no idea."

Lindsay no longer seemed to find reason to it. She rose wearily from her chair, then sloughed her way to the couch along the far wall.

She fell upon it and laid her arm across her eyes.

"What happened just then?" Donnie asked her. "Describe it to me."

"What's the point?" she asked with a heavy sigh. "Everywhere I go, I see…"

"See what?"

Lindsay tucked herself into as small a ball as possible, then turned to face the wall.

"Would you mind too horribly if I lie down for a moment?" she asked. "I'm afraid I feel one of my turns coming on."

27

AND ON THE BIG day, Summer searched Miracle Ranch high and low before finally she found Jack standing alone at the edge of darkness, where the furthest sliver of light stopped at the black shadow of the barn. He faced yonder, into the night. He spoke to someone who was not there.

"Jack," she called to him. "Jack, it's time."

He twitched his head, as if snatching himself from deep thought. "You ought not to sneak up on someone."

"I think I made plenty bustle tromping through that tall grass just now. You could hardly call it sneaking up."

"All the same."

She cocked her head to the side. "Were you talking to someone just now?"

Jack said nothing.

"Part of me expected to find you here with one of those Miracle girls working on your privates with her little mouth."

Still, Jack kept quiet.

"I know a guy like you has needs," Summer said, clearing her throat.

"You can't be expected to go too long without some kind of release. All I'm saying is maybe you'd better find it in town, instead of with these here girls. They ain't ready for that. Beth Ann's got big-time sex issues and she's about ready to pop. Brenna…well, Brenna's got a lot to learn about herself and I aim to help her get life figured. All in due time. For now, I reckon, Jack, it's best if you don't fiddle with those girls."

Finally, he turned to face her. He stepped closer into the light, giving her a good look. He'd quit all product from his hair, preferring to wear it long and parted down the middle. He'd ceased to shave, and grew a shaggy beard. Gone were the garish colors of his wardrobe, as he opted instead for white worn head to toe. Where once he might shiver and shake, instead he kept steady at the hand, and calm at the stomach.

"I would not spoil my seed on lesser light," he said. "If I so desire, I could repopulate the human race from right here on this very land."

He stepped closer still.

"If that is the destiny which lies before me," he said in a low voice. "If that is the role chosen for me by a power greater than us both, would you suggest I deny it?"

Summer tried two or three times to wrestle out the words. All she managed was, "No, Jack."

Again, he turned his back to her.

"Another thing," he said, "I've told you once, I've told you twice. Don't make me tell you again: my name is no longer Jack Jordan. Jack Jordan is dead. My name is Hux Pariah, and I am the new leader of Miracle Ranch."

When Jack first told Summer of the name he had chosen for himself, she had crinkled her nose and shrugged her shoulders.

"I like the sound of the two words," Jack had told her. "Huckster and Pariah."

"I don't think those words mean what you think they do," she had replied.

All the same, he wished thenceforth to be known as Hux Pariah, and so it became thus.

Summer waited until their breathing shared a rhythm. She counted the galaxies overhead. She gave Hux all the time in the world to stare into the darkness.

"Remember your promise," she whispered. "We're going to use this Ranch for good."

Jack looked elsewhere a moment, as if listening to someone. He nodded to a question no one asked, then said, "I am only an instrument, Summer. I am only a vessel."

"Knock it off," she hissed. "You hear me? I won't have nothing bad done to these kids."

Again, Jack fell silent. He stayed as such a good while before drawing a heavy sigh.

"They're out there," he said.

"Who?" When he didn't answer, she put a hand to his shoulder. "Who, Jack...I mean, *Hux*?"

He nibbled absently at the flesh in the meat of his fist.

"Things got pretty bad in Houston," he said.

"What happened?"

Instead of answering, Jack turned and headed for the barn. He brushed his shoulder against hers as they passed, saying only the words, "They are out there."

☀ ☀ ☀

Summer stood before the fifty or so Miracles gathered beneath the torchlight at the front of the barn. She waited to introduce Hux Pariah until they had fallen to their lowest depths. Only moments earlier, Summer announced that Barney Malone had finally left them to walk with Luther.

"Be not sad for Barney," she told them from beneath the open doors of the barn. "Rather, be happy. For no longer is he burdened with mortal constructs, nor is he bound by earthly desires."

The fact that only a handful of Miracles had actually known
Barney did not keep them from falling to their knees and pounding
fists against the earth with great consternation. For the better part
of the last month, Barney's stock had certainly risen, as stories and
legends reached a fever pitch—

"When Barney returns, we'll feast for days."

"I heard Barney is in Hollywood, helping actors and actresses kick
drugs."

"I heard he got a death metal band sober."

"I heard he could ripen a tomato upon command."

—and the Miracles could little help but despair at the news of
his passing. Summer thought it best for them to wallow a moment in
misery before sharing with them "the good news."

"While no human on earth could ever replace Barney Malone in
our hearts," she said to them all, "we are not truly left without rudder.
Luther would never allow his message to pass on with any single
mortal individual, choosing instead another vessel by which to receive
his ministry."

"Who is the vessel?" called one of the Miracles.

"When can we meet them?" cried another.

When Hux Pariah emerged from the shadows of the barn, he
raised high his hands and turned his face to the heavens.

"My fellow Miracles," he called aloud, "my name is Hux Pariah and
I shall now lead you on your journey with the Principles."

Summer stifled a laugh. She covered her mouth with her hand
and watched with detached bemusement as the Miracles seemed not
to know what to make of Hux Pariah. They scratched their heads and
exchanged whispers. Some shook their heads, as if shooing a fly. Others
stomped their feet and chortled through their noses.

"I told them this would be a hard gamble," Summer said to the air
around her. "What do you bet these Miracles will take one look at his
silly getup and tell him where to stick it?"

When no answer came, she took a look to her left, then one to her right, before finally turning again to face the spectacle before her.

Not all of the Miracles took the news with a degree of serenity. Lindsay Swanson, the new girl, screamed at such a pitch, she frightened a hoot owl from the branches of the crooked willow. She hobbled away from the throng on a pair of crutches, dragging alongside her a leg which she kept in a plaster cast.

"What troubles you, child?" Hux called after her.

"It's him!" Lindsay could not be consoled. "I can't believe it. It's him!"

The other Miracles took her into their arms. They stroked her hair. They whispered platitudes into her ear, but she would have none of it. She kicked her gimpy leg this way and that until finally unhanded, then did her level best to scoot free of them. However, her injury allowed her only so far, and she crumpled next to a rusty plow.

Hux held up his hands to silence the other Miracles. This had little effect, so he shouldered through the crowd of them until he arrived at the feet of the cowering girl. He reached a hand to her, from which she flinched, and said to her in a calm voice, "Lindsay, be not afraid."

Her lower lip quivered, but she made no sound.

"I wish you no harm."

She violently choked out the words, "It's you. I thought you were dead. All this time, I thought I'd killed you."

"Your entire life, I have been by your side," Hux said. "Forever shall I remain there."

Lindsay wept. Hux pulled her into him.

"Tell me what happened to your leg," he said. "How did you find yourself injured?"

"I don't know," she said. "The night I arrived…I've no recollection what horrible thing has happened to me, nor what horrible thing I may have done."

Again, Summer suppressed the urge to laugh. While she would never admit it, Summer was one of three people on the planet who knew what happened to Lindsay's leg. That night, after she'd slipped her enough MDMA to knock her silly, the girl acted a fool in front of each and every Miracle on the property. She'd danced and swayed. She'd sung and shouted. Lindsay Swanson had run from one edge of the property clear to the other, all the while professing love for the moon, the stars, the singing bullfrogs along the banks of Chambers Creek...all of it. She'd gone to such great lengths to rejoin the cosmos and the universe and the collective conscience, that when finally she slipped to slumber, she did so at a level which could not be disturbed.

While she slept, Summer and Hux went fast to work, fitting her leg for a plaster cast, while Donnie leaned against yonder wall with his head in his hands.

"What we are doing is immoral," he blubbered. "We should all hang our heads in shame."

"Quit your ballyhoo and help get this plaster set," Hux had grumbled. "When she wakes, you both will tell stories about how she'd carried on like a heathen, then broke her leg sometime in the night. Later, I'll lay hands on her and order her healed. At that point, we'll have everyone's full attention."

That night, Summer had watched as Hux lowered his hand to Lindsay's face. He stroked soft swaths against her cheek with his fingertips. He brushed askew a lock of hair behind her ear.

"This is truly fate," Hux whispered. "Who among us can doubt the fortune which has befallen me by seeing her returned?"

Much as he handled her in the moment, in the shadow of that rusty plow, where Hux held her close and murmured into her ear that it did not matter how she'd come to find her leg in that cast, nor did it matter what she'd done the year previous in the Light House trailer. In fact, nothing in the whole of her life mattered half a whip, because all that mattered was the here and now, and what she planned to do with it.

"By the power and love of Luther," said Hux, with both hands upon her crippled knee, "I command you healed."

The only sound in all the land was the collective gasp of the Miracles.

"Hereby, you shall no longer carry fear in your heart, nor tote it upon janky leg." Hux motioned to Summer and Donnie, standing ready with pump pliers, a steak knife, and a pair of scissors. They went to work removing the cast from Lindsay's leg. It took nearly a half hour, but when finally they freed her from it, Hux stretched out his hand. "Please, walk with me, child."

"But, I can't…"

"Oh, but you can." He smiled and turned his head to one side, as if listening to a whispered secret. "Luther just told me you could do it."

And, just as he'd promised, Lindsay rose to wobbling feet. She teetered to the left and swayed mighty to the right, but eventually found her footing.

"Now," said Hux, "you walk."

Not a single person doubted she could walk. Not the Miracles who watched with open mouths, and not Summer and Donnie, who were in on it. Certainly not Lindsay, who, at this point, would believe anything told to her, so long as it came from the lips of Hux Pariah. Summer clapped her hands hard against each other—first once, then twice—until the other Miracles joined her with a steady cadence of applause.

Lindsay felt the love. She put one shaky foot in front of the other. She hobbled from one side of the congregation to the other. Slowly at first, then gaining confidence, then soon maneuvering with nary a hint of a limp. All the while, the Miracles chanted.

"You are perfect."

"You are loved."

"You are a Miracle."

Hux rose both his arms in jubilee. He cried thanks to the skies above.

However, his work that night was far from finished.

Once he had recaptured their attention, Hux gathered the Miracles around him in a circle before the open doors of the great barn. Above them, the stars twinkled bright and cast a deathly pallor upon the proceedings.

"I want you all to close your eyes and think about your fathers. Some of you love him dearly and, still others of you may hate him. Over time, in Spirit Studies and one-on-one sessions with Donnie or Summer, many of you Miracles have confessed you've never known your fathers. You say instead of a daddy, all you've known was a giant daddy-sized hole in your life. Whether it's a hole or a real person, each and every one of you have a daddy and I want you to think of him right now. Go on, close your eyes."

Even Summer, sitting closest to him on the grass, did as she was told.

"You all see your daddy standing there in front of you?"

Most murmured assent.

"Marva, I know your daddy was a truck driver."

Marva nodded, her eyes still closed tight.

"That man raised his family in a pair of blue jeans, didn't he?"

Marva smiled, but did not open her eyes.

"You see that man standing before you in blue jeans? Were they faded, or maybe a little too tight in the thigh? How about you, Cassandra? What do you see? I don't want you to look at the grave he left behind, I want you to look at his face. What color were his eyes? How did he smile at you when you obeyed him, and how did he frown when you didn't? What color was his hair? Was it curly, was it short? Did he have a stubble when he kissed you good night? And you, Peter? You never knew your father but you've seen photographs. What does he look like in your head? Can you throw his phantom arms around you, and how does his breath smell when he whispers he loves you in his ear?"

Some of the Miracles wept. All among them smiled in rapture.

"There is something you want to tell that man. Something you've always wanted to say to him but, for one reason or another, you haven't.

Maybe you never thought much about it, but you're thinking about it now. You're thinking, man, Hux, what I wouldn't give to stand before that man once in my life and tell him about this thing I have kept locked in my heart in my stomach in my soul *in my very being*, but I never told him, and now what can I do with all of this? Luther has told us if we keep all this inside us, it will burn angry like a conflagration or rot like a cancer. I don't want to be sick, and neither do you. You want to be well. You want us all to be well. But it never will be, so long as you've got all that trapped inside of you.

"I want you to do something for me. You picture your daddy standing in front of you? You see him? Now, imagine your daddy's face has disappeared. There's nothing there. There ain't no eyes, no nose. No warm smile, nor frown from frustration. All of it has gone. Nothing remains but a blank slate.

"Now I want you to put my face there."

Hux stood before Tanya. He placed both hands on her shoulders.

"Tanya, what do you have to tell me?"

The young girl bit her lower lip until it nearly burst.

"I…uh, I—"

"Picture my face on your daddy. It is me standing there. You have something to tell me. You've held on to it for years. What is it?"

Tanya, bless her heart, could not keep it together. Her knees gave out. She crumpled to the dirt in a sea of sobs and both Marva and Jenny reached to help her.

"Don't touch her," ordered Hux. "She's a strong woman. She can handle this on her own." He genuflected to Tanya's ear. "Tell me what you need to tell me."

Tanya choked it out. "Why didn't you ever notice me?"

"That's my girl."

She was far from finished. "Why did you stay late at work every night and never duck your head into my bedroom to kiss me good night?"

"Yes. Yes."

"Maybe you think I'd never notice, but I did. I stayed up every night until I heard you come home because I thought maybe tonight was the night you'd come in."

"Of course you did."

"When I turned sixteen, you came home at ten minutes to midnight and I said it was because you promised you weren't going to miss my birthday. You weren't there when I woke up and you weren't there to take me to dinner, and you weren't there when I went to bed, but none of that mattered because, with ten minutes to go, you were going to come into my room and kiss me on the head or the nose or...but you didn't come in. Even though that would have made up for everything, with ten minutes to go on my sixteenth birthday. But you didn't, and I swear to Luther, the next day I quit staying up for you."

No one on the grassy lot dared so much as breathe. Most had opened their eyes to fix them upon Hux and Tanya at the front of the congregation. Some kept them closed, but from all of them streamed rivers of tears.

Hux took both hands and cupped her cheeks. He held her face an inch from his.

"Tanya..." She opened her eyes. "Tanya..."

"Yes?"

"I see you."

She could hardly catch her breath.

"I notice you, sweetheart."

Her lip trembled, like the death throes.

"I was a fool." Hux stroked her cheeks with his thumbs in wide swaths. "I was an idiot not to spend more time with you because you are perfect. You are beautiful. And you are a Miracle."

To seal the deal, he kissed her long and hard upon her forehead, which sent her to his arms where she could have stayed, she could have lived, and she could have died.

Behind them, every Miracle stood and exploded into applause. Their first instincts were to pile atop Tanya and whisper forevers into her ear. To take every drop of love and happiness from their bodies and souls and stick them right back into her every hole, but each and every one of them stood at bay, should Hux tell them not to move.

"Y'all come show sister Tanya some love."

And they did.

"All of you are *perfect*," Hux shouted into the throng. "All of you are *loved. All of you are miracles.*"

Never before had Summer seen such a spectacle of jubilation. Never in all of Luther's creations had love been stronger. Marva held tight to Cassie and, for the first time, noticed Rhiannons's cheek touching hers. The warmth between them kickstarted a chain reaction and Rylah turned to them both and whispered truths. Jesse's hand was held tight by Jason's, who in turn stroked fingers through Darla's hair. They spoke in murmurs, and they spoke in shouts.

"This week, I expect to see each and every one of you at the Big House." Hux retook his spot at the front of the congregation. "You are each going to tell me the thing you forever wish you'd told me. You will have my undivided attention. There will be no distractions between you and I." He put his hand on Tanya's head and tousled her hair. "You and I have a lot of catching up to do."

One by one, each Miracle nodded their teary heads. They raised their arms to the heavens. They breathed as one.

"In the meantime, why don't you come show Hux how much you love him?"

He raised high his hands to the night to better receive the lot of them.

Once finished, Summer escorted Hux to the Big House, much like a bodyguard delivering a dignitary. He'd grown weary after his proselytizing, and insisted he'd need a moment's rest. Summer kept pace with him from the distance of his heels. She had over a dozen things on her mind, but had yet to put words to them. She focused hard on her Principles and tried her damnedest to focus on the positive parts of Hux—

Like how he could march with his head high and chest puffed, no matter what levels of treason he'd committed.

Or how taut was his jawline.

Or how he operated with a deliberate focus.

—rather than succumb to her natural inclination, which was to reckon him a scoundrel. She closed tight her eyes and blocked away the bad stuff, much as she'd been taught. She let one fanciful thought multiply with another, then yet another, until finally she threw both arms around Hux's waist and held him dear.

Never one for sentiment, Hux did not allow the moment to fester. He unwrapped himself from her grasp.

"I plan to implement a few changes around here," he said.

"Just tell me what you want me to do," said Summer.

"From this point forward, let's reassign duties around here. I find it unwise that men and women share the same chores."

"But *Equality* is one of the Twelve Principles. It's important to—"

"What we have are a group of lovely young women digging gardens from their own feces," said Hux. "We shouldn't allow that."

Summer sucked on her lower lip.

"And I'm calling an end to all the feminism chatter." Hux looked at a distant point in the night sky. "All this empowerment only serves to fatten the girls."

"Jack…"

"Tell me you haven't noticed Rylah's put on a little weight. For the moment, it's in all the right places, but I've seen how quick that can get out of hand. It would be a crime to ruin a canvas such as that."

Summer's hands balled to fists. She shoved them into the pockets of her overalls.

"And those are the next to go." He pointed at her britches. "Those outfits are hideous. They're fine for the men, but the girls need to wear something a bit more free. It's nearly June and they'll require a bit more sun."

"You promised we'd use the ranch for good."

Hux nodded, his attention elsewhere. "And we will, Summer. But not a lot of good can be done with a cult full of frumpy fat chicks. It's our responsibility to keep them in shape. Now it's time for me to retire to the Big House. If you wouldn't mind, would you please send Lindsay to see me?"

"Lindsay…" Summer couldn't get enough air into her lungs. "I don't think…after everything that's happened to…you shouldn't—"

"The iron is hot," said Hux. "She's good and primed, and besides, she and I have a lot of lost time to make up for." Hux leveled his gaze at her, as if to place blame.

Summer could no longer see straight. She tumbled backwards into a pair of rusty, tumbledown gas pumps. She held onto the blades of grass around her, as if they might keep her from hurtling headlong into the night above them.

"I told you I was…" Summer's eyelids grew heavy. "I never meant to—"

"At any rate," said Hux, "when I ask you to do something, I expect you to hop right to it. Remember, it ain't me making all the decisions around here. That would be Luther, and it's probably best if you mind him."

Upon taking moral inventory of her current situation, Summer reckoned herself good and fucked. For the first time, she could find no one to blame but herself. Her cheeks flushed with blood and her heart filled with mighty shame. She took ample time to think back on her every decision since arriving at the ranch and tried her level best to decipher which one it was that led her so far astray.

Hux had no time for crisis. He turned his back to her and started again for the Big House. Over his shoulder, he called to her.

"I'm adding another Principle. It's called *Loyalty*. It's one you'd be smart to work on."

"Ain't nobody more loyal than me, Jackie."

Hux paused his parade. Whatever he meant to say, he thought better of. Instead, he said, "Show me how loyal you are by fetching Lindsay. Tell her I'll be waiting."

Hux disappeared into the Big House. This time, Summer did not follow him.

28

DONNIE'S MOMENT OF CLARITY wouldn't come until much later in the year, near about June, when he awoke with a start upon the linoleum floor of an RV pushed to the furthest reaches of the property. He couldn't recall how long he'd lived there, thanks to a somehow steady supply of booze and the speed by which the pages of the calendar had flipped. What he realized, however, was that he'd finally grown sick and tired of being sick and tired and it was high time he acted.

He shot like a bolt into his britches, which he found scattered across the camper. On the mattress in the corner, young Beth Ann stretched, yawned, and kicked away enough of the covers to show off her assets. She watched him dress and smiled coyly.

"Why don't you get back in the bed?" she asked him. "I got a favorite way to start the day and, if you give me a minute, I'm sure it will be your favorite way in no time."

"I've said it before and I'll say it again," Donnie said, shimmying into a dirty t-shirt, "this has got to stop."

"Ugh…" She rolled over, sticking her ass up high. "You sound like a broken record. You'll huff and puff all day long and never once make eye contact, but by the time midnight rolls around, you'll stand outside the window of my RV to howl like an alley cat. What do you say we cut out all the middle business and get right to the screwing?"

"I can't keep living like this." Donnie swung wide his arms, but misjudged the size of the skinny trailer. He skinned his knuckles against the wood paneling and knocked his knees at the cabinetry. He missed living in the Big House. He'd hooted and hollered when Hux ordered Donnie out to the yard, but placated him by sending Beth Ann around to his RV wearing nothing but a smile and a bottle of corn liquor crooked at her finger. It served to distract him a good month or so, but now Donnie put down his foot. "This is a horrible way to live."

"There's bigger trailers," Beth Ann said. "The one those two newbies moved into last week is twice the size of this. All you've got to do is pull rank on them and y'all can swap."

"I'm not talking about the trailer." Donnie pulled a pair of mismatched socks from beneath the mattress, then slipped into them. He did his level best to smooth the wrinkles in his slacks. "I'm talking about all of it. The drinking, the sneaking around…it's not good for my soul."

"We don't have to be so sneaky about it," Beth Ann said. "Everybody knows we're doing it."

"That's not the—wait…what do you mean *everybody knows*?"

She sat up and twitched her frisky titties. She moved to an imperceptible beat and twirled the ends of her hair.

"But sexual congress is specifically forbidden by the Principles," Donnie said. "Especially at a stage where—"

"Oh, Hux got rid of that stupid Principle a long time ago," Beth Ann giggled. "We've got new ones. Want me to recite them to you?"

Donnie racked his memory best he could. When had the Principles been changed? How long and how much had he been drinking? Did Beth Ann's slippery flesh taste of peaches or tangerines? He shook the images sneaking into his brain by plucking her britches from the floor and handing them to her.

She looked at them like they were foreign. "I asked Hux if we could make it an official relationship, like Rylah and Peter, or Cassie and Steven. I'd like nothing more than to walk hand in hand with you through the meadows, but he said no, on account of we reckon you get off on the sneaky parts of it."

Donnie could drive his hand through the wood paneling, but for fear it might get stuck. Instead, he ran his fingers through his hair and smashed sleep from his eyeballs with the palms of his hands.

"You're getting yourself all worked up," Beth Ann murmured. "You ought to take your pills."

Donnie moved a safe distance from her. "I'm not taking any more of those. They make me...I won't swallow another one."

"Then bring that over here so I can chill you out some."

She'd already loosed his belt buckle, but still he wouldn't go for it. He pushed her off him and collected himself.

"I've had it," he declared. "I've had my fill of it."

With that, he threw open the door of the trailer. He cut through the rows of green corn and the Miracles working them. He shielded his eyes both from the hot Texas sun and their faces—

"Good morning, Brother Donnie."

"Isn't the day glorious?"

"Praise Luther."

"See you in Spirit Study later today, Brother Donnie?"

—and marched the entire distance to the Big House. He reached for the doorknob, but found himself instead accosted by two big boys in overalls.

"Hux Pariah is not to be disturbed," said the fat one, a long-haired kid named Wayne. "Not without an appointment."

"That's ridiculous," said Donnie. His attempts to wrest himself free from the big boys remained futile. "I can see him whenever I like. Do you not know who I am?"

"We know who you are," said the other, a goth kid named Steve. "Still, you must have an appointment."

"You listen here—"

Donnie would not finish his protest, for he caught sight of the sidearm and holster hanging from the hip of one boy, then the other. Donnie looked to their faces and caught the same dead stare he'd seen in Summer's eyes before she...

Donnie ceased to struggle. He hung limply in their arms until finally he'd been relinquished. He rubbed circulation back to his arms and squinted into the sun.

"If you won't let me see Hux," he said to the two boys, "then will you please take me to Summer?"

Steve and Wayne looked to each other and swapped wry grins. They chuckled at something, but otherwise made no sound.

"What's so funny?" asked Donnie. "What's happened to Summer?"

"Summer's gone," said Wayne.

"What do you mean, *Summer's gone*?" Donnie asked.

Said Steve, "We don't have room for traitors around here. You either live close to the Principles or you can bail."

"The Thirteenth Principle is *Loyalty*," said Wayne. "You can lie about a lot of things, but eventually an impure spirit will expose itself."

Donnie shook the cobwebs from his head. Parts of a memory shouldered their way into the fog of his brain. He could remember one night with Summer at the door of his camper, breaking his liquor cache one by one, all save for the ever-winnowing bottle he held in his hands. How she screamed at him and shook him by the collar. How she told him he could little see what was going on before his own two eyes.

He could recall little more, yet still he felt the urgency in her message. Again, he tried for the door to the Big House, this time nearly twisting open the knob before he felt the vise-like grip of both boys tearing him from the door frame. Next he felt the hot air race past his face as they chucked him down the patio steps and into the sunbaked yard.

"We won't tell you again," Wayne said. "If I have to stomp good sense into you, you'll obey the orders passed down from Hux Pariah."

"Summer wouldn't have quit the ranch," Donnie said. "She would never have left these Miracles behind."

"Turns out," said Steve, "the only person Summer cared for was herself."

"I've heard talk her real name wasn't even Summer."

"Hux said there was no end to the lies told by that girl."

"Addition by subtraction. Miracle Ranch is better off without her."

As Donnie rose unsteady to his feet, both boys replaced their hands on their holsters. Donnie waved them off.

"No need, boys," he said, tired and resigned. "I can show myself back to my RV."

"Best you sleep it off," chuckled one of them.

"Have another drink," snorted the other.

But the last thing on Donnie's mind was another drink. No, he'd visited that well plenty times since his daddy died and he reckoned it best not to visit again. He looked at the land around him and remembered not for the first time it had been built on Twelve solid Principles, ones his father had lived and died by. The first of those Principles, Donnie remembered, was admitting you were powerless.

"To hell with the Principles," Donnie muttered beneath his breath. "It's up to me to save Miracle Ranch."

☼ ☼ ☼

When Donnie finally found Rylah in the old work shed, he nearly didn't recognize her. She'd long shed the bulky attire for a bikini top and shorts cut from the denim of her overalls. Where once her skin had been pale, she'd bronzed. Her long black hair had somehow tinted darker, yet nowhere near as dark as the coals of her eyes. In fact, Donnie thought perhaps it might not be her, as she'd yet to answer to her name.

When finally she turned to face him, she could not be more annoyed.

"Rylah Kincaid is the name of a dead girl," she rebuked him. "Hux said I shall forever be known as *Satin*. You know why?"

Donnie rolled his eyes.

"Because of the way my skin feels to the touch." She stuck a willowy arm below his nose. "Go on," she said, "feel it."

"Whatever your name is," Donnie said, already out of breath, "we need to get the hell out of here. There's no time to explain, but the longer we stay here—"

"Brother Donnie," said Satin, "are you drinking this early in the day?" She clicked her tongue against the back of her teeth. "There's never a day goes by when I don't thank Luther for freeing me from my chains and I only hope that—"

She stopped sudden. She looked to a point on the far side of the work shed, past the rusty tools, past the dusty work benches. Donnie turned, but found nothing by which could hold anyone's attention.

"Are you—?"

Satin said to no one, "You are right."

"Who is right?" asked Donnie.

"It is not for me to understand."

Donnie looked this way, then that. "Who the hell are you talking to?"

Satin turned again to look him in the eye. "You were saying?"

Donnie launched into it. It felt good, at last, to confide in someone. He told her how he had sat with his mother until finally she died. He recounted the tale of how he'd searched high and low the streets of Dallas until he'd found Barney Malone, preaching straight-edge on street corners. He talked of how he'd helped start Miracle Ranch and all the things they'd done to lure the Miracles.

And when it came time, he told her of what fate awaited his father, and how he'd never be found at the bottom of the old rock quarry. How Hux wasn't Hux, but rather a grifter named Jack Jordan, and somehow Summer Halifax had thrown in with him. Summer, who up and disappeared one day under the shadiest of circumstances, and now some of the Miracles carried guns and, if they knew what was good for them, they'd hightail it out of there before something dreadful happened.

Satin's eyes sparkled. She licked her lips and tucked herself into him somewhat close.

"And you're going to rescue me, Donnie?" she asked with a coo.

"Of course," he said. "I have failed too many people around me. I couldn't live with myself if I failed you girls as well."

"What ever will you do?"

"I'm going to get you out of here," he said. "I'm going to get you all out of here."

Satin said nothing. With a smile like that, she didn't need to.

"I want you to gather up as many Miracles as you can," he said. "Meet me tonight after evening Spirit Study, after sundown."

"Where?"

"By the doglegged curve in the road on the far side of the ranch," Donnie said.

"What do I tell the other girls?"

Donnie shrugged. "I'm afraid we can tell them nothing. Who knows how bad Hux has them brainwashed. Instead, just tell them it's part of a new Principle."

Again, Satin's head turned to the far wall of the work shed. She listened a bit to the wind, then nodded her head.

"I'll do whatever you say," she murmured.

"Perfect. I'll see you at sundown." Donnie clapped her on the back, then bustled out of the shed with only two things on his mind: one, he hoped the others would be near as easy to convince as Rylah had been, and two, how her bare skin felt leagues more sinful than satin.

29

THEY ARE OUT THERE.

Hux Pariah stood on the porch of the Big House and scanned the steadily purpling horizon. Although he saw no clouds of dust from approaching vehicles, nor telltale red lasers from the scopes of sniper rifles, he knew it deep down in his bones. It was the first thought when he woke in the mornings and his final prayer before he closed his eyes at night. It danced so often through his head that he no longer needed to say the words out loud in order to hear them.

No, he didn't.

They are out there.

No matter how many fences he ordered built, or torches he commanded to be lit. No matter how many men he had on hand to load their guns with powder or stand sentry at his doorway. He jerked with every rustle from the brush. He ducked for cover at every whisper of wind. Not a day passed when Hux didn't sick up a meal or two and, though he found his jawline awful striking as a result, there'd be no way to disguise the steady shaking of his hand.

"When will they attack?" he asked.

Any day now, Hux. Any day.

"I wish they'd do it and get it over with."

That's not true and you know it.

"I'm not scared," said Hux. "I'm ready for them."

Maybe you are, but are they?

Hux diverted his attention to his Miracles. About forty or so of them stood in the yard, each facing different areas which had been designated as *weak points*. Places where the fortifications could be exploited, or the defenses manipulated. Each of them had been given a weapon of some sort. Some carried a gun, while others brandished sticks and stones. They kept their heavy-lidded eyes pointed toward the various tree lines and dared not so much as blink, despite the hour growing long.

"Tomorrow, we should let them sleep in shifts," said Hux. "They'll be no use to me dog-tired like they are."

They'll be no use to you dead. Now is hardly the time to split your defenses.

"They're likely to collapse from lack of sleep."

If they collapse, then at least you will know the limits of their loyalty.

Hux nodded. "You're right, Luther."

I'm always right.

Hux surveyed the lot a final time, then stepped inside the Big House. He removed his sidearm from his shoulder holster and placed it on the kitchen counter. The one from his hip went to the kitchen table. Finally, he slipped the tiny Derringer from his ankle and handed it to the big boy named Boo who guarded the bottom of the stairs.

"Are they awake?" Hux asked him.

Boo answered, "They ain't made any noise for the past half hour, but I reckon they're still awake."

Hux nodded wearily, then ascended the stairs.

Some time ago, Hux relocated the dry goods storage locker to the top floor of the Big House. First, he had concerns of rats, roaches, or other vermin accessing their packaged foods. However, as time passed, he began to fear other Miracles sneaking past him, late at night, and poisoning their highly conditioned bodies with bowlfuls of pasta or cans of preserved meats. Rather than risk it, he'd replaced the wood door with one made of steel, and fitted it with a lock to which only he held the key.

Only recently had he come to realize that the room served not only to keep people from getting in, but could also be ideal when you wanted to keep them from getting *out*.

Hux stood at the door and rapped lightly with his knuckles.

"I'm going to open the door now," he called inside. "Should either of you think it wise to bum-rush me, I only ask that you think upon what happened last time you tried it, and how none of us wants that to happen again."

When he heard no further protest, Hux slipped his key into the door.

Inside, the dry goods closet contained enough sundries to feed a small platoon. Hux knew there'd come a day when outside forces might drive them within their own walls and he would not suffer for lack of his own preparation. The resulting siege could last days, weeks... months, even, and he would not be caught unawares. He'd stocked the camp with all the food and ammo he could lay an honest hand on, and then some. What had once been two bedrooms now housed shelf upon shelf of food that would last them through to the Tribulation.

It also housed Summer and Donnie, who stayed put on the floor as Hux opened the metal door. He clicked on the light as both of them covered their eyes with their hands and scurried like cockroaches for the shadows. He looked down upon them and shook his head.

"This is not what I wanted for us," he said to the room. "Not by any means."

Used to, Summer would plead and whine. She'd launch into a chorus of *let me go* and *it doesn't have to be like this*. Most of the wind quit her sails when Hux tossed Donnie in to join her. Donnie was quicker to break. A couple turns with the boys downstairs and the old boy learned his lesson. He'd gone meek as a lamb as of late. He'd come to fear the gaze of Hux Pariah.

Don't be fooled. He lies in wait.

"It will be any day now," Hux told them. "All this will be over."

Summer sighed. "You've been saying that for over a week."

"Any day now."

Hux's attention turned to a small pile of shredded paper. It had been scattered across the room like confetti. He kicked into the jumble of it and toed it aside with his boot.

"Is this what I think it is?"

Summer said nothing.

"I asked you to read it."

"I got better things to do than sit around all day and read the crap you write," she grumbled. "That was the ramblings of a crazy man."

"That was my manifesto." Hux was on the verge of losing his cool. Luther put a hand to his neck and squeezed gentle until Hux's heart rate settled. "That was my life's work."

"It was overwritten and paranoid," said Summer. "Nobody wants to read crap like that."

Hux could not take his eyes off the scraps littering the carpeted floor. "No matter," he said. "There are other copies. When the time is right, every newspaper, every TV, every website in America will be reading it."

"I'd suggest a good editor, then," said Summer. "You can't spell for shit."

"And you…" Hux looked to Donnie, who had yet to rise. He sat with his back against a giant case of toilet paper, one of the rolls he'd busted open to use as a pillow for his neck. "What great things we could have done together. I gave you everything you wanted. I gave you companionship, I gave you the pick of the litter…you could have lived out the rest of your years in absolute bliss. But you had to betray me."

"I kind of like it in here," Donnie shrugged. "Summer's great company."

"Sure, she is." Again, a bitterness took hold of Hux's mouth, one he was powerless to defend. "She's great company until she ain't. That's for sure."

Summer flipped him the bird.

Said Hux to Donnie, "I know your greatest fear, and that's to be alone. You stick with this one and that's exactly what you'll be: *alone*. She says she'll stand by you, but she'll crack at the seams before too long and she'll fix it so there's no one there but you to hold together the pieces. She'll run off anyone and everyone who might manage to possibly matter, then once she's got you all to herself, she'll show her mind to the door."

"Go to hell, Jack."

"I mean it," Hux said. "After you were gone, I was down in Houston picking up some tabs, and I got caught up in some nasty traffic. Turns out, some hobo had charged into an intersection with a samurai sword and was waving it to and fro, talking about how he'd been sent to defend the world from dragons."

"That's a fascinating story, Jack," said Summer. "Why don't you write that one down too so I can add it to yonder scrap pile?"

"I watched that hobo run from one side of the street to the other," Hux said. "I watched him hoot and holler until the police took him down with three bullets. Long after they carted him off, I could still hear the echoes of his carrying on, bouncing off the skyscrapers."

"Is there a point to all this?" asked Summer.

"Sure there is," Hux told them both. "For days or weeks after, I couldn't figure out what the difference was between him and us."

Hux knew he'd stung her, but not nearly hard as he wanted. So he went on. "Is it because we had a roof over our heads? Is it because we transacted thousands of dollars' worth of goods at a time? Really…I thought about it a good, long while and never once could I come up with the answer of what made us any different than that stark, raving hobo."

"I know what the answer is," said Summer.

"Do you?"

Summer rose slowly to her feet. She kept sacred the distance between them.

"We have each other," she said.

Hux dismissed her with his hand. He turned to face the door. He stepped no closer to the exit.

"I'm serious, Jack," said she. "That hobo is what happens when we let each other get too far from the other. You can take up with all the little girls you want, Jack—"

"Quit calling me that."

"Call yourself whatever you want," she said, "but there's only one thing keeping either one of us from going straight to ruin."

Yes. Only one thing. Keep that in mind.

"I'm happy now," Hux said. "But you couldn't let that be. Once again, you had to go and spoil it."

"You call this happy?" Summer pointed to the room into which she'd been locked. "You're half out of your mind, man. You don't trust anybody and you've gone completely off your rocker. This is how you get when I'm not around to keep you stable."

To what great depths she has fallen. She will say anything at this point to further bend your mind.

"We both know that's why you keep me locked up in here," said Summer. She took a step toward him. "Because you know I'm the one who keeps you from falling apart."

"You two can't be serious," moaned Donnie.

Hux silenced him with the wave of his hand. He kept his eyes fixed upon Summer.

"You tried to run," said Hux. "You were going to leave the ranch."

"I was never going to leave," Summer said. "You know how often I get worked up. Sure, I hem and haw over things, but in the end, do I ever go anywhere? It's like there are decisions being made outside of myself, and I just act on them. I have no way to explain what that force is—"

It has a name.

"—but think back from when we first met, until this very moment. Can you do that?"

"Okay."

"Have I ever left you?"

One thing Hux prided himself good at was the ability to sniff out a lie. He'd been doing it since his early days and reckoned he had a knack for it, one that could beat lie detectors to hell. However, he could make neither hide nor hair of how sincere the words spouting forth from his old friend were.

"What do you think?" he asked the room.

She raises a valid point. On the one hand—

"I think I'd be lucky if I found someone so devoted," said Donnie. He crawled on all fours to Summer's feet and tugged her by the ankles. "If you showed me half the allegiance you show this crack-up, I swear I would stick by your side through thick and thin."

Summer put both hands to her cheeks and flushed an unhealthy shade of red. While she found it impossible to speak, Hux suffered from no such affliction.

"A likely couple!" he scoffed. "Summer, to hell with this guy. Come with me."

"Don't listen to him," said Donnie. He scurried up the length of her, until he held her face in his hands. They fixed their gaze upon each other. "Summer," he said, "this idiot had his chance. He stuck you with a needle full of drugs and left you to OD in an East Texas emergency room. He's taken from you the only thing that made you happy and locked you for weeks in a storage closet."

"We've got quite the history," said Summer.

"Maybe now it's time to take up with someone new," said Donnie. "Somebody who won't put you through so much pain."

Summer smiled. "We won't get very far, you and me. We're locked in a storage closet."

"Like I said," Donnie said, also smiling, "you're great company. We can spend the rest of our days in this storage closet, for all I care."

Summer looked from Donnie to Hux, then back to Donnie. Hux could see the whirligigs spinning in her head. She closed her eyes then opened them.

You can't trust her.

"If I could trust anyone..."

She'll say whatever she believes is necessary to wriggle free from bondage. You'd forever look over your shoulder, waiting for her true intentions.

"You're right..."

Hux backed out of the room, stopping at the doorframe. He braced it with both hands and eyed both his prisoners. Neither of them moved a muscle.

"I'm going to step downstairs and brew myself a nice pot of coffee," said Hux. "Do you know how long it's been since I've had caffeine?"

Are you sure that's a good idea?

"I think it's a wonderful idea," said Hux. "Furthermore, I'm going to leave this door unlocked."

Like hell you are.

"If you join me downstairs, then all is forgiven."

Summer licked her lips. Donnie held his breath.

"If you choose to throw in your lot with each other," said Hux, "then you can remain up here."

Donnie took Summer by the hand. Hux did not wait to see how she received it, instead turning his back to them and again descending the stairs.

She's not to be trifled with. You should march back up to the top of those stairs and lock the door.

"I have no doubt in my mind what she'll do," said Hux. Even still, he ordered Boo to keep vigil at the bottom of the stairs. He walked into the kitchen and rustled an old can of coffee he'd stashed behind several boxes of herbal tea. He opened it and received its pent-up aroma straight to his face.

He closed his eyes and smiled.

"Oh, how I missed that smell."

Even if she walks down those stairs, that means nothing.

"I can't do this alone," Hux said. "I'm getting so tired."

You're far from alone. Those Miracles outside, they'd die for you. They'll do anything you told them.

"But for how much longer?" Hux poured hot water into a dented kettle, then set it on a gas burner to boil. "I see it every day. Their devotion is flagging. When I am inside these women, they no longer receive me with the vigor of the early days. When they work in the fields, they don't sing the songs as loud as they used to. I hear them whispering..."

Perhaps we should keep certain ones separate from the others.

"I see how they look at me each time I order them to stand down, after each unfulfilled prophesy."

I've been meaning to tell you, maybe we should go easy on all that End Times talk.

"I need Summer back by my side," he said. "Like the old days."

The two of them are plotting your downfall as you speak.

Hux shook his head. "She wouldn't let that happen."

You don't know her as well as you used to.

"I know her better than most people."

You can't trust anyone. I'm the only one...

The kettle kissed steam into the room and Hux removed it from the flame. He stood alone in the kitchen a moment, before he said, "How do I even know you're real?"

Take a look upstairs.

"I don't hear anything."

That's because they're gone, Hux.

"That's impossible. Boo would have—"

A window, a door...a hole in the wall. What does it matter? They've escaped.

"Summer wouldn't—"

See for yourself.

Hux dropped the kettle to the floor. Before it landed, he'd already crashed through the dining room, the living room, and bustled past Boo at the bottom of the stairs. He crashed up them two, three at a time, until finally he reached the landing, the hallway, and the metal door standing wide open.

Inside, he found no one.

Hux staggered into the room, empty save for all the sundries he'd collected for an Armageddon that may never come. He walked to the center of the room and dropped to his knees upon the discarded shreds of the manifesto that Summer had destroyed, rather than read.

"How do you like that?" he asked aloud. "She's gone."

I hate to say I told you so, but…

"I never thought she'd do it," Hux said. "Never in all my days did I think she'd go anywhere but where she belonged, which is by my side."

First thing they'll do is call the cops.

"Summer would never go to the police. She and I have an agreement."

Like "no hospitals"?

Hux swallowed thick. "Still…"

And if she would leave you, what's to keep all the others from doing the same?

Hux could no longer argue that point. While still down on his knees, he fought a fanciful notion that perhaps he might toss out a final call for help, one that might be answered by a power great enough to stay the coming tide from the bad guys down in Houston, or the cops in Corsicana. One that might finally give him what he really wanted, which was peace of mind enough to finally get a little bit of rest. Just a moment's fucking rest, because it never stopped, that piece of him upstairs never, ever stopped, not with all the booze in the world, not with all the money. He could be neck deep in little girls from here to Salvation and still that evil organ between his ears would keep right on cranking.

Cast down upon his knees, he closed his eyes tight and lifted his head to the sky and didn't care if it was Luther who answered, or some cranky God with whom he'd always been a stranger. He made a promise then and there, if one of them would answer him, he'd forever be in their service.

"Just please give me peace of mind."

Hux Pariah opened his eyes to see what sign he may have received, and found himself staring at the top shelf of the dry storage closet.

Up top, where he'd crammed a bulky box of purple powdered drink mix.

Kool-Aid.

30

SUMMER SAT ALONE IN the motel parking lot atop the hood of a beat-to-shit pickup truck. It was still early morning, and she'd smoked half a pack of cigarettes waiting in the muggy Virginia air. She had aimed to smoke a half pack more, when along came Craig in a pickup of his own.

He parked alongside her and sat in his cab a good bit before finally climbing out. Summer watched him take his sweet time rounding the vehicle until he stepped up alongside her and pulled her into his arms. He hugged her good and tight, like two friends who hadn't seen each other in a long, long time.

Which they were.

"Not the reaction I expected," she said when finally he released her.

He plucked the cigarette from her lips and took a long, steady drag. He looked her up and down.

"You look good," he said.

"Thanks."

"No, really. Last time…I mean, you look *great*."

"Easy, rider." She nodded her head toward the closed door of her motel room. "Not in front of the kids."

Craig followed her gaze and squinted. If he had something to add, he kept it to himself.

He handed her back the cigarette and said, "Texas, huh?"

She nodded.

"That's a crazy place," he said.

"You've got no idea."

Behind them, traffic passed along the interstate at a steady enough clip. Folks headed to work, but nobody drove slow enough to notice anything along the off-ramps, least of all the two of them.

"I heard some things on the news," said Craig. "There was a cult down there, maybe about fifty, sixty people. A bunch of hippies, they said."

"Oh?"

Craig sucked again from Summer's cigarette and nodded. "They loaded themselves up with guns and their leader made them drink a bunch of Molly. They went half out of their minds until the Feds showed up."

Summer took her cigarette back from him, but she did not bring it to her lips. Instead, she kept eyes on the door of her motel room.

"There was a bit of a to-do, but eventually they winded up with their asses in jail." Craig laughed to himself. "Being Texas and all, those kids were lucky they didn't end up shot to hell and back, or burned to death like those freaks down in Waco."

Rather than damage her throat with further cigarette smoke, she tossed the butt to the asphalt. She watched it smolder at his feet.

"The guy behind the whole deal," said Craig, "was the craziest of them all. I heard he slipped the drugs into their drinks and forced them to drink it. They put him on the stand to testify for himself and he talked up and down the room about folks who weren't there and taking orders from somebody who couldn't nobody see. Any time the cops would parade him in front of the other kids, they'd fall to their knees and chant hippie shit."

"Like you said," Summer smiled. "Texas is a crazy place."

Craig eyed her sideways. "You weren't nowhere near none of that, were you?"

"Me?" She took a minute before adding, "Texas is awful big."

"True that."

She nodded to a brown envelope he held in his hand. "You got something for me?"

"You know I do."

"Thanks a lot." She hopped off the hood of the car. "Let's step inside."

Craig didn't move. Instead, he eyeballed the front door of the motel.

"Is that a good idea?" he asked.

"Don't be silly." Summer led the way. "He won't bite."

Once inside, she did not click on the light. The room was dark, save for the television before the twin beds, switched to a cartoon which had been left on mute.

"Dear God," breathed Craig. "What happened to him?"

Summer closed the door behind them. "Things got a little messy leaving Texas." She rubbed the inside of her arm with her thumb and forefinger and wondered if that itch would ever quite get scratched. "I'm afraid our boy, he didn't—"

"Maybe it's best if I don't hear nothing about it," said Craig. "You asked me to get you some Florida IDs, so I brought them. Lucky for you I picked up the phone. Last time…"

Summer brought him around to the tottering table and switched on a tiny lamp. She took the envelope from Craig and dumped out the contents.

Drivers licenses. Two of them.

Social security cards, also two.

A pair of birth certificates.

Two brand new lives scattered across a scuffed tabletop.

"This is good stuff," said Summer. She picked up one ID, then the other. She held them beneath the lamp and flipped them from the front side to the back. "This is really good stuff." Over her shoulder, she called, "Hey, you ought to come check this out."

When no movement came from the far bed, Craig scratched his head.

"Hey, is he all right?"

"He'll be fine," said Summer. "You know how he gets."

Still, Craig shook his head. "Yeah, maybe...but I ain't never seen him like this."

"My name is Katrina Merriweather," she said to the room. "Will you get a load of that, Hux—I mean, *Andrew*. From now on, my name is Katrina Merriweather and your name is Andrew Catton."

And so it became thus.

Katrina escorted Craig to the door and stepped outside. He stopped before they reached his truck and pointed to the hills on the other side of the freeway.

"You know, Keith was born just over that rise."

She furrowed her brow. "Keith?"

Craig nodded toward the motel room door.

"Oh, yes."

"A little town called Lake Castor," he said. "Not big enough to land on anybody's map, and you could drive past it without ever knowing."

"Nothing wrong with that," said Katrina. "If that's what you're looking for."

He went on. "What I'm saying is, he's still got people over yonder. You could leave him in that motel room and haul ass down that highway with your new drivers license and be a whole new woman."

Katrina's gaze drifted northbound, then south.

"You don't have to worry about him," said Craig. "If you ask me, he shouldn't never have left Lake Castor in the first place."

"Maybe," she said. "Who's to say what we should have done with our lives? Right? All that matters is how things shake out when it's all said and done."

Craig spit sideways. He kicked gravel with his toe.

"Me and Andrew—" she smiled a bit "—*Andy*…eventually we'll probably move on, same as anyone else, I reckon. One of us will decide to settle down and put down roots and the other…" She sucked the insides of her cheeks. "But for now…"

She let the thought hang in the wind like a cattle thief.

Once again, Craig held her tight. Before climbing into his pickup, he stopped and took a final look at her.

"Promise me you'll be careful," he said. "Florida is no place to jerk around."

"Show me a place these days that is."

Craig slipped the truck into gear, then waved with two fingers as he backed out of the motel parking lot and, in a spray of gravel and rock, got himself onto the freeway.

Katrina stood there a spell. Behind her, the cleaning lady shuffled her cart past each door, placing a newspaper on the mat before each occupancy. After she'd slouched along, Katrina picked up the paper and sighed into the printed face of Donnie Williams. Above the photograph in large, bold type were the words: CULT LEADER BLAMES INVISIBLE WOMAN FOR DRUGGING FOLLOWERS.

"Front page news for two weeks now," she said with a sigh. "Ain't that something?"

Maybe Craig had a point. Maybe Andy would be better served by going home to his family. Maybe time for a change beckoned. Maybe she should hop on that same freeway and pick a direction and not stop until she got someplace she could call home.

She looked at that newsprint in her hands at the photo of Donnie Williams and saw not the drug-induced mania set within his eyes or the hair standing at end on all sides of his head. Rather than the lunatic he'd become in the mainstream media, she thought instead of their last conversation, as they stood at the gates of Miracle Ranch, hand in hand.

"Are you sure we should leave them behind?" Katrina had asked him, back when she preferred to be called Summer.

"Of course, we should," Donnie had answered. "We haven't time to argue. Hux has brainwashed them and they'll be coming for us."

"How do you know?"

For a moment, she'd seen something flicker in the young man and couldn't quite put her finger on it. His aura had darkened and something passed through him, like a wraith. She shuddered then at the gates same as she did back at the motel parking lot as she recalled it.

Donnie had opened his mouth and said, "Luther is telling me we should make a run for it."

"What did you say?"

"Luther says so," he told her. "For the first time in my life, I can hear him. It's so wonderful." Donnie hopped up and down. He spun round and round in circles. "Do you hear me? I can hear him, plain as day, and he's telling me to take you by the hand and run far, far from this place."

"Let me tell you something I've never told anyone in the whole, wide world."

"Sure."

"Luther's not real, you idiot. I made him up."

For what decision was there left to make? She'd long ago ceded control, just as she'd been told. Running to the gates with Donnie had been little more than Kabuki. She would never leave Andy Catton, or Jack Jordan, or Hux Pariah, or any number of names he had or would have. Should the comets converge in the heavens, then rain ash and ice from the sky, she would still be at his side, and he at hers. For there was a devil she knew, and a devil she didn't. There also was a planet hurtling through the solar system upon which she was supposed to walk, and she preferred to do it with a friend.

Katrina Merriweather stepped back into the motel. This time, she flipped on the light. The figure beneath the blanket still did not move. She sat beside him on the bed and listened to the shaky rhythms of his breathing and the labored spasms from the thing he called a heart.

Was she happy?

Hell, she could be anything she wanted in this whole, entire world, so why in good hell could she not be happy?

"You hear that, Andy?" she called to the lump beside her on the bed. "I'm going to be happy."

And so it became thus.

ACKNOWLEDGEMENTS

Without the following people, nothing would ever get done: Lana Pierce, Natalie Pruitt, Dan Morrison, Julie Malone, Bobby Gorman, Jason Pinter, Jedidiah Ayres, Todd Keisling, Benoit Lelievre, Jim and Yvette Arendt, Jennifer Asbury, Lorie Underwood, Geraud Staton, Mike Bourquin, The Wild Detectives bookstore in Dallas, Paul Snow and Meredith Sause, Michael Howard, Jeffrey Moore, Tracey Coppedge, Monique Velasquez and Piper Kessler, E.A. Aymar, Marilyn Hays, S. W. Lauden, and all the folks who come out to read or hear us read at the Noir at the Bar events around the country.

ABOUT THE AUTHOR

Eryk Pruitt is a screenwriter, author and filmmaker. He wrote and produced the short film *Foodie* which went on to win eight top awards at over sixteen film festivals. His short fiction has appeared in *The Avalon Literary Review*, *Thuglit*, *Pulp Modern*, and *Zymbol*, among others, and he was a finalist for the Derringer Award. He is the author of the novels *Dirtbags* and *Hashtag*, both available from Polis Books. He is the host of the monthly radio show and podcast: The Crime Scene with Eryk Pruitt. He lives in Durham, NC with his wife Lana and their cat Busey. Follow him at @ReverendEryk.

CPSIA information can be obtained
at www.ICGtesting.com
Printed in the USA
LVHW01s2116251017
553775LV00003B/3/P